CW00481957

An Irish Winter

Gift Aid

20 70950292 5705

BRAND KING

THE CHOIR PRESS

First published in the United Kingdom in 2020 by
The Choir Press

ISBN 978-1-78963-099-2

For my late grandfather Charles

Part One

Alice

—◦ **1** ◦—

It was a chilly day in mid-December when the rooks first came into my life.

I was in the lounge room of the cottage, wondering what on earth I was going to do with all this spare time, when two thuds came from the front door. It was so sudden and brief that my first thought was I'd imagined it. But then came the distinctive sound of wings beating against the ground. I moved tentatively down the hallway, through the kitchen, until I arrived in the small foyer by the front door.

Through the windows either side of it I had a good view of the area outside – the small grassy garden edged by empty planter boxes, the lichen-covered wall that bordered the neighbouring property, the path to the beach. Beyond, the winter sun sat low on a veiled horizon.

For a few silent moments I wondered if I really had imagined the whole thing. But then the flapping returned, descended into scratching, before a ragged, throaty caw gave way to deathly silence.

I steeled myself as I put my hand on the doorknob. But as soon as I turned it, I heard wings beating at the air and a loud, urgent caw sound out three times, each one a little further away than the last. Hopeful, I opened the door, only for my heart to sink again as I saw the black listless shape beside the doormat.

The poor creature. I bent down and looked for signs of life, but its chest was still, its wings limp and its eyes closed, the little black lids trapping its final panicked thoughts. What a horrible way to go.

I went to the kitchen, put the dishwashing gloves on, then carried the dead bird to the wheelie bin at the back of the cottage. I had the lid open and was about to drop it in when I heard another strange sound coming from a nearby tree. Looking up, I saw three rooks watching me. The largest of them, with a plumage of fine jet-black feathers, was making a noise like an old wooden door straining on its hinges.

I couldn't put the bird in the bin now. Instead I carried it across the garden, over the path and to the base of a tree beside the wall. The three rooks followed, keeping a keen eye on me as they hopped from branch to branch. I gathered some of the leaves that had been blown into a heap against the wall and shaped them into a kind of bed. Then I placed the dead bird down gently, taking care to adjust its neck so it looked relatively natural.

I returned to the cottage door and watched the two smaller rooks fly down to the grave. They poked at it inquisitively, then stood back and remained still, as if they couldn't comprehend what they were seeing. Meanwhile the larger rook remained on a thick branch, watching me.

Sensing it was waiting for me to go inside, I stepped into the foyer, shut the door behind me, then peered through the side window. The large bird glided inelegantly down from its tree – it looked as though a wing was bent – and perched on one of the planter boxes, its focus still on me rather than its dead mate by the wall. Finally I got the message and walked upstairs, taking up position by the window on the landing.

Satisfied, the large rook flew to the door and stared at the spot where its mate's body had come to rest. For a few moments it didn't move, as if it was running the event over and over again in its head, trying to make sense of what had happened. Then it lifted its head and let out a sound completely unlike any that had preceded it. It started at a high pitch, then descended mournfully, like a child's toy trodden on and kicked from a bridge. From the grave tree the other two called back with the same sound, their beaks pointed to the sky. Then the large rook flew awkwardly over and joined them by the body.

*

I watched the three birds through the lounge room window for what felt like an hour, imagining every movement they made as part of a mourning ritual. The small hops this way and that a dance; the dips of their heads a concession to tears; the pokes at the corpse – gentle farewell kisses.

Then the large bird hopped away, scanned the immediate vicinity and took flight. The smaller two followed close behind. They flew low along the path and on towards the beach, calling out loud enough that I could hear them through my double-glazed windows. Calling with that same high-pitched falling sound.

I put on my jacket and shoes and headed outside.

When I reached the grave site the body was gone. Or at least appeared to be. On closer inspection I realised the pile of leaves I'd made as a bed seemed larger than before. Making sure the mourning birds were still out of sight, I carefully picked away some of the leaves, digging down a couple of inches before I noticed the shiny black feathers beneath. They hadn't been poking at it after all; they'd given it a proper burial. Moments earlier I'd nearly tossed it in the bin.

I looked in the direction in which the rooks had flown off. Beyond the low-hanging tree branches, above the grassy dunes and through the sand and salt haze that hung over Lough Swilly, I could make out the hills above Buncrana, juxtaposed like felt against the slowly darkening sky.

I followed the path past the other cottages and down a short gradient. From there the beach was still out of sight as the dunes, topped with thin, hardy tufts of pale green grass, rolled and pitched for twenty or so metres. Amongst them, small birds darted in and out of the undulations. The path bent round and ran parallel to the beach here and for a short stretch was clear of trees. A strong wind was cutting across the lough and though it was icy cold I turned my face into it and revelled in the bracing sensation of being slapped in the face by nature. When I opened my eyes the small clouds that dotted the fading blue sky were stained orange and spread across the horizon as if by an old wiper blade. Streaking across them were the black figures of hundreds of rooks.

I continued along the path as it veered back up a slight rise and ducked once again under the canopy of large, mostly leafless trees. Here I could make out the beach through the trunks. I spotted a white-haired woman wrapped up against the wind, determinedly pursuing her walk along the sparse coastline. A little further along, an old man was struggling in the soft sand.

Beyond the gardens of Rathmullan House and some ropes that hung from thick branches for kids to swing out over the dunes was a cemetery. I'm not sure why but when I reached it I stopped walking. It wasn't that a thought had occurred to me or I'd heard something, it was more an unconscious thing, like being tapped on the shoulder by a memory I hadn't yet formed. It was instinct. The same instinct that made me look up. There, in the canopy of the trees, like a collection of abandoned crowns, were dozens of large brown nests. And above them, barely visible through the latticework of branches, I could just make out the shapes of what seemed like scores of rooks hovering in the sky.

I hurried along the path, cut past a children's playground and onto the beach beside the boat ramp.

It was bitingly cold. The wind, without the relative shelter of the trees and dunes, didn't so much slap me in the face as try to tear it off. I tucked my chin into my chest and turned to look back at the trees by the cemetery. What I saw made the conditions completely worthwhile.

Above the canopy was at least a hundred rooks, their wings spread but barely moving, pinned to the sky like kites. It was a remarkable sight, and all the while more rooks were joining in. They surfed the wind over the water, across the beach and then up the face of the trees, where they performed an elaborate 180-degree roll and became suddenly stationary in the sky, another black dot amongst the growing curtain. Best of all, there seemed no other reason for it than the sheer thrill.

I was sure that what I was seeing was unique and rare – perhaps even magical – but nobody else seemed interested. A young man was training his dog nearby, completely oblivious to the sky above; the old man I'd seen earlier was stumbling over the dunes; and the white-haired woman was disappearing around the bend further along the beach. I wondered if the display was a regular event and these were locals who had grown accustomed to it. Or maybe it wasn't as remarkable as I'd thought and I'd just been cooped up at work for too long.

I could have watched them for hours, but beaches have a way of making me want to walk along them, and now that I was out of the house, the idea of exploring a little appealed. I vowed to walk to the rocks at the other end and back again, and if the birds were still at it I'd sit and watch them until it was dark or they gave up.

The sand was a dull orange and lined at the high tide mark with a fringe of kelp, driftwood and crab shells. It was so different from back home, where the beaches were in-your-face attacks of primary colours and populated by people of a similar character. Here the beauty was in the shades, in the subtlety of endurance.

I walked down to the waterline and snooped amongst the small shore break. A tiny beige shell flipped over, revealed its empty insides, then flipped back again, as if to prove it wasn't hiding anything. A little further out, a large clump of brown seaweed floated menacingly in the shallows, while beyond that the lough was a nervous green soup, tipped haphazardly with the frothy shards of small cresting waves.

My senses were stirred. A sharp but pleasant redolence of salt, fish – the scent of the sea – hung in the air, somehow cleansing my palette without clinging to it. Soon I came across some writing in the sand, a name composed with meticulous handwriting. I imagined a child sweating over their work, their parent watching on, worried they had an artist on their hands. For a moment I thought fondly of the classroom, but quickly shook it off.

I continued, trying not to notice the persistent armada of rooks flying overhead. Instead I focused on another black shape materialising in the distance. This one was land-based, about six foot tall and, other than luminous green shoes, was dressed head-to-toe in black running attire. He was huffing and puffing, his forehead furrowed in concentration, as he jogged past.

As I reached the bend in the beach I simply couldn't ignore the flotilla of birds anymore. I looked back and, even from the best part of a kilometre away, could see the cloud above the cemetery trees had grown to immense proportions. I dug my heel into the sand, twisted it for a moment, then turned back. This was going to be too good to miss.

The runner approached again, his face as focused and determined as before. Had he not seen the birds? Surely when he turned at the boat ramp, as I assumed he did, he had noticed the giant cloud of rooks blacking out half the horizon. Was I really the only one who found it amazing? I felt like pointing it out – *look, nature being remarkable!* – but as he passed he seemed to make a concerted effort not to look at me.

His loss. When I reached the beach in front of the cemetery there must have been four or five hundred rooks holding a patch of sky above the trees; it was as if a rumour had spread and every bird in Donegal had come to join the party.

I sat on the soft sand and admired the show, satisfied that if it was a common occurrence then I really had made the right choice when leaving London. Then, from a branch high up in one of the trees, a large bird took flight. It beat its wings against the gale, dipping and swerving awkwardly, before it reached a spot above my head. There it began to circle, all the while looking down as if to study me. I was sure one wing was bent. Then, right on cue, it let out that falling, whistling sound and returned to the treetops.

Moments later, as if one organism, the entire flock dived in front of the trees, flew out over the beach and then climbed again, pausing above my head in a giant cone shape. For a moment they hung there in the same way they had above the trees. Then a single cry came from the cloud and they started swirling like a tornado. I held my breath. Another cry, that sound of a child's toy being stepped on, and in an instant the whole flock changed direction, calling back in kind. This repeated over and over, with each call responded to by the flock and instigating a sudden, perfect change in direction, the movement rippling through them like a shiver. Their paler undersides caught the dying light of the day as they turned, flashing from black to silver as if an eyelid falling shut.

It was the most remarkable thing I'd ever seen.

I sat on the cold sand and watched in veneration, only looking away once, when that man with the shoulder-length black hair ran by, puffing and sweating, so completely wrapped in his own world that he didn't even notice the miracle happening right above his head.

*

It was difficult to pull myself away from the rook display, but as the light faded so, one by one, did the birds. Soon all I could make out was the dim outline of two rooks circling above me. They called out every so often and though I was sure it was to each other, I let myself believe they were including me in the conversation too.

I returned home and put the kettle on, then made a kindling tepee in the fireplace, put a match to the balled-up newspaper at its heart and watched the flames, blue and gold, get to work.

I loved making fire. It felt primal and organic and there was something magical about staring into the flames and letting my mind go. No matter my problems and anxieties, the warmth of a fire and the dance of its flames had the balm.

The tepee collapsed on itself and I added some more kindling. Jets of heated air escaped from the timber and I watched the splinters of fresh wood catch light, turn dark, curl up and break off. I spread the burning sticks around, tossed some more kindling in and placed a small log on top.

Outside, the wind whistled through the trees and for a moment I thought I could hear a rook's call on it. I stood up, walked to the window and looked out at the shadows of the trees by the neighbouring wall. I squinted into the darkness and tried to distinguish a bird shape on the dark limbs but couldn't tell a rook from a stumpy branch. The fire crackled and I hurried back to it, feeding it some more kindling and another log the size of my foot. In the kitchen the kettle clicked off but I was lost in the flames, revelling in memory.

I'm lying in bed and there's an arm under my neck and another around my chest, and I'm looking out the window at lightning flash through cauliflower clouds on the horizon. I run my hand up the arm and begin to roll onto my back.

Then there was a knock at the door.

It took me a few moments to realise what I had heard. A knock at the door. Here. In Rathmullan. The wind threw some sticks at the roof and something small shook loose in the chimney and fell into the fire with a hiss. The knock came again and I was sure I heard a rook's call from amongst the howl of the wind outside.

I stood up, approached the windows by the door cautiously and peered outside. I could see a shape there, tall and dark, moving about with the wind. I reached for the exterior light switch and flicked it on. The shape moved, gained form, poked its head into the window. It was a woman, slim and beautiful, with long black hair in braids. She was wearing a dark blouse beneath a thin black leather jacket, from which she brushed off a leaf that had blown onto her shoulder and got caught in a crease.

'Hello,' I said, opening the door.

'Good evening, ma'am,' the woman replied. Behind her the wind was stirring up the leaves pushed against the neighbouring wall. 'Sorry to disturb you but I was looking for Wicklow Cottage. Is it near here?' She glanced at the varnished nameplate above my door. 'I noticed yours is Mayo.'

'I think it's just beyond the row of trees over there,' I explained, pointing in the relevant direction. She followed my directions, nodded and returned her gaze to me. She had dark, intense eyes, like they knew something I didn't. I couldn't.

'Thanks,' she said. 'It's been a hell of a day.'

I could see her car parked behind her now. 'Come far?'

She didn't answer directly, just brushed another leaf from her jacket, widened her eyes and said, 'Oh, yeah …' as if the story was too big to be told to a stranger in a doorway. Then she straightened, looked over my shoulder and asked if I had a telephone.

'Only my mobile,' I answered, 'though I usually have to go upstairs to get a signal.'

'Tell me about it,' she replied, and fished her phone from her jacket pocket. 'I was meant to call the owner of Wicklow Cottage ten minutes before I arrived, but I haven't had a signal for half an hour.' She looked at the screen as if she expected no better from such things.

I don't know what it was, but I felt at ease with the woman: she gave off a kind of big-sister energy, even though if anything she was probably a couple of years younger than me. I invited her in out of the cold and walked her through to the living room. The fire had died down a touch so, with the forceps, I picked up the half-burnt log, added another handful of kindling to the red embers, then placed it back on top. White smoke started crawling from beneath it almost instantly.

'I'm still getting used to the cold,' I told her, 'but I absolutely love having a fireplace.'

'You're on holiday here?' she asked doubtfully.

'No, I work in Letterkenny. I'm a drama teacher.' The kindling began cracking and popping with anticipation. 'What about you?'

'Oh …' she replied, flapping a hand in the air dismissively, 'work.' Then she quickly changed the subject. 'I'm sorry, I realise I don't know your name. I'm Janet.' She offered her hand.

'Alice,' I said, taking it and resisting the urge to comment on how smooth her skin was.

'Alice!' Janet replied, her voice shooting upwards like a small firework. 'I love that name. My best friend in high school was Alice. We had so much fun.'

I searched for some memory of a friend or indeed anyone I knew called Janet, but my mind drew a blank. It was possible this was the first and only Janet I'd ever known. I considered saying this but thankfully didn't get a chance to, as she asked if she could go upstairs to try and get a signal on her phone.

I showed her to the staircase and watched her walk halfway up before she stopped and looked down at me cheekily. 'I'd love a cuppa if you're putting the kettle on …'

'Shit, so sorry, of course.'

I hurried into the kitchen and filled the kettle. Upstairs I could hear Janet walking on the landing outside my bedroom, and I tried to remember if I had left the door open. I took two mugs from the cupboard and added teabags, then removed the milk from the fridge. Janet's voice fluttered over the landing and bounced into the kitchen. I was glad my first floor had been able to help her. Moments later she appeared in the doorway.

'Thanks for that,' she said, tapping her breast pocket.

'All sorted?'

'Yes, he was already on his way.'

I looked at the kettle as it grumbled angrily. 'Are you staying long?'

'Not sure,' she said, watching the kettle with me. I didn't want to press her on her work commitments as she hadn't seemed keen to discuss it earlier, and so for a moment neither of us said anything. With us watching it, the kettle reached its climax, flicked itself off and relaxed. I reached to pick it up but Janet's hand touched my arm.

'Alice, I have to go and meet the man with the key.'

'Okay,' I said.

'I'm sorry, he said he was just around the corner as he'd been expecting me.'

'That's fine. You should go.'

I was surprised by how her leaving so suddenly made me feel. As if she sensed this, Janet then said, 'But I'm coming back for that cuppa in ten minutes, okay?'

I smiled and nodded, trying not to give much away.

'Good,' she said, ''cause you need to tell me how it is a gorgeous girl like you ends up by herself in a place like this.'

*

I had to place my phone on the middle frame of my bedroom window to get a 3G connection. I tethered it to my laptop downstairs and booted up Spotify, then selected a Jamiroquai album and kept the fire burning. When I opened the door to Janet I caught a glimpse of the lining of her jacket. It was grey and looked incredibly soft. I found myself wanting to touch it just to feel how comfortable it was. But of course I didn't say anything.

I showed her through to the living room and then returned to the kitchen to flick the kettle on. 'How do you have it?'

'Just a splash of milk,' she called back, her voice less formal than it had been earlier. 'Half a sugar. Please. Thank you.'

I took the milk from the fridge again and placed it on the counter next to the two mugs. The kettle hummed into action, its contents having already made the journey once.

'Warm enough?' I asked, standing in the doorway between the two rooms.

'It's perfect.' She was wearing the same black denim jeans as before and sat with her legs crossed and her shoe tapping playfully in the air.

'You met the man with the key, then?'

'I did.' She pulled the oversized keyring from her pocket and put it on the coffee table. It was similar to the one Cormack had given me when I arrived. 'I guess I'll never lose it,' she said. 'But dear lord, the accent is so heavy here. I had to ask him to speak slower so I had time to translate what he was saying.'

'Oh, I know, I had trouble at first. It's funny how you get used to it though.' I could hear the kettle rumbling through the gears.

'How are they with yours? Is it Australian?'

'Yeah. They're okay. I lived in London for a year and a half before coming here, so I guess the edge has been taken off a bit.'

'Australia to London to Rathmullan.' Her shoe, matte black flats with a hint of sparkle that might just have been water, tapped eagerly in the air. 'Go on then, out with it.'

The kettle climaxed, clicked and relaxed. I backed into the kitchen and filled the two mugs.

'I moved there with . . .' I felt the end of the sentence catch in my throat. '. . . A boyfriend.'

'Oh yeah?'

'Yeah.' I realised I hadn't said his name in months. 'Max.'

'Max,' Janet echoed, surprising me from the doorway. 'He sounds like trouble.'

The teabags expanded and floated to the top of the mugs, gently relinquishing their contents in swirling brown eddies.

'Trouble finds trouble,' I replied, watching the steam curl out of the mugs. 'That's what Max used to say.'

I hadn't spoken about him since I left London and had tried – with work very much helping in this regard – not to think about him either. Now that the subject had been broached I wasn't sure how I felt about stirring it to the surface.

As if sensing my slight resistance Janet skilfully steered us to safer ground. She asked about my work and we sat in the living room, warmed by the fire, discussing my end-of-term production of *Bugsy Malone*. I relaxed more as a result and hardly noticed when we came back around to the topic of men once more.

'So, any cute teachers in that school?'

'Oh, no, not really.' I sucked my top lip into my mouth.

'"Not really" sounds like "Well, maybe".'

I chuckled shyly. 'There's one, Trevor, he teaches biology.'

'He'll know what he's doing, then,' Janet replied. 'Half the battle right there.'

'Yes, but he's married. Getting a divorce, but still married. Has two kids.'

'A nest-builder, that's something. But complicated.'

'I know. I think it's probably a bad idea, but he has amazing eyes ...'

'Bastard.'

'He brings me chocolates and has lunch with me sometimes, stayed back to help out with the play.'

'Chocolates? The man wants you. I say get as much out of him as you can – dinner, wine, flowers – make him earn it.'

'There's still the issue of him being married, AND being a colleague. It would be scandalous.'

'True. So what about around here? Are there any other humans in this place?'

'Really, I've barely gone out. Haven't been to the pub. Though I went for a walk on the beach this afternoon ...' My mind drifted back to the incredible display the rooks put on and for a moment the thought of it felt almost fictional, like something I had imagined or wished had happened.

'And?' Janet was eyeing me encouragingly, as if she could tell where my mind was and wanted me to follow through with the thought.

'And ...' The fire spat a cinder onto the carpet. *Look*, it seemed to be saying, *look what's become of me while you've been talking, blah blah blah.* I got up and fed it two thick sticks. Looking back, I saw Janet was still waiting expectantly for me to finish my story about the beach.

'Well, I saw a guy there,' I explained.

'I like where this is going.'

'But I don't know. He's probably a tourist.'

'At this time of year?'

'Or maybe he's just here for work, like you.'

'Or like you.'

I grinned at Janet's wisdom. It was a nice idea, however unlikely. And besides, now that the subject of Max had been brought to the surface and left to percolate for a while, I was beginning to suspect that I wasn't over him yet. I turned to gaze into the fire again and briefly lost myself in its uncomplicated embrace. I would never get tired of making flames to create heat. It felt such a natural, timeless pleasure, like picking fruit from a tree or drinking water from a stream.

'So, what did he look like?' Janet's voice was soft and gentle, not unlike the warmth of the fire.

'Oh, he wasn't anything really,' I explained. 'Just the only guy I've noticed in the village.' I sat back down in my chair. 'But like I said, I haven't really been out much.'

'Did he look married though?'

I laughed. 'No. I don't know.' I thought about the man's face. 'Actually, he looked kind of alone.' It seemed silly talking about someone I'd seen only briefly and would probably never see again. I described him quickly so that we could move the conversation on.

'He had black shoulder-length hair, about six foot tall and looked very serious. But he was running – jogging, that is. He seemed very focused on it, barely aware of other things going on around him.'

I was about to tell her about the rook display, but Janet jumped in first.

'Well,' she said, sounding more officious than she had all night. 'He sounds like more trouble than Max and more complicated than . . . what was his name? Terry?'

'Trevor.'

'Right, Trevor. Well, there's plenty of fish in the sea and all that.'

'Yeah,' I replied, trying not to think of Max.

Janet stood up. 'We need to go to the pub, then.'

'Now?' I was beginning to feel quite tired.

'No, I'm knackered. How about tomorrow night?'

'Okay. Sure, why not?'

'Great,' she said. 'It's been a long day.'

We walked to the door and hugged.

'I had a really nice time,' she said. 'Thanks so much for the tea. And the natter!'

'Me too,' I replied.

'Seven tomorrow?'

'Seven is perfect.'

'Great.' She winked and left.

When she was gone I sat in front of the fire for a few minutes, watching the flames burn out and the orange and red embers plead for my intervention. Then I took the empty mugs and quickly washed them up in the cool air of the kitchen. There was a vacuum where Janet had been and I didn't know how to fill it. I turned off the lights, went upstairs and picked up my phone. I checked my messages, flicked through a few apps, then settled on the photos. Without thinking I found my way to an old favourite of me and Max.

If you didn't know any better you might just think we were

spooning fairly innocently, but in reality he was inside me. The photo only had our faces and the top of my chest. His fingertips are just visible, cupping my left breast. I'd always found it an incredibly sexy photo, I think because of the subtlety of it, and because I can tell by the flush of my skin how turned on I was. It was taken when we'd been together about a year and were play-talking about how beautiful our children would be with his hair and my cheekbones, his nose and my eyes. There were no plans for London, no hints of what was to come. It felt like we were on a river, going where the water took us.

Suddenly there was a knock on the door downstairs. I wasn't quite sure whether I had really heard it, but then it came again, a volley of three quick thuds. I walked to the top of the stairs and saw Janet through the window, hugging herself against the cold. I quickly ran down and swung the door open.

'Hey, what's wrong?'

She stepped inside. 'Sorry. Really sorry. I left my key here.'

We walked into the living room and found the key, right where she had left it on the coffee table. It was such a big keyring, it seemed impossible to miss. We walked back to the front door and she thanked me and apologised again for interrupting. Then she paused and looked at me suspiciously.

'Honey,' she said, 'we're going to turn heads in that pub tomorrow night.'

B ecause life is better with wine, I drove into Ramelton the
following day and picked up a couple of bottles. The sky
was a motley grey, the road puddled black and blue, and the
farmer's paddocks, dotted with as many rooks as there were
sheep, a flaccid green. These were the colours of the Irish
winter. In the evening I tethered my phone to my laptop and
put *The War on Drugs* on Spotify. I got dressed with a glass of
Sauvignon Blanc always within arm's reach.

I wore my black jeans and a white t-shirt beneath a tight
blue sweater. I suspected it would be too chilly, even inside the
pub, to remove the sweater, but just in case I wanted to be
wearing something worthwhile. I thought heels would be too
much, so went with flats, but chose my Zaras, as they had some
pearl beads across the tongue. It had been an age since I'd last
dressed up properly; a female teacher's wardrobe needing to be
less interesting than the subject she is trying to teach her male
students.

It was twenty past seven by the time Janet's knock came at
the door. By then I was on my second glass.

'Hey!'

'Hey. Sorry I'm late.'

She looked fabulous. It just seemed so effortless for her –
dark blue jeans, topped by a black leather jacket, different from
the one she wore yesterday, the zip set off-centre. I immediately remembered her perfume, even before she gave me a hug.
When she did I noticed she was taller than I recalled.

'You've got heels! I'm going to change!'

'Too much, you think?'

'No, they're perfect!' I could feel the alcohol making me
giddy. 'Have some wine!'

I poured Janet a glass and then went upstairs to change into my heels. I could feel myself rushing; I don't know why. I had to slow myself down as I slid the shoes on.

Janet was frowning at her phone when I came back down, a face she pushed away as I approached. I was about to ask her about it, but she got in first.

'Oh, I love those,' she said, looking to the floor.

'I haven't worn them since, God, since London.'

'Oh, we're going to blow the minds of the locals tonight.'

I grinned. It was exciting, her being excited and me being part of it, but I couldn't get the image of her on the phone out of my head.

'Is everything okay?' I asked. I thought I'd give her the opportunity to reveal it.

'Oh, it's nothing,' she replied, dismissing my concern with an easy hand gesture.

'Nothing nothing? Or nothing something?'

'Nothing something that's probably nothing.'

'That's enough something to be something.'

For the first time I saw a flash of vulnerability in her eyes. It was just a moment but it was definitely there, and I felt with a nudge I might be able to get her to reveal it. But before I could say anything more she shook her head and opened the fridge door.

'Don't worry!' she said, holding her phone between us. 'This is easily fixed.'

Then she pulled out the vegetable crisper and placed the phone on top of a bag of tomatoes.

'There'll be none of that,' she said firmly, shutting the door and reclaiming her wine.

We had another glass each and then I ran upstairs again to get my flats; Janet, ever prepared, had hers in her handbag. We walked into the village, lighting the way with the torch on my phone, then leaned against the wall outside the pub and changed into our heels.

To my surprise there were about twenty people inside. No

one paid us a great deal of attention when we walked in, though a few heads certainly turned. We ordered a couple of glasses of white wine and sat at the bar, since there weren't any tables available.

It was a nice enough place. The dining area at the far side from the entrance was raised slightly and had windows that ran the width of the pub, providing a view of the lough. There were a few groups eating still, or sitting there having finished their meals, including a jovial collection of seven or eight, mostly men. The bar ran about half the length of the pub and had stools all along it, while opposite it were three tables with bench seats along the wall and wooden chairs on the other side. A few other small tables were crammed into innocuous spaces here and there. The PA was playing some tedious radio music.

'So,' I started, more than a little buoyed by all the wine, 'how was work today?'

'Oh, you don't want to know,' Janet replied, again dismissing the notion with a flick of her wrist.

'I don't even know what you do,' I persisted.

'It's complicated.'

'Oh, well ...'

She reached across urgently and touched my arm. 'Oh no, it's not that you wouldn't understand,' she said, adding, 'sorry, I didn't mean it to sound like that.'

'It's okay, you don't have to tell me.' I was curious about what she did, more so because she seemed so reluctant to tell me, but if it was a source of tension I didn't want it to get in the way of a fun night. I held up my glass. 'Let's talk about something else.'

Janet smiled and clinked my glass, but I could feel she kept her eyes on mine as we drank. It was an odd moment, like there was a slight shift in the nature of our fledgling relationship. I wasn't sure where it was going to go or if I liked it. But as always Janet seemed to read my mind and began to right the ship.

'The thing with my work,' she started to say, 'is that I'm not really ...'

Before she could go any further I felt a tap on my shoulder. Slightly annoyed I turned around and was immediately lost in a pair of deep hazel eyes.

'Trevor! What are you doing here?'

He kissed me on the cheek. I felt the hairs on my arm stand up as his stubble moved across my face.

'I'm a Polar Bear,' he said, pointing at the large group I'd noticed in the dining area.

'What on earth do you mean?'

'We swim in rivers, lakes, loughs during the winter. You know, for fun.'

He turned to Janet and offered his hand. 'I'm Trevor.'

'Janet.'

'Sorry,' I said, 'so rude of me.'

Janet brushed my worry aside with a wink. 'I saw you earlier today,' she said to Trevor. 'I thought you guys were crazy.'

'Crazy helps. But it's incredibly invigorating. And addictive. You should try it. We're here until Sunday, every morning at 11 am. Getting the locals acclimatised for the big New Year's Day plunge.'

'There's no way you're getting me in there,' Janet replied, putting her hand on Trevor's arm. I could see his smile broaden. Then she lifted it and pointed at me, at the same time getting up off her stool. 'But this beautiful lady,' she emphasised her point by raising and lowering her finger. 'This beautiful lady you should definitely persuade to go with you.' Then she slid past Trevor, throwing me another quick wink. 'I have to go pee,' she said and was gone.

'You're staying in the village?' I asked Trevor. I had my elbow on the bar, my left hand draped over my right wrist.

'With my mate Connor,' he answered, turning to his group and pointing out a balding man, his cranium orange under the dining area lights. Then he returned his attention to me, leaned in a fraction. 'You live here?' he asked. 'For some reason I just assumed you lived in Letterkenny.'

'You know what they say about assumptions,' I said, not really knowing what I meant. I reached for my wine.

Trevor nodded. 'Is that your housemate? Janet, was it?'

'Yes, but no, she's a friend from ... elsewhere.'

More nodding. It was interesting seeing him outside of work. He looked different, more relaxed, younger and slightly mischievous. It was cute. I had some more wine.

'Staying long, is she?'

'Depends. Why? You interested?'

'Might be. Though I was thinking more for Connor.'

I noticed beads of sweat in Connor's thinning hair. Squishing up my nose, I said: 'I think she's a bit out of Connor's league.'

'Well, that's a relief,' Trevor replied. 'Connor's married.'

I slapped him playfully on the arm. 'You married men are all the same.'

'Funny you should mention that, Alice,' he said, just as Janet reappeared and slid into her seat. 'I'm expecting my divorce to come through tomorrow.'

Janet stood up again. 'I think I left my phone in the bathroom.'

'Oh,' I said to Trevor, trying to sound like he was discussing a student. 'Oh, well, that's a relief, I guess ... for you, I mean.'

'It's a weight off my mind, but only because it means the legal arguments are over.' He reached towards the bar, then closed his fist as he realised he'd left his drink at his table. 'It's the kids though,' he continued, placing his empty hand in the pocket of his jeans. 'Divorced parents. Bedrooms in two different houses. Christmas ...' his voice trailed off as he clenched his jaw. 'Modern family, huh?'

I could see his hazel eyes starting to go red and instinctively put my hand on his arm. It was the first time we'd spoken in any detail about his children. At school our chats had always

21

been tempered by our environment – discussing divorce amongst Catholics was nigh on impossible. And then there were the students, omnipresent in all parts of the school. I'd heard him refer to me by my last name so often that when he used Alice it felt almost insubordinate.

'I'm sure it's for the best,' I told him. 'You're a good parent. Your children will recognise that. Kids are very perceptive.'

Trevor blinked the redness from his eyes and frowned. Something changed in him. His chest raised in a slight jerking motion, as if he'd hiccupped. 'Yeah,' he said dismissively. He looked about to add to this, but stopped short. I saw the muscles in his jaw tighten again.

'I should rejoin my lot,' he finally suggested. 'It was good seeing you.'

He turned and walked away, just as Janet re-emerged from the bathroom. She smiled at him as he walked past, then took her stool next to me.

'He's got a nice bum. Tell me you guys are hooking up.' She picked up her wine.

'We're not hooking up,' I told her. 'Actually, I think I upset him.'

'What?! How?'

'I told him he was a good parent and that his kids would see that. His tone completely changed.'

'Ahh,' Janet said, swivelling on her stool and fishing a phone out of her bag. 'I get that all the time.'

I looked confusedly at the device in her hand.

'Work phone,' she explained. 'For emergencies.'

'Oh …'

She continued as if it was nothing.

'The "You're not a parent, what would you know?" look. It's such nonsense. As if you're unable to understand kids unless you've destroyed your body trying to purge one from your womb' – she waved her hand dismissively in Trevor's general direction – 'or watched your wife do it.' She checked the screen on her phone, then placed it back in her bag. 'Nothing you can do about it, honey. Just be a friend – or a professional – and then leave them to it. Go off and enjoy your pristine vagina.'

'That's so unfair. I deal with kids all day. Just because they're not mine, doesn't mean I don't "know".'

Janet raised her glass, suggesting I do the same.

'To the mothers of other people's children!'

We clinked glasses and finished off our wines, then ordered two more. I really admired the way Janet took things in her stride, remained upbeat and determined to have a good time, even when she seemed to have other things to be worried about. I tried to follow her lead and put Trevor's attitude out of my mind.

Everything was going nicely and we were onto our third glass, when a sound started coming from Janet's handbag. The smile on her face dropped as if it had only been held there by magnets. She fished the emergency phone out and looked at the screen.

'Shit.' She answered and held it to her ear. 'What's wrong? Is she okay?' A pause was followed by a confused look crossing her face. 'Petra? Are you okay?'

For the first few moments of the conversation I watched Janet's face. I'd not seen her look so concerned before and even though I knew nothing of who she was talking to, I found myself on tenterhooks waiting to find out what had happened.

But just as quickly as it had tightened, Janet's face relaxed and she visibly breathed out, even looking at me and expressing her relief with a smile and gentle nod. 'Is he?' she said into the phone, before getting up and indicating she was going to take it outside where it was quieter.

I turned to have a drink of wine, mulling over the little titbits of information I had gathered about Janet in my tipsy head. Then, without realising it, I found myself looking back over at Trevor's table. He had his back to me and seemed deep in conversation with his friend Connor, whose sweaty head seemed doubly so now. Beyond them, through the dark window that looked across the lough, I could make out some lights and, with the moon finding a gap between the clouds, the vague outline of the hills above Lisfannon. I was about to turn back to my wine when I saw a bird fly past the window. First one, and then another. I wouldn't have thought anything of it, except they clearly weren't seagulls. The wings were shorter and flapped more urgently. It was a technique I had become familiar with.

I considered it for a few more moments, before the urge to pee overwhelmed me and I ducked into the bathroom.

When I returned Janet was talking to Trevor at the bar. Four pints of Guinness, the head of each a curtain of fine, creamy bubbles, were waiting in front of him. I sat on the stool, a little unsteadily, and picked up my glass of wine. Shortly Janet turned and put her hand on my arm.

'Alice, Trevor was telling me that they saw a seal out there today. It swam right next to them. Isn't that amazing?'

'Mmmm,' I said. 'Is everything okay with your ...' I pointed at her handbag.

'Oh, yeah, it's fine.'

'I was worried. You sounded really concerned there for a moment.'

'Forget about it,' she insisted. 'Trevor, Alice was telling me earlier that sometimes one of her students will call her "Mum" accidentally. Can you imagine what that's like for her?'

'No, I—'

'Don't your students ever call you "Dad"?'

'Well, no—'

'Oh I'm sorry. But your kids do?'

'Yes, of course—'

She touched his arm. 'So imagine what it must be like for Alice, Trevor. Being thought of as a mother by these kids, and feeling the same way back, but then having to let them go home every day to their real parents, who they will hug and kiss and trust with their laundry.'

Trevor looked this strange exotic creature Janet over, unsure how to answer. Instead he mumbled and acknowledged what she said with an awkward smile and an uncomfortable glance in my direction. I might have been thankful for it if I wasn't feeling so uneasy.

There were a few moments' silence then as Trevor reached for his drink and Janet did the same. Then Janet's emergency phone rang again, piercing the tension. She picked it up without the panicked reaction she'd had earlier.

'Petra? How did you get on? What's that?'

Connor was making his way down to the bar to help with the beers and was just about to introduce himself when I saw Janet's face drop.

'Don't answer it! Honey, listen to me. Are you listening? It's going to be okay, just promise me you'll stay upstairs and not answer the door. Okay? Good. You're doing great.' She stood up. 'Now, can you try and wake your uncle up? No, it's okay, he won't mind. Tell him I'm on my way and not to answer the door until I get there. Can you do that? Okay, stay on the phone, I'll be there in a minute.'

She took the phone from her ear and pressed it into her jacket, then looked at Trevor.

'I need a car. Who's got a car?'

Trevor volunteered and they took one step towards the door before he stopped.

'Shit. Sorry. Mine's parked in. Connor, can we take yours? I'll come.'

'I don't need a militia,' Janet said, her voice forceful and urgent but somehow still calm. 'I need a car.' She looked at Connor, whose hands were still hovering over the beers. 'Please. Now.'

Connor's hands folded up in a silent clap and he followed her out.

I was unsure what to do. I had stood up as Janet had, but now that I tried to put my hand on the stool behind me I found it kept moving out of my grip. I turned to make sure of it and felt the room drag behind the movement of my head. When it caught up it kept going, then bounced back and forward again. I sat on the stool, not quite getting it square.

'Are you okay?' Trevor asked.

'I am,' I told him, annoyed his concern was only for me. 'I'm worried about Janet and the phone thing . . .'

'Yes. There's trouble somewhere? Should we call the Garda?'

'Janet knows what she's doing,' I said. I adjusted myself on the stool and then reached for my wine, intent on wetting my lips so the piece of my mind I intended to give Trevor would come out unhindered. But instead everything went blurry and I passed out.

I woke up in my bed, undressed down to my underwear, a glass of water on my bedside table, a folded note beside it. Grey light framed the curtains.

My head throbbed and my stomach, the walls seemingly gouged with a trowel, felt hollowed out. I couldn't recall coming home or getting into bed. I eyed the note with trepidation then rolled onto my back and looked at the ceiling.

Flashes of the previous night came to mind, a disjointed series of images and snippets of conversations. Eyes, clothes, shoes, floor tiles. I tried to assemble it in order. There was wine, there was Trevor, there was Janet on the phone. My heart jumped. What had happened to Janet? I reached for the note.

Drink loads of water (no wine, ever again!). Meet me for lunch if you're up for it (I'll call). X Janet

I looked around but couldn't see my phone or handbag. It hurt just to move my head and a fresh wave of nausea came over me. I sunk back into the pillow and let life re-enter me at its own pace.

When I felt slightly more capable I had another look for my handbag; I was sure Janet would have left it nearby. I crawled to the end of the bed, scanned the room and found it on a chair that also had my jeans hung over the back. With all the effort I could muster I stepped out of bed, grabbed the bag and fell back onto the mattress. Everything was a struggle.

Once my head had stopped spinning from the exertion I dug my phone out and looked at the home screen. It was 9:13. There were messages from Trevor and from a number my phone didn't recognise but which had a UK prefix. I assumed it was from Janet. I opened Trevor's first.

Hey there Ms Phillips. I hope you're feeling okay. You know the best thing for a hangover is a cold swim? We'll be at the boat ramp at 11. X T

There was no way I was going for a swim. I opened the message from Janet. Only it wasn't from Janet after all.

Hey Alice its Max. I prized you're number out of a mutual friend who swore me not 2 tell there name. Sorry, but I needed to talk to u. Can we? xx

I stared at the message for a few more moments, reading over it twice, then tossed the phone aside, rushed out of bed and threw up in the bathroom sink.

*

Eventually I got up properly and, after a shower and a few slices of Vegemite on toast, started to feel better. I forced down a couple of glasses of water, had some Panadol and a coffee. I could feel life returning to my limbs, my stomach no longer ate itself and I was able to breathe properly. My head still throbbed, but it was less clamorous and slowly receding to an epicentre just above my spine. I dressed warmly and headed towards the boat ramp.

I took the path that ran parallel to the beach, but seeing the tide was out decided to cut across the dunes and walk on the sand. There was no breeze at all and clouds sat low on the hills across the lough, blocking their peaks, and the wind turbines halfway up, from view. For a winter's day it was fairly mild, which made my hangover that bit more tolerable. Small mercies.

I walked over the soft sand, across the marmalade-brown tidemarks and peered into the clear water. I felt a sudden impulse to immerse myself, as if doing so would wash away my hangover completely and take with it the feelings of embarrassment, insecurity, loneliness, heartache and everything else that anchored me to land. The water reflected the white clouds and said, *fly away, under the sea*. I shook off this strange reverie and looked down the beach, towards the bend.

The man I'd seen before, training his dog, he was at it again.

Further down was a couple and their child. The mother was walking slightly off to the side, leaving the father to hold the child's hand. Beyond them the lough widened and a blue fishing boat chugged optimistically towards the Atlantic.

I headed towards the boat ramp. It was about quarter past eleven so I knew I would probably miss Trevor and the Polar Bears entering the lough. Perhaps I would be there when he got back though and I could apologise and thank him for looking after me last night. My memory was blurry and potholed and I wanted to fill in the missing pieces. At some stage I was going to have to apologise to the pub.

I was trying to come up with what I might say to the publican when something unusual happened. From out of the trees by the cemetery a group of about two dozen rooks suddenly took flight. Half of them swooped out over the water and started circling about twenty metres offshore, a couple of metres above the surface. The rest landed by the waterline, spread out like a mini black wall, just beyond the reach of the tiny lapping waves.

Curious, I approached to see what they might have taken an interest in. As I did, two of the birds broke away from the wall and flew towards me. They traced an arc past my right ear, swooped behind me, then emerged on my left. Then they flew off towards the car park. As they did this they made that same squeaking toy sound that the flock had made when pitching and turning above my head two evenings earlier.

I continued towards the birds lined up along the water's edge. To my surprise they didn't fly off as I approached. Instead they jumped a few inches off the ground, flapping their wings excitedly, as if to make themselves bigger. But while they kept an eye on me, mostly their attention was out over the water, where their friends looked to be in a feeding frenzy. I'd never seen this kind of bird do it before, but they were diving into the water as if after baitfish beneath the surface.

The two birds that had flown towards the car park returned,

banked around behind me again, let out the squeaking toy sound and headed back once more. It was almost as if they wanted me to follow them. Then something in the sand caught my eye.

It was a name – Felix – written in elaborate handwriting. My memory was shaky at the best of times, and my hangover wasn't helping, but the way the four tails of the X curled off in search of something was distinctively familiar. I had the feeling I'd seen the same name written here before.

The circling, diving rooks were getting closer and the ones on the shore more excited in return. There was something unsettling about their behaviour and so rather than stick around to see what might happen, I started to move on. But just as I did I heard a heavy splash. I turned and saw a small patch of broiling white water about ten metres away. The circling rooks were above it, throwing themselves into the spray in a mad panic, but the disturbance was definitely not caused by them. Perhaps it wasn't baitfish after all, I thought. A sketchy memory from the pub came back – Janet saying something about a seal.

Then, a little further out and to the left, I noticed more splashing. This was bigger still and as opposed to the single eruption it was ongoing. Then I saw movement within it – pale arms wheeling through the air, turning the water a frothy white. I quickly realised it was the Polar Bears. As they approached, the rooks stopped diving into the water. They circled higher, then further offshore, where they maintained a cautious observance from about ten metres above the surface. The shore-based birds dispersed too. Whatever had been happening, the excitement seemed to be over for now.

I followed the Polar Bears along the beach and waited by the boat ramp as they emerged. Trevor certainly looked invigorated and wore a wide grin on his face; however, the freezing temperature was evident on his goose-pimpled skin as soon as it was exposed to the air, while doing nothing for his manhood in the tiny Speedos he was wearing. I tried (and mostly failed) not to look.

'Hi,' I said to him, giving a little wave as he walked shivering up the boat ramp. I thought I'd feel embarrassed seeing him for the first time since the night before, but his little swimming shorts made everything alright.

'How are you feeling?' he asked, either unaware or unconcerned about his state.

'Hungover,' I said. Hearing his sonorous voice and seeing him towel off without worrying that I was looking, brought all my insecurities about the night before rushing back. 'Embarrassed. Ashamed. Suicidal.'

'Oh, it was nothing,' he assured me. 'Hardly anyone noticed. Just me and the barman really, and we got it all cleaned up pretty quickly.'

'I'm so sorry that you had to do that. I feel terrible. Can I make it up to you somehow?'

He pulled a t-shirt over his head. Without any jeans on it made him look like he was standing in his underwear.

'I wouldn't say no to a coffee,' he said, 'since you offered.'

Trevor got into the back seat of a car and put on his jeans. I assumed he put these on over some dry underwear, rather than straight over his Speedos, though as I couldn't know for sure I found myself looking for a damp patch to show through his bum and crutch area for the next few minutes. It never appeared.

As Trevor was putting his shoes and socks on, Connor came shivering up the boat ramp, his head looking even balder coming out of the cold lough than it had in the pub. He said hello to me and I sheepishly replied in kind, then Trevor tossed him the car keys and told him we were going to the cafe and that he'd meet him at the house later.

*

We'd only just ordered our coffees when my phone rang. To my surprise it showed that Janet was calling; I didn't recall exchanging phone numbers with her.

'Hey girl, how you feeling?'

'Getting better. How are you?'

'Oh, I'm just fine. Was wondering if you wanted to meet for a coffee and something to eat? There's someone I'd like you to meet.'

'Oh God, who?'

'You'll see.'

'... Okay. I've so many questions. I'm actually in the cafe with Trevor right now.'

'Oh, great, I'll be there in ...'

Janet appeared in the window of the cafe, her phone to her ear. She spotted me and waved, then hung up and walked through the door. Trevor stood and gave her a kiss on the cheek. I realised then that he and I hadn't exchanged that greeting today. Janet and I did the same.

'Thanks for last night,' I said. 'I'm so embarrassed.'

'Oh, don't be. We've all been there.'

'I don't remember getting home, going to bed, anything.'

'Yeah, you were out of it. Mark carried you up the stairs like a fireman. I thought you were going to wake up and fall in love with him.'

'Who's Mark?'

'But don't worry, I kicked him out as soon as you were on your bed. Nobody saw that smoking body but me.' She winked at Trevor as she said this.

Janet was talking far quicker than I could think. I turned to Trevor.

'I thought you put me in bed.'

'Me? No, Mark had it covered.'

'Who's Mark?'

'Have you guys ordered?'

'Yes, but I'll get the waitress,' Trevor said, before getting up to find her.

Janet was checking her phone again – I wasn't sure which one. I had so many questions but could only get one out at a time. I put the Mark question aside for a moment.

'When did we exchange numbers? I can't believe how much I can't remember ...'

Janet bit her lip. 'Actually that was a bit sneaky of me. I unlocked your phone with your finger while you were passed out and saved my number on it. Sorry?'

I laughed. 'Don't be. It's kind of sweet.' I took a sip of coffee and could feel the hangover loosening its grip. 'Janet?'

'Yep.'

'Who's Mark?'

Presently a tall man wearing a black beanie and a black denim jacket with woollen lining appeared in the window. He was carrying a small plastic bag. Trevor cut him off as he entered the cafe and shared a manly hug and a chuckle over some story that I feared I was somewhat implicated in. Then Janet grabbed his hand and introduced him.

'Alice, this is Mark.'

She didn't say as much, but it soon became apparent Mark was Janet's boyfriend. The waitress came over, took their coffee orders and promised to come back to see if we wanted food. I hid myself behind my mug, unable to look Mark in the eye. He was incredibly handsome and the idea of him carrying me to bed while I hung limp in his arms, smelling of sick, was mortifying.

Thankfully he didn't mention it and after a while I began to feel at ease. It was also clear he was besotted with Janet, while there was a subtle change in her character around him. The confidence she always carried was still there, just tempered with a soft vulnerability that she gave away when he looked at her for more than a few seconds. It was as if she knew how much he could hurt her and struggled to find a way to overcome that with her usual bag of tricks.

We ordered food and settled into easy conversation. It was nice having Trevor there. He was a reassuring presence that somehow made me feel like I was okay, I was doing the right thing. He told

33

Janet and Mark I was a good teacher and the students liked me and that the other teachers, though they might not say it, were glad I had chosen to teach at their school. They felt it gave the students a sense of the world they wouldn't have gotten otherwise. It was nice hearing that, though in truth, of course, I didn't exactly choose the school, rather took the first job that offered me an escape from London and all the mess there.

It took a while for the conversation to move around to the topic of the previous night. I'd been happy to avoid it, given what had happened to me, but I was still curious as to what Janet's emergency phone call was all about and where Mark fitted into it all. It was only when Mark mentioned 'that guy last night' that the opportunity came up again.

Janet clearly wanted to change the subject straight away, but Mark, concentrating on speaking to Trevor, kept going.

'. . . But he was a good guy,' he explained. 'A stranger was standing at his door in the middle of the night and he didn't baulk.'

'Yeah,' Janet replied, 'well, I noticed the cricket bat had moved from the bedroom to behind the front door.'

'Ah, you think the worst of men.'

'That's because I've seen the worst.'

'Not this guy. I like him.'

I felt stupid not knowing who or what they were talking about, but finding a way to ask was difficult, especially as Janet had gone out of her way not to talk about work since I'd met her. And this clearly had something to do with work. Yet it was apparent that Mark was able to cut through this, even with me listening in. Janet's responses were begrudging, but she gave them, almost as if she knew that if she didn't he might spill the beans and tell me everything.

It was in this way, by staying quiet and letting Mark ask questions, that I was able to begin forming a faint outline of what it was Janet did and who the people were she was working with.

'Where are they now?' he asked.

Janet replied. 'They're down on the beach on a mermaid stakeout. I'm trying to give them time together without me, so left them to it.'

'I thought the mermaid thing was an issue.'

'It can be, but he's figuring out how to deal with it.'

'Neutral response, no encouragement?'

'Exactly. He's picking it up. There's hope for him yet.'

'I knew it.'

Janet rolled her eyes at Mark and quietened the conversation by picking up her menu. The rest of us followed suit instinctively. But I couldn't concentrate on the options; instead I was trying to put together the pieces of the puzzle. There seemed to be a child involved, probably a girl, and a man, the one with the cricket bat, looking after her. Suddenly it occurred to me that Janet wasn't here for work at all. She was here with her daughter and this other man was the father, a father who until recently didn't know he was one. But as soon as I came to that conclusion I realised how silly it sounded. There was no way she would have casually gone to the pub with me while her daughter was left with her estranged father. Perhaps the girl was being adopted by the man. But I was fairly sure that was rare.

Whatever it was, I was going to have to wait for more details to trickle out.

'Around here,' Trevor announced, placing his menu on the table, 'some folk refer to mermaids as merrows. Then there's the selkie . . .'

'Selfie?' Janet asked, perplexed.

'Selkie. It's like a mermaid, or a merrow, but appears like a seal when it's in the water. When it comes to land though, it sheds it skin and looks human. And if a real human, usually a man, finds and hides that skin the selkie will be compelled to be his wife and be unable to go back into the sea until she finds it.'

'Ugh,' Janet groaned. 'Men.'

'So the seals out there might be selkies?' Mark asked.

Trevor chuckled. 'If you're lucky. But if you're unlucky, you might come across the sea witch.'

'I like the sound of her,' Janet replied. 'What's her game?'

'Well,' he began, as if every word was true, 'she controls storms, tides, even the moon. She can hide sunken treasure and reveal it to sailors who have pleased her.'

'And how does one please her?' Mark asked.

'Money usually does the trick.'

'I've met some sea witches.'

'Ha. The most common belief of the sea witch around here,' he explained, for the first time using language that suggested it was a fairy tale, 'is that she will bring back the body of a drowned sailor if you cast a coin into the sea as payment.'

'Well,' Mark announced, picking up his plastic bag from the floor and looking at Janet, 'honey, you'd better make sure you've got some change.'

He removed some faded green shorts from the bag and held them over the table proudly.

'You're in?' Trevor remarked.

'I'm in.'

'Good man.'

'You guys are crazy,' Janet exclaimed, and then turning to Mark she added: 'especially you. Look at your hat and that jacket, it's not even a cold day.'

'It's because I don't want to do it,' he said theatrically, 'that I must.'

Janet shook her head. Trevor touched my arm, left his hand there and focused on me.

'Why don't you join us? There really is nothing else like it. You'll know you're alive, and you need something to remind you during term break. Soon you'll be swimming amongst kids again and you'll yearn for the icy water.'

It might have been Trevor's chocolate eyes, or maybe just

the caffeine; or it could've been the idea of seeing Trevor, and Mark for that matter, in their swimming shorts. Whatever it was, I suddenly felt like it wasn't such a bad idea. There was only one problem.

'I don't have a one-piece swimming costume.'

'They've got some in the charity shop,' Mark said. 'I checked, just in case I could convince Janet.'

'Not on your life,' Janet replied.

'Figured.'

'Well?' Trevor asked.

'If they've got one in my size.'

Mark nodded at me. 'They do.'

⸺ 4 ⸺

When I arrived at the boat ramp I could see Trevor talking to Connor and a few of the other swimmers. I gave him a wave, but having spotted an apprehensive looking Mark in his car I went to see if he was having any second thoughts.

As I approached I could see the grey sky reflected in the windshield and through it, leaning on the steering wheel, Mark looking at the clouds. I opened the passenger door and slid into the heated interior.

'Don't you think you're making this harder than necessary?' I asked.

Mark nodded but didn't respond verbally. He was focused on the clouds. I leaned back in the seat and closed my eyes. I felt that every moment spent warm and dry should be cherished as if it were my last.

'Ever thought about having children?'

His question took me by surprise. I opened my eyes and looked across, but Mark was still peering out the windscreen, looking into the sky above.

'Umm, a little,' I replied. 'Have you?'

Again he nodded without saying anything. I leaned forward and followed his eyeline. Two rooks were above the car, tracing a circle on the grey backdrop.

'Has Janet told you why she's here?'

'Kind of,' I replied sheepishly. 'Work.'

'Right. But that's not the whole story.'

His attention was still on the rooks.

'She's a child protection officer with the NSPCC,' he explained, finally leaning back in his seat. 'She brought a girl here to be with her uncle.'

I nodded gently, not wanting to fully endorse Mark's spilling of the beans, but also not wanting to stop him from doing so.

'Thing is, they're poorly funded.' He shrugged his shoulders. 'They can't afford to send an officer to Ireland, and even if they could, they wouldn't. It's not exactly their jurisdiction.'

'What are you saying?'

'I'm saying Janet shouldn't be here with that girl.'

'Legally?'

He tilted his head slightly. 'Well, it's a grey area. Officially the girl's in temporary foster care in Bristol.'

'So her parents don't know she's here?'

'The father will figure it out. I've met him. The mother is deceased.'

There was something about the way Mark was explaining the situation that was both formal and personal. It was like he was balancing on a wire and occasionally tilted one way then the other. I was sure there was more he wasn't telling me, but before I could probe further he changed the subject.

'What about you, though?' he asked, the corner of his mouth curling into the start of a grin. 'Why does a girl ... a woman who wants children come to a tiny Irish village where she knows no one?'

'I didn't say I *want* children.'

'But you've thought about it.'

'What are you getting at, Mark?' I looked out the window at the bodies gathered at the boat ramp. I could see Trevor looking towards us, squinting. 'We should get going.'

'When I met Janet,' Mark continued, 'she had a knife in one hand and a three-year-old under her arm.'

'Janet?!'

Mark nodded slowly, a nod that dissolved into another smile. 'Fiery woman.'

'But ... what?'

'The child wasn't hers,' he explained. 'Nor was the knife, for that matter. She'd relieved both of them from a drunk who was arguing with his ex. By the time I got there he was crying on the sofa.'

39

'You worked with Janet?'

'No, but our paths crossed occasionally.'

I shook my head inquisitively.

'I'm a police officer,' he explained, 'on the beat back then. Now a detective with CID.' He focused on me. 'So go on. Why Rathmullan? Why not stay in London, or go back to Australia?'

Some of the other swimmers were wading into the water. I could see their chests inflating as the cold registered and they took involuntary lungfuls of air. Then they plunged under the surface and swum eagerly away, as if they could bat the cold water from their bodies.

Even though I had nothing to hide from a police officer, I still found myself worried Mark was on to me somehow. His detective senses could probably tell I had a secret and, even if it wasn't illegal, it needed to be prised out of me and pored over for traces of moral guilt, of which he would find damning evidence.

I told him as much as I was comfortable with. 'If I'd gone home after Max and I broke up, it would have meant my whole time away from Australia was about him. I had to go somewhere and do something, however small, that was my choice, rather than a result of following Max. Everywhere in the UK felt too much like a consequence of London.'

Mark nodded his approval, then said, 'Kind of the same reason I'm going for this swim today.'

I smiled and reached for the door handle but felt Mark's hand on my leg. I turned and he took it away.

'The house the girl has been staying in,' he said, 'the foster home. It's our place – mine and Janet's.'

'Oh. Shit. Will you get in trouble?'

'Depends on the father. He's voluntarily given up care for the child while he fights a restraining order taken out by his girlfriend. It's a tactical move to gain favour with the court. That and taking anger management classes. Shows he's trying and has the child's best interests in mind. So if he finds out the girl is with her uncle in Ireland, the wisest thing for him to do is not to cause a fuss, complete his course, make good with his girlfriend and have the restraining order removed. On the other hand he might fly off the handle.' Mark grimaced. 'Which is probably what Janet is hoping for.'

'But why would Janet risk your job, her job . . .'

Trevor was waving at us from the boat ramp. Beyond him the water was broiling with pale arms and pink faces.

'Janet lived in foster homes from when she was four. Some good homes, some bad, but none that were family. She remembers a face that she believes was her mum and recalls numerous other people being around her from that time. Family members, perhaps. But she doesn't know what happened for her to be taken away, or why none of those other people wanted to take her in. She's never heard from any of them.'

'That's heartbreaking.'

'Yeah. So, for her the risk is worth it. Even if the girl goes back to her father, she'll know she has an uncle on her mum's side that, hopefully, will be there for her.'

By the boat ramp Trevor's waving was becoming more urgent. Mark flashed the headlights and breathed out heavily.

'Right,' he said. 'I guess we better go in.'

We climbed out of the car and eyed each other over the roof, before a rook called out and our attention was again caught by the circling birds. After a few moments Mark started to undress. I followed suit.

'I think you'd make a good mother,' he said, pulling his jumper over his head. I could see the hairs on his arms standing on their ends as the cold air hit his skin. I didn't respond to his comment.

'Janet can't have kids,' he finally conceded, opening the door and tossing his jumper inside. 'Believe me, we've tried. Uterine fibroids, apparently. Medical speak for an unwilling uterus.'

'Oh, I'm sorry. Is there a treatment for it?'

'Nope.' He shut the door solidly.

I placed my clothes on the front seat. It was difficult to know what to say. Talking about Janet's body like this felt like an intrusion, yet Mark obviously wanted to discuss it.

'I'm really sorry,' I offered hopelessly.

Mark blinked my apology away and focused on me with steely eyes. At first I thought it was just his way of dealing with the cold, but then he said, 'Perfectly good eggs though,' and I suddenly realised what he'd been getting at all along.

I was stunned. 'Mark,' I said, trying to gather my thoughts. 'Does ... are you ...'

'This is me talking,' he explained, 'not Janet. She hasn't said anything to me about you, about *this*. But I know she likes you. We've discussed potential surrogates before. Obviously it's a very personal thing for her, so I don't push it. But when it does come up again, it'd be nice to be able to suggest someone she likes. Someone who I knew was willing.'

'Jesus, Mark ...'

'Don't answer. Not now. Let's go swimming first.'

Although the breeze was light it cut right through me. I hugged myself, shaking.

Mark rubbed his forehead. 'Shit. I'm sorry. I didn't mean to dump this on you. I was just thinking out loud, really. It's just when you said that you wanted to do something over here that wasn't about Max, I just ... I'm sorry. Forget I mentioned it. Please.'

I nodded and looked towards the boat ramp, glad for Trevor's impatience to get me out of the conversation.

'We really should ...'

'Yes,' replied Mark. 'We should! Forget everything I said. Let's jump in!'

'Okay,' I answered, meaning the forgetting everything bit, but not resisting when Mark grabbed my hand and led me to the jetty.

The water was clear, but the sandy bottom somehow

imbued it with a green hue. I could make out clumps of seaweed here and there, like the islands of an atoll, while a flash of silver gave away a school of small fish by the hull of a nearby boat. Yet with the grey clouds reflecting off the surface it felt like we were jumping into the sky. The two rooks circled above and below us.

The drop from the jetty to the surface must have been about four metres, but it felt much further. Trevor was treading water to our left while the rest of the group were splashing around a little further along the beach, some swimming and some looking back to watch us. I could see Connor's balding head beaded with water.

I wanted a few moments to compose myself and build up my confidence, but Mark was of the mind that hesitation was fatal. He squeezed my hand.

'On three. One, two ...'

'Wait—'

'Three!'

He pulled me forward and I resisted. For a moment we stood hand in hand, our arms stretched, leaning away from each other like figure skaters. Then I said *fuck it* and let him pull me to the edge. We placed our feet on the wide timber beam and launched ourselves into space.

For a few moments we seemed to stall in the air, held in a spot in low orbit like the rooks above the trees; before Mark's hand slipped from mine and gravity speared us into the frigid water.

I'd never felt such an immediate, all-encompassing change to my sense of wellbeing. All the air was sucked from my lungs and I could feel my heart thunder into action. I'd instinctually kept my eyes closed as I entered the water, but now I opened them wide and tried to make sense of my environment. All I could see was bubbles. And then, as I struggled to get my bearings, I saw a shape coming towards me. I was already in such a state that I observed it with near indifference, like it was just another part of the maxed-out trauma.

A hand grabbed mine and pulled me upwards until my face erupted into the cold air. I gasped for oxygen but only got a mouthful of hair before dipping back under. The hand pulled me back up again and wiped the hair from my face. I desperately sucked in a lungful of air and leaned back on the arm that was wrapped around my back, holding me on the surface.

'You're okay,' Trevor said. 'You did it.'

For a few moments I could only breathe in and out. We drifted under the jetty with the current; the semi-darkness felt like a cave.

'Ready to swim?' Trevor asked. I could sense by his voice that this was more than just a recreational suggestion.

I nodded, rolled on to my stomach, put my head back under the surface and started kicking. Soon I was back from under the jetty and making my way up the beach; the rest of the group were about twenty metres ahead.

Once the initial shock subsided and I became relatively aware of my surroundings, I began to relax. The temperature of the water was frigid, but it wasn't actually as cold as I had thought. It was bearable and as my arms got moving and my legs kicking I could feel a distant warmth spreading through my limbs and around my chest. My toes and fingers, even my nose, these I could feel being abandoned as superfluous, but there was something incredibly reassuring about feeling my body looking after its essential parts.

Soon I caught the rest of the group. Some of them were standing, looking back at where they had come from as if to convince themselves that they had actually done it. I stopped with them – not for that reason, but because I wanted to see where Trevor and Mark were.

'You're like a feckin' fish!' Trevor said as he caught up to me, breathing heavily.

'We swim to school in Australia,' I explained. 'Where's Mark?'

Trevor looked around but couldn't see him either. Panic

suddenly reared in me until a woman in a blue cap spotted him.

'He's gone ashore.'

Sure enough, his tall, muscular frame was emerging from the water a few metres from the boat ramp, his arms wrapped around himself as if wearing a straitjacket. He looked over and waved away our concern as he trotted up the beach to reclaim his tracksuit pants and hoody.

The rest of us continued to swim up the beach for a few more minutes, before Trevor suggested we turn around. Some of the group moved closer to shore so they could wade, rather than swim, but I was really beginning to enjoy myself.

'I'm going to keep going for a bit,' I told him.

'Okay. Be careful, though. Hypothermia is deceptive. The more comfortable you feel, the more likely you are to be getting it.'

I reassured him I wouldn't be too much longer, then swam off. The water felt smooth, like I was sliding through velvet sheets. It was a full body embrace, getting into every pore, separating every strand of hair. It felt like returning home after a long absence and being hugged and coddled by family and friends. I'd forgotten how much I loved swimming.

I'm not sure how long I was in there for. As I glided across the sandy bottom, crabs nipping defensively at the water above them, tiny fish watching me cautiously through miniature eyes, there was nothing as mechanical as a clock to concern myself with. Time seemed a construct of another world. I straddled the edge of the drop-off, the other side of which plunged steadily into an azure-blue jungle of seaweed and aquatic mysteriousness.

It was only when I looked towards the beach and recognised the group of cottages which mine was part of that I realised how far down I had swum. I tried to perform a tumble turn under the water to begin heading back, but instead of rolling gracefully forward and swivelling around, I found myself tied in an ungainly knot under the water. My arms felt like prosthetics, clumsily tacked to the shoulders. I tried to kick to get some momentum but my legs, too, were unresponsive. I could feel my heart racing and my jaw, like a manic typewriter, begin chattering uncontrollably.

With great difficulty I managed to splash and scramble to the shallower water, until I was able to stand unsteadily on the bottom. The relief I felt at realising I probably wasn't going to drown was tempered by the fact that my head, exposed to the remorseless air, now felt like a block of ice. Then my vision began to blur. Where I thought the beach was suddenly looked like the hills on the other side of the lough. I started to move in the opposite direction and felt the sandy bottom drop away. I scrambled to get my footing again. Above me I heard strange sounds. Then a large shape splashed furiously in the water, moving towards me. In my confusion I thought it was a sea turtle. I reached for it, put my arms around its shell and let it carry me to the shore.

Trevor wrapped me in a towel and rubbed at my arms. Mark arrived moments later and concentrated on my legs with his towel. I was shaking still but coherence quickly returned.

'I'm s-s-s-s-so sorry,' I told them. 'I was ennnnnnjoying it s-s-s-s-so much I didn't realise how c-c-c-cold I was get-ting.'

'Just concentrate on getting warm,' Trevor said, wiping the hair out of my face.

Mark pulled my jumper over the top of me and Trevor helped me step into my tracksuit bottoms. Then, for the second time in two days, a man helped me into my house and put me into bed. This time it was Trevor and as he pulled the duvet over me and found a blanket to put on top of that, I saw those coffee eyes of his swimming with concern.

'Do I look that bad?' I asked.

'You were blue,' he explained. 'Like a Smurf. I was really worried.' He ran his hand through his hair, revealing momentarily the extent of its recession. I concentrated on his eyes.

'Thanks for saving me,' I said.

The cold still gripped me but I could feel the warmth of the bed and my clothes around me, like stepping into an air-conditioned car.

'It was the birds that saved you,' he explained. 'I was coming down the beach, anyway, with your towel. But these two birds kept flying around me and making a strange sound, then going out across the water. It was only when I saw they were circling around you too that I realised something was up. The strangest thing.'

I curled into a ball inside my duvet.

'You should take your swimsuit off,' Trevor continued. 'The dampness won't be helping.'

I'd forgotten I still had it on, but now that he said it I could feel its icy skin clinging to me like seaweed. I slid under the duvet, removed my jumper and tracksuit bottoms, then peeled the damp swimsuit off. Sneaking a hand out from beneath the duvet I dropped it where I imagined Trevor's feet were. Then I pulled the tracksuit bottoms and jumper back on and re-emerged. I looked around for Trevor, but he was gone. There was a knock at the door.

'Decent?'

'It's fine,' I said.

'I've put the kettle on,' he said, poking his head around the door, 'and lit a fire.'

'Both those things sound perfect.'

I embraced the cloudy warmth of my duvet for a few more minutes, then wrapped myself in it and joined Trevor down-stairs.

'I've moved the sofa in front of the fire,' he said, pouring hot water into two mugs in the kitchen. 'Go make yourself comfortable.'

I nestled on the sofa, a fluffy white ball of cosiness, and basked in the orange heat. Shortly Trevor brought my cup of tea, which I wrapped my hands around and integrated into my duvet cocoon. Then he settled in next to me, rubbing my legs through the duck down as he watched the dancing flames.

Life returned to my body by degrees and with each one I realised that, in spite of the brush with hypothermia, I had discovered something I'd forgotten I'd lost. I thought my attraction to the beach had been the pensive subtlety of its beauty, but it was more than that. It was the magic of the water there, of swimming where and when you weren't meant to, of entering a world of seals and crabs, fish and seaweed jungles, of not knowing what was over the drop-off. Maybe it was a sense of returning to where we came from or, less profound, simply the familiarity of the sea, having grown up on a large island surrounded by it. Whatever it was, I couldn't wait to go back in.

We watched the fire crack and glow, and then put on a DVD and snuggled together to watch that. Outside a drizzly rain turned into icy hail that covered everything in a white sheet. For now at least, being inside felt like the only place to be.

*

'Mark told me what happened,' Janet said, reaching over the cloud of duvet to give me a hug. In the kitchen Trevor and Mark were making tea.

'I was enjoying it until I nearly froze to death,' I told her. 'I forgot how much I love swimming.'

Janet shook her head. 'All three of you are crazy. Mark's still cold. I wouldn't let him touch me until he warmed his hands over the toaster.'

I'd become incredibly sensitive to other people's body heat and could feel Janet's warmth through the duvet. She looked towards the door that opened into the kitchen, then turned back to me, her voice lowered, an eyebrow raised.

'Trevor's been looking after you, then?'

I grinned. 'He's been very gentlemanly. I think he feels responsible for what happened.'

The fact was we *had* fooled around a bit – eager for any kind of warmth, I had let him get under the duvet with me and as I snuggled up to him, almost by accident, our lips met. It was a nice, comforting kind of kiss. The sort a husband might give his wife after a romantic dinner and before he volunteers to do the dishes. A gentlemanly kiss. Afterwards we settled back in front of the DVD as if it was normal. Janet and Mark had arrived ten minutes later.

But it was the swimming I really wanted to talk about.

'I'm looking forward to going back in,' I said.

'Are you serious?'

'Deadly! I might get a wetsuit though.'

'Well okay, you're mad,' she said, dismissing my enthusiasm. She checked the door again and then turned back and put her hand on top of a leg-shaped mound of duvet and squeezed gently.

'Mark told me about your conversation this morning.'

'Oh.'

'Don't worry,' she said. 'I don't mind.'

'I feel like I should apologise anyway.'

'Don't be silly! What for? It's nice that Mark trusts you. I trust you!' She squeezed my leg again and smiled.

I smiled back. I wasn't entirely sure if we were talking about him telling me about her job, her childhood or her womb. But then it became very clear. Janet's eyes moistened, she leaned forward and wrapped me in another hug.

'You're such a wonderful person,' she said. 'We've only just met but I feel so close to you.' She pulled back and wiped some tears from her cheeks.

'I feel close to you too,' I replied, unsure what was happening.

'It's a wonderful offer, Alice, but you've got your career to think of and, who knows, maybe you and Trevor—'

'What?'

'Oh, I know it's early days but he obviously likes you, and you're right, those eyes!'

'I—'

'Look, I need to think about it – you really need to think more about it – we don't even know if it'll work.'

'No, umm ...'

Janet shook her head at me. 'You're so sweet. And Mark! God, he's so desperate to have a baby. They say women have a biological clock. His has got one of those bunny-rabbit batteries in it.'

'Batteries ...'

'Let's talk again in a few weeks, when you've had some time to think about it.' She waved her finger between our two wombs. 'And don't let this,' she said, before pointing to the kitchen, 'stop that.'

Right on cue, Mark and Trevor came in with the teas and eyed us suspiciously. We did the same to them.

They settled on some chairs and the conversation shifted, before Janet announced they were leaving that evening. I assumed this meant the girl she'd brought over to see her uncle was leaving with them; however, as there was no elaboration on the subject, and I wasn't sure if Mark had told her this part of our conversation, I just had to put the pieces together. I wondered if I would ever find out who the uncle was. It would be odd, knowing something of the drama surrounding his private life, yet having to pretend I knew nothing at all.

'We'll speak soon,' Janet said as she hugged me at the door.

I wanted to say something to Mark when he hugged me, but Janet was right there, watching us like the mother of the baby might watch the father and the other mother of that same baby. It was all too bamboozling to find words for. It felt like one of those strange, visceral dreams, when you're convinced the events actually took place. I half expected to wake and have to touch my stomach to see if I was pregnant.

Trevor and I retired to the sofa and continued watching the DVD, though I wasn't able to concentrate on it. Soon Trevor started touching my leg again and searching for my hand. I let him find it and snuggle in a bit closer. Then he was kissing my neck. My body had completely thawed out now and I tossed the duvet aside, which only encouraged him further. We kissed for a while and then he took off my jumper and shirt and kissed my chest. All I could see was his hairline, which made him seem much older than he was. Still, he had a way that wasn't unpleasant. I let him slowly turn me on, my mind never quite where his was, but close enough. When he felt confident enough that he could remove my tracksuit pants and toss off his t-shirt, I had to stop him and ask if he had a condom.

'Ah Alice,' he moaned, 'I'm a Catholic, you know . . .'

I rolled my eyes.

'Don't worry,' he insisted. 'We have a special technique.'

—◦ **5** ◦—

The morning after I mistook Trevor for a sea turtle in Lough Swilly, he made pancakes, filled them with mushrooms and cheese, and served them to me in bed. I preferred sweet fillings but didn't say anything; his gesture was sweet enough. The sex we'd had was pleasant, and I wasn't as anxious as I thought I might have been, given he was the first since all the London business. When he left he told me he'd call and arrange to meet up during the week, if I wanted.

'Uh huh,' I replied.

The following day I drove to an outdoor adventure shop in Letterkenny and bought the only wetsuit they had for women. It was the kind of green you saw on aliens in low budget movies, but I didn't trust my car to make it into Derry to try another shop. Instead I convinced myself that no one would see it anyway and that all that really mattered was that it kept me warm.

*

Soon I was swimming every day. With the wetsuit I was able to spend an hour or more in the water, whereafter my body would radiate with the organic pleasure of use. I'd walk off the beach, through the dunes and up to my cottage, where I could strip off and shower and be having a coffee or hot chocolate twenty minutes after leaving the water.

I would plan my day around my swim, knowing that whatever drudgery might lay ahead, be it food shopping, cleaning or – when the time came round again – planning for classes, I would be able to tackle it with a clear mind and energised body. And that I had spent some time doing something for me meant I didn't feel any day was 'wasted'. For years I had concentrated on (and often failed at) being a better student, a better girlfriend, a better teacher. Now, every single time I swam, I felt I was becoming a better Alice.

In the water I saw giant schools of herring massed beyond the drop-off. Beneath them larger fish circled, dazzled by the wall of silver flashes. Occasionally seals would swoop, carving furrows through the school and somehow isolating individual fish to chase and easily catch. Beneath all this the depths of the lough remained mostly a mystery, save a few tall trees of seaweed that waved ominously in the current.

Most of my time was spent over the shallower water though. Here the current wasn't as strong, the water not as cold and the feeling that something might emerge out of the darkness to pull me under played less on my mind. There was still enough to see – crabs larger than my hand scuttled by watchfully, fish the colour of the sand and shape of a flat rugby ball spooked and swam off, while seals occasionally ventured near and observed me as an exotic outsider making her way through the water in an ungainly fit of noise and colour.

But always present, no matter the conditions or offensiveness of what I was wearing, were two rooks, circling watchfully over me like my own security detail.

*

My hopes that there would be no one around to see me in the hideous green wetsuit were quashed as Christmas approached. The population of the village swelled and pods of extended families traversed the well-trodden beach path from boat ramp to the rocks and back. Self-consciously I waited for a break in the traffic and then darted across the beach, sank into the water and swam away. Once in, I was fine. The water surrounded me and not only was my wetsuit mostly out of view, but I cared less about what the land people thought.

Still, it was hard not to notice them looking at me. Try as I might to concentrate on my stroke and the clumps of seaweed that floated by like jellied mines, occasionally, as I turned my head to take a breath, I'd catch a blurry glimpse of a group standing by the waterline looking my way, as if I were a circus act.

On one occasion, before the sting of the saltwater made my eyes completely useless, I saw the shape of a little girl in red pointing excitedly in my direction. Beside her was a large dark figure, crouched on his haunches. I kept swimming and soon they were behind me; when I came back they were gone. It was a brief encounter, but perhaps because of the feeling that swimming gave me, I allowed it to push upon the door to the memories of London. Tears came, each one adding minutely to the depth of the lough. And then I thought of Janet and the idea of carrying her baby. It gave me a warmth that I hadn't expected, a feeling of sisterhood. I drifted along with that feeling until a piece of seaweed entangled my arm and pulled me to a stop. Momentarily startled, I quickly removed the weed, the base of which seemed to be anchored over the drop-off. It gave me the creeps, so I angled inshore and completed my swim in shallower water and without the feeling of serenity I had found earlier.

*

Two days after he made me pancakes, Trevor came over for dinner and sex. There was no point colouring it any other way, though of course we didn't say as much. Afterwards he snuggled up behind me and there was an hour of him stroking my leg and kissing my shoulder before he finally fell asleep.

We saw each other once more before Christmas. On that occasion he came swimming with me, though without a wetsuit he couldn't stay in as long. He wound up waiting on the beach while I lost myself in the blissful, smooth waters of the lough, daring myself to go out a little further, stay in a little longer. Soon I forgot altogether that Trevor was waiting for me and had to jolt myself into the present tense when I came ashore. It really was the most perfect escapism.

*

On Christmas Day I tried to make a WhatsApp video call to Brisbane, but the connection was weak and it kept dropping out. In the end we exchanged a few text messages and that was the extent of my family Christmas. I felt a little sad for not being with them, but I was quietly proud of myself for getting through the last four months alone in Ireland, so surviving Christmas wasn't a big deal. I lit a fire and read a book, as red robins jittered amongst the evergreen shrub by the windowsill.

I waited until 11 am before messaging Trevor. I knew he was with his kids and ex-wife for the day, but figured by then most of the early hysteria would be over and he'd have a chance to respond. But he didn't, even though he had seen the message. I had two cups of tea and half-watched *Love Actually,* before checking my phone again and then deciding to go for a swim. My dad, in something of a seasonal miracle, had managed to buy me flippers and have them delivered in time for Christmas.

The beach was deserted. I imagined all the families I had seen over the last few days huddled around dinner tables piled with food, pulling crackers and drinking wine. I was a little envious, but there was something incredibly empowering about being alone at Christmas, just doing the one thing that made me feel most like myself.

The water was rippled like corduroy, green beneath serried grey clouds. A white-headed loon winged its way at low altitude across the lough, while my two lifeguards circled above me, enjoying their own game on the Christmas winds. Otherwise the scene was mine. I waded into the water until it was waist-high, then slid under the surface and kicked away. I was home.

I swam down to the jetty against the current, snaked around the pylons, and dared to venture just a little bit further. The sandy bottom continued for a little while, then the sea's floor became rocky and mired in seaweed. It covered everything, a pungent salad of brown green leaves and sinister seed pods that looked as if they had descended on the rocks one fateful night and suffocated everything beneath them. I turned around and let the current take me back.

Soon I was past the jetty and swimming the length of the sandy-bottomed beach again. The flippers made everything so much easier. I could propel myself without needing my arms, just rolling my body like a dolphin and coming up for air every twenty seconds or so. It was a mesmerising feeling.

I could have stayed out there deep into the evening, but the sun was no match for the clouds and before it was due, dusk was already making its presence felt. I made my way towards the shore.

It was only when I reached the shallows, breached the surface, tossed my hair back and sat amongst the small shore break, that I noticed the little girl staring at me. Her eyes were wide open and her two adorably small hands, stuffed into red mittens, were pressed over her mouth. It was like she was trying to stop me from hearing her breathe. I was sure it was the same girl I'd seen a few days earlier.

I looked up the beach to see if her parents were nearby, but my eyes were stinging after an hour in the saltwater and I couldn't see with any clarity beyond twenty or thirty metres. Even closer objects were a bit blurry.

A small wave washed over me and I let it push me down so my head was under the water. Then I raised it again, letting my hair fall behind me and cling to my back. I was having trouble getting the flippers off as my hands, for which I didn't have gloves, were icy cold and my fingers nearly useless.

The girl was still looking at me. I realised she was close enough to speak to.

'Hello,' I called out, raising a shivering hand to wave at her.

She was the cutest thing. Even under her red woollen beanie I could make out her long blonde hair – not unlike mine, I thought – and though I couldn't see them, I imagined she had blue eyes like opals. Hearing me call out to her, she released one of her hands from in front of her mouth and waved back, before clamping it back down again. I wanted to gobble her up, she was so gorgeous. But why was she alone? I felt the door open on memories of London again, but before anything significant got out I noticed a man appear in the dunes behind the girl, carrying what looked like a wrapped Christmas present. It jolted me back into reality and I was able to shake the thoughts away. I rolled into the deeper water and swam back into the lough. Taking one last look over my shoulder I saw the girl turn around as the man tapped her on the shoulder. Her cute little gloved hands dropped from her mouth and she stood there looking up at him, unsure whether to give him a hug or grab the present. I dived under the water, closed my eyes and let the current sweep me away.

*

When I finally got the flippers off and returned to my cottage, I checked my phone to see if Trevor had replied. He hadn't. I could feel myself getting annoyed by it but rather than let that feeling win, I had a shower instead.

Suitably cleaned, dried and dressed, I made myself a cup of tea and considered the half a bag of kindling I had left. After immersing myself in freezing seawater, warming myself by a log fire felt like the most natural response. I built a tepee of sticks over some scrunched-up newspaper, but after it collapsed a couple of times and the paper burnt out without the wood catching, I picked up my phone. Trevor had read the message but still not responded. I was annoyed that I was annoyed. I wasn't all that sure how I felt about our relationship, but being ignored really bugged me. Unsure what to do I fiddled around on my phone for a little while, opening and closing apps that barely worked, before finding myself going through old text messages.

Hey Alice it's Max. I prized you're number out of a mutual friend who swore me not 2 tell there name. Sorry, but I needed to talk to u. Can we? xx

I'd deleted and blocked his old number after we broke up, then changed mine. Our last conversation had been a fight I'd instigated about something stupid he'd done – staying out drinking again and not telling me where he was, I think. It was an excuse, and though he gave me many, it wasn't why I broke up with him. He didn't know the real reason.

I wasn't sure if I could tell him if he asked. He wasn't the inquisitive type anyway, so there wasn't much risk. On the other hand, maybe I wanted him to. A part of me yearned for his anger and indignation. It would free me somehow, confirm what I knew. And then, maybe, I could move on from it. I needed someone to tell me I had done the wrong thing, so that I could draw a line in the sand.

Hey Max. How are things with you? A

I looked out the window and could see a pale light illuminating the trees. Bending to get a better view, I realised the clouds were breaking up and a three-quarter moon was making its silent pilgrimage through the night. I couldn't remember the last time I'd seen a sky full of stars. A walk felt like just the thing. I put on my jacket, tied a purple scarf round my neck and grabbed a torch, then I left my phone on the mantlepiece above the fireplace. It'd be interesting to see who, of Trevor and Max, messaged me back first.

Usually I walked into the village – along the path during the day or, because that's unlit, via the Kerrykeel road at night. But I knew that would take me past all the Christmas lights and the warm glow of families in lounge rooms. I didn't particularly envy them, but neither did I need the reminder of what most people were doing today. What I really wanted was to find somewhere dark and quiet where I could look up and lose myself in the vastness of space.

I turned right at the end of the driveway and headed away from the village. I'd never been this way before, but now, under the gently shimmering Milky Way, I could make out the shadowy silhouettes of dozens of cottages and holiday homes that sat in chilled darkness, waiting for the summer crowds to arrive.

I shone the torch up driveways as I passed, searching for

signs of life; but most were empty. In fact, from my little group of cottages right around to where the houses gave way to farmland, the only other property that looked to be occupied was the one whose garden border wall I could see from my front door. There were two cars parked outside it and, though I passed the light over quickly, I thought I could see someone standing beside one of them, looking into the sky. Whoever it was, they were the northernmost residents in Rathmullan. I was the second.

Shortly I came to a paddock where my torch illuminated the eyes of a flock of sheep watching me from the top of a small rise. Thereafter the road cambered gently downhill before approaching the slightly wider road that carried on to Kerrykeel.

By this intersection there was a sandy track, just wide enough for a tractor, that cut through the farmland. It headed in the direction of the beach. I followed its deep, rutted tyre marks, edged around a wide puddle and then climbed a short rise, before reaching a metal gate, and climbing over that. Then I found myself on a wide, bumpy grass field. Beyond it I could see the lights of Buncrana on the far side of the lough, reflecting off the water. The moon, potted and scarred, was emerging from behind the last of the clouds, throwing its pale, ghostly light over Donegal. With the stars thick through the sky it was an awesome sight.

Then, from somewhere just above me, I heard a series of short, falling squeaks. My security detail. They sounded close and low, and for a whimsical moment I thought they might land on my shoulders. Then a series of heavy thuds echoed nearby. I swung my torch around and was startled to see a horse coming towards me, the white streak on its nose bouncing up and down as it neared. I backed away but it kept coming, pushing through my hand and nudging me in the chest. I wasn't sure if it expected food or was being aggressive, but it kept shoving and I kept retreating, stumbling backwards over the uneven terrain. Then I felt my backside push against a wire fence and a moment later a jolt of electricity zapped through me. I jerked forwards and screamed. At the same time one of the birds flew past my face, right between me and the horse, which tossed its head up, bucked around and galloped away, whinnying and sliding on the muddy grass.

I made for the gate, my backside throbbing. Unsure where the horse was, I scrambled to get to safety, but in a panic my foot slipped off and my knee banged painfully into one of the rails. The birds came closer again, sounding their distinctive alarm. Behind me I could hear the footfalls of the horse bustling towards me again. I carefully placed one boot on the lower rail, another on the next and then, just as I could make out two bellows of angry air jetting out of horse nostrils, I cartwheeled over the gate and landed, bum first, in a puddle. Behind me the fence rattled as the horse shoved its chest into it, its hot angry breath moistening my hair.

*

As I walked back towards the cottage the rooks continued circling overhead. Their urgent calls no longer cut through the night, but I became attuned to the way their wings beat at the crisp air. My heartbeat slowly returned to normal and soon it was just the cold wetness soaking through my jeans, along with the soreness of my backside, that lingered.

When I approached the property next to mine, one of the cars I'd seen earlier pulled out of the driveway. I dropped my torch's beam so as not to blind the driver, but they turned left and drove off without appearing to notice me. I carried on and instinctively looked up the driveway, and as I did I caught the shape of a man, dimly lit by light spilling out of the doorway. He had his hands on his hips and looked to be watching the driveway where the car had just been. On the other side of me there was the darkness of trees and uninhabited houses, so I doubted he could have seen me.

It was only a brief glimpse as I passed by, but there was

something eerily familiar about the man, even in the dark outline that I was able to see.

I got home a few minutes later, changed into dry clothes and tried the fire again. Until it was properly going I resisted the temptation to check my phone. When I did I found messages from both Trevor and Max.

Hey you, sorry for the delay. Lots of family dramas today, as I'm sure you can imagine. Talk soon. T X

Hey Alice, great to here from you. Up for a chat? xx

Trevor had replied three minutes before Max. But there had only been fifteen minutes between my message to Max and his reply. I hated that I noticed this. In fact, I hated everything that the two messages stirred up. I turned off my phone and picked up a book.

6

Trevor called on Boxing Day. There had been dramas: his son got the same present from two relatives; his daughter didn't like her parents living in different houses; a broken glass and a bloody finger. As his story went on I found myself wincing more and more. It was all so busy and hectic. Everything was about his children, his ex-wife, the push and pull of family life. There seemed no time for living.

'It'd be nice to see you,' he finally concluded.

'Uh huh,' I replied.

'How about I come over tomorrow, cook you a roast, just the two of us?'

'You mean your kids won't be coming?'

'Oh ... well, I can see—'

'I was joking, Trevor.'

Despite my reservations, the idea of having a roast dinner cooked for me appealed. I agreed, and promised to supply the wine. When the call ended, though, the feeling that his life and mine were incompatible quickly returned. I spun the phone between my thumb and forefinger for a few moments, then went to the fridge. I had half a bottle of Sauvignon Blanc, a remnant of the evening with Janet. I unscrewed the lid and put the bottle to my nose. It smelled reasonable: nothing kills Sauvignon Blanc. Outside the weather was abysmal: not a day for swimming. I filled a small wine glass, took a sip and squinted as the first tang of grassy citrus hit the back of my throat. It was immediately followed by a soothing warmth through my chest. I loved Sauvignon Blanc a little bit too much. I picked up my phone and opened WhatsApp, then typed and sent before I could second-guess myself.

Not sure I'm ready to chat yet.

I didn't know what I wanted from Max. Part of me wanted

him to draw out of me the truth about why I left him; part of me wanted him to fix everything and return us to the time and place we first fell in love. A not insignificant part of me wanted him to hate me. He replied before I'd time to take another sip.

Totes understand not being ready to chat. Glad ur cool to text tho. U still in Lon? xx

I took a large mouthful and read over his message a couple of times. He really had no idea. Outside, the rain made the world look like it had just been salvaged from the bottom of the sea. Two rooks huddled together on a thick branch near my neighbour's wall.

Ireland. It rains a lot, but the birds are friendly.

I topped up the glass and considered the logistics of going to the shop to buy another bottle.

Ireland?! I guess that explains ur ph number. Why there?

Why indeed. Beyond the wall I could make out the roof of my neighbour's cottage, a curl of smoke coming from the chimney. I recalled the shadowy figure of a man with his hands on his hips the night before.

Was there something you needed to discuss, Max?

I wondered if it was the father of the blonde girl I'd seen on the beach. I tried to remember whereabouts I'd come ashore and how that related to where the neighbour's cottage was.

Ha. Strait to the point. U can take the girl out of Brisbane ...

It lined up. I was about the same distance from the cottage as my exit from the beach. Perhaps she lived there. Or maybe she was just visiting. She may have been in the car that I saw pull out of the driveway last night. I took a sip of wine. There was something else about all this that was familiar but I couldn't quite put my finger on it, like the sound of a doorbell being pressed but the ringer not working. I looked down at my phone and saw Max's name illuminated. He was calling. I took another sip, a bigger one, and pressed Answer.

'Hi,' I said, butterflies flapping annoyingly in my stomach.

'Hello?'

'Yes, hi, Max.'

'Hello? Alice??'

'Max? Can you hear me?'

'What, are ya fuckin' with me? What's goin' on? Alice??'

I walked up the stairs and stood on the landing, by the window above the front door. One of the rooks flew to another branch and shook the rain off its feathers. The second followed a moment later and rubbed its beak into the first one's neck.

'Max? Can you hear me now?'

  . . .

'Max?'

  . . .

I looked at the screen. One feeble bar of the reception graph was illuminated. It still showed the call as connected, but there was no Max at the other end.

I hung up. Through the window I could see a little more of my neighbour's house, a top-floor window, probably a bedroom. It was too far away to see through it or even tell if the curtains were drawn, but it gave the house, the person or people in it, another shade of character.

Really bad reception here. Sorry, I typed.

The chilled edge had been rubbed off the wine now. I could taste peaches and . . . grapes. Mostly grapes. Grapes that had been left in the sun too long.

Sure. Shame tho, it wudve been nice to here ur voice again. xx

Rain continued to empty out of the sky as if it was on a continuous loop from ground to lough to ocean to cloud. I guess it kind of was.

So what was it you needed to talk about?

A blurred photo started the tediously slow process of down-loading. I left the phone on the bannister, went back downstairs and poured the last of the wine down the kitchen sink. A gust of wind spattered rain against the windows, the sound of tiny knuckles cracking. I turned the kettle on.

As I waited for it to go through the motions I imagined the photo travelling, pixel by pixel, through the sky from Max to me. I imagined the image being of him and his bride-to-be, both of them beaming as they showed off her engagement ring. The thought of it didn't upset me like I thought it might. He deserved it. Or perhaps more accurately, I did. His happiness was my punishment.

The kettle was growing ever more animated, a sound that reminded me of the coal trains that used to rumble through the suburbs of Brisbane when I was a girl. I dropped a teabag into a mug, then took the milk from the fridge and waited.

I wondered what the girl would look like. She'd be a brunette, or, actually more likely, she'd have jet-black hair. And she'd be thin and tall with big breasts. Max was always distracted by girls that, unlike me, had big boobs. I imagined him fucking her, beaming at the things like he had won a prize. I imagined her faking an orgasm.

The kettle clicked off and I poured the steaming water over the teabag, stirring it in gently and pushing the bag against the wall of the mug to encourage it further.

I'd never faked it with Max. In the early days there hadn't been enough time to. But, strangely, it was those encounters that I remembered most fondly. They felt genuine and spontaneous. Seeing him desperate to hold on, asking me in the moments before he came to promise we could do it again soon, just so he could have more of me; if we ever made love, it was during those days. After he mastered his body, and then mine, sex became a sport to him.

I fished the teabag out and added a splash of milk. Half a teaspoon of sugar and I took the mug into the living room and placed it on the coffee table. With some reluctance I then went upstairs to get my phone and see who the lucky girl was.

Except it wasn't a girl at all – at least not an adult one. It was an ultrasound. Tens of thousands of black and white pixels in the shape of an unborn baby in its mother's womb. There was no text accompanying it. I leaned against the wall, felt my breath catching in my throat and my legs begin to wobble. Then I quickly turned the phone off, ran downstairs and threw it in the vegetable crisper.

*

I ignored my phone for the rest of the night and instead tried to read, before taking sleep's invitation at the first moment of asking. There followed a fitful night of bad dreams that evaporated from my memory as soon as I woke, leaving only a residual feeling of the traumas my mind was inflicting on itself. In the morning I put on my wetsuit and, ignoring the rain, went for a swim. Only then, when safely in the water column, was I able to let go of the anxiety Max's photo had caused.

Trevor came over in the evening. He brought with him a large cut of lamb and enough potatoes and parsnips to feed a rugby team. Then he set up in the kitchen and chopped, parboiled and roasted for an hour and a half while I occasionally offered to help, but mostly talked and drank wine. I steered the conversation away from his family and kept it on school. It was safe ground and there was enough material that we sailed through the meal, then a dessert of Viennetta ice cream, and had retired to the sofa before any mention of his children came up. I listened vaguely and then suggested we watch a movie. When he started moving his hands over my leg suggestively, I let the three and a half glasses of Cabernet Franc get the better of me and dozed off.

The next day we went for a swim together. He didn't have a wetsuit, but still lasted for twenty minutes before going to shore and towelling off. Then he dressed in tracksuit pants and a thick jacket and followed me along the beach. It was sweet of him, I suppose, but I felt watched and coddled, as if I were another of his children. I enjoyed swimming for its escape from land, yet with Trevor following me I constantly felt tethered to it, like I was on a leash.

I slowly made my way towards the rocks, consciously spending longer and longer underwater as a means of stretching my link to Trevor. I grazed the sandy bottom, letting my chest stir up the sand, and letting buoyancy lift me above sporadic patches of seaweed. Then I rolled onto my back and looked at the surface of the water, at the grey light of the sky wobbling in the contours of the small waves. Amongst it were two black shapes circling at what appeared to be very low altitude.

My momentum slowed until a small blonde cloud of hair billowed around me. Then I slowly drifted towards the surface and enjoyed the sensation of the water returning me to the air that kept me alive. Everything felt in harmony.

I was in the middle of the water column, about a metre from the surface, when out of the corner of my eye I noticed something moving. But when I turned to look it was gone. Telling myself it was probably a seal, I continued to drift upwards, my lungs yearning for a fresh intake of air. Resisting the desire for oxygen, I'd found, was as invigorating as the relief from finally getting some.

Then I felt something pass beneath me – a caressing presence over my back, followed by a turbulence in the water. Instinctively I rolled around. Even though I'd barely thought about sharks since my first swim, my mind immediately went to that possibility. It was a primal thought, like not being afraid of heights until you lose your balance on top of a cliff.

But there was nothing there, just the deepening green haze of the lough, empty of anything bar seaweed, small fish and sand. It had to have been a seal.

My back was now breaking through the surface, my lungs beginning to cry out. I was just about to lift my head into the air when I saw something glint from amongst a large clump of seaweed and dark sand. The colours looked out of place - a flash of red and a streak of white, but with a transparence too. I breached the surface, filled my lungs and prepared to dive back under, but took the opportunity to glance at the beach. There, Trevor seemed happily occupied with something on the sand. I breathed out and in again and was about to dive back down, when I heard the falling squeak sounds. Above me the two rooks were circling low and then darting off towards shore, before returning. Ignoring them, I dived back under.

The current had taken me away from the large clump of seaweed, so I kicked with my flippers until I was above it once more. It occurred to me that the mysterious red and white object might be a jellyfish, but if so it must have been extremely lost; and besides, there was something unnatural about it. It was almost as if the thing was tangled up in the seaweed, as if the brown fronds had reached out and pulled it in.

I dived down until it was within arm's reach, and as I did the seaweed flared. For a moment I wondered if it was actually some kind of fish, like the Wobbegong sharks we get back home. I looked closer, trying to see if I was being fooled by its camouflage, and for a moment thought I could make out eyes and a mouth, even a nose, but when I blinked I realised it was just my mind trying to make something out of nothing. I refocused on the strange object caught in its canopy. And then, like staring at one of those 3D pictures, I suddenly realised what I was seeing: a Coke bottle, and inside it a rolled-up piece of paper.

The next few moments happened in a confusing blur. I saw movement out of the corner of my right eye, almost exactly as I had done a minute earlier. I turned my head and this time saw a dark smudge in the water, moving swiftly away. A moment later the movement of another dark object caught my eye, this time much closer and far less graceful. Right in front of me one of the rooks speared into the water and then spread its wings in an ungainly attempt to fly deeper. I flinched backwards, not wanting to drift above the bird and block it from resurfacing. My flippers touched the bottom and kicked up a cloud of sand and for the next few seconds all I could see was dark shapes moving above, beside and beneath me.

When I managed to gather my wits and swim out of it, the patch of seaweed and the Coke bottle were gone. I let the sand cloud settle slightly and swam back to the area, but everywhere I looked, the seafloor was barren of all but a few small rocks and startled crabs. Soon my lungs began to scream and I returned to the surface.

I could hear the falling whistles of the rooks still; however, they were further away now. I followed the sound and saw them circling a patch of water about fifty metres further down the beach, towards the rocks. There was more than a dozen of them now, throwing themselves into the water like I'd seen by the boat ramp a week ago. I tossed my hair back and noticed my two bodyguards still above me, circling silently, but edging towards the shore.

There I could see Trevor standing up to his shins in the water, looking my way. He was waving with both arms. I waved back and indicated I was coming in.

He greeted me with a towel, hugging me with it then rubbing my arms. 'Are you okay? What happened out there?' His voice was rushed, like all the words he needed to say were pushing up against each other.

'I'm fine,' I replied, putting one hand on his shoulder as I tried to peel a flipper off. 'I think it was just a seal.'

'I saw the seal,' he said. 'But the birds, it looked like they were feeding on something right where you were. I was worried that ...' his voice trailed off as he took a breath.

I tossed the flipper on to the dry sand and worked on the other. 'That I'd been eaten by a shark? Why didn't you come and save me?'

The flipper came off and I tossed it next to the first, then took the towel from Trevor and wrapped it around my hair. Trevor hadn't answered but I barely noticed, still trying to make sense of what had really happened myself.

We walked to where I'd tossed the flippers, but when I reached down to pick them up I noticed some writing in the sand.

Felix Listen

I stared at the words, trying to place the name.

'I saw that earlier,' Trevor said. 'I wonder who wrote it.'

'A frustrated girlfriend is my guess.'

Trevor looked at me. 'I would have come in if I thought it was a shark, you know.'

'I know you would,' I told him. I didn't doubt it.

We walked back along the beach towards the path that led to my cottage. My two bodyguards circled overhead. Trevor carried my flippers.

'What is it with you and the rooks?' he asked.

'I gave one of them a dignified burial a few weeks ago and they've taken a shine to me since.'

Trevor absorbed this information but remained quiet. I guess it was an unusual thing to hear. I looked to him when he still hadn't spoken after a few more moments. 'You okay?' I asked.

'Aye,' he replied. 'It's just been a strange time.'

I was about to ask him to elaborate when I saw a man and a young girl emerge from a garden and start on a path through the dunes. I looked up to the cottage above the garden, then further along, and realised it was my neighbour. They were about thirty metres away and as we were walking perpendicular to them, they were quickly behind us. However, it was enough time for me to recognise the red woollen hat and mittens of the young girl. I was certain it was the same one I'd seen on Christmas Day, standing alone on the beach and looking at me with her cute little hands covering her mouth. However, the man she was with now wasn't the one I'd seen with the Christmas present. My eyesight hadn't been perfect, but I was fairly sure his hair had been the same colour as the girl's. This man's hair was black.

'Do you want to meet my kids?' Trevor asked, jolting me out of my reverie.

'What?'

'I have two kids.'

'I know, I just—'

'I'd like you to meet them. You should. I don't want to keep things from them.'

'What things?'

'Us. This.'

'This?'

'Us.'

I didn't know what to say and couldn't keep repeating what he was saying. Instead I fell silent. It hadn't even crossed my mind, meeting his kids. It felt so official. We reached the path through the dunes so had to walk single file. Trevor fell in behind me.

'Well?' he asked, sounding a little put out.

'I'm thinking,' I told him, because I was.

We didn't say anything else until I opened the door to my cottage. I put my flippers under the staircase and began to walk up the stairs.

'How long will you be thinking for?' Trevor asked, as he removed his shoes.

'I don't know,' I replied, because I didn't. 'I'm going to have a shower.'

I got to the top of the stairs, crossed the landing and looked out the window above the front door. I half expected the rooks to be sitting on the opposite roof, watching over me. But I couldn't see them. I looked at the grey sky for a few moments and ran the last half hour through my head. I felt as though everything had been turned over, like I was drifting through the water column again, my back to the sea floor. It was disorientating.

Trevor came up the staircase. 'Hey, sorry, I shouldn't have mentioned the kids. Too soon. I don't know what came over me.' He paused. 'Actually, I do.'

'Yeah?' I asked cautiously.

'When you were under water, with the seal and the birds, I was worried.'

'That's really sweet of you, but I was fine.'

'I know. I know that you can handle yourself. That wasn't it. It was more that I was surprised how much I was worried about you.'

'Really, I was completely fine.'

'No. I'm not saying it right. What I'm trying to say is, I realised how much I cared for you. How much—'

'Trevor,' I stopped him. 'I care for you too.' I walked up and hugged him; our cold, damp bodies pressed together at the top of the staircase. Then we pulled apart and I could see he was still trying to finish his sentence. I didn't want to hear him say the word. It would change everything, drag me out of the soft, harmonious water before my lungs needed it. I put my finger on his lips. 'I'm going to have a shower.'

I kissed him on the forehead and backed away. Then I turned, walked to the bathroom and shut the door.

*

Trevor had a cup of tea and a cold roast lamb sandwich ready for me when I came back downstairs. The fire was burning and he'd filled the cane basket next to it with logs.

'I was going to put on some music,' he said, 'but you don't seem to have a radio. Which confuses me because I'm sure we've had music on before.'

'Spotify,' I explained, pointing at my laptop on the coffee table. 'I have to put my phone upstairs so it gets a decent signal, then tether it, perform a little pagan prayer ritual ...'

Trevor shook his head. 'Back in my day we had to put some cheese on a piece of string and dangle it in front of a mouse on a wheel. That powered the gramophone ...'

I chuckled. 'Oh, you're not that much older than me.'

Trevor's eyebrows arched upwards, amplifying the peaks and valleys on his forehead. 'How old do you think I am?'

He looked in his early forties, but I suspected he was actually late thirties. I decided to err on the side of caution.

'Thirty-seven?'

'Kind,' he replied. 'I'm forty-four. Forty-five in March.'

'Oh. Wow! You look good for your age.'

'You're ... thirty?'

'Thirty-three.'

He nodded. I nodded back and put the warm cup of tea to my lips. He was forty-four. Divorced. A father of two. I couldn't help it, I tried not to, but could only see him as someone in middle age now, with the baggage, physical and emotional, of a middle-aged man.

His eyes narrowed on me. 'Are you okay?'

'Uh huh,' I replied, blowing the steam from the top of the tea, both hands wrapped around it. 'Warming up.'

Trevor studied me for a moment, then gestured with a tilting of his head. 'I'm going to have a shower.'

I listened to his footsteps thud slowly up the staircase, shuffle across the landing and into the bathroom. He was going to be forty-five while I was still thirty-three. When I was forty he would be fifty-two. My uncle was fifty-two – he had something wrong with his back. I thought about my mother, who was sixty-four now and could easily pass for mid-fifties. When I was her age, Trevor would be seventy-six. Both my grandfathers had been around that age when they'd died.

I sat in front of the fire, watching glowing orange ripples radiate through morsels of timber left behind by the flames. I heard the toilet flush and then the pipes in the wall groan as the shower started. My phone came alive with a new message.

Wanna discuss this?

I looked at the photo Max had sent of the unborn child, while upstairs Trevor's feet squeaked on the shower floor. A soul-deep urge for a big glass of Sauvignon Blanc gripped me. I turned the phone over so I couldn't see the screen and tried to make do with tea.

How could I have a discussion about an unborn baby with Max when I couldn't talk about born ones with Trevor? Poor Trevor. He was probably thinking about his kids now, about his son and the two presents he got that were the same, about his daughter and how she would react to a new woman in Daddy's bedroom. Trevor, who would never cheat on his partner, who wouldn't even make a move on me until the divorce was official. Trevor, who read books, drank wine, could cook a good meal. It was silly to focus on his age. Janet was right: Trevor was a good person.

I took my phone upstairs, plugged it into the charger, then came back down to open Spotify. I skipped through my various playlists until I found something that matched how I felt: Sigur Ros.

Trevor entered the living room, residual shower water in his sandy brown hair glistening in the firelight, and sat next to me on the sofa with his hand resting on my leg. I could feel the weight of it through my jeans, no different to a dinner plate or remote control.

We sat without speaking, looking into the fire, listening to enigmatic Icelandic soundscapes emerging from tinny laptop speakers. My body had a pleasant throb to it from the swim earlier. I could feel myself relaxing into the cushions and into Trevor's safe arms.

He moved closer, put his head on my shoulder, then started nuzzling my neck. I felt a distant shimmer of arousal, like the sound of an ice-cream truck two neighbourhoods away. He continued kissing my neck and up behind my ear. His stubble tickled my skin and an instinctive, pleasant shiver rippled through me. Noticing this reaction, Trevor pulled back, smiled at me, at his achievement and moved in for a kiss. I watched him approach and kept my eyes open as his lips pressed on to mine. I could see crow's feet spreading into his temples and small, wispy tufts of hair in his ears. His hand slid up from my leg and mapped out the shape of my breast.

I put my hands on his chest, pushed him back and wrestled my mouth away from his. He looked at me perplexed, trying to conflate the data with motive.

'Can we just talk for a bit?' I asked.

'Let's talk later,' he replied. 'I've been wanting to do this all day.'

He moved in again, cradling my jaw with his hand. My head was against the back of the sofa, dimpling the top of the cushion. I kissed him back for a while, not wanting to upset him, but I couldn't shake the need to clear the air first.

'Trevor . . .'

Growing in eagerness, his hand dropped from my jaw to my neck. He slid his thumb around one side so my windpipe pushed against the webbing like a vacuum-packed beef fillet. Then he squeezed.

For a stupid, brief moment I was proud of him. He was applying the lessons I'd been teaching him in the bedroom. But the context was all wrong and he didn't seem to understand the difference between resistance and reluctance. I broke from his kiss and pulled at his hand.

'Trevor,' I began, trying not to make a big deal of the fact I couldn't breathe. 'I need to tell you something first.'

He released his grip, allowing air back into my lungs. I sat up and pushed him gently away. His face was paused in a strange middle ground between turned on and politely waiting. I took a few moments to get my breath.

'Trevor,' I started again. 'You're sweet.' I gestured at the air between us. 'This is sweet. Us, I mean, it . . . could work.'

'It could, Alice. It really could.' He sat back slightly. 'But I'm sorry I brought up my kids. It's too soon.'

'No, it's fine, I understand. Slowly slowly, that's all.'

'Of course. I'm sorry. I really like you and . . .'

'I like you too, Trevor.'

We smiled at each other and gently touched fingers. He really was a good guy and better than Max in so many ways. His enthusiasm was endearing and although I wasn't at the same place as him yet, I felt like I could get there in time. I just needed him not to race too far ahead.

We began kissing again, more gently this time. I closed my eyes and tried to imagine a future with him – reading in bed together, driving to work together, swimming together. Things that Max and I could never have done. It wasn't the future that I had dreamed of as a girl, or even as a young woman, but it was a realistic, adult future. It was honest and sincere.

It was with that in mind that I broke off our kiss once more and looked into Trevor's hazel eyes. For the first time I felt a pang of genuine, deep affection for him. He would never hurt me, never lie to me, never cheat or go behind my back. He would always be on my side and, if the love wasn't as all-consuming and instant as it had been with Max, it would grow over time. But the only way that could happen was if everything was out in the open.

'I never told you why I broke up with my ex,' I began.

Trevor shook his head. 'And you don't have to.'

'No. I do. It's been hanging over me ever since.'

The music shifted from one Icelandic soundscape to another. I took a breath and began my explanation.

'We'd been in London for about ten months. He loved it more than I did. He worked in events. He was always good with people – charming and gregarious. London was a good fit for him.'

'And for you?'

'I found it too fast-paced. Brisbane is laid back and so am I, I think.'

Trevor nodded. I squeezed his hand and continued.

'But I knew we wouldn't be there forever, especially with his visa only being good for two years, so I decided I would ride it out. I even started discussing where we would live when we went back to Australia, friends we would see again. I wanted to keep that link alive. But whenever I did Max would just grunt and nod and then change the subject to some new bar he had discovered or a minor celebrity he had lined up to appear at one of his events. He started spending more and more time with people I didn't know, while I spent more and more time at home alone. I felt like I was losing him.'

Trevor rubbed my leg. It only occurred to me later that it must have been difficult for him to hear me telling a story about someone I once loved.

'So I stopped taking the pill.'

Trevor's hand paused on my leg. He blinked and then, I'm sure unconsciously, let his eyes drift down to my stomach. I put my hand on his.

'It's such a girly thing to do,' I said, shaking my head, 'but I felt helpless and desperate and this was the only way I could think to keep hold of him.'

'So, did you—'

'About two months later I was at work when I started feeling nauseous. I threw up a few times and was sent home. It occurred to me straight away what it might be. I was already late. I popped into a chemist on the way and picked up a pregnancy test. But when I got home I noticed a blue jacket hung over one of the kitchen chairs and a handbag on the table. There was music on and I heard a woman's voice down the hall. I went straight back out the door. I'm pretty sure they didn't even know I'd been there.'

Trevor shook his head in a gesture of sympathy, but there was a rigidity to his movements now, like each part of the story was weighing him down more and more. In contrast I was feeling lighter with every word.

'I went straight to a doctor. I had to wait all afternoon to get in, but I didn't mind. I realised how silly I had been, how Max and I had been growing apart and that to bring a child in to it would benefit none of us, least of all the child.'

'Oh, but Alice—'

I squeezed Trevor's cold, hard hand. 'Please, let me finish,' I said. 'I didn't even ask the doctor to confirm I was pregnant. I just told her I was and that I didn't want to have it.'

Trevor ran his hand through his hair and looked into the fire. I ploughed on.

'She sent me to a family planning clinic. They told me it could affect my chances of getting pregnant again, then gave me an ultrasound. They wanted me to see there was a human inside of me, but I was adamant. They made me take the picture home, and I did, but only to put it in the bin. I went back and told them I was sure. A week later it was over.'

Trevor was now sitting formally on the couch, looking forwards as if attending a lecture. I spoke to the side of his face, holding back the tears as best I could.

'And the worst thing is that a week after that, while I was still at our flat 'sick' and secretly applying for jobs in Ireland, Max came home with a woman from work. His manager. She was wearing that same blue jacket and had the same handbag I'd seen that day in our kitchen.' I shook my head. 'She was sixty, maybe older. Max wasn't sleeping with this woman. They just popped in every now and then to go through his CD collection and choose some music for an event. He hadn't done anything wrong, yet I'd aborted his child.'

I collapsed into tears, relieved to have finally told someone my secret, but horrified at how much worse it sounded out loud.

I laid there in a ball by his side for what felt like minutes, as a gyre of mournful Icelandic string instruments filled the space where my story had just been. Then I felt a hand on my shoulder, resting there like a latch on a gate, before it lifted off just as mechanically. I reached for it, but Trevor stood and walked to the fireplace. He grabbed his keys and wallet.

'Alice, it's not for me to judge, but ...'

I watched him through tear blurred eyes. 'What ... what do you mean?'

'Oh, Alice, I'm sorry for what you went through, but ...'

'But what?'

'But ... this is Ireland, Alice. This is Catholic Ireland.'

I sat up. 'But Trevor, of all people, I thought you,' I furrowed my brow, 'with your *divorce* ...'

'Aye, it's frowned upon,' he admitted, 'but Jesus, Mary and Joseph, Alice, an abortion is something else.'

I wiped my eyes. 'Trevor, you can't be serious.'

'Alice, please, I think maybe we both need to step away for a little while.'

He walked towards the door, then turned back. 'You're a lovely girl, Alice. I'm sorry for what you went through.' I thought he was going to elaborate, but instead he squinted at me, as if I was fading from view. 'I'm really sorry.'

And then he left.

Part Two

Felix

—◦❧ **7** ❧◦—

I t was a cold day in December when I first saw my name
written in the sand.

Initially, I registered only an impression of valleys and
grooves, ridges like eyebrows; I strode over it without thinking
and kept running. I breathed icy air in, absorbed its gifts and
expelled carbon dioxide for the trees. My body was in rhythm,
the legs encouraging the arms, the arms opening the
diaphragm, the blood pushing the whole thing along. I was a
perfect machine in a harmonious world.

But as I continued down the beach the image in the sand
jostled for attention, sharpening in detail. A name. Each letter
eloquently crafted, the strokes of an even depth, the vertical
lines meeting the horizontal at the perfect juncture. Even the
dot on the *i* was a work of art, a tiny circle drilled neatly into
the sand. For the *x*, however, special care had been taken. The
four tails curled off like arms, reaching across the beach as if to
points on the compass, searching for something lost.

I pushed on, observing a thin veil of mist on the far side of
Lough Swilly, a small blue fishing boat chugging towards the
Atlantic, a seagull turning with the tiniest dip of its wing. My
fingers and toes were numb. The sun did nothing this time of
year, rising late and setting early, spending what little time it
had as a cowering orb behind bullying clouds.

The image came into focus.

Felix

I kinked my head back, as if looking over my shoulder might bring it into view again. I was a hundred yards past it now and would return to that point on my next lap, but still, the memory of it seemed absurd. Someone had written my name in the sand. Or another Felix's. I timed my stride so that I could leap across the delta of rivulets coming out of the sand sphincter and carried on towards the bend.

The wind, teeth bared, whipped across the lough, dissuading all but the hardiest souls from braving a walk. Up by the bend there was a woman with white hair, the rest of her wrapped in a thick black jacket. Her arms barely moved as she walked, making her look like a piece of sushi. Who else had I seen? I cast my mind back over the terrain I'd covered. An old man, battling his knees as much as the wind; a woman, younger and blonde, looking into the trees like she'd just discovered they shed their leaves; a young man with a skinny dog on a long lead. Any one of them could have cause to write Felix. It was almost definitely not *my* name.

I rounded the long, slow sweeping left-hand bend, felt it turn bristly underfoot where, for reasons known only to mother nature, small shells covered the sand. Then I reached the rocks, pushed off and headed back, the wind now in my face.

I passed the sushi woman, rounded the slow bend and aimed for the jetty and boat ramp that marked the village end of the beach. The wind stung my eyes, pulling out tears and streaking them down my cheeks. It was tough going but I enjoyed the sensation of effort and revelled in that feeling of air, crisp and icy in my lungs. There's a kind of alchemy that happens when I run, some unique chemical reaction that my body is only able to perform while exhausting itself. It distils its magic ingredients from the air, filters them into my blood, then pumps them through me, scraping the stagnant, maudlin crust off the inside of the veins and flushing the negative thoughts out of my brain. Perhaps that's the reason for my tinnitus. All that crust and negativity has been pushed to my ears, but hasn't jumped.

Felix Salten, author of Bambi. Felix Nussbaum, German surrealist painter.

The blonde woman had exhausted her fascination with the trees and was making her way towards the bend. I observed her casually, with just a couple of glances as I approached, otherwise keeping my focus on the white-capped water or the beach ahead. She looked to be late twenties, pretty, content. I'd not seen her before so perhaps she was a tourist, though there were very few of those this time of year.

I jumped the sand sphincter delta again and pushed on. Small white birds the size of teacups schooled in the shallows, poking at the damp sand with their long, thin beaks. Seeing me approach they scuttled forward, reluctantly taking wing when I continued to chase. Then they settled ten yards further up the beach and the dance unfolded again. This happened three times before they finally switched on and flew out over the water, rode the wind back around behind me and settled once more in the shallows.

Felix the house cat. Felix that Austrian guy that jumped out of the balloon on the edge of space.

A strong gust of wind rolled a piece of driftwood a few inches across the sand. The old man was making his way across the beach, likely aiming for a trail through the grassy dunes and to the path behind it. From there he could go left and back into the village, or right and away from it, popping out on Kinnegar Road, near where my cottage was, and where most of the holiday homes stood empty and cold, silently waiting for summer.

I shook out my arms, releasing the tension that had built up in the muscles around the elbow. So focused was I on this, and the coming boat ramp, that I forgot to look out for my name in the sand. I was on top of it before I realised, but noted the spot, pushed onto the boat ramp and turned back again.

This time I was able to study the writing as I approached. It definitely said Felix. The incoming tide had nipped at the base with a few small waves, smoothing the ridges and filling the valleys of each letter, but it was my name. Or another Felix's name. There were only so many of us. I continued down the beach, the wind at my back again.

The young man with the dog had moved closer to the waterline. He was letting his brown mutt sniff at the clumps of seaweed, sticks and the odd dead crab that littered the shore. Seeing me approach the dog barked and charged, gums raised, teeth exposed.

'Sally!' the man called, but Sally smelled blood.

It got to within five yards before the lead pulled tight and Sally yelped, performed a 360-degree flip with a pike and landed, confused, facing the other direction. The man gave another jerk and Sally, tail tucked out of sight, whimpered to his side. He demanded she sit and patted her kindly when she did.

'Good girl,' I heard him say, reaching for a treat from his pocket.

The blonde was halfway between the sand sphincter and the bend when we crossed paths again. She was already heading back towards the boat ramp so mustn't have gone all the way to the rocks. Seeing her face grow steadily nearer, I began to imagine the conversation we would have if she happened to wave and stop me. *You like running?* she would say. *Yeah*, I would reply. *You like walking?* Fireworks. I hadn't been with a woman for two years, couldn't even remember the last one I spoke to.

She was midway between the water line and the dunes, leaving a ten-yard gap of hard sand for me to run by on. I kept as close to the water as possible and didn't make eye contact as I passed.

The rocks loomed, a lumpy wedge of volcanic activity,

suspended in time. They emerged from a headland that jutted through the dunes and separated Rathmullan's beach from the next. Up close the molten layers looked like sheets of lasagne pasta, albeit well past their use by date. Grey through green, potted by erosion and slivered randomly by thick veins of milky quartz, they acted as a natural end point to a stroll from the village. Or a run.

As I approached, the encroaching tide pushed a set of waves a little higher up the beach. I followed them, not wanting to get my shoes wet, and saw, just as by the boat ramp, my name written in the sand.

Felix

I was sure it hadn't been there when I came by the first time, but I could've missed it. I pushed off the rocks, cast an eye over the writing again and headed back towards the boat ramp.

The sun, already smothered by clouds, had surely dropped beneath the horizon now, allowing a torpid, blue-grey twilight to seep into the sky.

I spotted the blonde woman as I came around the bend in the beach. She was higher up the shore now, sitting in the soft sand near the cemetery and looking up at the trees again. My lungs were stretched and I realised I was pushing harder, which I often did when thinking about something that frustrated me. I slowed my pace and tried to relax my thinking.

I passed the blonde and ran over the original writing of my name. By now the tide had reduced the letters to a ghostly impression of themselves. I turned at the boat ramp and splashed through a retreating wave that was finishing the job.

I'd met one other person called Felix in my forty years and knew of two cats (not including the cartoon). They were all over 300 miles away in England, and in the case of at least one of the cats, dead.

The blonde didn't look my way. She seemed to be having

some kind of transcendental experience, leaning back on her arms and looking skyward, as if expecting to be beamed into a spaceship. If the aliens took her, earth would be a duller place. I left her behind and concentrated on my rhythm, keeping my arms low to open up the diaphragm.

Rooks were streaking across the darkening sky, returning from secret feeding grounds on Inch Island, at Buncrana and all along the Wild Atlantic Way. The tide had encroached most of the way up the sand sphincter delta now, the bubbling fresh-water spring less than an hour from being absorbed by the sea once more.

Around the bend and to the rocks. I wanted to see the writing again, make sure I wasn't imagining things. It was most likely someone else, probably a pet. I could more or less accept that explanation; I just couldn't understand when it was written, and by whom.

The dark, roughly triangular outline of the rocks grew larger as the wind, stronger than it had been all day, pushed at my back. Finally I reached the spot. Only to discover there had been an addition.

Felix Stop

I stopped. There was no one else on the beach. I looked to the dunes, but couldn't see any bodies moving amongst the grass. Was it possible someone was playing a trick? No one knew me. I'd been here for three months and barely spoken to a soul.

I waited in the fading light for ten minutes, hoping the trick would play itself out, but nothing happened. The small waves of the lough continued to break onto the shore, making an echoing sound amongst the rocks. The wind played with this sound, carrying it through the crevices and cavities until it was distorted into something almost human.

Slowly the coming tide took the beach, inch by inch, wave by wave. Darkness absorbed the middle distance. I began to shiver, then gave up on the mystery of the anonymous sand author.

I jogged back to the boat ramp. The blonde was gone, to a galaxy far, far away, or to a packet of Pringles, I didn't know. I cut through the village, turned right onto the Kerrykeel road and then veered onto Kinnegar Road, making the plateau and then cruising the last half mile home.

As I turned into my driveway I noticed another vehicle parked next to mine and two people stood by my door. The taller of the two, a woman of about thirty with braided black hair that reached a few inches past her shoulders, was peering through the windows. The other was a blonde girl of around six; she had her arms folded and seemed unaware she was standing in a small puddle. As she turned and saw me I could make out the puffiness of her cheeks, the glint of moisture in her nostrils and the downward pointing corners of her mouth. A flash of recognition was followed by an instinctive smile, before the sadness reasserted itself. Her mouth opened to say something, then closed, before tears started to roll down her face.

I felt my heart thump. She looked so much like her mother it killed me.

Instinctively I paused five yards short of the pair, sensing that they would need a moment together before introductions could be made. Beside me, growing by the wall of the cottage, was a rose bush rendered all but barren by the winter. A single flower, perhaps a remnant of autumn warmth, still clung to its stalk, frozen in mid-blossom.

Petra touched the woman on the leg, getting her attention and directing it my way. The woman's hair had a red streak in it and fingernails to match. It caught my eye as she swung her head around, then tilted it back in a patent, if measured, display of relief. She squatted down next to Petra and wiped a few tears from the young girl's cheeks. They spoke quietly to each other for a few moments, before the woman squeezed

Petra's hands and encouraged her to walk towards me.

Petra started shyly before breaking into a run; I was all ready to receive her hug when she pulled up. She took in the speckled sweat on my face, the steam wafting magically from my shoulders, the unsubtle aroma of effort. Then she scrunched up her little nose and moved in, tentatively placing her arms around my waist and resting the side of her face on my stomach.

'Hi, Uncle Felix,' she said. 'You smell.'

'Hey, princess,' I replied, stroking her hair back gently, aware every part of me was lacquered with the tack of perspiration, 'I'm sorry that I smell.' It wasn't her mother's colour, but she wore a clip in her hair in exactly the same place. 'It's so good to see you.'

She pulled back and looked up at me, then her eyes reddened and, like a submarine submerging, tears enveloped them from behind. She planted her face into my stomach again and began sobbing. A few yards away the woman blinked back her own tears. The half-blossomed rose wobbled in the defused wind.

I dropped to my knees and wiped Petra's face. The similarities between her and my sister were striking, though strangely hard to put a finger on. It was more of an overall impression, rather than specific traits. It wasn't my sister's forehead that dipped, or her nose that started sniffing, but it was definitely her grief that Petra felt.

'Come on,' I said, noticing her shaking from the cold. 'Let's get you inside.'

At the door the woman held out her hand. I shook it and introduced myself. It was a dark red nail varnish, like cabernet.

'Janet,' she replied, handing me a business card. She tilted an eyebrow my way. 'You're a very hard man to get hold of, Mr Blunt.'

I opened the door and let Petra and Janet in, looking at the card as I shut it behind me:

Janet Lovell
Child Protection Officer
NSPCC

I showed them through to the living room which, thankfully, wasn't in a complete state. I'd left the heating on while I ran too, so the place was nice and warm. I was more prepared for this visit than I thought.

'Petra, would you like a drink of water?' She shook her head and sat on the sofa, rubbing the last of the tears from her eyes. 'Janet?'

'Any chance of tea?'

She was wearing mostly black, but with blue jeans and flat black shoes that revealed her ankles. I caught a glimpse of a small tattoo on the right one, though couldn't make out what it was.

'Sorry, I don't have any tea. Just never got into it. Coffee?'

'Oh, no, it's fine. Too late for coffee. A glass of water will be fine, thanks.'

I brought Janet her water and stood awkwardly in the middle of the living room. Petra sat on the front edge of the old beige sofa, her hands bunched together in her lap. I realised I had absolutely nothing to offer her that she might find interesting. Even my laptop, which she was eyeing, had no games on it (that I knew of), and there was no WiFi that she might use to go online with. I felt quite hopeless.

Thankfully Janet stepped in. 'Why don't you go and get cleaned up? Petra and I will be fine down here for a while.'

Petra looked at me and gave a hopeful smile. She didn't get that from her mother either.

My usual post-run routine was a few push-ups, some stretches and maybe a sixty-second plank. I'd follow that up with a hot shower, shampoo and conditioner, work up a good lather of soap, and then dry off and get changed into some fresh, clean clothes. At that point, dry, dressed, my body humming with the buzz of performance and my brain bathing in endorphins, I felt as good as I ever got. It was all downhill from there.

Without the luxury of that time though, I sacrificed the exercises and the shampoo and conditioner, and instead had the quickest of showers, staying under only long enough to wash the sweat off. Then I quickly pulled on some old jeans and a woollen jumper and went downstairs.

Janet was standing in the middle of the living room miming, while Petra tried to guess what each of her actions meant. I stood in the doorway watching. Petra had already established it was a movie and the first word was *The*. Janet skipped to the third word and made a gesture of placing something on her head very carefully.

'Hat?' Petra said.

Janet shook her head and made the same gesture with her hands, this time even slower and with a face that made her look posh.

'Oh! Crown!'

Janet nodded enthusiastically, encouraging Petra to follow the thought.

'Crown ... Queen!'

Janet grinned, but indicated she still wasn't quite right.

'Umm, not Queen ... King!'

Janet pointed and winked at Petra. She then indicated she was miming the second word. She lunged forward with her fingers flared like claws and her teeth bared like, well, teeth. Petra got it straight away.

'Lion! *The Lion King*!'

I clapped and sat in the lounge chair. There was obviously much to talk about but I wasn't sure when the time was to do so. I let Janet run proceedings, as she seemed to be the most competent of the two of us. As if on cue, she looked in my direction.

'Perhaps Uncle Felix would like to have a turn?'

'Oh no,' I replied, 'I'm not a very good actor.'

'It's not acting, Uncle Felix. It's miming.'

'Ahh, well I don't think I'm a very good ... mimer either.'

I expected Petra to push me further, and if she had I almost certainly would have caved, even though in that moment I couldn't think of a single movie title, or TV show or book that she might know. My mind, as it often did under pressure, fell blank. But instead she looked to Janet eagerly and then, when given the nod, jumped up enthusiastically.

She put her left hand, in the shape of a toilet roll, to her left eye and made a winding motion with her right just in front of her cheek.

'Movie!' Janet and I said together.

Petra indicated there were three words in the title and the first one, she motioned as if it was obvious, started with a T.

'The,' Janet and I said together.

For the second word Petra pointed at herself, then pointed at Janet and me, then at herself again.

'Us?' I said. Petra shook her head. She pointed at me again, then at Janet, then ducked her head and crouched slightly as she pointed at herself.

'We?'

Petra shook her head more vehemently. I felt bad for not understanding her. I looked at Janet, who had sunk back in the sofa, as if to take herself out of the game. Perhaps she wanted this to be an interaction between niece and uncle, I thought. But there was a seriousness on her face that hadn't been there a few moments earlier.

I refocused on Petra. She was pointing at herself again and making herself as small as possible.

'Small!' I exclaimed, surprising myself with how enthusiastic I was at having guessed it.

Petra shook her head, but made a little twirling motion with her finger, as Janet had before.

'Not small ... little?'

Petra sprung up from the floor and clapped her hands. I looked over at Janet triumphantly. She gave me an encouraging nod.

For the third word Petra again pointed at herself. She didn't make any other gestures, just pointed at her chest.

'Petra?' I suggested. She shook her head and kept pointing at herself. 'Me? You? Yourself? Myself?'

Petra kept shaking her head. I racked my mind for movie names that might fit, having stupidly not considered this tactic before. *The Little* ... God, I thought, how many movies were there that started with *The Little*? There must be dozens, a hundred even, and yet I couldn't think of a single one.

Finally Janet leaned forward, sighed ever so gently and then suggested Petra try to mime it in a different way. Petra dropped her hands to her side despondently, then, without the same determination as before, put her palms together in front of her, sucked in her cheeks and moved her head gently from side to side.

'*The Little Fish!*' I exclaimed, figuring it a recent child's movie I'd never heard of.

Petra shook her head. I hated letting her down. She sat down on the floor and, with her knees together and her legs straight, lifted her feet a few inches off the carpet. She then moved them up and down in a vague wave motion. I thought hard, but nothing came. Indeed, the harder I thought, the less knowledge I felt I had about anything. How to drive, open cans of soup with a can opener, long division, my own birthday, everything seemed to empty out of my brain. I looked to Janet, who was looking back at me as if it was the most obvious thing in the world. It had to be a fish of some kind, but what movies had fish in them? Then it came to me.

'*Finding Nemo!*'

Both Petra and Janet dropped their shoulders and looked at me like I was an idiot. Strangely, that they were both doing it made it feel not as bad as if Petra was doing it by herself.

'The Little ...' Janet explained. 'The title starts with *The Little*.'

'Oh, of course. Sorry, I'm ... I haven't played this for a while.'

Petra was still on the carpet. I tried to remember when the last time I had vacuumed was. She was kicking her legs higher now, really getting into it, while flicking her long blonde hair over her shoulder and pouting like a ... I looked at Janet again. She was mouthing the answer. Ma ma? *The Little Ma Ma*? That couldn't be a movie. Meanwhile Petra was going red from the effort, tossing her hair around in her own little world. Whatever she was being, she was loving it. For the first time since she'd arrived she had a smile on her face. Then it came to me in a flash.

'Mermaid! *The Little Mermaid*!'

Petra collapsed on the floor in exhaustion as Janet clapped her hands. Relief flushed through me, filling the gap left by the truncated post-run ritual. It was the best I'd felt for months. Then Petra sat up.

'That was soooo obvious, Uncle Felix.' She rolled onto her knees, stood up and hugged me. 'Was I a good mermaid?'

'You were the best mermaid I've ever seen.'

'How come it took you so long to guess, then?' She had her mother's wit.

'Well, I've never seen a mermaid before,' I explained. 'I couldn't believe my eyes.'

Petra studied my face. I'd contradicted myself and she hadn't missed it.

'Mermaids are real,' she told me, a hint of challenge in her voice.

I tapped her on the nose, an action I'd never done before but which came to me out of the blue, as if it was the most natural thing in the world. 'Are they?'

Petra nodded. 'Mummy's a mermaid now,' she said, as if merely saying what day of the week it was.

I bit my lip. Janet stepped in, resting her hand on Petra's back.

'How about we ask Uncle Felix if he can show us around his cottage?'

I took them up the stairs. I had two bedrooms and a bathroom, nothing special. My bedroom was relatively tidy, but they weren't interested in that. Instead they went into the spare bedroom, which had an old double bed that came with the house and which I'd never so much as sat on. Otherwise there was just junk in there – a guitar, sleeping bag, camping mattress, cricket bat, some fishing equipment. A bookshelf built into the wall was being used to hold two blown lightbulbs I'd replaced in my room but wasn't sure if I could recycle or not.

Petra poked around tentatively while Janet studied it for cleanliness. My niece yawned and sat on the bed. She seemed defeated.

'We've been going since five this morning,' Janet explained.

Blinking a losing fight against tiredness, Petra laid down on the mattress, her hands clasped together in a prayer under her left cheek. Again I was struck by how much she looked like her mother.

'Is this where I'm going to live?' she asked, her eyes already closed.

I pulled my green sleeping bag out of its waterproof cocoon, unrolled and unzipped it, then spread it like a moss blanket over Petra. From my bed I took a spare pillow, then lifted her head and carefully placed it underneath. As I did, her little hand reached out and touched my arm, her lips parted gently and I thought she was going to say something, but sleep pulled her back under before the words could escape.

*

Janet and I sat in the living room, her on the beige sofa and me on the maroon lounge chair. Beside me the fireplace looked post-apocalyptic: the white, lifeless ashes scattered like corpses, the back wall charred black. A clear plastic bag sat limply nearby, a third full of kindling, and next to that lay three logs the size of weightlifter's biceps.

'Warm enough?' I asked Janet.

'It's fine, thanks.'

She sat with her legs crossed, her hands held together as if they'd caught a bug. The part of me that saw a beautiful woman and converted that sight into desire was broken. She was more artwork than female.

'You run often?' she asked.

'Every other day,' I told her. I was happy for her to take the lead. There was bad news coming and she'd know best how to ease it into the conversation. 'I'd be dysfunctional without it.'

'Really?'

Perhaps I'd said too much. 'It keeps my head above the parapet,' I explained.

Janet looked briefly confused, then shook it off. 'What happens if you're unable to run?' she asked, sounding more like an interviewer now. 'If you get an injury or the weather is terrible . . .'

'I'll run in just about any conditions.'

'Okay,' she replied, her shoe tapping the air, 'so if you break your leg in a car accident. How would you manage not being able to run for six weeks?'

'I guess I'd find some other exercise to do.' I thought about being in hypothetical plaster. 'Lots of push-ups, maybe. Though it wouldn't be the same.' I didn't like the idea of running being taken from me. Running was the light, the only light. 'Anyway, I don't drive often so it's not likely to happen.'

Janet leaned forward and tipped her eyebrow towards me again. 'You do realise why I'm here, don't you, Mr Blunt? Why *we're* here.'

'I assume something went wrong with Michael.'

'Yes. He beat his girlfriend.'

I felt a tension grip me. 'What about Petra?'

'It happened while she was at school.'

Breathing easier. 'How's his girlfriend?'

'I'm not sure, to be honest. My concern is Petra.'

'Mine too,' I replied. 'I was being polite.'

'Petra has been with us for two weeks,' she explained, 'staying with foster carers while we' – she blinked her way through some alternatives, before settling on one – 'tried to get hold of you.'

'Sorry about that,' I said. 'I don't get much signal here and, well, I don't expect many calls.' I wasn't even sure where my phone was.

'That's fine. We're here now. For the moment her father ... Michael ... has signed a Section 20, which means he has voluntarily given over care of Petra to our organisation.'

'For the moment?'

The heating system groaned into another fit of activity. My tinnitus searched for the sound, raised its pitch.

Janet continued. 'He's playing the penitent card. He's been charged with assault, but the entire case rests on his girlfriend's evidence. If she changes her mind, the case falls apart.'

'He assaulted my sister, you know.'

'I know. The police have told me everything they can.' Her voice was neutral now, venturing no opinion either way. 'The hearing is scheduled for January third.'

Janet leaned back, creating a bit more space between us. I rubbed my temple with my thumb and looked to the floor. Her tattoo was yellow and green.

'What happens if the case goes ahead and he's found guilty?'

Janet gave me the same look as when I was trying to guess Petra's act during charades. It took a few moments for it to register.

'Stay with me? *Live* with me?!'

Janet blinked. 'Mr Blunt, besides her father, you're her only living relative.'

'Yes, but ...' my tinnitus climbed an octave, harmonised

itself, then drifted into the background again, 'I'm not ...'

'You're not a parent. I know.' Her voice was adamant now. 'But you are blood and in my experience it's far better for a child to stay with family than to be put into foster care.'

'I don't want that,' I offered. 'Her in foster care, I mean. It's just ...' I shook my head. I wasn't even sure what day of the week it was. Possibly Tuesday.

'To be clear,' Janet continued, 'if Michael is convicted, my agency will be making a recommendation to the family court on how we best think Petra should be cared for.'

I nodded, my mouth dry. 'Of course.'

Again with the eyebrow, this time with a squint thrown in. 'Mr Blunt, I'm here to see if you're capable of caring for a six-year-old girl. If Michael is convicted and I don't think you can do the job, I'll recommend she is moved into a home.'

I had a sudden, horrible image of a teenage Petra slamming the door of her foster home in my face.

'I don't know what to say,' I said.

'That's understandable. It's a bit of a shock. I guess the first thing is that, if things go that way, do you think you're capable?' Just a fraction, her voiced softened. 'I understand you've had your own struggles since your parents passed away.'

Janet somehow managed to juxtapose a look of professional indifference against one of disarming empathy. Frustratingly, it was impossible to tell which one was dominant.

'Honestly,' I answered, 'I'm not sure. I've never had any kids. I wouldn't know where to start.'

'That's okay. You'll find it's instinctual. I can see Petra already has a bond with you and you're comfortable with her.'

'You sound like you're trying to convince me.'

Her eyebrows rose like a golfer's backswing. 'Don't get me wrong, Mr Blunt. I'm here for Petra. My job, my intention, is to find the best arrangement for her. I *want* her to stay with you. But I can assure you that unless I am one hundred per cent convinced you're up to it, I'll not recommend that she does.'

Janet moved the conversation on to Petra's immediate needs – a warm bed tonight, breakfast in the morning, a shower and brushed teeth. Breaking things down into these smaller tasks made it less daunting. We went into the kitchen to see what food I had for breakfast. I could do toast and jam.

'That's fine,' she told me. She had her phone in her hand. 'Do you get reception here? Or have WiFi? I need to call the owner of the place I'm staying at.'

'No WiFi. I sometimes get reception upstairs, though it's better later at night. You're staying nearby?'

'I've booked a cottage just around the corner,' she said, walking through the foyer.

I listened to her footsteps drum up the stairs, cross the landing and stop outside Petra's bedroom. My kitchen was a deathtrap. There were knives and gas stoves, electric toasters and hot water taps. I stood against the kitchen sink, saw that my waist was just above it. That put Petra's head even further above, and therefore the unwashed dishes within range of her hands. I was going to have to wash and dry after every meal.

Janet's footsteps moved back across the landing and came down the stairs. She entered the kitchen still brandishing her phone, as if for evidence.

'I'll try at the other place,' she said, sliding it into her jacket pocket. 'I'll come around in the morning at, say, nine? We can go through some things then.'

'I'm not usually up before eleven ...'

Janet chuckled. 'I can assure you you'll be up well before nine, Mr Blunt.'

'Right. Of course.' I could feel my internal clock fretting. 'It's Tuesday today, yes?'

'*Wednesday.*'

'No, that's right. Wednesday. I forgot ... about Monday ... you can call me Felix, you know.'

Janet nodded faintly but didn't reply.

We went to her car and unloaded Petra's belongings.

Amongst them were some sunglasses with the *Little Mermaid* design on them.

'She really likes that movie,' I said, sliding them into my pocket.

'Every time we play charades,' Janet explained, handing me a red jacket, 'she mimes that movie.'

'That's cute,' I replied. 'I was like that with *Star Wars.*'

'Yes but, did you notice that when she was miming the mermaid word, she pointed to herself first? She thinks *she* is a mermaid.'

'Surely that's just a thing that kids do.'

'Make-believe is healthy. Fantasising about being a fictional character is normal. This is something else.'

'Is it really worse than most kids?'

'Most kids, Mr Blunt,' Janet exclaimed, again looking at me like I was an idiot, 'haven't had mothers that drowned themselves at sea.'

8

On Friday 23rd September 2016, my sister Patricia dropped her daughter at Michael's house in Bristol. She said goodbye with a hug and a kiss and watched her daughter carry her bag up the stairs. Michael stood in the doorway. It's unclear what was said between the pair, but it's believed there was an exchange of some depth, as it was another twenty to thirty seconds before Michael shut the door. He didn't slam it, but Patricia was still facing it when it was closed. I know all this from reading the police report, which included eyewitness accounts from two neighbours.

Patricia then got in her car, sitting in it for at least a minute before driving off. One of the neighbours believes they saw the curtain of Petra's bedroom move aside and a face, slightly back from the window so unidentifiable, look out.

Phone records show a terse exchange of texts between Michael and Patricia at around 11 pm that night. They revolve around Michael wanting more access to his daughter and his concern about Patricia's mental state and the effect it was having on Petra. Police say that while there is a level of aggressiveness to the messages, there is nothing 'out of the ordinary', given the circumstances. A phone call between the two happened shortly before midnight. It went on for twenty-three minutes. In his statement Michael claimed the conversation was along the same lines of the earlier texts, though never became more heated than a simple disagreement. He said that he found Patricia, both on the phone and at his house earlier that evening, to be acting 'strange and unlike her usual self'. Other than Michael's account, there is no way of knowing what was actually said.

Patricia lived in a terraced house on the other side of Bristol, by herself when Petra wasn't there. In the year since our parents died she had fallen into a mire of depression, and was on medication to help her cope. It's not clear what happened in the hours after the phone call with Michael. Police found half a bottle of red wine next to a single glass with a small amount still in it, a pen and a notepad with nothing written in it bar the usual stuff (shopping lists, random dates, doodles) all at her kitchen table, which is where they also found her phone. In the bathroom cabinet they found her anti-depressants. After talking to her doctor the police deduced she had either been reducing her intake, or stopped taking them altogether. There's no way to tell which, or why.

At seven the next morning a neighbour, who was just leaving his house to go for a run, saw Patricia get in her car and drive west. He didn't notice her put any luggage in, or even a handbag, though he admits he didn't pay that much attention.

It has always struck me as horribly ironic that someone going for a run, something I use to keep myself above depression, witnessed my sister falling victim to it.

Patricia's car was found in a car park by the harbour on Sunday. It had a parking fine attached to the window for £50. She'd hired a small boat with an outboard motor, the kind you don't need a licence to drive. The person who hired it to her said he thought it odd she didn't have any fishing equipment or diving gear, but other than that he didn't see any reason to be concerned.

That man's name was Paul. He was the shape of a space hopper, had lived in Bristol all his life and with his parents until his early forties. His wife was short, broad-faced but, comparatively at least, not as large. Their two daughters took after their father. I took Paul for lunch at a Spanish restaurant, where he ordered fish and chips and a Diet Coke. When I asked him if he could tell me anything at all, however trivial, about my sister the day she hired the boat from him, he said all he remembered was that she asked how much fuel was in the tank and how far she could go. This was in the police report so wasn't new to me. I asked him why that didn't strike him as unusual and he said that girls always worry about stuff like that. He told me this while his mouth was full of chips. I asked him if women regularly hire boats by themselves. He said no, they don't, usually they're with their boyfriends or husbands. Again, wasn't this unusual, then? Yes, he admitted, washing the chips down with Diet Coke from the can, he supposed it was.

Paul was the last person my sister ever spoke to. Her final human interaction.

The boat she hired was found drifting in the Bristol Channel five nautical miles from the coast. The fuel tank was empty. All that was in the boat was her purse and car keys. There was no note.

The coroner's report ruled that, while it was impossible to know for sure, in all likelihood she had entered the water to take her own life. It went on to detail the process that occurs in a drowning victim – the breath held instinctively until hypercapnia – the urge to breathe – kicks in and water is aspirated into the airways. The oxygen supply to the brain is reduced and consciousness fades, the point at which a state of calmness is often thought to descend over victims. The brain, by now overwhelmed by carbon dioxide, steadily shuts down its lesser important operations – speech, muscle movement, memory etc – focusing its depleted resources on maintaining core life functions. Death occurs when this is no longer viable, between fifteen and twenty minutes after submersion, depending on the temperature of the water. It's important to note, the coroner added, that after the initial anxiety relating to breathing, the victim will not have suffered.

Patricia's body was never found and according to an expert in tidal movements it was probably carried out into the Irish sea.

The coroner ruled it death by suicide brought on by severe depression, which had its roots in the tragedy of losing both parents to cancer within a few months of each other a year earlier, but was exacerbated by her reducing or not taking her medication in the days and weeks leading up to her actions. She chose drowning, according to the coroner, as it was the method least likely to result in a body being found; a conclusion reached by a check of her recent internet activity. This was the only indication that she had considered the consequences of her actions with regard to her daughter.

Child psychologists advised that we should be honest with Petra about what happened, though use soft language that she would understand. Naturally the role fell to Michael, but exactly what he said I don't know.

I held a memorial service a month after she went missing. Neither Petra nor Michael attended.

*

After Janet left that evening I went upstairs and watched my niece sleeping on the spare bed. She looked tiny under my sleeping bag, her delicate head engulfed by the duck down pillow. At rest, peacefully dreaming of mermaids, she looked less like my sister than before. Instead I could see Michael. His nose, his cheekbones, his blond hair. Perhaps Patricia was there under the eyelids. I wondered if the way she would look as an adult was set in stone, or whether environment and nurture had any influence. If he took her back would she become more and more like him as time went by, rendering her mother no more than a fleeting glimpse in an adolescent mirror? Would she seek that to be the case, especially as she matured and came to grasp what her mother had done?

She slept soundly, seemingly untroubled by the dramas surrounding her. Ever since my parents had died I'd struggled to sleep properly, rarely getting more than three hours at a time and waking up with my jaw clenched. Yet here was a six-year-old lost in a world of dreams, willing to accept that this room might be where she lived now. This room in a cottage I'd been in for three months, and still had trouble calling home. She had such resilience.

I went to my room and found my phone on the floor between the wall and the small set of empty drawers that amounted to a bedside table. It was connected to the charger but after pressing the home button and not getting a result, I discovered the power plug wasn't pushed all the way in. I reconnected it, observed a pale digital battery image flash on the screen, then left it on the table.

I took my duvet and a pillow from the bed and carried them into Petra's room, placing them on top of the blue camping mattress which I unrolled along the floor so it was parallel with the bed. Then I quietly brushed my teeth and put on some tracksuit pants, got under the duvet and, using the head torch from my old fishing equipment, read a book.

It was impossible to concentrate. My mind was full of worry about how I could look after Petra. I didn't know how to make food for a six-year-old. Did they eat the same as adults? And school – how, where, when? Would I have to take her there and pick her up, help her with homework? What if I didn't know the answers? There were so many ways I could fail her. But my biggest worry was that she was a girl. Her mind worked differently, with different concerns, a focus on feelings. I was numb inside. How could I empathise with a child when I had to run for forty minutes in freezing temperatures just to stir up a picture of how I felt about myself? And then there was her body. What on earth was I going to do when she got her first period? The thought terrified me and it was nearly five in the morning before I finally nodded off.

Sometime after eight I heard a gentle thump on the floor and then delicate footsteps creep past my head. I heard the bathroom door open and then Petra's voice make a shivering sound. I tried not to hear the tinkle of her pee going into the toilet, but there were no other sounds in the world. Then Petra crept back into the bedroom and got under the sleeping bag again. The sun wasn't yet up but the grey light of pre-dawn was evident through the curtains; I tried to go back to sleep but I could hear Petra moving around. I rolled over to look at her and saw she was fully under the sleeping bag.

'Morning, Uncle Felix,' she said, somehow aware I was awake. She must have had her hands above her face, as the sleeping bag was pointed upwards there, like a pole in a tent.

'Morning, princess. Did you sleep well?'

'Yes. Your sleeping bag is soooo cosy. Will it be my blanket forever?'

I wondered how she had come to think of this as a permanent move. I made a mental note to ask Janet about it when she arrived.

'If you want. But I can probably get you something else. A duvet maybe.'

'I like this,' she said. 'Can you zip it up around me?'

'Sure.'

I laid there, a little surprised I wasn't falling back to sleep, but equally unable to wake up properly. Then I realised what I had just agreed to do. 'Did you mean now?'

'Yes, please.' She was still completely covered by the sleeping bag.

I got up and went to the end of the bed. 'Are you ready?'

'Yep!'

I slid my hands under the sleeping bag and found her legs. Petra giggled. I lifted them up and curled the far side of the sleeping bag under them, then placed her legs back down. Then I knelt carefully beside her, slid my arm underneath her lower back, lifted and slid the next section of sleeping bag under her. Petra giggled each time but seemed to like being moved like she was a doll. I repeated the method beneath her upper back and under her head, until the two zip sides were completely on one side of her and she was sandwiched inside the bag like a Venus flytrap. Then I connected the zip at the bottom and sealed it all the way to the top. I could've got another half a Petra in there lengthways and two more sideways.

'How's that?' I asked the bump where her face probably was. 'So cosy.'

She shuffled upwards until her head poked out the top. Strands of blonde hair covered her face, but she smiled through them at me. 'Hello!' she said. It was the first time we'd looked at each other all morning.

Then she started lifting her legs up and down in the same way she had the previous evening during charades. 'Do you know what I am, Uncle Felix?'

I wasn't sure what I was supposed to do. Janet had indicated her mermaid obsession was unhealthy, but how was I meant to act when she went to it? Should I just acknowledge it, but not encourage, then change the subject? Pretend I couldn't guess at all? She had been so enthusiastic when mimicking it last night, I didn't think she'd give up that easily.

'Can you guess, Uncle Felix?'

I put on a monotone voice: 'Is it a mermaid?'

'Yep!' She kicked her tail enthusiastically. 'Just like Mummy!'

It was too much hearing her refer to Patricia like that. I got off her bed and sat back down on my mattress. Tiredness and the quick motion between her bed and the mattress made me dizzy; I laid down, covered myself with the duvet and looked up at the ceiling, blinking.

'What's wrong, Uncle Felix?'

'Nothing, princess.'

'Is it my mermaid? Don't you like it?'

Maybe this was a critical moment. Perhaps I could stop her infatuation with mermaids right here. It would be something to show Janet when she came round.

'Actually, real mermaids are quite bad,' I told her. 'They sing to men on boats and lure them into the water.' I nearly added 'where they drown', but thankfully stopped myself.

Petra fell silent. I was still staring at the ceiling, running the words back over in my head. They sounded okay, I thought.

Rational and true. Perhaps a little blunt, but I had to keep it simple.

Shortly I could hear sniffing coming from the bed. I looked over but Petra had lowered herself inside the sleeping bag again.

'Princess?'

Sniffing.

'Petra? Princess?'

'Stop calling me princess!'

Shit. 'I'm sorry.'

'I'm not a princess. I'm a mermaid!'

I got on to my knees and hobbled over to the side of the bed.

'You're a beautiful mermaid,' I told her.

'I don't believe you! You said I'm bad.'

'No, not you. Real mermaids, I meant . . .'

Her sniffing, I could tell now, had evolved into tears. She was gasping for breaths in between berating me.

'Mummy's a real mermaid!'

Shit. Shit fuck shit.

'She is, she's a beautiful mermaid, just like you.'

'You said she was bad.'

'Princess, I . . .'

The sleeping bag sprung up on either side, then thumped into the mattress. It did this twice, in time with her pertinent points.

'I'm NOT a PRINCESS!'

'No. Sorry. I forgot. You're a mermaid.'

Her crying had reached cruise altitude and there was no way in now. I decided to change tack.

'How about some breakfast?'

Crying.

'I've got . . .' What did I have? 'I've got muesli.' No response. 'Or I've got toast.'

Petra's crying stuttered enough to allow some words out. 'Nutella toast?'

'Oh, I don't have any Nutella, unfortunately.' Crying resumed. 'But I've got Marmite.'

'I (deep sniffing breath) hate (choking cry) marmite!'

'I'll see what else I can find. You hold tight, I'll be right back.' I patted the sleeping bag lump and ran downstairs.

*

Half an hour later there was a knock on the door, and Janet behind it.

'You're early,' I said, letting her in.

'I feared the worst,' she replied solemnly. 'How is she?'

'Oh, fine,' I lied. 'We're having breakfast upstairs.'

Janet put her jacket over a chair in the foyer, then went upstairs. I followed her, dressed in tracksuit pants and a blue hoodie.

Petra was still buried inside the sleeping bag. On the floor was my camping mattress, my duvet and pillow, a plate of uneaten blackberry jam on toast, an empty bowl of muesli, an empty plate with toast crumbs on it and Franz Kafka's *The Metamorphosis*.

'Good Lord,' Janet said, surveying the scene. Then she turned to me. 'Tell me you weren't reading her Kafka.'

'No, well, I was reading it anyway, and then I realised I didn't have anything for her to read, so I just read it out loud, but not to her, to myself.'

Janet closed her eyes, held them shut and sighed heavily. Then she opened them, shook her head and stepped into the room.

'Petra, honey, are you okay?'

'She's been under there all morning. I think she really likes—'

Suddenly Petra's head appeared. She wiggled herself out of the sleeping bag and jumped out of bed, where she rushed to Janet's side and buried her head in her stomach.

'Yay, she's up,' I said meekly.

Janet stroked Petra's head and then gently removed the strands of hair from her face as she pulled back. She crouched down to look her in the eyes.

'How are you? Did you sleep well?'

Petra shook her head. It felt like being stabbed in the back.

'Oh, that's okay. I find it difficult sleeping in new rooms too. Did Uncle Felix keep you company in here? Scare all the monsters away?'

'Uncle Felix said mermaids are bad.'

Janet didn't look at me as I thought she might. Instead she kept her eyes fixed on Petra's.

'Oh, he's silly. Boys are silly sometimes, aren't they?'

Petra nodded.

Janet continued. 'Do you remember yesterday when we were playing charades and you asked Uncle Felix why he didn't recognise you were a mermaid straight away?'

'Yes.' Her head rocked up and down from the back of the neck. I realised I didn't nod like that, somehow just nodded the front of my head instead.

'Do you remember what he said?'

'He said he's never seen a mermaid before.'

'That's right. So how could Uncle Felix possibly know anything about mermaids, if he's never seen one?'

Defiantly. 'He can't.'

'That's right. He was just being silly.' Janet turned to me. 'Weren't you, Uncle Felix?'

'I was. I'm sorry Petra. I didn't mean to upset you. Do you forgive me?'

Janet gave Petra a little push and winked at her. Petra took the cue and only slightly begrudgingly walked towards me. She placed her arms around my hips and plonked the side of her face into my stomach. I could tell she was forcing her bottom lip out and sniffing as if still recovering from her tears. I still wanted to soothe her. She looked up at me.

'Can we get some Nutella?'

'Absolutely.'

*

109

Janet sat in the living room as, upstairs, Petra had a shower and in the kitchen I made coffee. We spoke through the open door, with mermaids top of the agenda.

'The therapist says the best way to handle it is not to indulge her. She'll grow out of it in time.'

'Easier said than done,' I replied. 'What am I supposed to say when she's kicking her legs like a tail?'

'You can acknowledge she's a mermaid – without emotion – then change the subject.'

I entered the living room bearing a plate of ginger nut biscuits.

'Dammit, I was close – that was my first instinct this morning.' I took a biscuit and unconsciously used it to animate my points. 'I was right there, doing it properly, and then went and screwed it up.'

Surprisingly, Janet was supportive. 'Mr Blunt, it's okay. It's a steep learning curve. Just, maybe, stick with your first instinct in the future.'

I took a bight from the biscuit. 'Do we know how she came to make this association? It had to be Michael.'

'That's what we're all assuming.'

'I suppose it's not the end of the world.'

'It's far from ideal, Mr Blunt. By thinking her mother is a mermaid she is still associating her with being somewhat alive, even if it's not in a way she can touch and see. It's dragging out the trauma. She needs to let go.'

It seemed an absurd concept, expecting a six-year-old to let go of their mother? Especially the child of a woman who couldn't let go of her own mother's death.

'I never thought I'd say this,' I said, 'but there are parts of Michael that I hope she inherited, rather than from my side of the family.'

Janet seemed to know what I meant, as she didn't look at me like I was an idiot for the first time all morning.

We went for a walk on the beach. I couldn't remember the last time I'd been outside so early – the light was brighter and there was an actual sense that it was daytime. I'd become accustomed to sleeping in and only emerging to run in the hour before dusk; to me daylight was something that happened on the other side of the bedroom curtains.

The tide was up, leaving a narrow width of soft sand for us to stumble over. It was chopped with a month's worth of shoe and paw prints – all that remained since the moon last pulled the lough up to the cusp of the dunes.

'Someone rides a horse along this beach, Petra,' I told her.

'Really? Is it a black horse, like Black Beauty?'

'I don't know.'

'Why don't you know?'

'Well, I've never actually seen it. I've only ever seen its prints.'

'So … but …' It was fascinating seeing her little mind working its way through the logic. 'But how do you know it's a horse?'

'They're very distinctive prints. Have you ever seen a horse-shoe?

'Horses don't wear shoes!'

'They do. But they're not like your shoes. They're flat and they're made of metal and they're shaped like …' How do you describe the shape of a horseshoe, when a horseshoe is the way other things are described?

Janet stepped in. 'The letter U. Like a short, fat letter U.'

Petra processed this information in the silent bubble of her own world. She was holding both Janet's hand and mine, though I noticed that initially Janet had tried to stay far enough to the side that Petra couldn't reach her. It was only when a wave washed higher up the beach and she had had to move closer that Petra seized her chance.

'Uncle Felix?'

'Yep.'

'If you've never seen the actual horse, how can you be *really* sure there is one?'

'How else would the prints have got here?'

'I don't know. Are the prints here now?'

Petra looked in the sand around us.

'I think it only gets ridden at low tide.'

'So they're buried under the water?'

'They've probably been washed away by the water.'

'But maybe it's a seahorse.'

'I hadn't thought of that.'

She settled into her narrative. 'The mermaids ride the seahorses when they're tired from swimming.'

A large clump of seaweed, greeny-brown with leaves like a scorpion's tail and pitted with olive-shaped nodules, was tangled around a large dead tree branch, almost as if it had jumped out and wrestled it into the water. Janet and I swung Petra over it.

'And they jump over seaweed on their horsies when they're escaping from the sea witch.'

'Hmmm,' I offered, unenthusiastically.

Petra, undaunted: 'Uncle Felix?'

'Yep.'

'If you saw the shoe prints of a mermaid, would you believe they were real too, even if you didn't see the mermaid?'

Janet was communicating to me via her raised and slightly tilted eyebrows, and I read from them that I was to continue my campaign of un-enthusiasm. Frustratingly, this meant I had to let Petra's assertion that mermaids wore shoes slide.

'I would,' I said plainly, then fell silent and looked straight ahead.

Janet took the lead. 'Walking on this sand is difficult, isn't it? Shall we cut through the dunes and see if it's easier?'

Petra acquiesced without a fuss and shortly we were walking single-file along a sandy but firm track through the stringy grass of the dunes. I was up ahead, with Petra in the middle and Janet at the back. There was a slight headwind, nothing too fierce, but enough that I was sure I wouldn't be able to hear anything the other two said to me. Consequently I walked with the quiet calm of knowing I didn't have to make conversation, only looking back every so often to make sure I wasn't getting too far ahead.

To our right I could make out the path that ran parallel to the beach. We hadn't moved that far from my place and I could make out the collection of holiday cottages in the neighbouring property, the roofs of which I could see through my windows. A little further along, a couple of old ropes were tied to a tree branch, no doubt for local kids to swing out over the dunes and break their necks. I found myself telling Petra – entirely in my head – that it was too dangerous for her to have a go.

I looked back and saw Janet and Petra sharing a small conversation and pointing up at the cottages. Petra noticed me watching them.

'That's where Janet's living, Uncle Felix.'

'Staying,' Janet corrected her. 'Just for a little while.'

'That's where she's staying,' Petra repeated, her voice less enthusiastic.

Soon we were opposite the cemetery, the tops of the tallest gravestones just visible on the other side of the path. In the trees I could see dozens of nests but only a handful of the rooks that congregated there. They called to each other with a slow, foreboding cry of *arc*, as if every communication was laced with suspicion and warning.

Our trail through the dunes connected with the path and we followed that to the start of the village, where we cut past an empty children's playground. Petra studied the equipment, as if making a mental register of ways she could entertain herself. Janet checked her phone.

We continued out along the jetty and looked down at a group of eight people gathered beside the boat ramp. The women, of which there were only three, were wearing one-piece bathing suits, while all the men were in Speedos. Towels were draped over a nearby guard rail.

Amongst them was a woman with short curly white hair, her pale skin speckled with goose pimples. She had her eyes closed and seemed to be muttering something to herself, before she opened them again and tossed a coin into the water. Shortly she joined the rest of the group and they collectively counted out loud to three before rushing into the water, diving underneath as soon as it was over waist height.

'My Lord,' Janet said in the sombre tone she usually deployed when sceptical of something I'd said or done.

The water frothed white as the group swum about ten metres out. Then they turned and swum parallel to the beach, back in the direction we'd come. There were no gasps or sharp intakes for breath, no panicked darts for the shore and the refuge of towels and warm clothes. Instead there was a concerted and focused effort to stroke methodically, to keep moving, to appear as if this was a completely normal thing to do in December.

On the high street we stopped into a cafe and got a bite to eat and coffees for Janet and I. Petra had a hot chocolate with marshmallows. As I watched her spooning the melting sludge from the top of her drink into her mouth, her face still red from the crisp breeze outside, I remembered how I'd looked at her the previous night as she slept, and wondered if she had her mother's eyes. I tried to catch their colour in between her blinks and the times she closed them completely so she could savour the taste of the cocoa. It was harder than I expected.

'What are you looking at me like that for, Uncle Felix?'

'I was just trying to see what colour eyes you have.'

Petra dipped her long spoon into the cup and scooped the last of the melted marshmallows from the top. 'They're blue,' she said. 'Like Dad's.'

I nodded. I was a little disappointed, though not as much as I thought. She had called Michael *Dad*, not Daddy. It felt significant.

'Petra?'

'Yes, Uncle Felix?'

I poked my tongue out at her and flared my eyes. She giggled shyly.

'You're funny,' she said, picking up the glass and putting it to her lips.

I loved it when she called me Uncle Felix.

Janet was looking at her phone again, that professional facade betraying a modicum of something, frustration perhaps.

'Everything okay?'

'Everything's fine, Mr Blunt.'

'I really ... I'd prefer Felix.'

'Uncle Felix,' Petra suggested.

Janet ignored us both. 'So, Mr Blunt, do you have a girl-friend ... or a partner?'

Petra's blue eyes shifted from Janet to me. She had chocolate in the corners of her lips.

'No,' I replied, 'not at the moment.'

It was a surprisingly intimate question. Perhaps, I thought, she was breaking the ice. 'Do you?' I asked. 'Boyfriend or partner?'

Janet's eyebrows ducked, buckled, formed into short, fat letter U's. I had misread the situation.

'Mr Blunt, I need to know if any other adults might be spending time in the same house as Petra.'

I looked at my niece, who smiled back at me.

'Oh,' I said. 'I see.' I picked up my coffee. 'No. No partner of any kind.'

Petra's spoon clinked against her half empty glass.

*

We walked home without any further discussion of partners. Once there, Petra settled into a colouring book and Janet checked her phone twice more. It was clear something was troubling her, and I was trying to figure out a way of broaching the subject when she slapped her knee.

'Right,' she said. 'I might leave you two to it.'

Petra looked over, smiled without showing her teeth and returned her attention to her colouring book. 'Okay,' she said casually.

Janet met my eyes, nodded and stood up. I had the distinct impression she was holding herself together by not breathing. We walked to the door.

'Have you got food for dinner?' she asked.

I had some cheese in the fridge, some muesli, ginger nut biscuits, maybe a few bits of bread.

'No. I should go shopping.'

'Petra might want a nap this afternoon. You can't leave her.'

'Of course. Umm ... I think they serve food at the pub.'

'Okay ... no wait, no!'

'No?'

'No, no, you're trying to create a home for her. A pub isn't a home.'

'Okay, but—'

'I'll bring something round. My treat. There's a chippy next to the café. I had a peek at the menu and they had a selection of burgers and salads too. I'll get us all something and come round at six. How's that?'

'Err okay, fine, great.'

Janet looked relieved. Emboldened by this, I asked: 'What are you doing this afternoon, then?'

Her ability to communicate using her eyebrows was astounding.

'Probably none of my business,' I conceded.

'Have you got your phone?'

I pulled it from my pocket and brandished it triumphantly. 'Fully charged.'

'My number?'

'I put your card ...' I looked around, patted my shirt.

'Don't worry,' Janet said, 'just check your missed call history.'

A list of numbers filled the screen, with three featuring regularly over the last fortnight.

'Ah,' I exclaimed, 'these are probably you.'

Janet cast her eyes over them. 'That one's my mobile and that's our office. I don't recognise the other one. But save those two.'

I obeyed dutifully. The third number – a mobile with a UK prefix – I assumed to be a scam call of some kind. There really was no one I could think of that would have any need to contact me.

'Good,' she said. 'I'll see you at six.'

With that she left, retrieving her mobile from her pocket before she'd even taken two steps from the door.

9

Janet arrived with burgers and salad at six and the three of us ate at the dining table; we talked about horses, briefly of mermaids, and about school. Then Janet went to leave but discovered she had a flat tyre. I offered to change it, but Janet wasn't having any of it and decided to leave the car there to deal with in the morning. She left the keys with me just in case I needed to move it, as it was blocking my car in. She was wearing a leather jacket with impractically placed zips that suggested it was fashionable. Her perfume and makeup was such that I noticed Petra staring at her as she stuffed chips into her mouth. I wondered if she had a date. Was it possible, after being here two days, that she had met someone? I was so removed from the dating world that such a thing seemed plausible. Either way, I knew better than to ask her about it so thanked her for dinner and watched her walk speedily into the night.

Petra and I washed up and then played Ludo for a while, before Petra started yawning, which in turn made me start yawning. Soon we were both looking at the Ludo board with our chins in our hands.

'Bedtime?' I suggested.

'Bedtime,' she nodded.

We went upstairs and brushed our teeth, then Petra got into bed, looking tiny beneath my giant sleeping bag.

'Are you sleeping in my room again, Uncle Felix?' she asked.

'Would you like me to?'

'I don't mind if you want to sleep in your bed,' she said, then rolled onto her side and bunched up her shoulders. 'I like it when you're in here though.'

How do children make you feel so special with so few words?

I was at the top of the stairs, about to go down and make sure everything was locked up, when my phone rang. I looked at the number and saw it was a UK mobile. I didn't answer. Doors locked, I changed into my tracksuit pants and an old shirt and got under my duvet on Petra's floor. I read half a page of Kafka, turned the headlamp off and fell asleep.

I drifted quickly into a dream. I was sitting on the rocks at the beach, looking out across the lough. Somewhere a woman was singing. It was a beautiful song and I was entranced, but then a drumbeat came in, completely out of time to the singing. Moments later I was shaken awake.

Though I was in something of a daze I still had enough wherewithal to look to the bed for Petra. She wasn't there and neither was the sleeping bag. I panicked and sat up, then turned and found her kneeling on the other side of me. She had my mobile phone in one hand while two fingers of her other hand were pressed against her lips, trying to keep me quiet.

'Petra! What's wrong?'

'Shhhh, Uncle Felix,' she whispered loudly. 'Janet says we shouldn't open the door.'

I looked at the bedroom door, which was open. Then at Petra. I was very confused. Then the knocks came from the front door again. Things quickly fell into place. I took the phone from Petra's hand and saw that Janet was still connected on the other end. I spoke into it, but there was only a rustling sound and muffled voices.

Four solid thuds at the front door. I sat up.

'Janet said she'll be here in a minute and we should wait.'

Straight away I thought of Michael. Petra looked concerned, but also a little curious. Did she wonder if it was her dad? How would she react if it was? Would she run down and hug him, call him Daddy in a fit of excitement? How did I get this attached in such a short space of time?

'You stay here,' I told her. 'I'll just go and make sure it's not a baddy, okay?'

'But Janet said we shouldn't open the door.'

'I won't open it if it's a baddy.'

'What if it's a goody?' she asked. Her whisper was nearly as loud as her normal voice.

'If it's a goody then we'll want them inside, won't we?'

She didn't seem sure, and I was even less sure what I was going to do when confronted with Michael at the door. All I knew was that hiding from him felt wrong, both for Petra's and for my sake. I stood up and got to the doorway, then heard Petra moving behind me. I turned and saw she was holding my cricket bat in both hands.

'Here, Uncle Felix,' she said, struggling with its weight. 'In case it's a baddy.'

'Thanks.' Then something which had been in the back of my mind ever since I had woken up bubbled to the surface. 'How did you unlock my phone?'

'I pressed your finger against it while you were sleeping,' she whispered.

She said it with such innocence, as if it was as conventional as learning to use a microwave, that I could only nod and move on.

I took the bat downstairs and looked back up to the landing. Petra was peering through the railing.

'Stay in the bedroom, please,' I told her, 'just in case it's a really ugly baddy.'

She nodded and rushed inside the room, closing the door behind her.

I placed the bat down in the corner behind the door, then looked through the window. I saw straight away that it wasn't Michael. Relief flushed through me, but the anxiety it pushed aside didn't fully disappear. I had the feeling this was a test run for the real event.

I opened the door to a tall man in a black, wool-lined denim jacket. He nodded politely.

'Good evening,' he said, 'sorry to interrupt. I was looking for Janet Lovell. I saw her car parked here.'

'Yeah that's hers,' I said, unsure how much I should reveal.

The man stuck out his hand. 'My name's Mark,' he explained. 'I'm her boyfriend.'

'Ohhh,' I replied. 'I thought she came here alone?'

'She did.' He scratched the side of his head. 'I'm surprising her.'

I told him she was on her way and that her car had a flat tyre.

'I offered to fix it,' I said, 'but she wouldn't let me.'

'Yeah, that's Janet,' Mark replied. Then he winked. 'All the more reason to do it.'

I gave him the keys then trotted upstairs to tell Petra everything was okay.

'It's a goody?' she asked.

'It's a goody,' I told her. 'Janet's boyfriend.'

'Mark!'

She skipped out of her room and down the stairs. I wondered how much she knew about her father. Did she think of him as a baddy, after all? Baddy instead of Daddy.

Janet arrived just as we got the flat tyre off. She had a balding man called Connor with her, who seemed baffled by the whole ordeal. Everyone came inside and our stories were spliced together to explain the how and why of everything. Mark and I finished changing the flat tyre and then he and Janet got in his car while Connor got in his, leaving hers behind.

'I'll be round in the morning,' she told me, trying to maintain her professional facade in spite of much of it having fallen away. 'Around nine.' Mark coughed. 'Ten.'

'I'll be up.'

Then they left to go to the pub and I watched from the doorway, waving alongside Petra, who was so excited by it all that she wouldn't sleep for another hour and a half.

*

My father was diagnosed with pancreatic cancer in November of 2014; my mother received her breast cancer diagnosis a week before Christmas. They were both given six months to live. They did everything together, my parents, so dying of the same disease at the same time was apt, in a grim kind of way.

Mum used to tell me that things come in threes, so when I lost my job in January of 2015 there was more apt grimness to admire.

Shortly afterwards, my girlfriend Carly, whom I had an unhealthy attachment to, announced she wanted us to take a holiday to Bali.

'I've just been fired,' I protested.

Carly was staring at a bookings website. 'You'll get another job,' she reassured me. 'I've found these cheap flights.'

I squinted at the screen. 'My parents are both due to die around then.'

'Oh, that's right,' she replied, pushing her top lip out with the bottom one. 'It's just, I've always wanted to go to Bali.'

I broke up with Carly, spiralled downwards and moved in with my dying parents.

Before he was unable, my father, two thirds the size he used to be, called me to his bedside and espoused his philosophy.

'Life,' he explained in a voice I barely recognised, 'is unfair.'

That pretty much summed it up. Pushed to elaborate, he told me about one of his work colleagues, a chap called Charles Furst.

'*Furst in name, first in life*, that's what he used to say,' he said, then added, 'He was an arsehole.'

Charles Furst was racist, sexist, he stole from work, cheated on his wives and forgot his children's birthdays unless they were living under his roof.

'Such an arsehole,' my father insisted.

When he was fifty-seven Charles Furst won the lottery. Three and a half million pounds. He retired early and moved to Spain, where he lives to this day. The last my father heard he had a twenty-three-year-old girlfriend and a dog called Ronaldo.

'I could be wrong about the dog's name,' he said. 'The point is ...' Even in his last few weeks my father would use his hands to colour his speeches, raising and lowering them as if tossing coins into a glass. 'The point is your mother and I have been good, honest people. Faithful, hardworking, always remembered your birthdays. Maybe we could have been more fun' – here his voice trailed off – 'but, well, your mother ... the point is I'm sixty-six. I was retired for six months, and now look. Meanwhile, *Furst in life* has a dog called Ronaldo.' He sank back into his yellow pillow. 'Such an arsehole.'

There was no moral. He didn't tell me to therefore seize the day or throw caution to the wind. He didn't even say I should go and buy a lottery ticket. He just left it at that. *Life is unfair.*

After he died and after my mother died, but before my sister died, Carly took me back. It was a brief rekindling born out of pity. At that stage I took what I could get.

One afternoon, as Carly and I strolled along the banks of the Avon, I shared my father's story about Charles Furst. I added that I didn't understand why my father hadn't been able to provide a moral spin.

'I thought that's what parents were meant to do,' I said, 'even if they know it's probably not true.'

Carly nodded and hummed, then asked what kind of dog Ronaldo was. I changed the subject. I told her that I'd seen a psychologist while we'd been broken up, and that the psychologist suggested I write down my regrets on a piece of paper, since I had trouble articulating them.

'The problem was,' I explained, 'after I wrote them down, I couldn't bring myself to give the piece of paper to the shrink. It felt like handing over my clothes and just being there naked, you know?'

'Uh huh,' Carly replied.

'So anyway, I still have the piece of paper,' I went on. 'I don't know why. It feels like a part of me. Throwing it away would be like throwing a piece of me away, even if that was probably the idea.'

'Where is it now?' she asked.

I removed the piece of paper from my back pocket.

'Can I read it?'

Even though I suspected she would ask that, and I kind of wanted her to, it still came as a surprise. More, I think, that I had deliberately fostered a situation where this could happen and then, suddenly, it was. It was always easier to create miserable situations than positive ones.

Carly sucked away the last of her ice lolly and tucked the wooden stick into her back pocket, then she took the piece of paper from my hand. There was no formality to the way she opened it, no melodramatic build-up. She just unfolded it and scanned the list silently, as I drank some Coke and watched her eyebrows rise and fall. Then she looked at me in a way I hadn't seen before.

'We should burn this,' she said.

'We don't have a lighter,' I replied, hoping this might stop the idea dead.

She frowned at me, looked to my hands and took the bottle of Coke. Then she drank the last of it, rolled up my bit of paper and stuck it in the bottle.

'Where's the lid?'

Because I was an idiot, I handed it to her. She sealed the bottle, then hurled it into the river. It bobbed on the surface about ten yards out. It all happened really fast.

'My name was on that,' I complained limply.

'There are plenty of other Felixes in the world.'

'My last name was on it too.'

She ignored me and quickened her pace down the path. 'I appreciate you letting me read the list,' she said, after I had caught up. 'Honesty is important in relationships.'

One of the regrets I'd written was falling in love with her.

'I feel like I should be honest in return,' she continued.

I felt thirsty.

'When we were broken up, I slept with Peter Beard.'

'Oh.'

'And this guy called Ray, who I met in Bali.'

'I see.'

'I was upset!' she pointed out.

'I was upset too,' I argued, 'but I didn't sleep with anyone.'

'We weren't together. And you broke up with me, remember? You can't be pissed off with me.'

I looked back. The bottle was reclining in the water as if it knew there was nothing I was going to do about it. We continued quietly to the end of the path, then turned and came back. The bottle was heading towards the harbour.

Carly broke up with me a week later.

10

The next morning we had breakfast (toast) and then, after Janet arrived, the three of us went for a walk on the beach. The tide was further out than it had been the previous day, so we were able to walk on the hard sand. Lumps of brown and green seaweed littered the high-water mark, along with thin yellow things that looked like alien arms waving slimy bonbons. A low cloud covered the hills on the far side of the lough, while the water showed the gentle pulse of the distant Atlantic in shallow corrugations.

I felt my phone vibrate in my pocket.

Looking in the direction of the boat ramp, I recognised the man training his dog, Sally. Some way beyond him a woman was walking towards the village. It was difficult to be sure, but I thought I could make out blonde hair. Beyond her, other human forms blurred into the terrain.

I took my phone out and looked at the number. It was the same UK mobile that had rung previously. I pressed *Ignore* and placed it back in my pocket. A few moments later came a short vibration. I squeezed Petra's hand and winked at her when she looked up at me.

We walked along peacefully, discussing crabs and seaweed and horses, until we came across the sand sphincter. Petra studied the round hole, its circumference creased with eroded valleys, then looked at me inquisitively.

'What is it?'

'This is the ... err, it's a spring.'

'What's a spring?'

'It's where water trapped underground comes to the surface.'

Petra watched balloons of fresh water emerge from the heart of the spring and spill down the delta of rivulets. She walked its short length, looked out over the lough and came back again, then peered closer at the bubbling water. I wasn't a hundred per cent sure about the mechanics of the feature, but it seemed to make sense and was a lot better than telling her I thought it looked like a cat's bum.

'How do you feel about me leaving you two to it for a few hours?' Janet asked, phone in hand.

'That's fine,' I told her. 'I was thinking I needed to go shopping for food, so maybe after we've walked up the beach and back we'll do that.'

Petra broke away from her observations. 'Are we going to buy Nutella?'

'It's the only reason we're going,' I said.

'We also need toilet paper and Coco Pops.'

'Oh, okay. I'm glad you're coming.'

Petra smiled then returned her attention to the sand sphincter.

'Uncle Felix?'

'Yep.'

'Do you think this is where mermaids have baths?'

'I'm not sure,' I answered. 'I think it's just where water comes from under the ground.'

'Yeah. But can we wait here and see if any mermaids come?'

'For a little while.'

Janet grinned at me and then said goodbye to Petra from a few steps away. 'I'll see you later this afternoon, okay?'

Petra nodded and looked as though she was going to go for a hug, but Janet quickly turned and started walking away. I watched Petra's face to see if she was upset, but she had other things on her mind.

'I want to take a bath here.'

'It might be a bit cold, don't you think?'

Petra considered it. 'Yeah,' she finally said. 'But when it's warmer, like in summer, can I take a bath in it then?'

'We'll have to get you a swimming costume.'

'I've got one, but if you want you can get me another one.'

While we waited for mermaids to emerge, I found myself looking up the beach at the shrinking figure of the potential blonde. I wondered if the hair belonged to the same woman I'd seen staring at the sky while I'd been running the other day. The day I'd seen my name written in the sand.

I was distracted from this reverie by the sight of Petra scrawling a P in the sand next to the hole. She added an E, then a T, an R and an A.

'You've got lovely handwriting,' I told her.

'It's a stick,' she corrected me, 'not a hand.'

'Ah, of course.' She didn't get that literalism from my side of the family.

'Do you want me to do yours?'

'Yes, please.'

As she carved my name into the sand the memory of seeing it written two days ago emerged from behind the fog of all that had happened since. The perfectly dotted *i*, the ends of the *x* reaching out like they were trying to grab something. It seemed almost dreamlike and for a moment I wondered if in fact that was what I was remembering.

I cast my eyes up the beach for the blonde, but before I could spot her a splashing sound caught my attention. Turning, I saw some broiling white water about fifteen yards out, where something had broken the surface and then gone under again. I kept looking at the spot, but nothing reemerged until, just as I was about to give up, a little head poked out.

'Petra,' I said quietly. 'Look.'

'Nearly finished, Uncle Felix.'

I crouched down and gently touched her shoulder. Her back was to the water. 'Petra,' I whispered. 'It's a seal.'

Petra spun around and scanned the water eagerly. 'Where?'

I pointed in the direction of the twitching black head. Its body poked above the water behind it, a convex protuberance of blubber that the seal displayed proudly.

Petra took a sharp intake of breath. 'Ohh!' She hopped on the spot and pointed. 'I see it! I see it!'

Then the seal flipped backwards, revealing its pale grey underside, and disappeared from sight.

Petra stared at the place where it had gone underwater for a few moments, not saying anything, daring not to breathe. Finally she whispered: 'I think it's gone away.'

'I think so too.'

We waited a little longer, then both turned back to where she had been writing my name. She had almost finished, with only the *x* to go. She picked up the stick and carved two lines into the sand, as if marking the spot on a pirate's map.

'Beautiful,' I told her.

'It's not finished.'

She took a few steps to the left and started writing more letters. She wrote a *u*, then an *n*, followed by a c. When she was done she stood back and admired her work.

'There,' she said. 'Now when the mermaids come to have a bath they'll know we were here and want to meet them.'

'Perfect.' I took comfort from the fact she referred to them as *the mermaids*, rather than *Mummy*.

We continued down the beach, keeping our eyes on the water for mermaids or seals, but not seeing any more of either. I thought I could pick out Janet up ahead, crossing the soft sand and making her way towards the car park. I guessed she was going to meet Mark in the cafe. The blonde was gone.

Further ahead I could see a couple of swimmers emerging from the water at the boat ramp. Maybe this was a regular part of village life and I was completely unaware, having never been on the beach before two in the afternoon. If Petra stayed with me, my life was definitely going to change. I looked at her face as we walked along, at its sincere reflection of her every thought, every feeling, every moment of curiosity. How do we learn to hide all that? Why do we? I wished that she never would.

'Uncle Felix?'

'Yep.'

'What are all those birds doing?'

Up ahead a large group of rooks were crowding around a spot just above the waterline. It was an unusual sight. I'd run along this beach over a hundred times and never seen this many in one spot before. Not on the beach.

'I guess they're looking for food,' I said, though they seemed to be looking out across the water, rather than at the sand.

As we approached, the birds spooked and took off. They wheeled away in a group and settled in the trees by the cemetery. Petra and I reached the spot where they had been gathered and stopped dead.

'It's your name, Uncle Felix,' she said softly, almost as a question. 'But it also says *look*.' She looked up at me. 'Is that your last name?'

The arms of the *x* were curling outwards like octopus tentacles, searching for something to cling to, something they could grab and drag in to the water.

'No. My last name's the same as yours,' I told her.

'Is there another Uncle Felix here?'

'I don't know. Might be.'

'But also they might not be an uncle because they didn't write *Uncle*.'

I wished I had her innocence. I stared at the writing, searching for some logic to explain what I was seeing away. It was entirely possible there was another Felix in the village and, for whatever reason they, or someone they knew, wrote their name in the sand occasionally, along with the word LOOK and the word STOP. Maybe they were autistic, and this was how their carer told them to stop walking up and down the beach and pay attention to the view.

'Maybe it was a mermaid,' Petra suggested, as if sensing my confusion. 'Maybe the mermaid is in love with the other Uncle Felix who isn't an uncle and she wants him to look at her because she's pretty.'

'Maybe,' I replied, then grinned. 'That actually sounds like a pretty good explanation.' It wasn't what I was meant to say, but it sounded a lot better than what I had come up with.

Petra's face blossomed, then she put the side of it onto my arm and looked up at me.

'Are we going to buy some Nutella now?'

─•◎ 11 ◎•─

When Janet announced she was going back to Bristol and leaving Petra with me it came as a surprise. She'd spent four days looking as though at any moment she would sigh, ask Petra to wait in another room, and then tell me she doubted I could look after myself, let alone a six-year-old girl. But when the time came she actually smiled and told me I had surpassed her expectations.

'They weren't high to start with, were they?' I suggested.

She didn't answer. Instead she explained that she would be in touch with developments in the court case and that she hoped for the best.

'You should make the most of each day,' she added, 'just in case.'

Mark shook my hand and, in a strangely more officious tone than when he arrived, told me to 'be safe'. Those words echoed in my mind for some time afterwards. Then he hugged Petra and stood back to let Janet say her farewell.

If there was any part of her that thought she should maintain her professional distance from Petra, it melted away the moment she caught her blue eyes. They embraced, shed a few tears, then parted.

Petra watched the car drive away, then turned around and fiddled with the autumn flower bud by the cottage wall.

'Janet was nice, wasn't she?' I asked.

Petra frowned and turned to me. 'I'll see her again, won't I?'

'Of course. Probably. If you want.' No answer felt right.

Petra returned her attention to the flower. The petals were a deep pink, like it had been late to the paint bucket.

'Uncle Felix?'

'Yep.'

'Did my dad do something wrong?'

I could feel my phone in my back pocket. 'He ... what did Janet tell you?'

'She said he'd been naughty so had to go away and get better for a little while.'

'Okay. So, yes, that.'

'Is he in trouble?'

'A tiny bit, but the important thing is that you're okay. Aren't you?'

'Yes,' she said plainly. 'Is what he did wrong shouting?'

I went to her side and watched her stroking the sepals that held the bud in its pensive state of pre-blossom. I tucked a strand of hair behind her ear.

'Did you hear him shouting?'

'Sometimes,' she answered, then added, almost in defence – though of herself or of him, I couldn't tell – 'but not at me.'

'Everyone gets upset from time to time,' I told her, 'but it's not okay to ... shout at someone else, even if you feel they've done something wrong. That's why you're staying with me.'

'Staying, not living,' she said in that un-emotive voice.

'Would you like to live here?'

She shrugged her shoulders. I tried not to feel the sting of her indifference. 'Was Mummy naughty too?' She finally asked, her mind elsewhere.

'No. Mummy was sad because *her* mummy died. Do you remember Nanna?'

Petra nodded.

'Well Mummy was very close to Nanna and ...' I was digging myself into a hole. Petra looked at me to finish my sentence, but how could I tell her that her mother had died because she couldn't live without her own mother? Where was that going to lead?

But again Petra was on another wavelength. 'Was she also sad because Dad shouted at her?'

My blood went cold. 'Did you see Dad shout at her?'

She nodded sheepishly. 'I heard it. And I heard Mummy shout at Dad.'

'Wh ... when did you hear this, Petra?'

She turned to me and explained quickly, as if she could only keep the plug off for a few seconds. 'One day Mummy came to pick me up at Dad's and I was playing upstairs with a new doll house he got me and I didn't want to leave because I hadn't played with all the rooms yet and they started shouting and it was my fault.'

'It wasn't your fault, Petra. Mummy and Dad disagreed about other things too.'

'But Mummy was upset with me when we went home.'

'She was probably just sad that she had argued with Dad. I'm sure she didn't mean it.'

'She asked me if I wanted to live with Dad instead. But I didn't mean I didn't want to go with Mummy. Just not yet because I was still playing.'

Her hand came away from the flower, dropping by her side as her face broke into tears. She stepped towards me slowly and, not saying anything more, bawled her eyes out into my stomach. I wanted her to say that she missed her mother, that these tears were for that alone. But underneath all the complications of where she was living or staying, of Janet, Michael and me, there was a six-year-old girl whose mother had abandoned her.

I comforted her as much as I could, but had the sense that she already felt alone in a way no father, uncle or guardian could comprehend. We stayed like that for half a minute or so, until she wiped away the last of her tears and then went inside, up the stairs and into her bedroom. The door closed gently behind her.

I looked at the flower, at the way it bobbled defiantly in the breeze. I wondered what was going to happen to it in the spring. Would it just pick up where it left off, seeing out its colourful destiny? Or was it serving another function? A note left on the door reminding anyone coming by with an axe that the plant is just resting for the winter. I turned to go inside but then remembered something. I pulled my phone from my pocket and checked for reception. One bar. I dialled up my messaging service.

'Felix, it's Michael. I know Petra's with you. Whatever you think you know about the situation is irrelevant and probably wrong. She's my daughter and there's no way I'm going to let her grow up under the influence of another manically depressed and suicidal Blunt. Once I've dealt with this court case I'm coming to get her. In the meantime I don't want you filling her head with lies and grief that she doesn't need. You're not equipped to be a parent and you know it. Keep her fed. Keep her warm. Read to her and indulge her mermaid games, but DO NOT be a bag of miserable shit around her. Call me so we can discuss this.'

I pressed three and deleted the message.

*

Slowly, Petra came around, but where previously her light looked as though it might break through the clouds, now she seemed to sit behind them, lost in a fog of introspection. I'd catch her with a toy in her hand but not playing with it in any way; or at bedtime when I turned out the light she would say goodnight while staring at the ceiling. A young, delicate mind wrestling with oversized traumas. It frightened me to think what kind of adult she could turn in to.

We passed the days by visiting the village charity shop and raiding their DVD and board game collections. If the weather was favourable we walked on the beach and looked for horses or mermaids, but, for different reasons, didn't see either. On one occasion Petra got excited by some splashing in the water, but we soon realised it was just someone swimming. Madness at this time of year. I kept an eye out for the blonde woman too, but she, along with any new inscriptions of my name in the sand, wasn't to be found. All the while Michael continued to call, leaving messages I would delete without listening to.

It was early evening on a Saturday before it occurred to me that Christmas was two days away. Petra and I were driving to the village shop for pasta sauce when suddenly all the decorations that had been wrapped around power poles and stuck in front gardens, but which by day I'd ignored as dull obscurities akin to street signs, were now alerting me to the pending festive emergency. Petra craned forward on her seat and watched them go by.

'Do you think Santa's going to find me, after all?' she asked, a wisp of excitement in her voice. She turned to look at me.

'Is that what you think?' I answered, thinking fast. 'That he wouldn't find you here?'

'We don't have a tree,' she pointed out.

I was a terrible parent.

'And Dad sent him a letter last year saying I was living with him now.'

Naturally.

'Santa always knows where children are,' I explained, surprised at how readily to hand that information was, 'and he knows if they've been good or bad.'

'I've been good,' she confirmed matter-of-factly. 'But if he knows then why did Dad send him a letter?'

'Well, perhaps he wanted to make doubly sure.'

'Have you sent him a letter to make doubly sure too?'

'I have,' I lied, parking the car around the corner from the shop.

'Really!? I wanted to see the letter too. Dad let me write what presents I wanted on his letter.'

'I sent Santa an email,' I explained, 'and told him that you wanted a … Little Mermaid … dress.'

Petra's eyes studied my face in a way I hadn't seen before. It was like she was absorbing how my face looked when it said unexpected things, so that when it was proved to be a lie, she would know to look out for this face in the future.

But then there was a change and her face lit up, her blue eyes wide with the miracle of Christmas. 'How did you know that I wanted a Little Mermaid dress?'

My heart fell back into its cavity.

I wanted to say 'Uncle Felix knows best', but this sounded cheap somehow. Instead, I said: 'I wanted it to be a surprise.' Which I immediately regretted as I thought she might feel guilty about making me tell her. But Petra took it a different way.

'I'll pretend I don't know,' she quickly said, putting her hands over her eyes as if this could stop the knowledge going in.

'Don't know what?' I challenged her.

Petra shook her head, her hands still over her eyes. I opened my door and walked around to open hers. She stepped out, peeking through her fingers.

'Hey Petra, what do you think Santa's bringing you for Christmas?'

She shook her head and walked towards the shop with me. Mumbling through her hands she said: 'I don't know. How could I know?'

Back at the cottage Petra excitedly brushed her teeth and went to bed. She asked to see the email I sent Santa, but I told her only adults can know his email address, otherwise children all over the world would be emailing him constantly and he'd have no time to feed the reindeer. It was as if Christmas provided a limitless narrative through which adults could weave their own fibs.

Once she was in bed the reality set in. Where was I going to find a Little Mermaid dress the day before Christmas? I sat on my bed, tethered my phone to my laptop and went online. The connection was weak, but slowly I was able to get on to eBay to confirm that such a thing as a Little Mermaid dress existed. They were inexpensive too and cute, in their way. And they all took about a week and a half to get here.

Most sellers seemed to be in China. I searched through the listings and narrowed my criteria, but no one in the whole of Ireland was selling one. Even if they were, I wasn't sure how I would go about getting it here in time. I searched the websites of major retailers in Letterkenny, then in Derry, Belfast and Dublin. No one sold Little Mermaid dresses. I began to let panic in and in its wake I started to dream up excuses for Santa.

It didn't occur to me until sometime later that Disney might have their own stores. I punched that into Google, waited an age for the internet to work, then found there was a store in Belfast. Three hours' drive away. The day before Christmas.

*

The promise of shopping for a Christmas tree was enough for Petra to acquiesce to the long drive to Belfast. We stopped twice along the way for toilet and chocolate milkshake breaks, but still made it by 1 pm. The Disney store shut at six. I was proud of myself for making it happen.

After a lunch of croissants and salad we walked through a shopping centre and found a homewares shop where a handful of thin, tattered boxes of Christmas trees remained in a corner. Petra fiddled with the branches of the display model, noting how they folded up towards the 'trunk' for easy storage. After some consternation regarding the smell of the plastic she finally nodded her approval. I was curious as to whether she'd had a real tree at Michael's but didn't ask for fear of the answer. A tree requires decorations, so we got some of those, and then we needed two stockings so Santa the gift wizard could fill them with more of his magic, and finally some cookies so we could leave them out for his reindeer.

'I don't think reindeer eat cookies,' I told her. But of course, they do.

I had no idea how I was going to purchase all the presents required to satisfy her Santa expectations. It seemed with every step I took towards being a functioning parent, the hallway got longer.

As we left the shop Petra announced she needed to go to the toilet. We looked on the site map of the place we were in and then navigated our way to the nearest loos. We were a team. I usually hated shopping, but Petra was a natural who understood how to treat it as an exercise in hunter-gathering, rather than the chore impinged on us by a consumerist society I usually saw it as.

When we found the loos, however, she looked at me anxiously and asked if I could wait outside the door.

'You mean the bathroom door?'

'No, the toilet.'

A mother and daughter emerged from the bathroom. 'I don't think they let boys in there, Petra.'

She started squirming on the spot. 'I really need to go.'

A narrow hallway with yellow floor tiles and lit with sterile lights showed the way, the female toilets on the left, male a little further down on the right. At the far end a double door with black windows and a green and white EXIT sign glowing above it, punctuated the hierarchal order. I put our shopping on the ground and squatted down beside my niece. I had no idea how to approach this.

'What did Mi ... Dad do when you went shopping with him?'

'I didn't go shopping with Dad.'

'Oh, you went with his girlfriend?' I couldn't remember her name and actually wasn't sure I'd ever attempted to.

Petra nodded. 'She went in with me, and Mummy used to too.'

'You go to the toilet by yourself at home, though. This isn't any different.'

'There's lots of people here ...' Tears started to form in her eyes.

'Okay,' I said, terrified of a scene. 'I'll go with you.'

I picked up the tree and the bags and walked behind Petra as she skipped down the hallway. Just as she got to the entrance I asked her to wait. I swapped the bag to my other hand and grabbed Petra's, then we pushed open the door.

I whispered and mouthed sorry to half a dozen women as they looked at me in shock, quickly washing their hands, gathering up their daughters and rushing out. Oblivious, Petra found an unlocked stall.

'This one's free. Yes!' she announced triumphantly and made her way inside.

I stood by the door, looking at the air conditioning ducts on the ceiling while her pee tinkled into the toilet bowl. I could feel my face growing red as I tried to ignore the sounds from the other cubicles around me. Finally she was done and I encouraged her, not that she needed it, to wash her hands. Then we exited swiftly and I breathed out for the first time in an age.

'Don't you need to go, Uncle Felix?'

Up until then, I hadn't. But the idea of her standing inside a men's bathroom horrified me. I would hold on.

'I'm fine,' I told her.

'Mummy said that if you hold on too long you drown in your own pee.'

Mummy and drown in the same sentence; she existed on a different plane to me. But the more I thought about it, the more I needed to go. We would be here for another hour at least, and then there was the drive back to Rathmullan. I'd never make it.

'Will you be okay standing in the hallway outside the bathroom?'

She nodded tentatively.

We walked back down the hallway, past the women's bathroom and to a spot a little beyond the men's door. I gave her the bag of cookies, decorations and stockings and stood the boxed tree upright beside her, as if an armed guard ready to fire plastic pine needles at anyone who came too close.

'I'll be right back, okay?'

She nodded.

'One minute, okay? I promise.'

She nodded with more insistence, though said nothing. I opened the door, took one last look over my shoulder, then darted inside.

The urinals were all taken and so were the stalls. I lined up behind the small queue of men checking their phones, then, impatiently, double checked the cubicle doors to see if any just had the engaged levers pushed across inadvertently. No luck. I returned to the back of the queue for the urinals, having lost two places.

A minute passed, then two. How big were the bladders of Belfast men? Finally my turn came and I unleashed an eager flow. I pushed it out as hard as I could, causing myself a little pain so that I had to ease off. Then I quickly zipped up and ran my hands under the cold water tap. I didn't bother with the hot air blower, just wiped them on my jeans as I made for the door.

When I opened it I found Petra standing where I'd left her, with a middle-aged woman. They were talking quietly until Petra saw me.

'That's him!' she announced excitedly. In any other tone it would have been an accusation.

The woman gave me a sympathetic, if slightly judgemental, look. She had short hair the colour of tea and a striped cardigan over a beige blouse. Glasses with frames the shape of kiwi fruits reassured me, in the way glasses do.

'I saw this young girl by herself so checked to make sure she was okay,' she explained unnecessarily.

'Thanks,' I replied, then added necessarily: 'It's so hard by yourself.'

The woman looked down at Petra. 'Is Mum not shopping with you today?'

Petra shook her head slowly.

'I'm her uncle,' I explained quickly. A shade of suspicion fell across the woman's face. 'Her mother is my sister.'

'Mummy's a mermaid,' Petra offered, helpfully.

'Is she?' the woman replied.

'I'm Felix,' I said, trying to change the subject.

'Claire.' The woman shook my hand and then turned to Petra. 'But my students call me Mrs Hoolahan.'

'You're a teacher?' I asked.

'Year three,' she confirmed. Then she gave me a knowing look. 'Now, have you done all the shopping you needed to do?'

Mrs Hoolahan was a godsend. I left them in a cafe a few shops down from the Disney store, having dialled her phone to ensure her number was right and that she had mine. As an extra precaution I took a photo of her driver's licence too, with the promise to delete it as soon as I was back. Petra sucked a hot chocolate through a straw benignly as she watched me fuss over these details that I hoped were going to keep her out of harm.

Walking in the Disney store was like being hit by a sugary wave. The floor was a sickly chessboard pattern of pink and white squares, while the aisles were populated with big-eyed dolls that looked ready to swing from the shelves and rain buckets of glitter on me. Teenage girls dressed like cartoons and with smiles surely painted on drifted between customers offering cheery advice, as music consisting mostly of bells slurped out of the speakers like syrup and stuck in my ears with the same annoying consistency. I felt like a dark cloud drifting apologetically through a picnic.

I soon realised there was a Disney princess for every occasion – woodlands, castles, the Middle East, colonial America. I raced around, looking for an underwater version, died a little when I came across a *Star Wars* section, before finally seeing a sparkling emerald green dress hanging from the wall. A flared hem in the shape of a fish tail confirmed I had arrived at the mermaid's lair.

I rifled through a stack of boxes on a table beneath the dress, quickly realising they were all for ages four to five, or ages eight to nine. Beginning to panic, I waved awkwardly at an overly spritely attendant, who wore on her head a silver tiara and on her face enough makeup to fertilise a desert. She glided over, ratcheting up her smile along the way, as if she was installed with a sensor that detected anxiety. I couldn't tell if she was fifteen or twenty-five.

'Do you have any of these for a six-year-old?' I asked.

'Oh I'm sorry,' she sung, her voice on a velvet slide. 'Those are the last we have in stock. Maybe you'd like to get her something from *Frozen*? That's our biggest-selling franchise at the moment. Girls love *Frozen*.'

It briefly crossed my mind that she may be a robot.

'She's expecting a Little Mermaid dress from Santa. Do you really not have any more? How can a Disney store not have any left in a six-year-old's size?'

The smile never dropped from the attendant's face. 'It's the day before Christmas, sir,' she explained. 'Maybe she'll fit into a different size?'

She unhooked the dress that was hanging from the wall, looked at the tag and said it was for ages four to five.

'How does this look?'

'I really don't know. Maybe?'

The attendant pointed at a young girl perusing a nearby table's contents. 'Is she about that size? Or her?' She pointed at another. 'What about her in the pink dress?'

'Okay, I get it, please stop.'

They all looked different from Petra, somehow, like children you see in the distance, or on TV, cardboard cut-outs without personalities or distinct voices. I could feel my willpower scraping at an empty barrel. I needed to go for a run.

'I suppose it would be better to buy her the larger dress, so she can grow into it.'

'Mmmm,' the attendant hummed, sowing doubt inside me in the key of D minor.

'What?'

143

'Well, the reason we have so many dresses left in that size is because they usually grow out of the franchise by that age. These are really for girls that are just fast growers. Is your daughter a fast grower?'

So much of what she was saying was frustrating.

'I don't think so, and I hope she grows out of it too. We're expecting her to.'

'Okay, well maybe she'll fit into the four to five. It's only slightly smaller than the six to seven.'

'I think it being too small would be worse than too big.' I pictured Petra smiling from inside my giant sleeping bag. 'Let's just go with the eight.'

'Are you sure you don't want to get her one from *Frozen*?' Her voice was inviting, almost flirtatious. I tried not to hear it. 'Seriously, I've not met a six-year-old yet that doesn't love *Frozen*. And we'll *definitely* have her size.'

Still, it was a compelling argument. If it was as popular as she was claiming, then Petra was bound to know about it. And surely that it fit would be better than a mermaid dress that didn't.

The attendant winked at me, beckoning me to follow, which I did like an idiot. 'We'll just have a look,' she said, like we were sneaking a chocolate before dinner.

The *Frozen* section occupied almost an entire wall of the store. More than *The Little Mermaid* and *Star Wars* put together. Young girls and frazzled parents were sifting through the various trinkets, filling plastic baskets with plastic toys. The sales assistant picked a dress from the wall, long and blue and somehow more real than the Little Mermaid version. Unnecessarily, she held it up against herself.

'Here,' she said, 'this is for six-year-olds. Does that look about her size?'

'I ... can you maybe ...'

I took the dress from her and held it beside me so the hem hovered above the floor. The shoulders came to just above my waist. I recalled Petra hugging me when I returned from my run on the day she arrived with Janet, remembered her face pushing into my stomach.

'Yeah, that's about right.' I could imagine Petra in it, see her twirling around and doing whatever the characters in *Frozen* do.

The attendant hung the dress back on the wall and picked up a box. Her smile had evolved slightly, become almost fiendish.

'Trust me,' she said, less flirty now and more like a manipulative older sister. 'She'll love it.'

The last whimper of my dying argument choked to the surface: 'But she thinks she's a mermaid.'

The attendant, however, had scriptwriters. 'When she sees this, sir, she'll *know* she's Elsa!'

I looked at the character – Elsa, apparently – on the box. She was blonde, like Petra, and stood tall, with a confident look on her face. It was very convincing, and most of all, I reasoned, it wasn't the thing Janet had said I wasn't to encourage.

'Okay,' I conceded, already feeling pangs of guilt.

'You won't regret it.'

I suspected I would. I followed her to the sales counter, scooping up handfuls of Little Mermaid paraphernalia along the way, just in case. The sale was rung up and seventy pounds later I was out the door.

I then quickly ducked to a nearby Waterstones and bought a book, some pens and other small knick-knacks that I could gift myself, along with some wrapping paper. I put the Disney-branded bag inside the Waterstones one and hurried back to the cafe.

'All done, and thanks,' I said, sliding in next to Petra and squeezing her on the leg. I saw her eyes dart down to the bag and gave her a playful glare when she looked up and saw me watching her. She pursed her lips together and giggled.

I deleted the photo of Mrs Hoolahan's driver's licence off

my phone in front of her, even though she told me not to worry. Then, without having planned to do so, I reached into the Waterstones bag and searched for something to give her.

'Here,' I said, handing her a postcard. 'For you.'

'How nice. Maybe I can write to Petra and she can write back. Would you like that?'

Petra nodded. I opened a packet of gel tip pens which Santa had bought me for Christmas and wrote my address on the postcard. She thanked me and looked to Petra again.

'Maybe if Santa gets you some postcards for Christmas you can write back.'

'I hope he does,' Petra exclaimed, as if I wasn't right there.

I was exhausted but managed the three-hour drive back to Rathmullan without too much hassle. Petra was asleep when we got there. I carried her up to bed and tucked her in, then went downstairs, set up the Christmas tree, covered it in decorations, wrapped a dozen different presents, put out a plate of cookies for the reindeer, taking a bite from each of them, before finally going to bed at 2 am. I was wired and over-tired and didn't fall asleep until three.

Four hours later Petra woke in a blizzard of excitement.

'He found me!' she yelled from downstairs, then ran up and knocked on my door before entering. 'Uncle Felix! Santa found me!!'

─•❧ 12 ❧•─

Petra ran presents from the tree to my bedroom for the next twenty minutes, her blonde hair like a cape as she flew out my door. She would bring up one for her and one for me, then tell me I could open mine first and feign excitement when I removed the wrapping paper to reveal a pack of playing cards or a notepad. Then she would carefully, but with considerable speed, unstick all the tape from her presents, fold back the paper and, before she had even seen what it was, start making a wow sound. Then what it *really* was would sink in and I'd be able to tell how genuinely excited she was.

'Ohhh, I've seen this before but I like it anyway,' she said, waving the *Frozen* DVD Santa had brought her.

Her *Frozen* dress came in a box with a see-through window, which meant it had some bulk to it. This helped for distinguishing it as her main present from Santa. Just in case, I wrapped it in red paper, which was different from all the rest, and also added a red card, inside which I wrote a note from the big man.

'You have to come down to open Santa's big presents,' she explained to me.

Petra ran downstairs and I slid out of bed. I checked through my wardrobe and found an old red sweater that I never wore. It was the most Christmassy thing I had.

On the way through the kitchen I put the kettle on and quickly added some ground coffee to the cafetière. Petra called out impatiently.

'What are you doing?'

'I'll be there in a heartbeat.'

'You can't make a coffee yet,' she called back.

One day, I thought, she'll discover this stuff and understand.

'Uncle Felix?'

'Okay, okay,' I replied and walked through to the living room.

She was standing there with a small package, wrapped in the same paper she'd carefully removed from around one of her presents. 'This is for you,' she said. 'It's not from Santa. It's from me.'

I kissed her on the head then took it from her excited hands. In the kitchen I could hear the kettle grumbling towards the boil. The present was about the weight of a cricket ball but was unquestionably square-shaped. I wondered what she'd found in the house that fit the bill and had somehow personalised, but nothing came to mind. Had Janet, perhaps, somehow sent her something to give to me? I moved it around in my hands, trying to unpick the mystery.

'Open it!' she demanded, jumping on the spot, one eye always on the red-wrapped present beneath the tree.

Far more carefully than I had done with the presents I'd wrapped for myself, I peeled the paper from around her gift. Suddenly it all made sense: it was a coffee cup. I spun it round to look through the window of the display box it came in. Written on the front, in a big cheesy font, were the words: *World's Greatest Uncle*

So that she wouldn't see my eyes swell with tears I pulled her close and gave her a lingering hug. In the kitchen the kettle reached its crescendo and switched itself off.

'Do you like it?' she asked.

'It's perfect. When did you—'

'Mrs Hoolahan helped me choose it,' she explained, 'when you were shopping for the postcards.'

'I'll have to send her one with a thank-you note,' I said.

'It's from me though, Uncle Felix.' She swivelled on one foot. 'Mrs Hoolahan just helped me choose.'

I gave her another hug and told her it was the best present I'd ever received. Happy with that, she quickly reached under the tree for the red wrapped presents. She handed me mine and told me it was from Santa. Her patience was remarkable, but she was determined to open her present last of all. I quickly tore off the paper and remarked at how great Santa's taste in books was. Then it was Petra's turn. First she opened the card.

'To Petra,' she read out loud, 'you have been a very good girl this year – brave, polite, clever and helpful. I hope you like this present. P.S., Your Uncle Felix told me what you wanted, but Santa knows best!'

She turned to me, her brow furrowed slightly. 'He got your email, Uncle Felix,' she said suspiciously.

'Sounds like it.'

She unpicked the sticky tape without the delicacy of earlier, then pushed back the flaps of wrapping paper to reveal the box. The blue dress glittered through the plastic window, shimmering with all the magic of the franchise. For a few moments she didn't say anything, just seemed to absorb its unknowable Disney wizardry. She turned to me, showed me the box so that I could witness the miracle, then stared at it again. There was no obvious emotion on her face, but the excitement of earlier had definitely dropped away. I tried to give it a shove.

'You going to put it on?'

Petra nodded slowly and walked with equal moderation up the stairs.

Perhaps this was actually going to be okay, I thought. Maybe her belief in the all-knowing wisdom of Santa would convince her that *Frozen* was where her heart needed to be now. *The Little Mermaid* was old news.

I reboiled the kettle for the few seconds it required and then added the water to the cafetière, stirring the ground beans first clockwise, then against the current. When I was satisfied they were suitably drenched I put the press on and slid it a few inches down the glass cylinder. I struggled with the box that

149

surrounded my new coffee mug for a few seconds, before finally tearing it open. I ran it under the cold water tap briefly, then dried it and put a splash of milk in the bottom. After adding half a teaspoon of sugar I carried the two items into the living room.

Upstairs I could hear Petra's footsteps in her room. Sometimes when she was playing I could hear her talking to her toys and conjuring up a world for her and them to coexist in. I couldn't hear that now, but the way her feet moved in small increments across the floor suggested she was putting the dress on and looking at herself in the mirror. Shortly her steps moved along the landing and back down the stairs.

She came through the door, dressed as she had been before. I put my hands back together quietly.

'It fits,' she explained and sat amongst her other gifts.

'Oh. Good. That's a relief ... for Santa. You don't want to wear it though?'

'Ummmm, not right now. It's more for wearing to balls and stuff.'

'I see. Well we'll have to organise one of those, then.'

Petra nodded and read back over the card from Santa. Then she picked up a Little Mermaid brush, removed it from its blister pack and ran it through her hair a couple of times before putting it on the floor.

'Uncle Felix?'

'Yep.'

'Can I have some Nutella toast?'

*

We had a Christmas breakfast of Nutella on toast, coffee and orange juice. In all the rush of going to Belfast to get the Little Mermaid dress that I didn't end up getting, I hadn't thought of buying a turkey or Christmas pudding. Petra, like she seemed to do with so many bumps in her life, just took it in her stride.

We then settled in to watch some DVDs, but soon a maudlin fog seemed to settle on us both. I stood up and looked out the window at the charcoal trees set against grey, still clouds. My leg joints felt taught and anxious. In the reflection I could make out Petra running the Little Mermaid brush through her hair.

'Uncle Felix?'

'Yep.'

'If I brush my hair with this brush the mermaids will see it and come to the bath.'

'Will they?'

'But only girls can use the brush.'

'I see.'

She looked over and made a face to apologise. 'So you can't use it.'

'That's okay.'

'And I think that the mermaids don't like boys, which is why they haven't come to the bath yet.'

I decided now was not the time to remind her of the truth about mermaids and their vicious ways.

'I can't leave you there by yourself, Petra.'

It was clear that she had thought this through. 'But maybe you could go for a walk,' she said.

I looked out the window, saw the branches still against the clouds. 'Or a run,' I said.

Petra looked at me, and I looked at her. It was a good plan. I ran it over in my head a couple more times, tried telling it to an imaginary Janet, before concluding it was foolproof. 'Shall we?'

Petra clapped her hands, almost as if she was surprised her idea had worked. 'Shall we?!'

*

It was a little after two in the afternoon when we cut down through the garden, wound our way over the dunes and came onto the beach. The tide was well out and, as expected, there was no one else around. Petra was rugged up in her warm red jacket, with her red gloves and red woollen hat. She had spent ten minutes pulling the Little Mermaid brush through her hair and then carefully arranged two thick strands to hang from under the hat over either side of her face. Even though her hair was blonde, her eyes blue, she was unquestionably a Blunt girl.

I was in my full-length running gear – black leggings, black shorts, a long-sleeved black running shirt, black gloves. For contrast I had bright green running shoes. We walked towards the sand sphincter but Petra stopped me about twenty yards short of it.

'I think this is as close as you should get, Uncle Felix,' she explained.

'Okay. I'll run down to the boat ramp and back to the bend in the beach over there, then I'll turn and go back to the boat ramp. I'll do that a few times. I'll have to run past the sand sph ... the err mermaid bath, but when I do, I promise not to look at you, okay? I'll run higher up the beach so the mermaids won't see me near the water.'

Petra considered my suggestion and then agreed to the terms. I gave her a hug and headed off.

Almost immediately I could feel it all coming back. First there was the reluctance, the natural inclination to stop exert-ing myself, to save my energy for potential emergencies, to prevent possible injury. My breathing was short and ineffic-ient, a gasping for air as a short-term fix to the sudden increase in demand. But I knew to push on, to relax. My body would soon reconfigure itself, switch to endurance settings and spread its resources strategically. By the time I reached the boat ramp I could feel my natural rhythms falling into place.

I turned and immediately looked for Petra. I had glanced over my shoulder a couple of times as I ran away from her and saw her standing diligently by the sand sphincter, looking out over the lough. Now she was a tiny red smudge just under a mile away; but it was a reassuring smudge, and I hoped a relatively happy one. I wondered if I should perhaps pay someone to put on a mermaid costume and swim past one day. Or would that be the opposite of what Janet said? Probably that.

Gradually the red smudge grew bigger and as it did my stride relaxed. Regular running made regular running enjoyable, and though I hadn't gone for a while, I knew I had about fifteen minutes of pleasant cruising before the struggle returned. Then it would slowly grip my hamstrings, holding them fractionally tighter with every stride; the walls of my lungs would feel thinner, like deflated balloons unable to hold a decent quantity of air, and my calves would ache, telling me they'd been stretched to their limits. All that was to come though; for now every stride felt like it could be taken at a sprint and I played with the idea of one day running a marathon.

I passed behind Petra, who pretended she didn't see me coming. When I reached the curve in the beach I turned around and headed back towards her. The water was calm, with just a gentle three-inch swell rolling on to the shore to deposit its cargo of brown seaweed and driftwood.

Again I passed behind Petra and again she pretended I wasn't there. I wondered how long she would wait, given the chance. Were six-year-olds usually this patient? Where was the short attention span I'd heard so much about in today's youth? Was she an oddity, or was her obsession with mermaids so intense that it overpowered her natural inclination to seek new stimulus every few minutes? I didn't have a TV connection, just a screen and DVD player, but this hadn't been an issue for her. She was perfectly content to entertain herself with the few toys she had, keeping conversations going amongst her dolls all afternoon. Her imagination was all the stimulus she needed.

When I turned at the boat ramp I realised that I had been so focused on my thoughts that I hadn't looked over my shoulder to check on Petra. I quickly squinted down the beach to look for her red smudge. She was there. My hamstrings were beginning to tighten a bit now – a little earlier than usual – and I could feel a dull ache forming in the calves.

I was still about half a mile from Petra and able to make her figure out a little clearer, when I noticed she was standing with her hands over her mouth. It was the same way she stood when we saw the seal a week and a half ago. I looked out across the water but couldn't see anything, though wouldn't expect to at this distance. Then my eye caught something else. Up on the sand dunes behind her was a man. He was watching Petra. And then he started walking towards her.

Petra still had her back turned. I started running faster. It was probably nothing, maybe even a trick of perspective where the two of them were actually separated by a significant distance. But I had a bad feeling. I pushed harder. Even if I could run at my fastest I guessed it would take me a minute and a half to reach her, but as it was my legs were weary and my lungs stretched. The man's shape began to take form and it became more and more apparent he was definitely approaching Petra who, in blissful ignorance, was still fixated on the water.

With a few hundred yards to close, my legs started to feel thick and heavy. I began to slow, my shoulders to roll and my head to jerk forward with each stride, as it tried to gobble up more oxygen from the space in front of me. The man was standing behind Petra, his hand reaching out, touching her shoulder. I called out, but my voice lacked power. Every resource was taken up by my legs and chest. Two hundred yards felt like as many miles.

I don't know which was worse – realising that it was Michael, or being relieved that it was him and not someone even worse. By the time I reached them, puffing breathlessly, my legs like jelly, Michael was on one knee, accepting Petra's forehead pushed into his chest as part of her awkward hug. In her right hand was a wrapped Christmas present.

'Michael,' I huffed, sucking in air, my hands on my knees. 'You're here.'

'Felix,' he said, his jaw tense. 'You weren't.'

*

Through the obstinate yellow grass of the dunes we walked back to my cottage, me in front, Petra in the middle, Michael at the rear. Petra carried her father's gift like a plate of jelly.

'Did Santa bring you lots of presents?' her father asked.

'Yes.'

I didn't look back but I had the feeling she was nodding with the front of her head.

At the cottage I put the kettle on then quickly ran upstairs to get changed. Back in the kitchen I made coffee, putting Michael's in a plain green mug, and mine in my Christmas present from Petra. Then I shouldered the door open to get into the living room, just in time to see Petra tearing the wrapping paper from her father's gift. Her eyes widened with astonishment as the Little Mermaid dress appeared before her. Two Disney miracles in one day. What were the chances? I peered closely at the top right hand corner of the box as she showed it to me: for ages six to seven. Perfect.

'Perfect,' I told her, then handed Michael his coffee. 'Dad knows best.'

Years ago, Patricia and Michael were arguing and in the midst of it he grabbed her around the throat, squeezed until she started choking, and then shoved her against a wall. She stayed with a friend for the night and intended to go to the police the next day. But while she was having breakfast the next morning she started getting nauseous. Instead of going to the police station she went to the pharmacy to get a pregnancy test. Petra arrived eight months later.

Michael looked down at me from his six-foot-two-inch height, his blond hair hanging languidly over his forehead, his blue eyes cold and insincere. He thanked me for the coffee, glanced briefly at my mug, then returned his gaze to his daughter.

'Are you going to put it on for Daddy?'

Dad, I thought. She calls you Dad.

Petra nodded. In her eyes I could see the excitement of having the dress she wanted, but outwardly she was refusing to let it show. She took the dress out of the living room and up the stairs. Michael sat on the sofa as his daughter's footsteps sounded above us.

'How has she been?' he asked.

'Happy,' I replied, still standing.

'Good. That's some—'

'How did you find us?'

For a moment he looked shocked, then he chuckled gently to himself and leaned into the back of the sofa. 'You told me,' he said with a grin. 'When you came to say goodbye to your niece.'

'I didn't tell you the address.'

'It's a small village, Felix. Yours is the only car with English plates. But of course you didn't want to be found, did you? Wanted to hide away and indulge your self-centred misery. Live off the money from your parents—'

I took half a step towards him. 'Mention them again and—'

'And what?' His voice went up a few decibels. 'You'll hit Petra's daddy? On Christmas Day? By all means, Uncle Felix,' he presented his right cheek, pointing to it invitingly, 'do me the favour.'

He hadn't even blinked – showed no sign of fear at all. He just looked at me nonchalantly, said his bit, pointed at his cheek and then drank some coffee.

I was standing too close to him now, but didn't want to step away and show that I realised my aggression was ineffective. Instead I chose to reiterate my point. I pointed at his blue eyes with a forceful finger.

'Don't mention my parents again.' I held the position for a moment, then stepped back and sat on the lounge chair beside the tree. I would have taken a drink but my hand was shaking too obviously.

Michael watched me, then kinked his head slightly as Petra's footsteps moved about in her bedroom. I tried to match them to the sounds I'd heard that morning when she'd tried on, then took off, the Frozen dress. Perhaps there was less movement this time, but it was difficult to tell what it meant. Michael put his mug on the coffee table and sat forward.

'Felix, she's my daughter and I'm going to take her back.'

'You're—'

'Settle down,' he replied, raising his palm. 'Settle down. I'm not taking her today. That's not going to help me.'

'You hit your girlfriend. There's no way a court will award you custody.'

'Felix, what you think you know and what happened are two vastly different things. If you ever managed to keep a girl-friend for more than a few minutes you might actually learn one or two things about women. What makes them tick, what turns them on, the lies they're capable of,' he looked at me pointedly, 'their capacity for forgiveness.'

'Patricia never forgave you for assaulting her.'

'Assault's a big word, Felix,' he said, flashing Petra's blue eyes my way. 'Watch how you use it. Besides, I never forgave her for turning my daughter against me, for telling her not to call me Daddy, not to hug me in the same way she hugged her mum, or you, or her grandparents.'

I clenched my jaw. Michael continued.

'Patricia was a complicated woman. She wasn't happy, not before I met her, not while we were together, and not after-wards. You know as well as I do how she was. She was more comfortable knowing how bad things could be, than seeing they might be good. She was joyless, especially towards the end.'

'She had depression, Michael. She was a *single* mother.'

'Maybe so. But your sister was poisoning my daughter with her negativity and when your parents passed it got worse. Petra would slump in the sofa when she stayed with me, exhausted from trying to keep her mother's spirits up. In the end she just went up to her room and closed the door without saying anything. It would take me half the weekend to coax her out, and then we'd have one day together before she had to go back.'

'Maybe there were other reasons why Petra was hiding in her room.'

Michael dismissed this suggestion with a crinkling of his eyes and a twitch of his head.

'What happened is terrible,' he went on, pencilling a thin attempt at empathy. 'But in all honesty, I was going to go to court to become the primary parent anyway. It was in Petra's best interests. As it was, when your sister made her decision and Petra came to stay with me, I had to deal not just with what she'd put into my daughter's head, but also with her grief. The fact that she's as optimistic as she is, is a miracle. It's obviously not just her hair that she gets from me.'

Petra's footsteps could be heard coming down the staircase. Michael lowered his voice slightly and rushed through the end of his sermon.

'But if you think I'm going to risk her nurture, again, to another Blunt, you are mistaken. I may not be a perfect adult, Felix, but I'm a functioning one. I make mistakes like everyone else and then I correct them. I don't lose my job, I don't lose my girlfriend, and I don't run away.'

Petra announced herself from the kitchen, telling us to be ready.

Michael focused the shallow estuary of his eyes on mine. 'And I won't lose my daughter,' he said, before dropping them to the mug in my hand. 'No matter how *great* an uncle you think you are.'

The living room door swung open and Petra jumped in.

'I look like the mermaid from the beach!'

*

I left Michael to try and coax some enthusiasm out of his daughter and took a shower. I could feel the run in my legs, but not the pleasant strain that I usually got. Instead they were tender and hurt, in all likelihood torn. Michael had turned up and I'd crippled myself.

I stepped out, listened downstairs to make sure they were still there, then went to my room. I noticed my phone on the dresser, picked it up and saw a message from Janet.

Merry Christmas, Mr Blunt. I hope you and Petra are having a good time, and that Santa came. Janet

Did she think I'd forgotten about Christmas?

Merry Christmas, Janet. We had been having a good Christmas (with presents) until Michael showed up (with better presents).

I pulled on some fresh underwear and black jeans, a long-sleeved shirt and then a blue jumper over the top. I was brushing my hair when the phone rang.

'Hi Janet'

'Mr Blunt, hi. He's there? How did he find you?'

'Oh, he knew which village I was in and then drove around until he spotted my car.'

'What kind of guy ...? But how did he know which village you were in?'

'I ... may have told him before I came. It was just idle chat.'

'That's okay. How's Petra?'

'She's okay. A bit quiet, though she's containing her excitement over his present.'

'What did he get her?'

'You wouldn't believe it – a Little Mermaid dress.'

'Oh, for fuck's sake. I suppose she loves it?'

'Over the moon. She's been talking mermaids ever since.'

'What did you, or Santa, get her?'

'I thought it a good idea to steer her away from the franchise, so got her a *Frozen* dress. Girls her age love it, apparently.'

'The franchise? Mr Blunt, what's happened to you? But that was good. We'll make a parent out of you yet. Have you spoken to Michael, figured out what his angle is?'

'He knows what he's doing. Knows he can be here but can't take her back. I get the impression he thinks his girlfriend's going to drop the charges. What will happen then?'

'Shit. I was worried that might happen. The aggressor apologises and promises to change, tells her he'll lose his job, lose access to his child. Then the victim feels sorry for him. The case relies on her testimony, so if she changes her mind the police have no choice but to abandon the case. Happens all the time.'

'And so ...'

'If there's no assault charge and the restraining order is dropped, Michael will likely terminate the Section 20 agreement and seek to take Petra back. Without those legal issues hanging over his head, we won't be able to convince a family court that he can't provide a safe home. There won't be anything we can do.'

'So, that it?'

'Why don't you try and have a good a Christmas as you can with Petra, Mr Blunt? We can discuss this in a few days.'

'Is there really no other option?'

'If the case is dropped, I guess you could apply to the family court for custody. But it'd be an uphill battle.'

'Right.'

'Let's see what happens over the next little while and try and do the best for Petra in the meantime. Give her the best home she can have, while you can. You're her only link to her mother – make sure you're a good one.'

They were nice words and of course she was right: this was about Petra. But it was also about my family beyond Petra. It was about the Blunts: my parents and my sister. Me. If Michael could hit Patricia and hit his current girlfriend, and who knows who else in between, if he had that in him and was deemed a fitter parent than me, what did that say about us, about the Blunts, as people?

I went back downstairs and stood at the front door. I could

hear Michael talking in the living room and Petra talking back – a conversation between father and daughter. Outside, the night had well and truly set in, but there was a dim light shimmering behind the darkness. I opened the door, walked to the cars and looked up. The sky was clear yet littered throughout with a million stars. There was a sound behind me.

'Uncle Felix?'

I turned to find a little mermaid standing in the doorway. 'Hey.'

'Where are you going?'

'Nowhere. Just getting some fresh air.'

She smiled. 'I thought you were going without taking me.'

'Oh, I wouldn't do that.'

She dropped her arms to her side to present herself in the way the model did on the box. 'Do you like my dress?'

'You're the most beautiful mermaid I've ever seen.'

I walked to the door and let her hug me, her face turned sideways into my stomach.

'I saw a mermaid at the beach.'

'Did you?' I said, shutting the door behind us. 'Was it blubbery with a round face and flippers?'

'It wasn't a seal, Uncle Felix.'

'Was it as beautiful as you?'

'She was the most beautiful mermaid ever!'

'Well I wish I'd seen her then.'

We entered the living room, where Michael was looking at his phone. 'No WiFi? No reception?'

'It's a hideout. I can't risk being found.'

The next half hour or so went by amicably. All that needed to be said had been. On Michael's part, anyway; bringing anything else up would only cause an argument. Petra had witnessed enough of those.

Then, Michael announced he had to leave. He was back to work after Boxing Day and had a flight from Belfast early in the morning. He knelt on the floor and called Petra in for her hug, which she again gave with her forehead pressed into his chest. He gently turned her head so the side of her face was there instead. Then he whispered something in her ear, kissed her on the forehead and stood up. He stuck his hand out and shook mine firmly.

'I'll be in touch soon,' he said, not with a grin but with the firm, confident expression of someone who knows the natural order of things will assert itself on me soon enough.

I watched his car turn left out the driveway towards the village and disappear. Then I lingered, hands on hips, powerless but for the scrap that came from Petra staying behind with me for now. In the darkness I thought I could make out a figure walk by the end of the driveway – feminine, long hair above a trailing scarf. My mind playing tricks.

If you ever managed to keep a girlfriend for more than a few minutes . . .

I walked to the flower that had grown in the autumn and hung on to the naked vine ever since. It was still there, its pink petals contained in its partially opened bud, somehow brighter in the starlight than in the day. The moon was up now, too, its special, ethereal kind of light lending depth to the earth and distance to the heavens. The sky in negative.

I went back indoors and put *Frozen* in the DVD player.

—∽ 13 ∾—

Petra was desperate to go to the beach and show the mermaids her dress, but for two days after Christmas it rained constantly. Instead she wore it around the cottage and told me all the ways the mermaids in the lough would recognise her when we finally went.

'My hair is brushed like a mermaid and I've been practising what I'll say with my mermaid doll and I've written what I'm going to say on the mermaid notepad that Santa got me ...'

More than once I found myself watching *Frozen* alone while Petra played upstairs.

On the 28th the rain finally cleared and we headed for the beach. I expected there to be quite a few people, but as we crossed the dunes I only saw one couple walking by. The woman had a towel wrapped around her hair and was wearing a green, full-body wetsuit. I wondered what there was to see on the sandy seafloor. Faded hoof prints from horses, perhaps. Petra concentrated on jumping across puddles on the path as the gently rolling dunes gave way to the beach.

We walked down to the sand sphincter, where Petra set out her stall and looked determinedly across the lough.

'You have to stay away, Uncle Felix, so the mermaids aren't scared off.'

'Even with your dress on and your hair brushed?'

'Yep.'

Clearly there was no room for negotiation. 'Okay, I'll go for a walk down to the rocks. You be careful.' I wasn't running, as my legs were still sore from the sprint I put in when Michael arrived on Christmas Day.

Petra nodded. She had the dress underneath her jacket but pulled over her tracksuit pants and a long-sleeved shirt. It was a tight fit and it didn't escape me that if I'd got the one for eight-year-olds it would have been perfect for this situation. We'd made it work though and so with Petra at her station, I strolled off, never looking away for more than twenty seconds or so.

When I reached the bend in the beach where it turned towards the rocks, I realised that if I went too far around I'd lose sight of Petra. Instead I looked out across the water. A yellow channel marker bobbed gently to the distant pulse of the Atlantic; a flock of rooks milled curiously over a patch of water half a mile out. My mind drifted. How was I going to return to my old life if Michael took Petra back? She'd only been with me for two weeks but it felt like a cricket bat had been swung through my timeline and I'd landed in a parallel universe. Would I have been a good parent if it had happened to me? Would I have kept the darkness at bay with a mouth to feed? Or would I still have slid towards it as my sister had?

I started walking slowly back towards the sand sphincter. Petra was sitting patiently next to it, her eyes fixed on the tiny waves as they folded onto the beach, empty but full of promise. I wondered what she thought about as she sat there. She must have an internal dialogue going on, a way of continually justifying what she was doing, of stoking her belief in the face of mounting evidence.

I walked on the hard sand just beyond the reach of the water, taking small, tentative strides that didn't put too much stress on my leg muscles. Little waves washed up, leaving damp, ruffled arcs on the sand. I followed them up the beach, noting the consistency of their spacing, and also the randomness of their design. Chaos and order working perfectly together.

A few waves ahead I saw something deposited on the sand, then roll back with the receding water. It caught a sliver of veiled sunlight and glistened, showing its solid surface. The next wave came, smothering the object and pushing it further up the shore, before abandoning it in retreat. The object rolled back awkwardly and came to a halt as the next wave built on the shallow shoreline. I watched this idly as I approached, not thinking too much about what the object was.

But as the next wave covered it, rolled it over and retreated back to sea, the distinctive nature of the thing became apparent. It was quite unlike any other shell I'd seen there before. Usually they were the saucer type – small and beige-coloured with ridged backs. But this was cone-shaped with a tiger-like pattern made of brown lines over a porcelain-white background. It looked as though it belonged in the Caribbean, not the north coast of Ireland. As it rolled to a stop the bottom of the shell was exposed, revealing a cavity with a narrow, leg-shaped entrance. It was about the size of a deformed tennis ball.

I stood over it, a long-forgotten school lesson returning from oblivion to remind me that the inhabitants of these shells shoot poisonous darts at tourists fossicking for mementos. This one looked abandoned though, like an out-of-fashion bikini. I could only muse at the circumstances of its arrival on a beach in Donegal.

I saved it from the clutches of the next wave and gave it a hearty shake. Nothing tried to kill me. I held it in the palm of my hand and admired the beauty of the thing, the magic of its design. The base culminated in a narrowing spiral, like a tornado. How often nature mimics itself. In another context it might have been a seed pod snapped off a tree, a crocodile egg or a cloud. It seemed remarkable that an animal could evolve such an exotic home for itself. I dropped it in my jacket pocket.

Up ahead Petra was still sitting diligently by the sand sphincter. Her patience was remarkable. A Blunt family trait. In my and Patricia's case, perhaps, it had been detrimental. Rather than fight aggressively against our melancholy dispositions we tried to outlast them. Patricia couldn't. I was still wrestling mine. If Petra had inherited the patience, I could only hope she hadn't got the melancholy into the bargain.

The sun had settled in behind a narrow, black cumulus cloud, illuminating the edges of it like a cindering log. I watched veins of light streak out from behind this curtain and scorch gold the stratus clouds higher up. In the foreground the trees of the cemetery stood still, bare-boned, watching on in mute appreciation.

I stopped when I saw the writing at my feet.

Felix Listen

There had been no one in the vicinity the whole time I'd walked to the bend and back. Nobody knew I would be here today. Maybe they could have guessed, or perhaps they did this every day and I only saw it when I was here. Or maybe it had nothing to do with me. Maybe lots of things. It was starting to freak me out.

Felix Listen

What did it mean? If not for me, then what could it mean for someone else? I just couldn't think of a context in which this could be applied to another individual. It was ridiculous, but the most plausible explanation was that it was for me. But listen to what?

I removed the shell and eyed it suspiciously. The tiger pattern had glossed slightly from rubbing against the fabric of my jacket. I tapped the sides and then tossed it a few inches in the air and caught it, as if these actions might unravel the flimsy trick being played on me. Nothing happened. I brought it slowly towards my ear. A small wave washed up and bit at the bottom of the letters in the sand. I realised I could see shoe prints around them. Someone had definitely been here. But who? The only people I'd seen on the beach had been the couple walking by as Petra and I crossed the dunes. The woman in the green wetsuit.

Another wave washed up and took a little more of the writing away. Up ahead Petra's occupation of the sand sphincter was unwavering; I saw her brushing the strands of hair that hung from under her woollen hat.

Felix Listen

Who was the woman in the green wetsuit? What did she want me to listen to? Was it even her at all? Was it the blonde? I looked around but the only things of note on the beach were me, Petra and this lost tropical shell. With nothing to lose I put it to my ear and heard my tinnitus amplified by the echo chamber of an abandoned home. A relentless scream that only I could hear. But nothing else.

I walked past the writing and didn't look back. If it was meant for me, if it was some silly game someone was playing, I would patiently outlast them.

I approached Petra and expected her to tell me to steer clear, but to my surprise she let me come right up to her.

'How's it going?' I asked.

'I don't think they're here today.'

'Really? How can you tell?'

'Because the birds aren't circling over the water.'

'The birds?'

'The black birds. I think they're her friends.'

I looked back out to where I'd seen the flock of birds earlier. They were gone though, dispersed across the peninsula now that their water friend had sounded.

'Maybe this will help,' I said, showing her the shell.

Petra gazed at it with mild awe. 'What is it?'

'I believe it's a mermaid telephone.'

Her eyes widened. 'Really?'

'Well, I don't know for sure, because I'm a boy and mermaids don't answer when I call.' I nodded for her to take it. 'Maybe you'll have more luck.'

I wasn't sure what I would do when she tried it and nothing happened. Was I just building her up for a disappointment? Is that what parenting is? Either way, it was too late now. She took the shell, admired its glossy texture, then put it to her ear.

Slowly she turned towards me. 'I hear singing,' she whispered, 'and waves.' The blue of her eyes was purer than any gem on earth. 'It's beautiful.'

She offered me the shell and I let her put it against my ear. Again, all I could hear was the relentless scream of tinnitus. It wasn't that my hearing outside of the tinnitus was damaged. In fact it was excellent. But when no other sounds are there to take my attention, all I can hear is that endless beeping.

'Beautiful,' I told her.

We sat by the sand sphincter for the next five minutes, taking turns listening to the shell, until Petra put it down and said the song had finished. I thought she was going to ask me to go for a walk again, but instead she cuddled up to me for warmth.

'Petra?'

'Yes, Uncle Felix?'

'What did Dad tell you about what happened to Mummy?'

*

Behind us, low beneath the treetops, the sun crept from its cloudy hideout and threw a faint shadow of our huddled union onto the sand. It stretched towards the water, the waves tickling the top of my head. Above us, where the clouds had been blown away, the sky was a fierce shade of blue. A blue of defiance, of fighting the night. A fight it would lose. Across it a jet was flying, its contrail lit a burnt orange. I considered the possible journeys: Dublin to Reykjavik; London to Montreal; Bristol to heaven.

'He said she went for a swim one day and didn't come back.'

'Did Dad tell you Mummy was a mermaid?'

Petra's head was under my arm, resting on my chest. I could feel her move it but couldn't tell if it was a nod or a shake. For a few moments she didn't say anything. But then her head moved again and looked at the shell in her gloved hand.

'I just know she is,' she explained.

My adult mind wanted to know how she *just knew*. What logic had she applied to come to that conclusion? Had she, by chance, seen *The Little Mermaid* just before it happened? Just after? Had she googled something along the lines of girls that swim and don't come back?

But asking felt like questioning her faith. She wasn't expecting her mother to come back, so even if she wasn't using the word *dead*, believing that she was a mermaid she would never meet wasn't such a bad position to take. I quite liked the idea myself. Not just of my sister being one, but of mermaids existing at all. I couldn't recall the last time I'd believed in anything beyond what my eyes could see. Childhood never comes back.

Dusk was beginning to settle over the lough. The hills on the opposite bank were relinquishing their enervated tones of green to the merciless march of night.

'Shall we go home and light a fire?' I suggested.

Petra's head moved again; this time I was sure it was a nod. We stood up, brushed the sand from our backsides and took one last look over the water. Rooks were dotted across the sky, returning from their feeding grounds, while seagulls argued with each other over patches of water.

'Uncle Felix?'

'Yep.'

'Do you believe Mummy is a mermaid too?'

Why does so much of a child's life involve an adult having to lie to them? Santa Claus, death, mermaids. Did my parents lie to me this much?

'I believe that if you believe something enough, then there's no reason why it can't be true.'

Perfectly vague. An indisputable theory.

'So you DO believe she is one?'

'I . . . believe.'

Why wasn't it working on her?

'I ... do ... believe. Yes.'

Petra hugged me. 'I knew you would. Dad believes too.'

I was in heady company, part of Petra's mermaid alliance.

'I believe in your horse that rides along the beach too,' she offered as compensation.

'Thanks,' I replied. 'That means a lot.'

'Do you know why I believe in your horse?'

'Why?'

She pointed towards the boat ramp. 'Because it's coming this way.'

Sure enough, a horse and rider were galloping towards us. Petra giggled at her own cleverness as the animal approached, then backed into me as it got closer. I held her tight and we both waved at the jockey – a short, thin man with a weathered face – as he guided his steed past us. In his wake ran two tall dogs, white-haired and scruffy. They looked at us as they passed, their mouths hanging open excitedly, but stayed in pursuit of the horse and rider. We watched them disappear around the bend and continue towards the rocks. I showed Petra the hoof prints in the sand when her excitement had ebbed.

'See, a short, fat letter U.'

She studied it with the wide-eyed amazement that only a child has. That look of genuinely learning something new, something that has no precedent – not just a piece of a puzzle, but the whole thing. Around the hoof prints were the paw prints of the two dogs. Petra's gaze shifted from one to the other.

'Those are from the horse and these are from the doggies.'

I pushed my boot into a patch of sand between the two animal prints. 'And this is from the human.'

Petra put hers next to mine, then we stood back and admired our work. Horse, man, girl, dog. It was strangely compelling. Like something you'd see in a fossil museum with a plaque explaining the scientific theory on how the four distinct entities came to be in such proximity.

We started walking back to the cottage, but stopped as we reached the dunes to watch the horse and dogs run by again. I imagined a new set of prints being dug into the sand.

'Uncle Felix?'

'Yep.'

'What do mermaid footprints look like?'

I had her now. 'Mermaids don't have feet.'

Petra considered this for a moment, then shook her head. 'No. They have a tail. They can come up to the edge of the water,' she explained matter-of-factly, 'or up the little stream that comes out of the bath.'

'Sounds about right.'

We crossed the dunes, entered the garden and made our way up the hill to the cottage. The sky was grey-blue now, with a patch of cloud darkening it entirely in the south. The rooks returning to their colony were everywhere, travelling in loose pairs or groups of three or four. As they passed over the holiday cottages beyond my garden wall they whistled to each other, as if to announce they were home.

Inside I scrunched up three double pages from a newspaper and put them in the fireplace, then built a tepee of kindling over the top. I sparked a match and lit two edges of paper before dropping it in the middle. The flames started cautiously, like emancipated zoo animals peering out the opened door of their cages. Then they pounced, growing through the kindling with ravenous appetite. I watched them settle into the base of the fireplace and then added a few more sticks. When they too burnt down I added a femur-shaped log and sat back to admire my creation.

I could hear Petra's footsteps come out of the bathroom and into her bedroom. She shuffled around in there for a few minutes and then emerged, before pausing and going into my bedroom. Then she left there, crossed the landing, came down the stairs and through the kitchen. The living room door swung open and she walked towards me, curiously wrapped in her red jacket. In her hand was my mobile.

'This was beeping,' she explained, handing it to me. 'I think you had a message.'

She knelt in front of the fire and warmed her hands in the heat. I tucked a strand of mermaid-brushed hair behind her ear.

There was indeed a message, along with three missed calls. Ominously, they were all from Janet.

Mr Blunt, please call me ASAP. Janet

I looked into the fire, at the tongues of orange light dancing around the log that was, for now, too thick to be consumed outright. At its base, though, the bark was already glowing with radiant red cinders, like city lights on a Friday night. With every passing moment the flames grew bigger, spread wider, burnt away another layer of the log's defence. It was a battle lost. Petra basked in the warmth of their victory.

There was no signal where I was, so I left Petra with instructions not to get too close to the fire, and went upstairs. I stood by the radiator in my room and returned a call to Janet's number. She answered after two rings.

'Mr Blunt, hi.'

'Janet. Sorry I missed your calls. We were on the beach.'

'That's okay. How is she? How are you?'

'She's fine. I'm okay. We saw the horse today. I'm not sure if you remember that conversation?'

'I remember. The short, fat letter U's? Did she see the prints?'

'She did. And some dog prints. We put our shoe prints next to them. It was ...'

There was no point.

'Mr Blunt? Hello?'

'Yeah. Sorry. I'm here. Has it happened?'

'The case? I'm afraid so. His girlfriend has withdrawn the charges. The police have dropped the case.'

'How long have we got?'

'Michael's lawyers have requested the restraining order be lifted immediately. It'll likely be approved tomorrow, at which point he'll probably also cancel the Section 20. There's nothing we can do about it.'

'Okay. Okay ... okay.'

'I'm sorry, Mr Blunt. You've done a fantastic job. Petra will always know she can rely on you if she needs to in the future.'

'What damage will be done in the meantime?'

'We'll just have to hope that Michael has learnt his lesson.'

A fissure of frustration opened inside of me. 'Have you ever met him?!'

'Yes. I'm sorry, Mr Blunt. I'll be in contact when I know anything more.'

I tossed the phone onto the bed and rubbed my hands on the radiator. How was I going to tell Petra? What was I going to tell her? That her father wasn't a woman-beating arsehole after all? Forget everything you think you know?

I went downstairs and sat on the chair by the fire. Petra was still camped in front of it, warming herself up. She looked back at me, studied my face, then returned her attention to the fire.

'Were you angry, Uncle Felix?'

'No,' I lied, wondering just how many times she would make me.

'I heard you on the phone.'

'Oh. What did you hear?'

'Not any words. Just your voice got louder.' A crackle from within the fire; a hiss and a jet of white smoke. I suspected Petra had put a piece of kindling on while I was upstairs. 'Your voice never gets loud.'

She turned her head again, tilting it backwards and to the side in a display of flexibility that only a six-year-old could manage. 'I like that it doesn't get loud.'

The fire had control of the log now with small flames attacking it on all sides, like teeth taking corn from the cob.

'Does Mike ... Dad's voice get loud?'

She nodded emphatically, her gaze back on the flames. '*Really* loud.'

'Does he yell at you?'

'Sometimes, if I've been bad.'

I tried to make my voice jovial. 'What kind of bad things do you do?'

'I don't know. Stay in my room when he calls me.' Her voice trailed away. 'Wet the bed.'

I'd washed her sheets twice since she'd been staying with me. Bone-dry.

'Have you ever seen him be mean to ... err ... his girlfriend. Sorry, I can't remember her name.'

'Karen.'

'Karen. Does he yell at her?'

'Yep. He gets angry with Karen. Sometimes she comes and sits in my room after.'

'What do you do when she does?'

'Sometimes we play with my toys. Sometimes we talk about Mummy.'

'Karen asks about Mummy?'

'Yep. She asks me what we used to do when we lived together, what games we played.'

'Do you like talking about that with her?'

'Yep. I like Karen.'

'She sounds nice. Do you miss her?'

'Yes.' She nodded with all of her head.

'Do you miss Dad?'

'Mmmm.'

I knelt in front of the fire, picked up the log with the fire tongs and let Petra scatter some kindling on the glowing embers. Putting the log back down I turned to her.

'It must be nice to have another girl in the house that you can talk to about stuff. About mermaids and dresses and hair. I'm glad Karen is there.'

'Am I going to live with Dad again, Uncle Felix?'

'Do you want to?'

'I don't know. I thought I was living here now.'

A tide started to wash over her blue eyes.

'Your dad,' I started to say, though didn't know how to finish the sentence. Did I tell her the truth? Tell her that her father assaulted her mother while she was pregnant? Tell her that when Karen came to her room after an argument it was so she could hide from Michael's fury? Or would telling her do more harm than good? Why was it so much easier to lie to children?

'Your dad has been trying to get better,' I explained, 'because he was naughty.' Smoke started to grow from the base of the fireplace. The kindling cracked, popped and hissed, as gas escaped from the heated tendons of wood. 'And now he is nearly ... better ... so ...'

The fire burst into life with a rush, sending hungry orange flames up all sides of the smouldering log. Petra focused on them, her arms folded beneath her chin, resting on her knees.

'But Janet said I might be living here now.' Her voice was reluctant but defeated, merely articulating the injustice.

'Janet thought Dad was going to take longer to get better,' I explained, reluctant and defeated myself. 'But he has made a remarkable improvement.'

'What about the mermaids?' She argued, her father's side coming out. 'I have to wait for them by the bath so they can tell me about Mummy!'

'I'll talk to them for you.'

'But you're a boy!' Her head dropped between her knees. Tears came. 'I want to stay here!'

'What about Karen?' I suggested, stroking the top of her head. 'She misses you too. You'll be able to tell her about the horse and the bath and the birds. And maybe one day you can visit with Karen and show her all those things.'

It was an awkward feeling, suggesting Michael's girlfriend come here, but it was all the ammunition I had. 'You can visit anytime you want,' I added. 'I'll *always* be here for you. I promise.'

Petra's crying slowed and she leaned into me. A gust of wind blew over the chimney, pushing the smoke back down so it clouded the fireplace.

'I wish you could stay with me, Petra, I really do, but it's not up to me. Your dad wants you to live with him.'

Petra stood up, her head still bowed into her chest, and wrapped me in a hug. Her jacket was unbuttoned and as I moved my left arm it got caught underneath. I could feel the material of the clothes she was wearing; I was expecting it to be a jumper or tracksuit, but instead it had a stickier, artificial texture.

'I want to live here,' she said, her head on my shoulder, her tears gluing our cheeks together. 'With you and the mermaids.'

'Can mermaids live indoors?'

I felt her head nod. 'If you kiss them.'

'I'll try and find one and kiss it, then.'

She slapped me gently on the chest. 'I wanted to find you one.'

I pulled back and wiped the tears from her face. She did the same to me. 'I promise that no matter what, you'll always be able to stay here with me. Whenever you want. Okay? And if your dad gets angry, you tell me. Promise?'

She nodded with all of her head. I looked down to where my arm was still stuck inside her jacket flap. I could see now what she was wearing underneath. It was the *Frozen* dress.

'Are we having a ball?' I asked.

'I wanted to surprise you.'

'I *am* surprised.'

'It's kind of sticky.'

'You can change.'

'I want to wear it.'

'How about I put on something neat and then we have dinner together with some candles?'

176

We dined on pasta that night. Petra told me more about the mermaid she had seen in the lough on Christmas Day and I told her about the writing I'd seen after I found the shell. We decided the latter was definitely written by the former and that perhaps, after all, mermaids would like me, even though I was a boy. Petra said this was probably because they had seen me with her. I added that her mother was my sister, so she might have put in a good word for me too.

'Oh yeah!' Petra exclaimed.

It all made perfect sense and when the meal was over we sat on the sofa together, Petra in her sticky *Frozen* dress that she got from Santa, and me in the suit jacket that I last wore at her mother's memorial service. We watched *Frozen* again, all the way through. The songs were now burnt into my brain. Petra danced to them in front of the fireplace before tiredness got the better of her. I carried her to bed and put her under my giant sleeping bag, then I rolled out my camping mattress on her floor and made sure that no monsters dared come near.

*

The restraining order was lifted and the Section 20 cancelled. Michael came for Petra the next day.

He turned up just after eleven in the morning with Karen. I'd never met her before, only seen her in silhouette at the back of the house when I went to say goodbye to Petra. She was younger than I expected, no more than twenty-five or twenty-six years old. Blonde, though with dark roots, and pretty, in a simple, innocent way. A small tattoo on her left wrist of a red love heart flashed whenever the sleeve of her pink sweater rode up her arm. I wondered how the relationship had started, where they met, how Michael had groomed it.

Petra planted her face sideways into Karen's stomach and wrapped her little arms around her tightly. I wanted to be angry at Karen, but seeing the way they embraced, the genuine affection between the pair, that want quickly fell away.

Michael walked past me, throwing a dismissive sideways glance in my direction. 'Felix,' he muttered.

He went inside to gather Petra's belongings, which had been stacked by the door. I thought they might stick around for a little while, have a cup of coffee, but it quickly became apparent Michael didn't intend to spend any more time around me than necessary. Within a minute Petra's stuff was packed into the boot of the car and he was coaxing her into the back seat. It was all happening so fast.

'Can I use your bathroom?' Karen asked, her West Country accent sprinkled liberally with bits of Essex and London. 'We haven't stopped since Dublin.'

I directed her up the stairs. Outside Petra was in conversation with her father, the car door open like an animal trap. I had expected something else, a formal handing over, but this felt like a heist.

I darted into the living room and picked up the pack of postcards Santa had bought me in Belfast. I took half a dozen out and scribbled my address on the first of them, then walked back through the kitchen and into the foyer. Michael was blocking my view of Petra, who he had shepherded towards the back seat. I could make out her little shoes squirming on the gravel driveway.

'Thanks,' Karen said, coming down the stairs. 'He was so determined to get here.' She rolled her eyes.

The hissing gurgle of the refilling toilet cistern echoed from above.

I studied her face, the layers of makeup, the elongated eye lashes. Was this really Michael's type? She was the polar opposite of my sister. She caught me staring and smiled; I worried that she thought I was checking her out. But then her face changed, shifted from a bland, going-with-the-flow countenance, and became serious. She glanced outside then squinted one eye as she addressed me.

'You probably hate me, right?'

I didn't answer.

'That's okay. I don't blame you. Petra's such a sweet kid, it's tough losing her.' Her voice had lost its pop-culture references. She sounded like her own person. 'That's kinda why I ... you know, with the case? I couldn't be responsible for keeping him from his daughter.'

I checked outside and spoke through gritted teeth. 'But he hit you, Karen. You've let him get away with that.'

'It wasn't as simple as that. He gets angry, and I can be a right bitch. It's combustible, yeah. But he isn't a bad guy, and besides,' she shrugged her shoulders, 'if I have to tread carefully so that he can be with his daughter, it's hardly a choice.'

'He could have visited. We could have worked something out. You didn't have to sacrifice yourself like this.'

'It's not a sacrifice, Mr Blunt.'

It was odd hearing her use my surname. I had a flash of Janet speaking to me, explaining how things worked. It didn't feel so different.

'My dad was locked up when I was a little girl,' she began, like it was normal. 'I saw him once a month in the clink until I was twelve. He got out when I was fifteen and by then I thought he was a right prick for not being around, for leaving my mum to raise three shitty kids by herself. I still barely talk to him.'

So much hidden behind fake tan and eyelash extensions.

'I won't let him hurt her,' she assured me. 'I promise you that. And he knows if he does anything to me again, I'll take his daughter from him. He knows I'll do it.'

Outside Petra's shoes were dangling above the ground. I put the postcards in Karen's hands.

'Can you make sure she gets these?'

Karen looked at the picture on the top card. 'Is that the Titanic?'

'Yeah,' I replied. 'Karen, please, if anything happens, let me know? And make sure she writes. I don't want her to forget me.'

Her face cracked back into its simple, youthful prettiness. 'How could she?' she said, winking, then went outside and got in the car.

The back door thudded shut, with Petra inside it. Michael turned and looked to me triumphantly. He took two steps in my direction, before Petra opened the door, ran past her father and planted a hug around my waist. She wasn't crying and didn't say anything. The Blunt genes coming to the fore. I stroked her natural blonde hair and held her tight, before she broke away and ran back to the car.

'Anything else?' Michael called out. I assume he meant Petra's belongings but the way he had his hands on his hips suggested he thought I might have something to say.

I looked around the foyer. All traces of Petra were gone, loaded into the boot of a hire car bound for Dublin. Then I remembered.

'One more thing,' I said, ducking back into the living room.

I turned the DVD player on, pressed eject and removed the *Frozen* disc. When I turned back Michael was filling the doorway. I put the disc in its box and handed it to him.

'Her favourite.'

He didn't say anything for a few moments, just looked down on me with his mouth pursed strangely, as if there were some words in there but he didn't know if he should say them. Tired of waiting for his lead, I offered my hand.

'Good luck,' I said. 'Take good care of her, please. Karen too.'

Michael shook my hand, though I suspected it was an unconscious act. I held it only as long as was polite. His mouth was still curled in that stupid way.

Finally he started. 'You've always been a cowardly little gripe, Felix. You didn't stand up for your sister years ago and you're too afraid to now.'

'This is about Petra. I only want what's right for her.'

'Yeah you've really fought a battle. I turned up and gave her a better Christmas present and now I'm taking her back. At what point were you going to make your case?'

I was seething but couldn't find the words. I felt my arms shaking with adrenalin.

He started warming into his diatribe. 'This is where you're meant to be, Felix. The middle of fucking nowhere, alone, out of harm's way. Leaving the rest of us to get on with the important and difficult things in life – making babies, having jobs, girlfriends, sex. When *was* the last time you got laid?'

I threw my right hand at his throat, gripped tight and pushed him into the wall. I could feel his Adam's apple roll under the webbing between my thumb and forefinger.

'If you ever hurt her. I will fucking—'

His left hand shot up and grabbed my throat, squeezing so hard that I felt my eyeballs swell in their sockets. He grabbed the wrist of my right hand, the one I had on his throat, and pulled it away with frightening ease. I still had my left hand free, but rather than use it to attack back I pawed hopelessly at the hand restricting my breathing. Michael sneered as I melted in his grip, before he dropped me to my knees. I groped like a pug at the air mercifully allowed back into my lungs.

He cleared his throat. 'I'm changing her surname from Blunt,' he announced. 'I should never have agreed to it in the first place. It's held her back six years already.'

Then he stomped off, got in the car and started the engine. I clambered to my feet, stumbled through the kitchen and out the doorway, just in time to see the car peel off down the driveway. As it turned left and onto the street, the last thing I saw of Petra was her face in the back window looking at me, the mermaid shell phone pressed to her ear.

Part Three

Alice

The messages started coming in at five past two in the afternoon. I imagined the senders gathered on wide verandahs in breezy dresses and loose-fitting shirts, holding up beers to the cloudless sky. Fireworks explode over the city, mosquitos feast on naked ankles, and startled fruit bats take wing through the humid night. 2018 had begun.

In Rathmullan it was two degrees and raining. Ever since Trevor left I had remained indoors, oscillating between the bedroom and living room, passing through the kitchen and bathroom as needs arose. I didn't go swimming or even leave the house to get firewood from the shed out the back. I lived in my tracksuit pants and wore my duvet as a cocoon. Occasionally I'd catch a rook flying by my window and wonder if it was checking up on me.

My mind felt as if it had been injected with a gel that didn't set. Thoughts and memories floated about aimlessly, never taking root and quickly fading away. At one stage I made myself a cup of tea, only to find upon returning to the sofa that I already had one there. As if to rub everything in, I got my period and was doubled over with cramps.

It was partly Trevor, partly Max, but mostly an annoying sense of guilt for the decisions I had made that led me to where I was. Thirty-three and single, thousands of miles from home, cold, lonely and with no prospects of any of it improving.

When midnight came I was in bed, reading a book without

absorbing the words. Out the corner of my eye I saw my phone light up and a message appear on the screen.

Happy New Year, gorgeous girl! Doesn't look like I'll be coming that way for work again, so you should definitely get your arse to Bristol! XX

I imagined Janet dancing in a packed pub, the red streak in her hair given a fresh rinse, her arms raised as she tempted Mark with sideways shunts of her hips.

Happy new year. I hope you're having fun. I'll look into it for term break. X

So the uncle had lost his niece. I wondered if I'd ever figure out who he was. I put the phone down, reached over and turned off the bedside light. Perhaps, I thought, I just needed to look for a man as miserable as I was.

—◦ 15 ◦—

Felix

After Petra left I went into her room to tidy up, thinking I could just roll up my sleeping bag and pull off the sheets and that would be that. But as soon as I saw the sleeping bag pulled aside as if she'd just got out of bed, I lost it. I slumped against the cupboard, slid to the floor, put my head in my hands and bawled my eyes out.

I sat on the couch and tried to read a book, but nothing went in. I watched DVDs and ate cheese on toast. I lit a fire and poked at it incessantly, adding pieces of kindling like a jigsaw puzzle, trying to keep the flames evenly spread across the width of the fireplace. Hours ticked by. The sun came up. I snoozed by the fire but didn't sleep deeply. Then I moved to the sofa and managed a few proper hours there. The sun set again; my windows darkened; I re-stoked the fire and ate some more cheese-based foods.

I was back to where I had been two and a half weeks earlier: alone in a cottage in Ireland, with no friends and no partner. No family. But where previously I'd accepted this as my lot, even searched it out, now it felt purposeless. Petra had given me relevance, like I had a stake in the future.

Perhaps a stronger person would have used this realisation to make some life changes; to me it just highlighted how much I'd wasted mine. In forty years I'd had a couple of false starts at love and been a parent to a child for two and a half weeks. Rather than kick me into gear, being a significant part of Petra's life made me want to end mine. I knew I couldn't change. I'd spent my whole life trying not to.

That's when the Blunt trait kicked in; some time around

midnight, just as 2018 was getting underway. The hopelessness and despair pulsed through me, made ruinous suggestions and hatched easy ways out, and then a heavy blanket settled over all that anxiety, tucked it into a manageable ball and stowed it in a darkened nook. It would weigh me down and clamour for attention, but I knew I could endure it. I'd survived worse. Not for the first time it left me wondering what had happened to Patricia. Had the medication left her natural resistance out of shape, so that when it was gone she was exposed? Or had it saved her for as long as it could?

I watched the fire die down and went up to bed. Having barely slept the night before, I was out quickly. When I woke there was grey light coming around the curtains. I didn't know where my phone was so couldn't tell the time, but feeling well rested I got up, stumbled downstairs and put the kettle on. I tossed two slices of bread in the toaster and dug the jam out of the fridge.

I ate my toast and drank my coffee, staring out the window at the charcoal trees. Without the sun behind them I could make out greater details on their lifeless limbs as they rocked in the wind. I could see smaller branches, twigs, knots in the trunk. And I could see birds coming and going. Two rooks sat on a thick branch and nuzzled each other, occasionally looking down, before returning to their flirtation. I watched them for five minutes, only giving Petra's words a moment's animation in my memory.

I think they're her friends.

Then I shut her out again and dressed for a run.

— 16 —

Alice

The following morning I showered, dressed and breakfasted, then set out for the village to get supplies. I still felt in a funk about everything, but knew that sitting at home by myself wasn't going to fix a thing.

It was freezing, with an icy wind scything in from the north and pushing a flotilla of beige sea foam up the beach. A small fishing boat was limping in from the Atlantic with a single hardy seagull perched on the forecastle. Seeing it, I thought to look out for my bodyguards, and found them circling overhead.

With the weather as it was it should have been a quiet day on the beach, but no sooner had the jetty come into view than the crowd of people around it did too. I squinted though the haze of salt and sand and could make out hundreds of bodies gathered by the overflowing car park. Something was happening.

As I got closer I realised that many of the people had their bare legs exposed, some were wearing bathing caps and there were towels slung around shoulders. I entered the murmuring mass and noticed a logo for a hospice in Letterkenny printed on t-shirts. Shortly a male voice called out from the midst of the group asking for everyone's attention. I recognised Connor's balding head as he climbed onto a bench and started giving instructions.

I picked my way sheepishly out of the crowd, exiting via the path that ran beside the children's playground, but only got halfway along it before a Trevor-shaped shadow formed in front of me.

'Hello,' he said. 'Happy new year.' There may have been an emphasis on the *new*.

I could sense he was trying to get a read on how I felt about him, but I couldn't tell if it was out of fear I might say something in front of the young girl holding his hand, or in hope I would ask for his forgiveness. Either way, seeing him brought back all the feelings of guilt he'd so callously dragged to the surface when I saw him last.

'Happy new year,' I replied, with no emphasis whatsoever.

He sighed gently, looked to the girl, who was blessed with her father's eyes and, I assumed, her mother's red hair, and squeezed her hand. 'This is Tess. Tess this is—'

'A colleague of your dad's. Are you going swimming today?'

The girl nodded and explained that her brother was too scared to go swimming in the cold.

'Girls are much braver than boys, aren't they?' I said. Tess nodded and smiled back at me. I looked to Trevor, whose creased forehead relaxed slightly. Perhaps he thought I'd seen the light on childbirth.

'Will you be joining us?' he asked. 'It's for a good cause.'

For a moment I imagined myself telling him to fuck off and punching him in the face, but instead I apologised and said no, and though I meant it to be directed at his daughter, it still made me feel slightly ill. Then Tess broke from his hand and ran after a friend she'd spotted. Trevor kept his hazel eyes on her, then cleared his throat and turned to me.

'Look, about the other night. I've been thinking.'

'For yourself?'

'Ahh yes. I think I may have been a little quick to judge. Ireland's changing, there's talk of a referendum on repealing the eighth. Maybe I can change too.'

I was caught off guard. He was apologising, in a roundabout way. Adapting. For a moment I didn't know how to react; annoyingly my instinct was to feel I should apologise for asking him to be someone he wasn't. It brought on a fresh wave of nausea.

'Oh, Trevor, no, don't,' I choked out.

'Don't change?'

'Don't be what you're not comfortable being.'

'I was comfortable being with you,' he said. 'The last few days have made that clear to me.'

The word *comfortable* wobbled between us like the sea foam I'd seen on the beach. Was it too much to hope for something more exciting than comfortable? Or was comfortable exactly what I needed? Max had been exciting.

'And you're right,' he continued, filling in the space where I hadn't replied. 'I'm a divorcee. I'm not one to judge.'

'But you did judge, Trevor.'

'I was hasty,' he argued. 'Instilled instinct.'

'So you don't mind that I had an abortion, now? Is that what you're saying?'

Trevor looked around anxiously. 'Alice, please,' he whispered.

Tess returned to her father's side and grabbed his hand. 'Sarah's getting an ice cream, Daddy.'

Trevor smiled at his daughter and told her she could have one after the swim. Then he looked back at me.

'Fancy getting an ice cream later?'

'Too cold,' I replied.

I hurried up the hill without looking back, then turned for the shop, loaded up on what I needed and walked back towards the beach. By then the group of swimmers were gathered on the beach between two flags. Around them dozens of onlookers armed with camera phones recorded the moment. Connor led the countdown from five and then in a fit of screams and yelps two hundred pale bodies ran into the waist-deep water and straight back out again. People cheered and clapped and half the contingent quickly wrapped themselves in towels and the hugs of impressed family and friends. The more hardy of the lot prepared themselves for another plunge though, counting down from five again and then running into the same icy patch of windswept water as before. Perhaps twenty or so went a third time.

I watched on from the top of the hill. A little beyond the waist-deep water I could make out Trevor keeping an eye on everyone. Bobbing a few metres to his right the broad grin on his daughter's face actually looked genuine.

I pinched my shoulders up and began along the path towards home. Shortly though I noticed two rooks sitting on a white fence looking at me. I looked up but couldn't see my bodyguards circling.

I'd bought a loaf of bread so opened it and removed the crust slice, tearing it into small pieces as I carefully approached the birds. As I got closer they started making the cawing sound I'd first heard after I buried their friend. It sounded like they were discussing what to do. I crept nearer, keeping the bread dangling from my fingers. I was within half a metre, the birds looking ready to take my offering, when they suddenly turned their heads to the left and took flight.

Startled, I jumped back. Then I heard shoes thumping into the pavement, turned around and saw the black-haired runner looking me over, his eyes narrowed as if he was trying to place my face. A gust of wind brushed my hair across my cheek. I wanted to say something, anything, but couldn't arrange any words from the jumble of syllables caught in my throat. Then his attention was taken by the crowds down on the beach; he muttered something to himself and a furrow deepened in his brow. He was still jogging and drew close enough now that I could hear his breathing, almost feel the crispness of the air he was sucking into his lungs. Then he was past me, his green shoes pounding rhythmically into the pavement. I hoped he would look back, but he kept his focus straight ahead, turned the corner by the White Harte and disappeared.

I continued along the path until I reached the cemetery. My two bodyguards had settled onto a branch a few metres above my head and called out optimistically. I still had the bread in my hand so offered it again. With a quick kink of their black heads they hopped down and settled on a brick wall.

'Do you have a name?' I asked the first one, as it gently pulled the bread from my hand.

The second one patiently waited its turn and then, hopping closer, pecked little bits of bread while it was still held between my fingers. Then the first one moved in and nudged my hand for more.

'How about Cameron? Cameron Crow. Do you like that?'

The rook didn't seem to mind either way. I gave it another piece of bread and studied the second one.

'You look like ... Russell? Nah, you're way too sweet for that.'

The bird nibbled at the bread and eyed me curiously. It was remarkable how quickly the situation was normalised.

I stayed with them for ten minutes, chatting happily with my back to the path, until they both stopped eating, ducked their heads suspiciously and looked to my right. Turning, I saw the black-haired runner standing fifteen metres away. His face glistened with sweat as his chest rose and fell with each heavy breath. He must have only just stopped, having reached the top of the small rise and seen me.

Slowly he walked closer, wiping moisture from his forehead, eyelids and from the end of his nose. His legs were hidden beneath black compression tights, making them look as though they were carved from liquorice.

'Looks like you've made some friends,' he said as he neared. His voice had a melancholic, almost nostalgic timbre. 'I didn't want to frighten them off.'

'Thank you,' I said, 'and yes, they are.'

He nodded. I noticed now, as he drew level with me, that his eyes were damp and looked heavy somehow. His forehead was creased with a frown that seemed unrelated to the present moment.

Once he had passed by he started jogging again and continued along the path towards the village, no doubt to circle around and repeat. I ran what I had said over in my head. *They are?* I should have said *I have.* I was such an idiot. I looked back at the rooks. Cameron was cleaning his beak on the wall while the other one eyed my hand in hope.

'You look a bit like that guy,' I said, giving him another piece. 'But he doesn't look like a Russell either.'

I continued on down the path until I reached the little track that took me up to my cottage. The rooks settled in a tree above me and watched as I tried to find things to do in the garden. But after fifteen minutes it was obvious that the black-haired runner wasn't coming around again.

───❧ **17** ❧───

Felix

I adjusted my leggings, opened the door and was slapped in the face by a bitterly cold wind. I enjoyed running for how it made me feel alive. But sometimes it really rammed it down my throat.

I turned left out of my driveway, jogged down the road and then cut through to the path. Here I passed the trees I could see out my living room window, though, focused on running, didn't think to look for the rooks. A small car, at least ten years old, was parked by one of the cottages. I realised I'd seen it numerous times before, just never registered that it probably meant someone was living there.

Lumbering down a short slope and along a section of exposed path I passed an old woman walking her dog. Then there was a short, sharp rise. Just over the top of this I was able to look across the dunes and see that the tide was well out, the water chopped up and rough.

I continued towards the village, past the cemetery and through the narrow gate that heralded the end of the path. There started a short road that rose slightly before dipping down towards the main part of the village – the children's playground, the car park by the beach, the corner pub. Usually it was an empty road, but I was surprised to find cars parked along both sides of it and, as I crested the rise, scores more tucked into every available spot.

That was when I saw the blonde woman. She had her back to the path and was approaching two rooks sat on a fence by the football pitch. I knew it was her even before she turned around and the wind brushed a lock of hair across her cheek.

She was strikingly attractive, a simple, classic beauty that was only accentuated by the hint of sadness in her eyes. What I would have given to be in a better place myself, and armed with the guts to stop and talk to her.

But as a bank of trees cleared and the car park came into view I was shocked to find it completely full. Hundreds of people were milling on the beach and even in the water, splashing about in a melee of pale bodies, white water and sand. There must have been some festival on, though why anyone would want to celebrate anything by swimming in this weather was beyond me.

By then I had jogged past the blonde and though the desire to look back one last time was strong, I didn't want to seem obvious. Instead I continued down to the pub and turned right. I'd just have to do laps through the village and back along the path.

When I turned up the Kerrykeel road the wind was in my face again, but by the time I got to the cemetery the tall trees there took the brunt of it. I turned on to my road and pushed up a slight incline, then cruised along the plateau, past the woman I'd seen walking her dog, and down to the turn off through to the path again. My legs were feeling good and the air, icy and sharp, stung my eyes, drawing out tears. I filled my lungs with large breaths as I rolled down the short slope, careful to watch my footing on the gravelly terrain, then settled back into my stride.

Though I tried to focus on running, worrying only about keeping a steady pace and avoiding puddles, I couldn't throw the thought of the blonde woman. It wasn't just that she was pretty and that I'd seen her before – that she must be a local – it was the sadness writ on her face. It felt like a way in. *My sister drowned herself*, I could say. *My cat died*, she might reply. Imagining this conversation was a sordid and real kind of bliss.

I was half expecting to see her at the same spot as before, but as I came up the sharp rise before the cemetery, I found her by the grey stone wall. Initially I thought she was just looking over it at some headstones, but as I got closer I realised she was actually feeding two birds. Furthermore, she seemed to be talking to them. It took a few moments for the reality of this to sink in. They were rooks – wild birds that usually spooked easily. Yet she had them taking bits of food out of her hand. Not wanting to disturb them and ruin her experience, I stopped.

The woman must have heard me though, as she turned to look, so I began walking again so not to appear weird. She stood with the rooks on the wall either side of her, as if with a flick of her wrist she could direct one to attack. Not that she looked the type. In fact, the sadness I'd seen before was less present now, so much so that I wondered if it had ever been there at all, or whether I'd projected my own onto her. I needed to say something. The words were waiting for me.

'Looks like you've made some friends.' I wished Petra was there to hear me.

My comment didn't elicit an immediate response, and a raft of explanations cascaded through my mind: she was deaf, she didn't speak English, she could smell me.

'I didn't want to frighten them off,' I added, seeking more clues.

'Thank you,' she replied, 'and yes, they are.'

It was solid English, but I couldn't place the accent. Possibly it was just Irish. It wasn't as though I'd spent much time talking with locals to get used to their inflections.

I wanted to say more but the way she was looking at me and the way the birds were doing the same behind her, I had the feeling she was waiting for me to move on. It was disheartening, but not unexpected. I nodded at her politely and then, when a few strides past, started jogging again.

Rather than risk the awkwardness of crossing paths with her on my next lap, I instead stayed on the Kerrykeel road past my driveway, until it reached a horse paddock. I could have kept going, but my legs were beginning to tire. Instead I turned around and went home.

*

I woke on Tuesday feeling no better than the day before. Even the run, vaguely present in my legs, couldn't lift me. Greyness felt ever present now, a thick, heavy cloud on my shoulders against which I had to fight with every step to stay upright and squint to see through.

I had breakfast and stared out the window. It was all returning – everything I had put off for three weeks and dared to believe might even have left behind. Yesterday, unaware of the time, I had been up and gone running by 11 am. But already I was sliding back into old habits: it was after one in the afternoon and I hadn't yet finished my toast. Tomorrow it would be half past, by the end of the week it would be gone two. There was no fighting it. This is what my body and mind had settled on as its coping plan. Sleep late and stay up through the night. A constant shroud of darkness to shepherd me through the no man's land of functioning depression.

I read for a while until a passage sent me off on a train of thought. I was thinking of Petra and the look on her face when she 'heard' the singing in the shell. Her imagination was so vivid, so sure of itself. It was the same look she had when she opened Michael's Christmas present – the look of a miracle happening in her hands. There was no filter through which she rationalised her experiences, no way she distilled the fanciful from the real. Everything was possible. She believed in mermaids and so her days were filled with things that could be explained by their existence. Was it so different from believing in melancholia and seeing things that reaffirmed that belief all day?

A wave of nausea washed over me. The charcoal trees were still against the grey sky; no birds sat in their limbs. I couldn't remember the last time I'd imagined anything fanciful. And then, as if my mind wanted to prove its power over me, I did.

It was only a few days ago. I'd found the shell and seen my name written in the sand. **Felix Listen.** And for a moment I'd thought that someone, somehow, had meant for me to listen to the shell. I'd even entertained the notion it was a mermaid. And then, before I'd even put it to my ear, I'd quashed the conceit.

I got dressed into something warm and made my way through the garden and across the dunes.

The tide was a fair way up the beach, though looked as though it was receding. Clumps of seaweed littered the high-water mark just short of the foot-high drop-off of sand that indicated its maximum reach. Towards the village the air was hazy with smoke from wood fires and sand kicked up by the wind. I could make out two or three people in the distance. There was no one to my left, but as I looked across the lough, in the direction of the bend, I spotted someone swimming about twenty yards offshore. They weren't using their arms to stroke through the water, just rolled their body as if a dolphin propelling itself.

I recalled seeing a woman in a green wetsuit, her hair in a towel, man by her side. It was the same day Petra came to the beach in her *Little Mermaid* dress and I found the shell. The same day I saw the writing in the sand telling me to *listen*.

I started towards the bend and the rocks beyond it. The swimmer was heading in the opposite direction. We crossed paths on the village side of the bend, no more than 25 yards apart. It was a woman. I could see her hair trailing behind her like a cape, a boat sail detached from the mast. In the water and wet from it, it was hard to tell the colour, but it was too light to be black. Her wetsuit was definitely green though. I scanned the beach in the direction of the village, the dunes near where I'd seen her last time, but couldn't see a man in wait. She breached the surface again and turned her head to take a breath. I saw her catch sight of me. My heart thumped, but I pushed back at it and continued around the bend.

Above me the sky seemed to be alive with rooks, dozens and dozens of them flying across the lough and towards their nests behind the cemetery. Everything was a memory of Petra now – she'd given meaning to the mundane. I found myself having a conversation with her as I walked along, asking her where the birds were flying, where they had been. They've been playing with the mermaids, she said, having a tea party on a secret island. In return she asked me where all the seaweed that washed up on the beach came from. Restricted by my adult imagination I told her the facts as I thought I knew them: it grew in vast forests under the sea. Mermaids could use it to hide from sharks, she replied. Everything made sense in the mermaid world.

When I reached the rocks the tide had claimed all but those highest up the beach. I looked them over and idly wondered if my shoes would have enough grip to handle their slippery surfaces. Then I took a few steps to the water's edge and saw the writing in the sand.

Felix Climb

I looked back down the beach but the woman in the green wetsuit was out of sight. There was no one in the dunes and the holiday home above them looked cold and empty. With nothing to lose I found a small ledge, put my shoe on it and climbed upwards.

The rocks were about three times my height, but they were cracked and bouldered and I was able to find good foot- and hand-holds to make my way. Near the top I began to hear a strange sound. It started off as a high-pitched whine and at first I thought it was my tinnitus making one of its sporadic changes of tone, but after rubbing my ears and listening more intently, I realised it was coming from the other side of the rocks. As I climbed higher it morphed from a whine into something else. Something, strangely and faintly, like singing.

I reached the top of the ridge and looked over the edge. There was a straight drop down into a shallow cove of water and then a narrow beach. At the top of that there was a cave. The sound appeared to be coming from inside it.

I walked along the top of the ridge, closer to the water. There was no way of getting down there without either jumping or by getting into the water and swimming. Neither option appealed. Instead I sat and tried to make sense of the sound. The wind was picking up again, whistling through the rocky nodes and crevices and the trees above the headland. The more I focused my hearing, the more the tone of my tinnitus swelled, like the microphone had been turned on to it. I ran through the possibilities, trying to explain it away. It could just be water bubbling up through a narrow vent inside the cave, not unlike the sand sphincter further down the beach. It could be birds or some other animals in a nest, crying for food from parents. It might just be my imagination making something out of the natural movement of wind and sea. In fact, the more I listened for it, the less it sounded like anything at all. Soon it started to fade, as if every explanation I conjured for it turned the volume down another notch. Then it was gone.

I climbed back down the way I had come. The writing was still there, inexplicable and bizarre. I stared at it for a while, wanting it to be a mermaid, but knowing it would be something tedious and stupid. My ears rung with tinnitus, it was cold and I missed Petra. I went home angry with myself.

— 18 —

Alice

The water embraced me like an old friend. It was murky from overnight rain, and there was a small chop on the surface, but when I dived down and let my flippers propel me along, I felt at home. I swam to the rocks and poked amongst the small coves and pools created by the high tide. Then I climbed out of the water, sat on a dry ledge and looked over Lough Swilly, at the distant buildings of Buncrana and the snow-capped hills above. The small fishing boat I'd seen coming in the previous day was heading out again, a steady, muffled roar coming from its diesel engine.

Beyond the rocks another long expanse of beach curved around, culminating in a rocky headland similar to the one I was on. It occurred to me that I'd never gone any further on the beach than the rocks on which I currently sat, and no further north at all, other than to the paddock with the horse and the electric fence a week ago.

There was still a few hours of light left in the day, so I decided to head back and do a bit of land-based exploring. I shuffled off the ledge and put my flippers in the water; then something caught my eye. To my left, where the small waves washed onto a sheltered beach, there was a cave. And at the mouth of it, leaning nonchalantly against the wall, was a Coke bottle.

I slipped into the water and swam up to the narrow, sheltered beach. On either side large dark rocks jutted out of the headland like ridged scales on a giant dinosaur. They were three times my height and rough, like a tree splintered by lightning. I doubted any sun warmed them until April.

I sat in the shallow water and peeled my flippers off. As

opposed to the main beach, there was no seaweed on the sand. It looked spotless, as if it had been picked of all imperfections – broken shells, stones, sticks – even the layered mark of the last high tide seemed to have been smoothed over.

And then there was the Coke bottle. It looked like a garden ornament, placed there for a particular kind of aesthetic. Or else it had been left by someone going inside the cave. Going in but not coming back out? Maybe they were still in there. And maybe, as I was trying not to believe was possible, it was the same Coke bottle I'd seen on the sea floor during my last swim.

I left my flippers by the waterline and walked up the narrowing beach. The walls seemed to grow steeper as they closed around me. At the cave mouth I saw that the ceiling sloped down from half a metre above head height, until it was shoulder-height a few metres in, whereafter it disappeared in the blackness. Unless at the very back, crouched down and looking out, it was unlikely anyone was in there. I reached down and picked up the bottle. The lid was still on and inside it was a piece of paper. I couldn't believe it.

The lid unscrewed surprisingly easily. I tapped the base like a sauce bottle and slid my finger in to try and ease the paper out, but it had partially unfurled and wouldn't come. It looked to be a sheet from a ruled notepad, as I could make out the blue lines through the blank side. There was also a sweet smell and a hint of stain on the paper. I wondered if, like the New Year's Day swim, there was a tradition of throwing bottled messages into the lough. There could be hundreds bobbing around out there.

As I fiddled with the note some of the writing began to show; I could see a few letters but not make out any words. I saw an *i* and an *x*, both lower case, that looked like the end of a longer word. I tried for a little longer before noticing a commotion in the water behind me. Turning, I saw a black cloud of rooks swirling over the surface about fifty metres away. Beneath them the water broiled with movement. Suddenly, from the headland above me, the falling squeak sound of my bodyguard rooks called out. I looked up and saw Cameron and Russell perched above the cave mouth, heads lowered, wings spread, pointing at the commotion like they might launch towards it. Above them more rooks were flying from over the dunes to join the action. Just as they had previously, the birds were diving into the water, as if to feed on fish, but none ever emerged with anything in its beak.

Gradually the commotion moved further offshore, until the cloud of birds circled over a spot about two hundred metres away. None of them seemed to be entering the water anymore. Cameron and Russell slowly tucked in their wings and relaxed.

I returned my attention to the bottle but was unable to get the note any closer to coming out. I tucked it into the leg of my wetsuit, put my flippers back on and started making my way home. Cameron and Russell circled overhead, whistling benignly every so often to remind me that all was well.

I was just rounding the bend in the beach when I saw the black-haired runner emerge from the dunes. Only this time he was walking. He was dressed in jeans and a thick black jacket, his hands buried in the pockets like they were holding his stomach in. It was definitely him though. His sombre, insulated demeanour was unmistakable, and his hair had a certain resistance to the wind, like it had once been coated with gel and now tried to replicate the feeling naturally.

I didn't think he had spotted me yet, so I sounded, brushed along the bottom and then broke through the surface again half a minute later. By then he was by the waterline and beginning to walk towards the bend. I swam along the surface until we were directly opposite one another, with only twenty metres or so separating us. I wasn't sure he'd seen me, until his head swung in my direction and, as much as we could given how mine were stinging, we locked eyes.

I was surprised by how nervous it made me feel. There was something so cloistered about him, so defiantly alone.

He watched me swim by and I watched him watch me. The

moment, given its isolation, felt as though it warranted a wave. Yet for some reason I couldn't bring myself to risk not being waved back at. Soon I was past him. By the time I came ashore he was disappearing around the bend.

*

Showered, dressed and sat in front of the fireplace with a cup of tea, I studied the Coke bottle cautiously. Since bringing it back a heavy feeling had come over me. This might be someone's confession, or a letter to a long-lost love. It could be a private correspondence meant never to be found, or only by someone much further away. What if it was from someone in Rathmullan? They might have their name on the note and one day I'd hear the same name in the pub or at the shop and I'd have to pretend I knew nothing so personal about them. It felt like a breach of a confidence that I hadn't been entrusted with, like glancing through a window and catching a moment of intimacy.

I weighed the bottle in my hand, pressing my thumb into it like an avocado.

Alternatively, what were the chances they had written anything that revealing, or even included their name? And whatever they had written, wasn't it done with some expectation of the message being found? Even if it had been intended for someone on the other side of the Atlantic, or Iceland, or even down the west coast of Ireland, there must have been some hope that one day it would find an audience. I could always put it back in the bottle and return it to the sea. I could even take it to the coast and toss it into the Atlantic.

That was what I would do. It was the perfect excuse to go on a proper trip out of the village. I unscrewed the lid, tapped the base and gripped an edge of the note with tweezers. There was little resistance.

I held it in front of me. The note retained its cylindrical shape, its message still hidden, but already I felt a connection to the author, just from the mere fact they'd made the effort. It was so much more personal than email. There was an intimacy to handwriting, to the way a person circles their o's and curls the tails of their y's. I put it down on the coffee table and added some kindling and another log to the fire. The gentle orange glow that had been bouncing off my walls died back and the soft fizzing and hissing of the new meal began. Soon veils of white smoke started snaking up the chimney.

I was eager to read the note, but wanted to savour it too. The moment needed to be just right. What if it was a confession of a love lost? I couldn't absorb that in front of a smoking fire. The flames needed to be licking the wood and warming my skin. I wanted to feel the heat inside and out.

I was delaying. I felt guilty, like I'd stolen someone's postcard. As soon as I read it the crime would be complete.

A piece of kindling popped, releasing a tiny pocket of heated gas, and in an instant flames exploded around it, roaring warm life into the fireplace. I was being melodramatic. I took the note between my fingers and unrolled it.

My dearest Felix,

Never a day goes by that I don't think of you. I still boil water enough for two mugs of tea. Sometimes I talk to you like you're in the next room, nodding off before you've eaten your tea. You were such a gentle and kind man, yet the space you've left is rough and pitiless. I don't dream at night, but of you coming through the door, only to vanish before I can reach your hand. My stomach is forever in knots, wishing just to know that you're at peace. I know you're not coming back, so I'm sending this out on the waves that took you.

Fleetingly yours in life, forever yours in death.

Siobhan

I felt terrible. I rolled the note back up, put it in the bottle and screwed the lid on tight. It was going back in the sea, there was no question about it now. If this poor woman had lost her husband somehow, I couldn't hold on to her heartbroken words for a minute longer than necessary. I grabbed my jacket and car keys and went outside.

It was still light, but dusk was pawing at the sky. I wasn't sure how far it was to the Atlantic coast exactly, but guessed it to be no more than half an hour. I put the key in the ignition and tried not to think about how I'd feel if the bottle was washed straight back onto a cliff and smashed into pieces.

But when I turned the key nothing happened. Over and over again I tried, pushing the accelerator and waiting and every other trick I'd seen over the years. Soon it wasn't making any proper sounds at all – just a muted click, like a magnet snapping together with another.

It was a problem for another time. I threw my car keys back inside and walked down to the beach.

The tide was out much further now, the shallow lower beach, like a ledge beneath the higher one, had about fifteen metres of its bank exposed above the waterline. Just hurling it out there would be no good though. Having swum up and down the beach I knew where the deeper water was, where the stronger currents were that would aid its journey towards the Atlantic. I headed for the rocks.

19

Felix

There was nothing to do at home. There never was, but now that absence of things to do felt deeper – a vast void of nothing. I had wasted most of my life, unwittingly at first, but then out of habit, and now, using the skills I'd learnt, I was committed to wasting the rest of it. What I called patience was actually fear. The fear of challenging that which challenged me. I never chased my dreams, pursued love, believed in anything greater than what I could see and touch. I wasn't just an atheist, I was spiritually nihilistic. I avoided hope so that the pain of disappointment avoided me. I'd taken myself to the edge of society and then slid out as soon as a crack appeared.

Why was someone writing my name in the sand? I couldn't let it go. The thought of it wouldn't let *me* go. I tried to read, but my eyes washed over the words, absorbing nothing. Someone was writing my name in the sand and I needed to know who.

Outside, the thick branches of the charcoal trees were even more stark and lifeless without the rooks perched on them. Somewhere behind a blanket of thick, impenetrable cloud, the sun was skimming the horizon.

I stood up, walked to the window, rested my head against the cool glass. A chair that I'd never sat on was tucked under a table I'd never eaten from. Both were damp and weathered, furrows of green lichen blending with the wood as if that was the plan all along. Everything was finding a way to fit in.

It was absurd that my name was written in the sand. Once was a coincidence, twice was peculiar, but what was it now – four, five times? It was a concerted effort. Harassment. If it was a mermaid, she had some explaining to do. I needed to know. I needed there either to be a rational explanation, or an extraordinary one. I couldn't just be patient while it played out. That had got me nowhere ever.

I grabbed my jacket and went back to the beach.

*

The tide was further out than it had been earlier, the water sucked into the Atlantic for further instructions before being shoved back into the lough to carry them out. I walked swiftly around the bend and towards the rocks.

Felix Climb

I cast my eyes over the writing, as if it might give up some more clues, then looked out across the choppy water. There was nothing much to see – a few seagulls, some waves breaking on a sandbank, a yellow channel marker. I walked down to where the waves of the retreating tide were clawing at the sand, like a cat sliding off a car roof. A few small clumps of seaweed floated about and some pale, uninteresting shells rolled in the foamy white water. I didn't know what I was hoping to find, but this wasn't it.

I turned my attention to the headland. The tide had gone out enough that the smaller rocks were now exposed. I started climbing. Shortly I was standing on the ridge and looking across the narrow cove I'd seen earlier. I tried to focus my hearing on the cave, but there was just the monotonous screech of my tinnitus.

I walked along the ridge towards the beach, then climbed down once I'd passed the waterline. With the steep wall of rocks looming on either side and the sun nearing the end of its efforts for the day, the place already had the eerie feel of twilight. A feeling emphasised by a single rook that watched me suspiciously from the cave entrance.

I started walking up the beach, expecting the bird to take

flight, but instead it lowered its head and opened its beak, then let out a falling whistling sound. I stopped in my tracks, wondering if it was the kind to attack. Perhaps it was protecting an obscurely located nest. Or maybe this is where they came to die. Petra would know.

As the stand-off continued I began to hear another sound. At first I thought it was someone approaching from atop the rocks, but soon realised it was coming from the cave itself. It was a voice – not singing, but a woman's voice in conversation. I focused on the dark void, searching for a shape. Then the voice stopped. For a moment everything fell still. The wind dropped away, the rook stopped its whistling and the waves seemed to take a breath. Then a shape appeared, small with beady eyes. A second rook. It hopped out of the darkness, its head lowered, pointing at me as if a fighter jet poised for launch. Then behind it a larger shape emerged. A woman with blonde hair. *The* woman with blonde hair.

'Hi,' she said, sounding far more confident than she had yesterday. She looked down at the rook, then back at me. 'Tell me, what *is* your name?'

— ❦ 20 ❧ —

Alice

The retreating tide had exposed more of the ridge, allowing me to climb up and walk a few metres beyond the water-line. But when I looked over the submerged rocks I realised it wasn't enough. I'd need to stand on the very end of the ridge line to have any hope of reaching the deeper water.

Unsure what to do, I climbed down to the narrow cove. Though the day still had some light left in it, between the rough grey walls of the cove it felt as though dusk had already arrived. A stiff breeze whistled through the gap and made a hollow thumping sound as it encountered the cave.

I approached the entrance and peered inside. The walls curved inwards invitingly and even though darkness kept secret any danger lurking inside, I felt inexplicably drawn to enter. I took a step, felt the strange embrace of the place, then took another. There was a curious, intangible femininity to the cave; in the way that ships and guitars are female, so too was this hollow. I let it wash over me, and then froze, as a tremor on the wind signalled there was something behind me. Turning, I was relieved to see Cameron and Russell land on the beach. They tilted their heads, as if to say, *Are you serious?*

'It'll be fine,' I reassured them.

I returned my attention to the cave. The walls were nuggety and rough, like an old man's face. They curved gradually around, narrowing to a width of only a metre or so, at which point the darkness became impenetrable. I looked back at the two rooks, who waited for me to take the lead, then continued deeper inside. Russell followed me in.

Given its location so close to humans, I had expected the

cave to have the stale whiff of an old toilet. But instead there was the crisp perfume of the sea. Was it possible no one ever came here?

Russell hopped along behind me as I ran my hand along the ceiling. The surface was cool but not damp and while the light allowed I could make out features in the stone. There were thick fissures of milky quartz and smooth sections, where it felt as if the stone had been sanded.

The ceiling lowered the further I went in and soon I was on my knees trying to reach the end. I ran my knuckles along the cool surface, picked up a handful of sand and let the grains sift between my fingers. It was dry and parched like an outback riverbed. Behind me Russell's presence was only noticeable from the sound of his little feet hopping in the sand.

I felt around in the darkness, vaguely wondering if I might find more bottles, but also drawn to a deeper mystery I couldn't identify. And then my hand found something. It was smooth and cylindrical, about the length of a baseball bat but slightly larger at each end. Next to it were similar objects of varying dimensions. I wondered if maybe someone had tried to light a fire, but when I lifted a piece to my nose it didn't smell like it had seen flames.

There was something about this cave. A feeling I couldn't put my finger on. It was like putting on someone else's clothes and realising this was how you should have been dressing your whole life.

I searched amongst the driftwood for more clues to the unidentifiable mystery which I felt I was just scratching the surface of, and then my hands came across something soft. Instinctively I flinched. Russell did the same, his beak catching a famished ray of light as he jumped back.

'It's okay,' I told him. 'Seaweed.'

Tentatively I reached to the spot again and picked up the damp leaf, feeling along its length until it widened and I got to the main body of the plant. But something was wrong. From outside the cave Cameron whistled in that strange diving way, provoking Russell to poke my arm. I looked out but my eyes were adjusted for the darkness and all I saw was a glaring semi-circle of light.

The rook poked my arm again.

'What is it, Russell?'

I spun around on my knees and crawled until the ceiling was high enough that I could stand. Cameron whistled again from outside.

'Is he always like this?' I asked Russell.

Suddenly I noticed the silhouette of a man standing on the beach. He had his hands on his hips. I'd seen the exact same pose before, though couldn't place where.

I moved a few steps closer to the cave mouth. It was obvious the man couldn't see me yet, as he was tilting his head as if he could zoom in on the sounds he was hearing. Russell hopped ahead of me and joined Cameron, trying to look big and dangerous with wings spread and heads lowered, but succeeding only in looking incredibly cute.

I was about to step into the light when I realised I still had the Coke bottle in my jacket. With my car out of action it might be days before I could toss it into the Atlantic. I placed it against the wall in the darkness. It had made its way there naturally, after all; in time it might find its way out. Then I stood upright and moved into the light.

*

Strangely it wasn't a surprise to realise the man standing on the beach was the black-haired runner. Somehow, in a way I was unable to put my finger on, it made perfect sense. For a moment I wondered if the driftwood was his and he was coming to start a fire in the cave, but it still felt like a woman's place and somehow I knew this couldn't be true. Then, as my eyes adjusted for the light, I could see there was something else going on. He looked conflicted, like the source of the sound coming from the cave was more than just a riddle to be explained.

I stepped into the light (though remained in the cave enough that I could still feel its embrace) and watched his face register my appearance. Surely he remembered me now. To help him along, as he appeared a little confused, I glanced down at my bodyguards. Russell and the man really did bear an odd similarity.

'Hi,' I called out, as clearly he wasn't going to say anything. 'Tell me, what *is* your name?'

The man furrowed his constantly worked brow. Such confusion, such indecision. He stalled on the spot, like a rook in the wind.

'John,' he answered, sounding far more English than I remembered. 'What's yours?'

'Alice,' I told him. 'I've seen you running. Like, not just yesterday. Before ...' I backed up half a step to better feel the strange power of the cave. 'I've seen you a few times,' I explained, 'you're very fit.'

Admittedly it was a bit silly, but men usually respond to compliments. However, he just looked uneasy. By my feet two attack rooks stood ready to launch.

'I enjoy running,' he explained, relaxing slightly. 'It keeps me ... on top of things.'

'I feel the same way about swimming. I go almost every day. I just love it.'

'Is there a pool near here?'

'Pool? Oh. No. I go out there,' I said, pointing over his shoulder. 'It's gorgeous.'

He twitched his head, as if a thought had been fired at him from a hundred metres away.

'Do you wear a green wetsuit?'

'That's me!' I exclaimed, the excitement of being recognised briefly overpowering my feelings about the colour of the suit.

Again the furrowing of his brow. He took a step forward, prompting Cameron and Russell to whistle at him. He stopped, looked from them to me.

'Are you writing my name in the sand?'

'What? No. Huh?'

'Someone has been writing my name in the sand and every time I've seen it ...' again he looked like he was hit with a thought bullet. It was quite endearing. '... Most times, I've seen you.'

I was feeling quite comfortable in the cave but the light was fading fast, and talking at John from a distance like this made it feel like we were combatants. I stepped fully out of the cave and as I did I felt the strange, soothing allure of its walls let go of me. The flickering lights of Buncrana started to flare over John's shoulders.

'That's odd,' I said, resting a hand against the cold cove wall. 'But I haven't ...' My head began to spin like I was on my sixth glass of Sauvignon Blanc.

'Are you okay?' John asked, taking a step forward that I was only alerted to by Cameron and Russell's whistles.

'I'm fine,' I told him, taking deep breaths. I leaned my back against the rocky wall.

'I didn't mean to frighten you.'

His voice had changed, the truculence sapped out of it. He now sounded more like I imagined he would, a less breathy version of his voice from yesterday on the path. I raised a hand to indicate I was okay. The initial contrast from being in the cave and leaving it had knocked me, but gradually I was feeling better.

'I haven't been writing your name on the beach,' I continued. 'I didn't even know your name until just now.'

He seemed to believe me as his head dropped slightly, like the answer might be on a piece of driftwood.

'Well, someone has. I really don't understand it.'

He sounded despondent, far more than seemed necessary for what was surely nothing more than a coincidence.

'John's a common name,' I reassured him.

'My name's not John. It's Felix.'

213

I was still feeling a little shaky so it took a few moments for what he said to fully register. But when it did I felt a stab of nausea. Suddenly the cold, high walls of the cove, the narrowness of the beach and even the darkness of the cave felt ominous. As if on cue Cameron and Russell took flight and joined their friends in a mass exodus across the sky. Did they not see this man as a threat anymore, or did they not see him at all?

I didn't want to say his name. Saying it felt like recognising that I knew it. He might slide back into his suspicion I was behind the writing on the beach. Indeed, now that he had mentioned it I felt a wisp of recognition, not just from the message in the bottle but from seeing it written in the sand myself.

'Seriously, are you okay? You look like you've seen a ghost.'

He was closer now, just three or four metres away.

'I'm okay. I think I should just go home.'

I started to move off, unconsciously sliding my back along the wall to keep my eye on him.

'Do you know who's been writing my name?' he asked again. 'I just want to know why.'

'It's not me,' I said. 'I've got to go.'

I was past him now and started to walk quickly, looking back a couple of times before reaching the climbable rocks. There I groped in the dim light at the wet surfaces and tried to get a foothold. My shoes slipped and I cut my hand on a barnacle, but after a minute or so I was over the other side and jogging back down the beach. I looked back before the rocks merged into the darkness but didn't see Felix, or John, or whatever his name was following me. I crossed the dunes, ran up the path to my cottage and locked the door. I didn't know what had just happened; what I did know was that I needed a drink.

21

Felix

I told the blonde woman my name was John. I wanted to see her reaction. But she didn't flinch or betray her knowledge in any way, just accepted it as fact. She told me her name was Alice.

What she was doing in the cave I didn't know, but she seemed at home there. The two birds at her feet (the same two she was feeding yesterday?) watched me carefully, primed to attack. It was the most bizarre situation. Part of me wanted to play along with it, with the weirdness of a beautiful blonde woman who talks to birds writing my name in the sand, slowly luring me to her cave for reasons yet to be revealed. The other part of me – the stronger part – knew that that was nonsense.

She said she'd seen me running on the beach and offered a compliment on my fitness. The conflict for understanding raged in my mind. Maybe she was homeless, mad and lived in this cave. From here she had watched me jogging up and down the beach, slowly developing an infatuation. She'd seen where I lived and somehow found out my name, perhaps by intercepting my mail. Then she'd developed her crazy plan of writing my name on the beach and luring me into her cave. But she looked too clean to be homeless. Maybe she bathed in the sea.

The birds are her friends.

'I enjoy running,' I told her, 'it keeps me ...' I was going to say sane, but worried it might be a sensitive subject, opted for '... on top of things.'

It worked, as she revealed that she was the swimmer in the green wetsuit. I recalled seeing her walking with a man recently. Was he an accomplice or another victim? Too many things contradicted each other. I couldn't bottle my suspicion any longer.

'Are you writing my name in the sand?'

I took a step towards her, but her birds whistled and ducked their heads. She was a pale silhouette against the black mouth of the cave, her hair stirred up by the breeze, dancing behind her.

She denied it and then stepped out of the cave. As she did a faint veil of light fell upon her face, the last vestiges of the day falling from the sky. Suddenly she looked vulnerable and uneasy. I felt guilty for accusing her.

'Are you okay?' I asked, concerned she might faint. I moved closer but the birds were having none of it.

She leaned against the wall to gather herself. I felt terrible for being part of her discomfort. Pursuing the crazy witch homeless mermaid theory was exhausting for both of us. I wished we could just forget the last few minutes and meet on the beach like normal people. She reiterated that she hadn't been writing my name in the sand.

'Well someone has,' I said, the final drop of doubt spilling out.

'John's a common name,' she explained.

It wasn't just innocent children I was finding ways to lie to; it was beautiful women too.

'My name's not John,' I confessed. 'It's Felix.'

Alice's face changed, like someone had whispered something in her ear. Did she know me after all? I didn't understand what was going on and it frustrated, exhausted and excited me all at once. As if to underscore this the two rooks suddenly took off, not to attack me, but to fly away like normal birds. Something was happening and I had no idea what it was. Again my mind oscillated between the rational and the irrational. Alice clung to the wall.

I took a step closer, wanting to help, but heartbreakingly she flinched, seeing me as a threat. Her face was pale, her breathing laboured.

'Seriously, are you okay?' I asked. 'You look like you've seen a ghost.'

She didn't answer. Instead she slid along the wall, keeping her eyes on me as she scuttled past. I asked her if she knew who was writing my name, but she just denied it was her again, then clambered clumsily over the rocks, slipping – and I'm fairly sure hurting herself – in the process. Then she was gone.

Darkness was falling quickly now. I could just make out the tops of the small, choppy waves of the lough, lit by the timid orange lights of Buncrana. Somewhere out of sight they crashed onto the shallow sandbank, while seals, seagulls and other creatures of the aquatic night patrolled nearby, sensing their moment.

I walked to the entrance of the cave and leaned a hand on the roof. Staring inside, I could barely make out the walls and could see nothing of how deep it went. But it smelled of the sea, of seaweed, wet sand and cold rock. It didn't smell like somewhere a person lived. I left it behind.

As I climbed over the rocks and left the relative confines of the narrow cove I could hear the waves crashing on the sand-bank more clearly, almost as if they were getting closer. I jumped onto the main beach and walked up to where my name had been written. There was no change or amendment. With the wind having worked at its edges for the afternoon and the daylight now all but extinguished, it looked less like a concerted effort to antagonise me, and more like a relic or some child's scrawl, already forgotten by the author. I rubbed my shoe through it until it was unintelligible. The next tide would finish the job.

Walking back along the beach, I felt my exhaustion rub against exhilaration. I couldn't pinpoint the exact causes for any of the sensations, but there was no doubt they centred around Alice. If she didn't live in the cave, she must live in the village. Was that her husband or boyfriend I'd seen her with the other day? And why did she react the way she did when I told her my real name? So many questions. I hated the idea of sitting at home dwelling on them. That was all I ever did. What I wanted was answers, or failing that, a drink.

*

I walked towards the village along Kinnegar Road. With the stars behind a thick blanket of cloud and the last gasps of twilight extinguished, I navigated by the density of shadows. On either side trees loomed, their ink-black presence juxtaposed against the caliginous sky, their absence indicating the direction of the road before me. It was like walking through a tunnel with only the grey promise of light at its end.

But after a few minutes I noticed a different kind of light up ahead. It was dim and seemed to be moving, swinging from side to side as if scanning the road. Yet its source was unclear, as all I could make out was the weakening flare of the beam and not the point from where it came.

I observed it curiously for a while, trying to figure out an explanation, when the single street light that lit up a puddle of road atop the small rise suddenly revealed a person walking in the same direction as me. Though I couldn't see much of them, other than their hooded figure, I assumed the light source to be a torch in their hand. Shortly they exited the pool of street light and the dim flare resumed.

By the time I reached the street light they had turned onto the Kerrykeel road and were momentarily out of sight. I quickened my pace. When I made the turn the gap between us had nearly halved and the street lights that lit the run into the village gave the person more depth. I could see the way their hips moved to each side as they walked, and their head swivelled delicately, rather than in sharp bursts. Beneath an orange light by the cemetery I caught a wisp of hair escape from under the hood.

She turned down the high street, towards the cafe. As she

did, she looked back, spotted me, then looked ahead again. Then almost straight away she looked back. It was Alice. I wanted to talk to her but this hardly seemed the location – and besides, she ran off.

I stood on the corner of the high street and watched her stretch out past the Presbyterian church and the doctor's surgery and into the puddle of lights outside the cafe. Cars lined both sides of the street. She stopped and looked back, then made an obvious gesture of pulling her phone from her pocket and holding it in front of her, like she was dialling a number. I raised my hands in innocence, turned and walked away.

A few minutes later I pushed through the two doors of the Beachcomber pub and ordered a beer. The place was lightly populated, with one man sitting on a stool at the bar, a Guinness and a glass of white wine in front of him, and another man and a woman sitting with two lagers at a booth nearby. I took my beer to the restaurant tables on the raised section and sat looking out across the lough through the bay windows.

That first sip was absurdly refreshing, like rain on a cracked riverbed. The bubbles tickled my tongue and the alcohol flirted with my senses. I couldn't remember the last time I'd had a drink. Having one suddenly felt like a window had been swung open and spring air was sweeping in, vibrating the cobwebs. I heard a door squeak and thud behind me – someone coming from or going to the bathroom. I took another sip and settled back in my chair. Someone should bottle this stuff, I thought.

Then I heard a female voice, turned and saw Alice sitting at the bar next to the balding man with the Guinness. Almost as soon as I saw her, she saw me. Our eyes locked for a moment and I saw in her a flash of that fear I'd seen at the rocks. She didn't move but to nod her head and flick her eyes to the balding man, who was having a one-way conversation with her. This was too much. I put my beer down and offered my palms to the ceiling, then gestured to the seat opposite me. Her face softened and that undeniable beauty I'd seen earlier warmed it. She blinked, looked at the man she was talking to, nodded at him, then looked back at me. She raised a hand, two fingers actually, slightly apart to indicate she'd be with me shortly.

Then she slid into the chair opposite.

'Hi,' she said, her blonde hair hanging like the train of a wedding dress over her shoulder. 'Felix.'

'Hi,' I replied, running a hand through my own hair. I was suddenly very conscious of how I looked. My heart was beating in my ears and with it the tinnitus was screaming. All my senses were alert, like they expected something catastrophic. 'Alice.'

I reached a hand across the table and she met it halfway with hers. It was cold – I was well aware mine was too – but touching her skin warmed everything inside me.

'We've both got some explaining to do,' she said.

'Shall we toss a coin to see who goes first?'

'Why don't you go,' she suggested. 'I have a feeling mine will make more sense to both of us that way.'

22

Alice

At first, when I saw him from the high street, I thought he was following me. I made to look like I was calling the police but he walked off in another direction and I felt guilty for running. He was probably just going to the shop. Then when I saw him alone in the pub, looking out the window, I realised it was just a coincidence. It was still a little scary, but also exciting. So much about the day had been, from finding the bottle and the love letter in it, the experience in the cave, then realising the black-haired runner had the same name. It felt as though everything that had happened in the last few weeks had been shaken through a sifting pan and finally, here we were.

I'd found Connor in the pub and had been having a friendly chat with him (he didn't know about, or was too polite to mention, Trevor), so waited until a break in the conversation came up. Then, at Felix's suggestion, I slid into the chair opposite him.

He looked a little nervous, but it may just have been me projecting. I tried not to betray any obvious feelings, wanting to give the impression I was calm and self-assured. But inside, my heart was racing. Felix suggested we shake hands by way of reintroducing ourselves. A sweet gesture. His touch made me nervous.

I watched his face as he repeated my name. For all his conflict of emotions earlier at the rocks, what I saw most in him now was a quiet, patient defiance. There was no malice there. I had no idea what had happened in his life, but already I was impressed by how he had endured it. It added a lustre of strength to his appearance, which was handsome in a young Sean Penn kind of way.

It was clear we both needed to explain ourselves. I suggested he go first so I could fill in the gaps with my own story. What I didn't expect was just how much of mine was already a part of his.

'My niece arrived a few weeks ago,' he started, and my heart jumped into my wine. 'A woman called Janet brought her from Bristol ...'

As he explained the story of Petra and the background to the whole horrible ordeal, I saw the fuzzy idea of the mysterious uncle sharpen into the man before me. Without thinking I'd used the template of the black-haired runner to put his characteristics onto. It was as if he had been created through witchcraft: a sprinkle of Janet's words, a drop of imagination, stir in a few glimpses of tight-fitting running attire.

'So, between her thinking there were mermaids out there, my name appearing on the sand, you swimming by and then appearing in the cave, things have gotten a little weird.'

'You have no idea how freaky this gets.'

I proceeded to tell him my side. Of meeting Janet and hearing about him (though not specifically of him) and of the rooks and swimming (I didn't tell him about Trevor) and even of seeing his name written in the sand myself. He shook his head in disbelief and took a long drink.

'It gets just a little weirder,' I continued.

The furrow in his brow bent into the shape of a rainbow.

'Earlier today, when you saw me in the water, I had been at the rocks already. When I was there I found something: a message in a Coke bottle.'

'Are you serious?'

'Yeah! Crazy, hey?'

'Depends what the message was.'

'Exactly. And this is why I was so freaked out at the cave. The message was a love letter from a widow to a husband lost at sea. His name was *Felix*. Isn't that fucking crazy?' I took a drink of Sauvignon Blanc, satisfied everything was finally on the table.

Felix breathed out heavily, then broke into something nearing a laugh. 'It was from a woman to a dead fisherman?'

'Yes! She must live locally as it didn't look like it had been in the water long.'

His laugh came, high in the back of the throat first, like a cartoon car trying to start, before tumbling down into his chest. It was infectious and soon I was laughing with him, though I wasn't entirely sure why.

'So that's who's been writing my name on the beach,' he choked out. 'A fisherman's widow?!'

'I guess so!'

With everything finally out in the open we relaxed. He no longer thought I was a crazy stalker and I no longer thought he was the ghost of a dead fisherman. It was lovely seeing him smile rather than frown. He had new mannerisms, like rubbing his cheeks after laughing. We were Alice and Felix, two single thirty somethings in a remote village in Ireland. We bought more drinks, then a couple more. I regretted not eating first.

It was ten o'clock when we left the pub. We walked up the high street side by side, laughing and talking like we'd known each other for years. Then we turned on to the Kerrykeel road and the lights of the village began to thin out. It wasn't until we turned onto Kinnegar Road that I stopped to think what was happening.

'Wait a sec,' I said. 'Where do you live?'

'Up here,' he indicated. 'You're up here somewhere too, aren't you?'

'Umm, yes. How do you know?'

'I was behind you coming in, remember? You ran off?'

'Oh yeah. I didn't know you'd been behind me all the way along here.'

'I was further back,' he explained, as we carried on down the dark road.

By the time we reached my driveway Felix had grown quiet. I was feeling really hungry and needed to pee. I wasn't sure what our parting should be. So much had transpired throughout the course of the day and night that it was hard to tell where we were now. Especially after four glasses of wine. I wanted to hug him and agree to meet tomorrow, but he seemed to be stalling. It didn't feel like the right time for a kiss.

'You live here?' he asked, his face again painted with surprise. 'With the porch light on?'

'Yeah. Oh hey, are you any good with cars?'

'I can change a tyre.'

'Oh, okay, never mind.'

'I can't believe this is you.'

'Why? Where are you?'

'Basically next door.'

He pointed over the wall that bordered the driveway. It was dark but I remembered the cottage with the smoke curling out of the chimney, the top-floor window.

'Holy shit. We're neighbours.' I groaned in drunken, hungry surprise.

'Crazy. So tomorrow, how do you feel about revisiting the cave and seeing if the bottle is still there?'

'Umm, yeah, sure. I was going to leave it though so the tide could take it away naturally.'

'I don't want to remove it. I just want to see the handwriting and be one hundred per cent sure it's the same as on the beach.'

It seemed a reasonable idea. And I was glad to have a plan to see him again the next day. 'Okay. What time?'

'About one? The tide should be out again by then.'

'Deal.'

He looked me over and smiled, then hesitated. I really needed to pee so tried to move things along quickly. I reached in and gave him a hug, but must have done so in a slight drunken rush as his arm got trapped between us and it was an awkward few moments as he tried to pull it out to complete the embrace properly. Even in my state the sense of having his arms around me was intoxicating. I held it for longer than my bladder wanted me to. Then we parted ways and I went home and straight to the bathroom.

—◦ **23** ◦—

Felix

It was hard to know where to start, though the beginning seemed like a good place. I told her that I had gotten up one day three weeks ago, looked out the window at the charcoal trees against the grey sky, at the empty cottages beyond the wall, went for a run, and that was about the last time anything had been normal.

Alice listened on with growing fascination, her lips parting, head shaking, her blue eyes exploding with a thousand stories of her own. I could tell she was dying to jump in, but she held back until I'd recounted the whole saga. Only then did she reveal that she'd known Janet, had heard of me through her, even knew of Petra.

She then explained her tale of finding a Coke bottle with a message from a fisherman's widow – a fisherman with the same name as me. Suddenly everything fell into place. The writing on the sand, her reaction to me at the cave. It was an absurd chain of events, but it led us to this table at the pub. I felt a weight fall off my shoulders and then realised I was talking and laughing with a beautiful woman who seemed to be enjoying my company. I forgot all about Michael and losing Petra. Being with Alice was fun. I could feel my cheeks cracking from actually smiling for the first time in an age.

We walked home and, naturally enough, it turned out she lived in one of the cottages on the property next to mine. Her roof had been visible through my living room window. Suddenly the rooks on the branch made more sense. I really couldn't believe what was happening and tried to suppress the nagging expectation that something would happen to derail the whole thing.

'So tomorrow,' I said, 'how do you feel about revisiting the cave and seeing if the bottle is still there?'

Alice agreed, though I think she was a little drunk by this stage and wanted to go to bed. It had crossed my mind that we might kiss, but I hadn't kissed a woman for two years and wanted the circumstances to be just right. Instead I motioned to shake hands, but she was already leaning in for a hug and my arm got trapped between our bodies. I think I managed to untangle it without her noticing; then we hugged properly. She smelled like the sea.

*

I couldn't sleep. It was earlier than I usually would anyway, but even still, my mind was racing. I felt I had to do something, tell someone, convert what I was feeling into an action somehow. I hadn't been excited about anything for years, and now that I was, I didn't know what to do with it. I began to distrust what was happening.

I put a pot of water on the stove and tried not to look out the window at the trees I couldn't see in the darkness, and the rooftop I couldn't make out behind them. Looking felt like desperation. I had to temper this, somehow, bring myself down off this unsustainable peak.

I recalled Carly, two years ago now. How she'd sought comfort in other men when I wasn't enough of one for her. I reminded myself of what Michael said, that I couldn't keep a job or a girlfriend. He was right. I couldn't. Alice would see that soon enough. In fact, she would probably meet Michael somehow, someday, and fall for him. He was taller, stronger, blond like she was. He had a job and could keep girlfriends of all ages. He was an alpha male and I was a beta, or whatever the next one was.

The water came to the boil and I added some salt and a bit of oil, then half a packet of pasta. The Carly and Michael train of thought had worked well. I stirred the pasta in and stared at the swirling water as it brought itself back to the boil. I needed to do a piss.

Upstairs I checked my phone. No messages. No missed calls. I hadn't heard from Petra since Michael took her away. I wondered if I ever would. Soon he would change her name, erasing my family from her life completely. Did she think of it like that? Did she understand what was happening?

Back downstairs the pasta needed a gentle stir to keep it from sticking to the pot. When it was done I drained it and added some sauce to the pot, cooked that a few minutes then added the pasta back in. I was fed. The rest of the night passed uneventfully. I was off the peak now, just as I'd hoped. It was disturbing just how easily I was able to descend to the valley floor.

*

I was sitting on the rocks, listening to singing coming from the cave. I wanted to climb down but my legs wouldn't move. Then the singing became the sound of lovemaking. I tried to run away but my legs refused to carry me. The sound grew louder. I turned away but waves crashed on to the rocks and the wind blew the spray into my eyes, forcing me to look back. Alice emerged from the shadows and leaned up against the cave mouth wall. Then Michael appeared, put his hand around her throat and squeezed. Alice grabbed his arm, stroked it, pulled him close. I willed myself awake.

I couldn't shake the dream and didn't want to go back to sleep, but was desperately tired. I dozed fitfully, not trusting my subconscious, then got up at midday for a shower. I had coffee and toast and looked out the window at the charcoal trees and Alice's roof behind them. I hated myself; hated the conviction of my subconscious. It felt like a cancerous weight that grew denser every year. I could clamber beyond the event horizon occasionally, but I was always sucked back into its black centre.

Finally one o'clock neared and I pulled on my jacket and closed the door behind me. I knocked on Alice's a minute later and listened to the gentle thud of her footfall echo down some stairs and to the door. It swung open and there she was, just like in the dream.

'Hi.'

'Hello.'

I wasn't sure if we could hug again, as last night's felt like it was a reward for the day that preceded it. Consequently I hesitated, hovering in the doorway like a soap bubble. As I did I found myself analysing her face to try and gauge her enthusiasm for seeing me. Was last night just some drunken fun? Did she see me now in the fresh light of day and second-guess herself? Was she regretting everything and looking for a way out? It was hard to tell. There was an initial smile, possibly out of politeness, then her eyes twitched a little, as if adjusting to the reality. She stepped aside and invited me in, slightly hidden by the door.

'Do you want a tea? Coffee?' she asked.

'I'm okay, thanks.'

'Right. Well I'm nearly ready.'

I realised for the first time she had only one sock on.

I could feel the empty space where a hug should have been. My chest and the inside of my arms, the side of my face, all the places where my body would have felt the pressure of hers, they were aching for what they had missed. It was like being penniless and hungry, walking past a bakery.

Alice raced back up the stairs and moved around her bedroom. Her cottage wasn't unlike mine, just slightly smaller. The stairs led to a balcony that led to the bathroom and bedroom. In the dining area, where I stood, I could see her green wetsuit hanging over a clothes rack beneath the staircase, a superhero costume waiting for its moment. Two white candles, half melted, sat in old silver candelabras on the dining table. I wondered if she lit them when she ate by herself.

Her footsteps moved swiftly around the upper floor. Was I early? Perhaps a few minutes, but she may have been expecting me to be late. She would read this as eagerness, desperation.

Shortly she came back down the staircase, nearly slipping on the first wooden step in her socks. I motioned to catch her, even though the table was in my way. She rescued it though and made it the rest of the way without incident.

'Have you got a torch?' I asked. 'It's pretty dark in the cave.'

'I've got my phone torch. That should be okay, shouldn't it?'

'Sure.'

She sat on a chair at the dining table and pulled her shoes on. Her hair fell either side of her head as she did, reminding me again what I'd missed out on by not getting a hug. I found myself staring at it, not speaking. It looked freshly washed, with a faint shine of moisture still on it. I remembered how it smelled last night. I was pathetic.

'Sooooo, did you sleep well?' she asked, looking up from the chair, her face slightly red from the contortion she was in.

'Yes,' I replied. Why was I always lying? 'Mostly. Kind of . . . it was okay.' I'd said too much.

'I'm not sure if that's a very specific description or very vague.'

'How did *you* sleep?' I asked, hoping to deflect attention from my awkwardness.

'I was out like a light,' she answered.

So not lying awake thinking about me all night. Of course not. What was there to think about? Nothing.

'Good,' I said. I could feel the door shutting, the last of my defences coming down.

She finished tying her laces and ducked into the living room, reappearing moments later with her phone. She checked the screen, made a face that suggested she had received some communication, but ignored it and picked her coat off the hanger.

'Right,' she said, breathing out theatrically, as if to emphasise how much of an effort this whole thing was. 'Shall we?'

I nodded and we left, walking side by side along the path until we reached a cut off through the dunes, at which point I followed behind her. We spoke about the weather (there was some blue sky earlier, but now it was gone) and the likelihood the tide was out (which I already knew it would be). The absence of fun and light heartedness that we'd experienced the previous evening was obvious. There was no way she couldn't have noticed it too. It was unravelling before it had even begun. I felt incapable and useless, without a single arrow to fire at the charging armies of misery.

We crested the final dune and saw the beach, cold and life-less. On the flattest section, right by the water line, the sand glistened with the moist sheen of an old man's cigar. Tiny patches of white water dotted the lough like dandruff. Without saying anything Alice turned left for the rocks and I fell in beside her, perhaps a half-step back.

What was she thinking? Regret? She seemed to be walking faster than I remembered from last night. She wanted this over and done with, then she could make her excuses and that would be that. I'd have to see the roof of her cottage through my window for the rest of time, a constant reminder of another failure. No. I'd move.

'What are you thinking?' she asked.

'That I should have hugged you at the door.'

It just came out, exactly like that, without any filter or conscious act on my part. I was mortified. There's not playing it cool and there's being utterly, desperately, hopelessly pathetic. She might have excused a lack of practice, but there was no way she could accept this level of incompetence.

'Why didn't you?' she asked, not breaking stride.

I hadn't stopped or turned around and ran. I couldn't. I was like a dog. I hated myself with every thought.

'I don't know.'

Because I was afraid you'd not want me to, or not hug me

back. Because the hug last night could probably never ever be beaten and so even a friendly, well-meaning hug would feel like a seismic shift backwards.

We continued walking in silence for a few more seconds. It was definitely only seconds, but it felt like hours. The wind was blowing her hair around, making it dance off her shoulders. Everything was a tease. Her beauty and nature combining to put me in my place.

'What are you thinking now?' she asked.

I hadn't realised I'd stopped until I noticed Alice getting smaller. I looked down and my shoes were stalled in a no man's land of mid-beach nothingness. A couple of yards up the beach was the high-water mark from the morning's mediocre tide. It was distinguishable by clumps of brown seaweed and the dry corpse outline of sea foam. Ten yards down the beach the tide, now nearing its lowest point, slapped at the wet sand with its little waves, rolling small shells and sticks in the shallows.

Alice had stopped and was watching me with her arms folded in frustration. Then she shook her head and started back towards me. This was it. I'd ruined it. I dug into the mess of thoughts in my head and mounted a last-ditch defence, but Alice cut me off before I could string anything meaningful together.

'Felix, stop ...'

‒‑ 24 ‑‒

Alice

The wine knocked me out. I managed to make two pieces of toast and a cup of tea, but I was asleep on the sofa before I finished the latter. I woke up some time in the early hours feeling like someone had put their hands around my neck and shaken me. My head throbbed and my throat was parched. The tangy, sour taste of Vegemite clung to the inside of my mouth. I thought I'd be able to get a glass of water and crawl upstairs, but as soon as I stood up, I felt nauseous. The water went down and came up a few minutes later, along with the toast. I slept face down in bed and woke around 11 am.

I couldn't recall what time Felix said he would be over, but remembered him saying something about sleeping until two in the afternoon. I aimed for then.

In the meantime I had a brutal hangover to deal with. I took two Panadol and put on some coffee, then looked through the pantry and realised there was next to nothing my stomach felt like putting in it. I ate a slice of bread just to fill the gap.

Curled up on the sofa, I tried to will my body to recover. I really didn't want to feel like this around Felix. We'd had such a good time and laughed so much, to then show up to our 'second date' looking and feeling like a boat wreck was going to be such a let-down. I wished I had his number so I could ask to put it off until tomorrow, or maybe just meet tonight instead. Then a lightbulb went on in my head.

Hey you, how are things in Bristol? Have you and Mark recovered from your NYE shenanigans yet? Speaking of recovering, I had a few drinks last night with a certain neighbour. It's a long story how we met, but we got on so well! And he's just a little bit handsome (you kept THAT part really secret) I'll give you all the details later, but for now, any chance you could give me his number? Xx

She was going to freak out. Just waiting for her reply made me feel better. But as it didn't come and time was getting on, I headed upstairs for a shower.

I had only just got dressed, ran a quick brush through my hair and not yet put any makeup on when the knock came at the door. I had been hoping to have a proper breakfast before he arrived too.

I rushed downstairs and unlocked the door. Despite the fact that I still felt mostly rubbish and looked even worse, I was still eager to see him. My memories of the night before were broken and missing in places, but the feeling of it, of the wonderful connection we had, was bright. I just hoped he felt the same way.

When I opened the door he stood there awkwardly. I said *hi* and he said *hello* and then he waited like a delivery guy hoping for a tip. I felt that after all we'd been through a hug was warranted, but now that it came back to me I remembered he had been reluctant about that last night too. I had to lead it then and now here we were again. Was it possible I had misjudged the whole thing?

I invited him in and asked if he wanted anything. I hoped he'd want a cup of coffee first so that I could make some toast, but he grunted a *no* and waited for me to react. I had the impression he wanted to be somewhere else. Accordingly I went upstairs to finish getting ready, then rushed back downstairs, nearly slipping on the stairs in the process. He was in the same spot, as if moving anywhere else would have indicated an interest in me or my things. I didn't understand his attitude at all. It was like he was a different person.

I tried to make conversation as I put my shoes on but his

answers were confusing. I teased him about it but the joke fell flat. The next hour was going to be hard. I grabbed my phone and saw that Janet had replied with Felix's number, then she'd added:

OMFG! It had crossed my mind that you might be good for him. Drag him out of his shell a bit! Seems you read my mind. I want details ASAP! Xx (Ps. I've got some news to share too ...)

My original message had been sent only an hour ago. How was I going to tell her that it had already gone belly-up? And what was her news? Had she found a surrogate?

The walk to the beach was horrible. We talked about things so boring and meaningless that I don't even recall what they were. None of the excitement and laughing from last night was there. My hangover wasn't helping, but Felix was a bag of sand.

When we started towards the rocks the conversation stalled completely. I was disappointed as much as annoyed. It was as if he'd dangled this cheerful, complex, sensitive persona in front of me only to take it away and replace it with a maudlin bore. I had liked him. Now I wasn't so sure. If only he'd say something.

'What are you thinking?' I asked, because I refused to believe he wasn't thinking about *us*.

'That I should have hugged you at the door.'

His answer took me so much by surprise that at first it didn't register. I just kept walking as the words ducked and weaved amongst the swinging hammers in my head. Then, once it sunk in, I struggled to make sense of it. It was as if he was still at my front door, his conversation only now catching up to his body. I didn't know what to say, so just put it back to him.

'Why didn't you?'

He said he didn't know. It wasn't much to go on but I felt

235

encouraged. I really wanted to just sit down and make him talk. We could end this thing or push it along right now, but this wordless middle ground was extremely frustrating. As he wasn't going to say anything more, I thought I'd try again.

'What are you thinking now?'

It was like throwing a ball to a dog that you couldn't train to sit or heel or roll over. If nothing else, I could prompt him to burp out unexpected thoughts with a simple question. Only this time he didn't say anything. The glimmer of hope faded and snuffed itself out. I didn't have the energy to go through with this. When I turned around and realised he had stopped about five metres behind me, I figured he was either thinking the same thing or was having some kind of existential crisis. Maybe his body was here on the beach, but his soul was still at my door, wanting to hug. Either way, I was done. I began to walk back towards him. I would suggest he go to the cave alone, maybe hang out in there and have a chat to himself. I'd tell him I wasn't feeling great and perhaps we could meet up for a coffee one day if he felt like it. When his body caught up with the rest of him. He started mumbling a defence but I could barely understand him. I cut him off.

'Felix, stop ...'

He had tired eyes, from not sleeping or from battling himself, I didn't know. There was a complexity here that I didn't have the energy for right now.

'Felix, look,' I said and tried to think of the best way to put it. The hangover made my brain feel dry.

But Felix's eyes had changed. They were the same eyes I'd seen at the cave yesterday when he thought I'd been writing his name in the sand. It really was too much for me to deal with right now. I tried to shake his gaze off.

'Felix, listen,' I said, but as I did he stepped back, ran his hand through his hair and for a moment looked as though he was going to throw up. Perhaps he was as hungover as I was, I thought, but then he straightened, raised his hand and started to speak.

'Let me start again,' he said.

There was something in the way he was speaking, a timbre in his voice that hadn't been there since he arrived but that I recalled dimly from last night. It tickled a pleasant memory, not of anything specific, just of a presence, an experience. It bought him a few more seconds.

'What do you mean?'

'Just, please, wait here. I'll be right back.'

He started walking up the beach.

'You're going home?'

'No. Just over the dune. I need a minute, thirty seconds. Please.'

'To do what? Felix?'

But he was already off, climbing over the front ridge of the dunes and down the other side. I stood there in the middle of the beach, my headache ebbing but my stomach rumbling for food. A few seconds passed and I wondered if maybe he had actually gone home. Maybe this was how he dumped all girls he met, with some vaguely eccentric display of weirdness.

But then he reappeared and paused on top of the dune. He was fifteen metres away and the wind was tossing his hair across his forehead, but I could still see his eyes, feel them locked onto mine. He smiled. It was the same as the one he'd shared with me across the table the night before. He was also handsome again, in an endearingly awkward way.

He strode up to me, raised the smile a few watts and said, 'Good afternoon.'

'Good afternoon,' I replied, timidly resisting being pulled into this strange game.

'I didn't sleep well last night,' he explained. 'Actually, hardly at all.'

'No?'

'No, I was thinking about you all night.'

I didn't know what to say. My hunger rumbles were replaced by a butterfly. Then Felix leaned in, put his hand gently behind my ear, and kissed me.

*

It was hard to tell how long we kissed for as time stopped and the world, my headache, hunger and frustration with it. I had no doubt Felix was a bundle of complex neuroses, but when he kissed me like that, I didn't feel like it mattered.

When we pulled apart, our fingers had become intertwined, as if during the embrace our bodies had reached out like Velcro to cling to each other.

'I was thinking,' he said, turning us to walk towards the rocks, 'the writing on the beach, the bit that doesn't say my name, that seems like an odd thing for a grieving widow to write.'

'Yeah, I guess.' Now I felt like the discombobulated one.

'It'll be interesting to compare the handwriting.'

I giggled stupidly.

My head was spinning and I'd lost the power of speech. So many thoughts were racing through my mind I didn't know where to start. I wanted to know what had just happened, but simultaneously I didn't want to risk derailing it. Was he so fragile that he could turn cold and unemotional at a moment's notice? I wasn't sure I could live with that.

'Sorry about before,' he said, squeezing my hand. 'I haven't ... I'm a bit out of practice.'

'That's okay,' I managed to say. It was lovely hearing his proper voice again. I squeezed his hand back. I wanted to add more, to ask some questions, to tell him I was out of practice too, but none of those things felt right (and some not true). For now it was enough just to rub his arm. There was time for all things.

'What's it like out there,' he asked, shifting into a casual tone, 'when you go swimming?'

And just like that we slid into an easy conversation like

nothing had happened. Soon we were chuckling and making little jokes, bit by bit making our way back to the happy place we'd been in last night. It still felt like tentative ground, but it was our ground.

*

The narrow beach was strangely clear of seaweed, shells and sticks, even though these things littered the high-water mark on the main beach. Cameron and Russell, who I hadn't noticed until then, settled on the rocks above the cave entrance and watched us with their jittery heads. They seemed to have decided Felix no longer posed a threat.

I took the phone from my pocket and turned on the torch. Even before its light took effect, I could see the Coke bottle was gone.

'The tide must have taken it,' I suggested.

Felix kicked gently at the sand near the cave mouth, sending a small cloud of grains into the air. 'It's dry here,' he said. 'Doesn't look like it gets seawater often.'

We walked into the cave, the sterile white light of my torch revealing veiny slivers of quartz like scar tissue. As opposed to yesterday I didn't have the same feeling of bold fearlessness while inside. It wasn't that I now felt the opposite, rather that I was aware of its absence. I wondered if I had imagined it altogether.

'Didn't you say there was some driftwood?'

I shone the torch to the spot I'd found it but only the seaweed remained. The patch was much larger than I had imagined – about the size of a living room rug and thick, like the padding in a dog's bed. Indeed, if it wasn't for the fact it was made of a repulsive lump of kelp it could well have passed for an animal's mattress. But there was nothing comfortable about it at all. It had long, flat, rubbery leaves, like the fly flaps on a butcher's door, and spindly fingers the width and texture of power cables, nobbled with jellybean-like tumours that looked ready to burst open at any moment. That there were forests of that stuff in the same water I was swimming in made my skin crawl.

We poked around for a few minutes, looking for signs of inhabitation – graffiti, burnt wood, cigarettes – but it was remarkable only for its lack of these things.

'You would think a place like this would be a hang-out for local kids,' Felix said, facing me now with both hands holding the ceiling. I turned the torch off. The dim light from outside accentuated the features of his face – the cheekbones and jawline, the stubble that seemed as much a part of him as his legs.

'Maybe it's too cold in the winter and the last king tide cleaned most of it out.'

Felix nodded, though I wasn't sure he was convinced.

'The writing after my name,' he said, shifting into thought-fulness. 'The first time it said *stop*. Then *look*. Then *listen* and *climb*. What do you think it means?'

'I don't think it was meant for you. It was the fisherman's widow.'

'But why was she telling a dead person to stop, to look, to *climb*?'

I shook my head and shrugged my shoulders. I didn't know and wasn't sure I wanted to, and in any case couldn't think on an empty stomach. 'I'm really hungry,' I said.

Felix blinked and I had the feeling I had derailed some other train of thought he was on, but he quickly got himself back together again.

'Do you like Nutella pancakes?' he asked.

'Oh God, yes.'

— 25 —

Felix

'Felix, stop ...'

I felt my heart thump in my chest.

'Felix, look ...'

This wasn't happening. It couldn't be happening. It was just a coincidence. This kind of thing does not happen.

'Felix, listen ...'

I stepped backwards, tried to keep my head from exploding, my stomach from jumping out of my throat. I needed a moment. Just one moment to get things lined up, distil reason from the weirdness. There was no way Alice was doing this deliberately. It was too fluid, too accidental. If I hadn't been acting so fucked up she wouldn't have begun this conversation. It wasn't her, but the words were ... the words were normal words. Surely.

Petra would know what it all meant.

Alice's eyes were glazed, the lids and cheeks narrowed around them. She looked anguished and annoyed, her face drained of colour. She was an intake of breath away from dismissing me. I wanted to know what she was going to say next, but from the way she was looking at me I didn't think it was going to be what I wanted to hear.

'Let me start again,' I said.

I climbed over the dune, took a breath and closed my eyes.

Life was unfair. Why hadn't my father given me a moral, a crumb of hope when he told me this? And why did I think he should? Life *was* unfair. Charles Furst was an arsehole and life gave him three and a half million pounds and a dog called

Ronaldo. My father was honest and life gave him a depressed wife, a suicidal daughter and pancreatic cancer. You can laugh at it, you can rage against it, you can be a victim of it. Life was unfair, regardless.

The look on my father's face as he lay there, only a month and a half of life left in his shrunken body, was of surprise. Surprise that it actually *was* going to end like this. Somehow, in the face of the mounting evidence, year on year, he had held on to the hope that life would somehow balance itself out in the end. And only then, with a few weeks left to live, did he concede that it wasn't going to happen.

What the sixty-six-year-old man had given up on, his six-year-old granddaughter had in spades. Life was unfair. It took away her mother, it gave her an angry father, it threatened her with a genetic disposition to depression. But a mermaid who rode seahorses through seaweed to hide from sharks, and who had rooks as friends, waved at her. Petra had less control over her life than anyone, yet she shaped it with a vivid imagination and a Blunt-like determination to endure. Life may have been unfair, but you write your own stories. Perspective was everything.

I climbed back over the dune and saw Alice standing there, the wind whipping the hair across her face. She looked annoyed but she also looked beautiful. I walked up, explained myself as little as I could get away with, then kissed her.

Things moved smoothly after that. We reached the cave and discovered the Coke bottle and driftwood were gone. There was no way the tide had taken them out, so perhaps a mermaid had. I didn't know and I didn't particularly mind either way. It was interesting to consider the possibilities but they felt less important now. Alice was looking at me differently. I enjoyed the tension, the positive energy that flowed between us now. I approached her, trying to look as masculine and cool as possible. I felt I could be a better person with her.

We chatted about the writing on the beach as I edged closer, drawing her towards me. I was just about to dismiss every-thing we'd said as incidental and pull her close for a kiss when she said she was hungry. It scuppered the moment somewhat but I didn't mind. I liked the idea of making her pancakes, so I offered. She accepted and we headed back towards my place, getting halfway before she decided that she wanted to kiss after all, and pulled me to her by the front of my jacket.

Alice admitted she was hungover, so I put the electric heater on in the living room, sat her down with a coffee and busied myself in the kitchen with flour, eggs and milk.

'You're reading Kafka?' she called out.

'It was Petra's favourite.'

We had the pancakes with Nutella and also with bananas and yoghurt. Suitably fed we then settled on the sofa and started to watch a DVD. Alice fell asleep on my shoulder and I carefully slid over so that her head was in my lap. We stayed like that until the movie finished. Then I switched it off, swivelled myself from under her, cradled her head and legs and carried her up to my bed.

'Undress me,' she said, her eyes still closed, her hair falling across her cheek.

We lay together under the duvet, stroking each other's skin, drifting in and out of sleep. Kisses lapsed into cyclical breath-ing, caresses became cuddles. We made love in the hour before sunrise, slowly and gently, our lips never more than a twitch of the head apart. Then we slept through until two in the after-noon, like all good people should.

*

When I pulled back the curtain that afternoon the sky was grey, the window flecked with spittle. There seemed no end to the rain that wanted to fall on Rathmullan. In my time there I'd come to realise it came in a variety of forms, but all could be put under one of two umbrellas, so to speak. There was rain you could go out in and rain you couldn't. This was the latter.

We had breakfast in bed.

I suspect Alice felt the same, but waking up and realising everything was okay was a relief. I was nervous – there was a beautiful woman in my bed, after all. But I wasn't afraid of ruining it somehow. Whenever those doubts crept into my mind – and they did often, for a lifetime of habit doesn't disappear overnight – I just told myself that it was in my hands, that in this moment everything is fine, so there's no reason the next moment will change, or the next hour, or tomorrow. It became a mantra and soon I was able to quieten the doubts and enjoy the present tense. Alice made it easy. Her smiles were like bursts of flame into a hot air balloon, and I reciprocated them unconsciously every time she shone one my way. The anxiousness she'd displayed the previous day was gone, possibly along with the hangover, but I like to think I played a part too.

We made love again, fell into a blissful half-awake slumber for an hour, then emerged and made love once more. The sun, whatever it had been doing, gave up on us.

'I want to make you dinner,' she said, walking her fingers across my chest.

'I'll wear my running gear.'

'I wouldn't turn you away if you did.' Her digit explorers found an unmapped tuft of hair and began investigating. 'But I don't know that my wetsuit will be making an appearance.'

'I like it,' I offered, stroking the outside of her thigh with the back of my fingers. 'It brings out your hair colour.'

She sunk her teeth into my chest, flicked her tongue across my nipple. The explorers expanded their party and spread out, slid across my face and dived into the forest they'd been searching for. We made love again. It wasn't that we needed the release, it was just the only way we could get closer to each other.

Alice left around six and told me not to come over until eight. I watched her leave, watched her turn back when a few steps from my door to see if I was still looking. The moon was up early, pouncing on a rare gap in the clouds to spread its magic over Donegal. Alice's hair was platinum under its spell, fanning out behind her like a silver-dipped peacock.

I showered reluctantly, because I smelled of Alice, could still feel her hands on me. It was only the promise of new imprints that coaxed me in. I dressed in black jeans and a navy-blue collared shirt, then picked out my dress jacket, the only one I had. Perfect for wakes, Disney balls and candle-lit dinners. There had been no mention of wine but I suspected Alice would want some. I drove to the village shop and browsed their budget range of Chilean Merlots and Sauvignon Blancs, choosing a bottle of the latter. Then I knocked on her door. It was four minutes past eight.

No one has ever been so beautiful. She wore a strapless dress the colour of the sea at sunset, a blue that outlasted the day and would survive the night. It was slightly longer at the back than in front and flared from the hips, like a lampshade leaning back on itself, impressed by what it contained. Her hair, beguilingly curly at its ends, fell down over her chest like ivy. Black heels shaped her calves into pieces of art. For a few moments I was too afraid to breathe.

'Hug me,' she demanded. It was probably makeup, but it looked as though stars shimmered on her face.

I stepped inside and put an arm around her back, dared pull her towards me. She smelled of summer.

'That wasn't so hard now, was it?' she whispered. I felt immortal.

'Ohhh wine,' she then exclaimed. 'Excellent choice!'

There was classical music coming from the living room, which the two flames above the silver candelabras danced to, like angels at gunpoint. Alice put the Sauvignon Blanc in the fridge and removed an already opened bottle from the door. 'I may have got a teensy head start,' she said, pouring some into a fresh glass and topping up her own.

We toasted to happiness and to Felix the fisherman, then

once more to his widow. Then I kissed her, because it was killing me.

'We're having pasta,' Alice explained with a hint of apology. 'I didn't have anything else and I wanted to get ready.'

'You look incredible,' I told her. 'And I love pasta.'

We ate, talked, drank, washed up, drank some more, laughed and played charades. Neither of us did *The Little Mermaid*.

If life played out on one long piece of celluloid and I was presented with that film by an angel at the Pearly Gates, and that angel said I could either go on through to heaven or I could choose a section of the film to live over and over again, I would seize the scissors from that angels hands and cut out the forty-eight hours that started when I got my act together on the beach, and ended the day after this dinner, when we kissed for the last time by the sand sphincter.

*

Like so much else that happened when we were together, it came about naturally, as if all that lovemaking had synchronised our thoughts as well as our bodies. We had just finished with the breakfast dishes and were entwined in the kitchen, our gazes out the window. That's when we noticed the rain had stopped. In the same moment I thought *run*, Alice thought *swim*.

Twenty minutes later we kissed by the sand sphincter and went in opposite directions. Alice waded into the water, pulled her flippers on and swam towards the rocks – I wished Petra could have seen her – while I started jogging towards the boat ramp. It was perfect. Running had always been something I did alone, yet somehow I'd found a way to share it.

There was a brisk, cold breeze at my back, gently encouraging me to get to the boat ramp so that I could turn and hurry back to Alice. It's remarkable how every little thing fits a romantic narrative when you're in love. There wasn't a moment during that downwind leg that a single negative thought entered my head. The world had relented and I was happy.

When I turned at the boat ramp I saw the dark grey cloud the wind had carried with it. It was moving low and fast, like a stingray ominously stalking the peninsula. Icy white veils of rain fell in its shadow, dousing the land in a glistening, freezing rinse, as if to cleanse it of anything without embedded roots.

I pushed on into the ever-increasing wind, before the first of the hailstones struck me on the forehead. In an instant the air was full of them, frozen raindrops the size of peas filling the atmosphere and stopping me in my tracks. I knelt down and covered my head. It was as if the cloud had frozen and was coming shattering to the ground.

Then, almost as quickly as it had started, it stopped. I looked up and saw the beach had been turned from a damp orange vista into a frigid white ice sheet. The cloud moved on and the sun started to break through. I reached down and scooped up a handful of sand and ice, the latter of which was already beginning to melt. Two substances that should have been alien to each other, fighting for dominance.

It was then that I heard the distant call of the rook. I looked up and saw the bird flying low over the beach ahead, its wings flapping franticly. A desperate whistle carried on the wind in front of it.

I started to run. The bird angled over the waterline, spread its wings and banked hard right, letting out another sharp whistle as it arced behind me and came up on my left, before heading back down the beach. I could feel my shoes slipping on the ice. I passed the sand sphincter, looked for signs of Alice but could only see the tame green chop of the lough. Then the rook came again, fired out its frantic whistle and banked around as before. I watched it fly thirty yards over the water and then dive under. Moments later splashing erupted on the surface, an arm flailed through the air and blonde hair wrestled with the water. Both rooks emerged from the commotion, pieces of seaweed in their beaks.

I tossed my shoes on the beach, barely noticing the word carved into the melting hailstones.

SWIM

I plunged in. The coldness stole the breath from my lungs and I instinctually gasped for air, taking in a mouthful of saltwater instead. I could still touch the bottom so stood up, never losing stride, and coughed up what I could. Then I caught my breath and started swimming again. Alice was gone, only the two rooks throwing themselves into the water giving any indication of where she had been.

I swam desperately to the spot, took a big breath and dived down. It was green and empty. I looked in every direction, swam to the bottom and pushed armfuls of sea out of my way. Every now and then a black shape would appear on the edge of my vision and I'd jerk around, but it would be one of the rooks, hopelessly out of its element, joining me in the search.

I returned to the surface, breathed out and in again, then returned to the green emptiness beneath the waves. It was a desert, without even a clump of seaweed or rock for decoration. That Alice was in it somewhere, drained of air, that she was dying in this barren, lifeless place was an injustice. It wasn't fair. I returned for air, went back under.

There was nothing under there, not even a fish.

She had been gone for maybe three minutes when I breached and started treading water. I looked to the rooks for help but they were circling hopelessly, their wings dripping with water, their heads ducked, emanating hoarse whistles. I tried to figure out which way the current was flowing and match it with where I'd entered the water, but as soon as I started swimming in the direction I thought I should go I was crippled with the fear of swimming further away from her.

There was nothing I could do. I was a bobbing cork on an indifferent ocean, a bottle at sea.

The rooks' whistles became mournful and as I drifted beneath them, shivering, my fingers already locking into useless claws, their pitch began to match that of my tinnitus. The saltwater started to sting my eyes and I was no longer able to feel my legs. I looked around me but the waves and the hills beyond them blurred into one. I began to sink.

Then the pitch of the rook's calls shifted. I could hear the whistles again, one far away, one close. I kicked, lifting my chattering mouth out of the water. Twenty metres away a blurry black shape was hovering over the water while closer a bird slid across the chop in a frantic and aborted landing, taking flight by my left ear while letting off that hopeful whistle again.

I rotated on to my stomach and flung my arms into the water, one after the other like the prop of a paddle steamer. The blurry, hovering rook gradually came into focus, joined now by the second one. I don't know how long it took me to reach them, but by the time I did Alice looked as lifeless as the seaweed wrapped around her neck.

I put an arm under her chin and pulled her into my chest, then kicked and pawed at the water, trying desperately to ride every tiny wave a few inches closer to shore.

Alice's face was blue, her lips purple. I dragged her onto the beach, laid her on her back and breathed air into her lungs. A woman appeared from the dunes, thin, late fifties, short, white curly hair, a face wrought with distress.

'I was walking past and saw—' she started to explain unnecessarily.

'Ambulance!' I told her between breaths. 'Call a fucking ambulance!'

She already had her phone out, but by then Alice's heart had stopped.

*

The ambulance put a wheel in the sand sphincter as it raced towards us, bouncing out at an angle that briefly saw it heading towards the water. By then I had been breathing air into Alice's lungs and pumping blood on behalf of her heart for ten minutes. The woman who had appeared from the dunes offered to help but I ignored her, only stopping when the paramedic shouldered me out of the way and took over. I rolled onto the sand, flat on my back, and stared into the sky. The grey clouds were eclipsed by a circling black mass of rooks, their wings beating as one against the cold air, as if they were trying to push it into Alice's lungs.

'Letterkenny University Hospital,' one of the paramedics told me, as she lifted Alice's stretcher into the back of the ambulance.

'Is she ... How is she?'

'She's breathing and we've got a pulse, but it's weak. University Hospital.'

The door slammed and beneath a screaming siren and a cloud of birds, Alice was taken away.

'That poor girl,' the woman said. 'What happened?'

'I don't know.' I hauled myself to my knees. 'It looked like some seaweed was wrapped around her. She might have got tangled up ... somehow.'

The woman moved a finger from her head to her stomach and then to each side of her chest. 'The witch is in that water,' she muttered.

I squinted at her face, trying to place it. But my head was a mess and I was desperately cold. I got to my feet and thanked her for her help. 'What was your name?' I asked.

'Siobhan,' she replied.

'I'm Felix.'

I shook her hand and thanked her again. 'I'm going to the hospital.'

Siobhan nodded awkwardly. Her face had changed, like she had something else to say but didn't know how. I was too cold to think about it though, and had somewhere else to be.

The reception office at Letterkenny University Hospital was at the end of a short hallway and looked like the square face of a 1980s arcade game character. I approached with trepidation, not sure I wanted to know what they had to say. A short, wide nurse with crew-cut hair and a tattoo on the back of her left arm waddled over from a photocopier at the rear of the office.

'Someone was brought in earlier,' I explained cautiously. 'A woman from Rathmullan?'

She moved a mouse around an old-school mousepad that was frayed around the edges, clicked a few times and then bit her lip.

'Yes,' she said. 'I see.'

'What do you see? How is she?'

'She's still being treated in our emergency department. I can't tell you any more than that at the moment.'

'So she's alive?' The words sounded giant coming out of my mouth, shaped by a god.

The nurse's eyes lifted from the screen for the first time during our exchange. 'I only know that they are treating her still, sir. As soon as I know anything more, I'll let you know. Are you family? We have no identification on the patient at all.'

'I'm ... a friend. Her family ... she's Australian, but she's working over here.'

I gave the nurse all the information I had, which wasn't much. I didn't even know her last name or which school she worked in.

'I'll make some phone calls,' I told her.

I dialled Janet and gave her the news. She was distraught, more so when she realised she didn't know Alice's surname either; but she gave me the phone number of a man called Cormack, who owned Alice's cottage.

'I'll call you back when I know more.'

Cormack had her details, including the school she worked

at. He also had a key to her cottage so agreed to try and find her purse and passport and bring it to the hospital.

The nurse left a message with an automated service at the school, which didn't go back until next week. Then she suggested I get a coffee, take a seat, try to relax. I managed one out of three.

Half an hour later a doctor appeared from a side corridor and gave the nurse a clipboard. They had a short conversation, before the nurse gestured in my direction.

The doctor was a woman in her late forties with short, stylised black hair. She had green eyes behind semicircle glasses with orange rims and wore a white medical blouse. She gave me a professional, neutral smile.

'Ms Phillips is in a critical condition,' she explained. 'She has suffered from diffuse cerebral hypoxia, in other words a lack of oxygen to the brain. We won't know how severe any damage has been until we perform a CT scan. Currently she's in a coma so we'll defer that scan until her condition stabilises.'

I grabbed the top of my head.

'A coma isn't necessarily as bad as it sounds,' she continued. 'It's the body's way of focusing its resources on healing the brain. However, the longer it goes on, generally, the worse the prognosis. The next few hours are critical. Much depends on how long she was underwater for.'

'I think it was about three or four minutes. Maybe five. It's all a blur.'

'You were there?'

'I pulled her out.'

'You did an excellent job. Five minutes in cold conditions is survivable, especially with CPR performed afterwards. But you need to be prepared for possible side effects if she does pull through. Cognitive functions can be impaired when the brain has been starved of oxygen.'

'Can I see her?'

'For now she's being monitored closely. It's best we let the nursing staff do their jobs.'

I tilted my head back, hoping to contain the tears to the back of my eyes. The doctor must have noticed.

'Perhaps I can let you look through the window, briefly.'

We walked down a side hallway, through two swinging doors and down another hallway, before taking an elevator up two floors.

'Do you know how it happened?' she asked as we jerked upwards.

'She swims there all the time,' I explained, shaking my head. 'When I found her she had some seaweed wrapped around her neck, but it was only a small piece. Perhaps she got tangled in something bigger ...'

'Seaweed grows in forests, so it's possible.'

'Yeah. It's just ...'

The elevator slowed, a metallic beep emanated from a speaker somewhere and the doors slid apart. I followed the doctor out into a hallway, in which we turned left.

'Go on.'

'It's just she looked like she was fighting something, rather than struggling against seaweed. Maybe a seal?'

'Seals can be inquisitive. My partner dives and says they approach without much fear. She's never mentioned any attacking.'

The doctor stopped by a double door, looked through the reinforced glass windows and then gestured for me to follow suit. I peered in and saw Alice, her hair tucked to one side and over her shoulder, with a thin, opaque tube snaking out of her mouth. Another tube came out of her nose, and both these connected to others that ran into machines that had wires and moving parts with red lights and green lines. It looked ad-hoc, like it had been made up on the spot, found to work and then left alone in case anyone accidentally touched it and ruined the magic. Her body had gone into a natural state of coma to preserve itself; this was what humans had come up with in support.

A nurse moved around the room, observing things, writing them on a clipboard. The doctor watched her work, as if expecting to catch her out.

'I don't know what to do,' I said, feeling hopeless.

'I'm not sure if a next of kin has been advised.'

'I'm working on it.'

'That would be a great help.'

*

Cormack turned up with Alice's passport and purse an hour later. He was short, mid-forties, with neatly trimmed dark hair and a thick set body, like he played rugby, or at least used to. I told him there was no update on her condition, but the next few hours were critical. Repeating the doctor's words gave me a feather of comfort.

'She was a lovely lass,' he said, seemingly unaware he was using the past tense.

As I waited behind a couple of other people at reception, I began flicking through the passport. Other than the last few weeks I realised I knew almost nothing of her past. I knew she'd been living in London before coming to Rathmullan, and that she grew up in Australia; otherwise she was a mystery. The couple of days we'd spent together had been all about the present.

Going through her passport I could see she'd been to Bali, New Zealand and Thailand during the last eight years. Such exotic destinations. Did she go with friends, with a boyfriend? Did she meet men there? What had she been like in her twenties? Did she have casual sex? Often? Did she meet men in nightclubs? Was I the kind of guy she would have spurned if we'd met on a night out when she was twenty-two? I barely knew her at all, and yet here I was acting like her other half. Maybe I was just the guy that happened to be with her at the time. We'd spent forty-eight amazing hours together, but were they more relevant than passing time with some guy she'd met on holiday? How does one measure these things?

At the back of the passport was a name and two numbers –

254

one of which had been crossed out – to call in case of emergencies. It was probably the nurse's job, but she was busy. I found a quiet corner and dialled.

'Yo.'

'Hi, Max?'

'Yeah? Who's this?'

'Hi Max, my name's Felix, I'm ...'

'I'm not buying anything, mate. Fuck off.'

And that was that. I wasn't sure who he was, but given he sounded Australian and the crossed-out number didn't look like a UK mobile, I guessed it was an ex-boyfriend. I had no idea what their relationship was like now and whether she would want him to know about her situation.

I looked in her purse and found a card with a list of emergency contact names and numbers. Max's was on there, along with a series of people with the same surname as her. All the phone numbers looked foreign. Was this the time to tell her parents? Suddenly the scale of what was happening and how many lives it was going to affect dawned on me. I returned to reception and waited for the nurse to become available. As I did, my phone rang.

'Hello?'

'Listen, mate, I don't know how my number got on your fucking database but I want it removed now!'

'Wait—'

'You're a bunch of fucking cunts! I'm putting this number on social media and telling everyone that you're a scamming cunt and get them to spam the fuck out of you with prank fucking calls. See how you fucking like it!'

'No, Max—'

'And I'm fucking blocking you. Suck a dick.'

And that was that. Strangely it made me feel better. Alice's ex-boyfriend was a twat.

I gave the nurse the passport and showed her the contact list in the purse.

'I've already called the number on the passport,' I explained. 'It's the same guy – Max – on the list there. He's . . . I've spoken to him.'

'Okay, thanks,' the nurse said. 'I'll contact the others.'

I wanted to listen in but the nurse went to a phone at the back of the office. Again the feeling of hopelessness came over me. There was nothing I could do but wait for news. I got a coffee from a vending machine and sat on a moulded plastic chair in the foyer, where I fiddled with my phone, vaguely wondering if Max's threat would bear fruit.

An hour went by. I gave the nurse my phone number and told her I was going for a walk. Outside it was early evening and the stars were already fighting with the city lights for ascendency. Hungry, I found my way to the high street and took shelter from the cold in a cafe. I ordered a small pizza and a Coke. A few minutes later my phone rang. I picked it up eagerly.

'Hello?'

'Yes, hello, we heard that you've recently been involved in an accident.'

'What? Really?'

'Yes. We can offer you backdated insurance. All it will cost you is the price of sucking a dick.'

I hung up. A minute later another call.

'Hello?'

'Good evening, sir. Tell me, how many cocks does a cock-sucker suck if a—'

Three more calls like this came in over the next ten minutes. Half of them didn't even bother to hide their numbers.

I ate my pizza under the glare of a fizzing white light. Teenagers came and went, plates were left on tables, top forty music played through crackly speakers. It was Friday night and Letterkenny was going about its business.

'Hello?'

'Hi, please hold for Her Majesty the Queen.'

I typed a text message.

Max, this is Felix. I called you earlier to tell you that Alice Phillips has had an accident and is in a coma. Call me if you want more details.

But when I sent it I received an error message. It took a few retries before I remembered what he said about blocking my number. It was baffling that Alice had ever been involved with such a prick.

At nine o'clock I walked back to the hospital. The prank calls had tapered off but were still trickling through. Some were actually quite funny and I answered them, even knowing what they were likely to be, just to see how creative the person was. I needed the distraction.

At reception the nurse shrugged to indicate that there was no more news and so I took a seat. Ten minutes later a man with receding brown hair and a dull coloured sweater emerged from the side corridor the doctor had come from earlier. He spoke to the nurse on reception who, after exchanging a few words, pointed to me. I straightened in my chair, my back stiff and backside numb.

'Hi,' the man said, 'I'm Trevor.'

We shook hands and he explained he was a colleague from school.

'I get the messages from the school's answering service,' he explained, sitting two seats away from me. 'What happened, exactly?'

'She was swimming and I was running along the beach, and then I saw she was in trouble.'

'In trouble? How?'

'It looked like she was ... wrestling with something.'

'Wrestling? With what?'

'I don't know. Maybe a seal.'

'Seal attacks are very rare.'

A short Asian woman came by, pushing a trolley containing blue towels and white sheets, a green bin bag on each end. She parked the trolley by a wall, pulled her right foot behind her to stretch her quad, then kept going.

'Well, it might have just been seaweed. She had some wrapped around her throat when I got to her.'

'She must have swum into a forest of it.'

'Yeah ... possibly.'

'Probably. She got into similar trouble a week or so ago. Sounds like it was the same spot.'

'Really? How do ... Did she tell you?'

'I was with her. Well, I was onshore, she was swimming.'

I nodded cautiously. I was tired and the sterile lights of the waiting area had made my eyes sore. Everything felt difficult. Perhaps sensing my confusion, Trevor elaborated.

'We'd been seeing each other,' he explained.

'I see.'

'It was a good thing you were running past when it happened,' he went on. 'Sounds like you got there just in time.' He reached over and patted me on the shoulder. 'The nurse tells me you've been here since the afternoon. You don't need to stay. I can wait now. Give me your number and I'll let you know when something develops.'

'I'm happy to stay.'

'Really, it's okay. I spoke to her mother in Australia, reassured her that we're doing everything we can and I'd keep her updated. There's nothing more you can do. Get some rest. You look knackered.'

'You spoke to her mum?'

'The nurse had called her earlier and she called back not long after I arrived. She wanted to speak to someone who knew her. I'm going to call again shortly, now that I've been to see her.'

'How was she?'

'Distraught. Worried. Talking about flying over.'

'I meant Alice.'

'Unconscious. Breathing. Alive. Seriously, you should go home. You've done good.'

He was a colleague and, apparently, a lover. He already seemed more a part of her convalescence than I did. I'd spoken to the ex-boyfriend and got a dozen prank calls; he'd spoken to her mother and discussed travel plans.

'I guess I should.'

'I appreciate what you've done. You may have saved her life. You're a hero.'

I grinned as best I could. The lights really were getting too much in there and I could feel my phone vibrating constantly with more prank calls. I stood up and gathered my jacket from the seat between us.

'Thanks,' I said. 'Please call me when something happens. The nurse has my number.'

'You're on the list. And here, this is mine.'

He took out his wallet and removed a business card. I looked it over.

Trevor Whitmarsh
Polar Bears Club
Treasurer

'Thanks,' I said, seeing more and more how everything fitted together.

I headed for the exit and looked back as I reached the doors; Trevor was at the reception desk conversing with the nurse. She was nodding and responding as if he were a doctor. Somewhere two floors up, Alice was in a coma, her brain slowly losing touch.

*

I didn't check my phone until I got home. There were thirteen more prank calls and one from Janet. She'd also sent a text message.

How is she??

I went upstairs so I could reply.

Still in a coma. Her friend Trevor is with her now.

She wrote back straight away.

Okay. Thanks.

Then another message.

How are you?

I replied: *Confused.*

It's a difficult time.

Very.

I wish I could say something to make it easier for you. Just, hang in there, I guess.

Any news from Petra?

Well, I've been meaning to contact you about that. Her father has put the house up for sale.

They're moving? Where to??

He's under no obligation to tell us (or you) unfortunately.

What?! How will I know where she is?

Wherever he moves to, she'll be registered at the local school. So she'll reappear officially, but neither you nor I can get that information.

So that's it?

Unless he reoffends. In which case the local child welfare charity will be contacted.

I have to wait until he hits his girlfriend again?!

Hopefully he'll let you know where they've moved to.

This is fucked.

Janet didn't immediately reply. I laid on my bed, stared at the ceiling and listened to the tinnitus screaming in my ears. I had exactly the same amount of people in my life as a month ago, and yet I felt I'd lost everything. It was a couple of minutes before another message came through from Janet.

Do you have Trevor's number?

*

I called Trevor the next day and he returned it a few hours later. Nothing had changed. The following day I called again and got the same outcome. Hopes declined with every sunset. Then on Monday Trevor called me and said I should come down. Alice had woken up.

'Be prepared,' he advised, his voice sombre. 'She has some cognitive issues.'

I drove to the hospital and made my way to reception, where I was met by a counsellor whose name I didn't catch. She had jet-black hair, sad eyes and a tan. She explained Alice was awake and speaking, but had moderate paralysis on both sides of the body.

'She also has memory loss.'

'Memory loss? How bad?'

'She remembers that she was a teacher. She remembers some of her students and colleagues. Indeed most things up until about a month ago she has no problem recounting, with a few noticeable blank patches. She has no recollection of the event that led to her drowning, or of swimming in general, nor does she remember the name of her village or what her house looks like.'

'She doesn't remember swimming at all?'

'I'm afraid not. It's possible this is a trauma reaction, as opposed to a cognitive issue related to the hypoxia. However, she's also struggling to form new memories, so it could be that the part of her brain that performs that function also stored these particular memories.' She pressed a button to call the elevator. 'There's lots we understand about the brain, but much more that we don't.'

The doors opened and we stepped inside.

'Her parents are here and also friends and colleagues from school. She recognises all of them, which is positive. We find that the more familiarities a patient sees as they come out of a coma, the more the memory can be jolted back into action.'

The elevator stopped on the first floor, where a gurney with an old man on it was wheeled in by a large nurse. The counsellor and I shifted to the side.

'I understand you effected her rescue?'

The nurse looked at me out the side of his eye, casting it over my physicality.

'Yes,' I said, unsure how else to respond.

'She's unlikely to have a memory of that. However, it's possible she may recognise you as a face she saw around the village. Her friend Trevor said you run on the beach, so there's a chance you and Alice have crossed paths. The brain is a curious thing. It stores all kinds of information, some of it seemingly innocuous. But sometimes one of those tiny, irrelevant little memories can be the catalyst for unlocking something much bigger.'

The words *Alice and I made love numerous times in the forty-eight hours before the accident* formed in my mouth, but I couldn't bring myself to say them. Everyone seemed to have settled on the narrative, and our relationship was on the cutting-room floor.

The doors opened and the nurse pulled the gurney into the hallway, wheeling it to the right. We turned left.

'So, who knows?' the counsellor went on. 'Your face might be the tiny detail that opens the floodgates. And if we can bring her up to date, she might start forming new memories with more dexterity.'

We reached the double doors of her room. I wanted to look through the window, but the counsellor was still talking.

'Her speech is laboured and, like I said, she has some paralysis in her limbs. We're hoping these improve with time. Just stand by her side and make eye contact, say hello, ask if she remembers your face from the beach. If you're comfortable doing so, touch her hand. She probably won't feel it anyway, but anything can help at this stage.'

'What if she doesn't say anything to me?'

'Try and make a conversation and if she stays blank too long I'll step in, try and encourage her and then, if nothing is working, you can just wish her well and step away. No one expects anything miraculous; they're all extremely glad you happened to be there when she got into trouble.'

The counsellor pushed open the doors and let me in. Other than Alice there were five people in the room. On one side of the bed was a man of about sixty with short greying brown hair, broad shoulders and a comfortable paunch. His face was tanned and creased and his forearms, which were exposed by the short sleeves of his t-shirt, had a thick matting of hair. He stroked his daughter's unresponsive hand lovingly. A woman who could only have been Alice's mother sat opposite and sprung to her feet as I entered, wrapping me in a hug. She was of a similar height to her daughter, with slightly duller hair but the same blue-green eyes.

'Thank you for saving my girl,' she said, wiping a tear from her cheek.

'That's okay,' I replied stupidly.

Her husband came over and shook my hand firmly, looking like he might also lean in for an embrace, but finally edging back again and slapping me on the shoulder. He tried to say something but tears filled his eyes and it took all he had to stop them from spilling out. His wife put a hand on his chest but he backed away with a series of small nods to compose himself out of the limelight.

'Mrs Phillips,' Trevor said formally, 'as you've guessed, this is Felix. Felix, Alice's mother.'

'Hello,' I said.

'Please, call me Sophie. My husband's name is Peter.'

I turned to Peter and nodded. He seemed to appreciate being able to respond non-verbally.

'Trevor tells me you were running by when it happened. We're just so grateful. So grateful. I don't know what to say.'

We were only a few steps in from the door and Trevor had managed to put himself between me and Alice, blocking my view.

'You don't have to say anything,' I offered. 'It was just luck.'

'Thanks!' Peter called out from the bedside, his voice low and forced, falling apart at the edges. 'Just, bloody, thanks.' Then he ducked his face out of view again.

The counsellor moved in now and suggested I try talking to Alice. Sophie stepped aside as Trevor's hand hovered in mid-air, helpfully showing me the way to the bedside.

The other two people in the room, a woman in her fifties and a man in his thirties, I presumed to be fellow teachers. They stood in a corner and nodded back to me as I looked their way. Then I dared to settle my eyes on Alice, her body prone beneath blank white sheets, tubes coming from her limp arms, her hair frazzled and confused, resting on her shoulder. I looked everywhere but her eyes, afraid of what they'd say; but soon there was no other choice.

She looked back at me silently, her eyes searching my face like a child trying to understand the TV news. I forced a smile, said 'Hi' like an idiot, then added 'How are you?'

There was no recognition. When we'd made love half a life-time ago we had kept our eyes locked on each other's, our foreheads touching, sweat dripping down our temples. It was unscripted. A spontaneous, organic manifestation of the close-ness we both felt but hadn't yet developed the bravery to articulate. When we climaxed, maintaining that eye contact had seemed more important than abandoning everything for the pleasure. As a result the orgasms seemed to happen around us, to these bodies we were inhabiting, while Alice and I fell down an iris-shaped hole, wrapped in the universe. It was impossible to imagine it ever being compromised. It felt like discovering a truth – pushing through a door that only opened one way.

Yet Alice showed no signs of knowing who I was. She stared for a few more moments, blinked, squinted, then looked to her father.

'Water,' she uttered slowly, like the word had been chopped

in two and glued back together. Peter put a straw to her lips.

The counsellor stepped up and asked Alice if she recognised me. Alice's head moved slowly round and focused on the counsellor. She looked at her with the same blank face that she'd just shown me.

'Do you recognise Felix?' she repeated, pointing my way. Alice's eyes moved to me, then back to the counsellor. It was as if she was speaking another language. 'Do you remember seeing him on the beach while you were swimming? Do you remember the beach? Felix would sometimes be running while you were swimming. Have a look at his face, Alice, have a good luck. Can you do that?'

I felt like a dog in a pound being sold to a sceptical customer. Should I wipe my face with moisture to give the effect of sweat? Should I have worn my compression tights? Alice tilted her head my way. I had the impression she felt I was a stranger trying to nudge his way into her life, somehow. She eyed me with distrust, contempt even. How could she have possibly known someone like *this*? She looked down the bed to her feet.

'Trevor,' she said, the two syllables gliding together on the *v*.

Trevor stepped forward, bumping me gently to the side while grabbing her hand. It looked pale and dead in his, like a fillet of fish left on the cold-room floor.

'Trevor,' she said again. 'School tomorrow.'

'Not for you,' he replied, rubbing her hand as if it made any difference. 'You've got to rest and get better.'

'She's remembering school really well,' the counsellor remarked. 'She's determined, too. It's a good sign.'

The woman who had been in the corner moved towards the bed now and suggested she might bring some students in to see if that stimulated more memories. Trevor cut her down before the counsellor could answer.

'I don't think it'll do her or the children any good, Simone,' he said. 'She needs rest.' He looked at me sideways and then moved a little closer to Alice. I backed away to give him room. He took more.

'I imagine there might be some resistance from the children's parents,' the counsellor suggested, 'though it's worth considering. All ideas are welcome.'

'She needs rest,' Trevor reiterated.

I moved away from the bed, unsure what to do with myself. Sophie moved closer, shuffling me further back, then Simone took up a position in the line-up. Soon I was by the door, my only view of the woman who'd taken my breath away in her blue dress being her two inert feet, beneath sheets like dust protected furniture.

Seeing me near the door the counsellor mouthed a *thank you*, then returned her attention to Alice. I backed away, hesitated, then pushed through.

I was waiting at the elevator doors, letting the tears well to the surface, when someone called my name. Looking back down the hallway I saw the other teacher jogging towards me. He was good-looking, with sharp blue eyes and shoulder-length blond hair. Well-built too. I guessed he was the PE teacher and hated myself for fleetingly wondering if Alice had ever fancied him, or maybe even dated him like she had Trevor.

'Sorry, mate,' he said, catching up to me. 'I'm Max. We spoke on the phone the other day.'

It took a few moments for the name to register, but then it fell into place like a Tetris block.

'Oh. Max. Of course. Hi.' I tried to blink out the tears as I shook his hand.

'Listen, mate. Sorry about the other day. I thought you were one of those scammers selling insurance and shit. They fuckin' shit me.'

'Yes,' I replied, unable to shake the image of him as a twat. 'Unwanted calls are annoying.'

'Yeah, sorry if any of me mates gave you a hard time. It was only when Peter rang that I realised you were for real. I deleted all the posts about it. Hopefully you didn't get too much hassle.'

The elevator door slid open and two female nurses emerged and turned off down the hall. Max watched them, squinting, as if to sharpen his focus.

'Some of them were actually quite humorous,' I offered.

He turned back. 'I've got some funny mates.'

I made to enter the elevator but Max grabbed my arm.

'So you were running past, ay?' he asked, a smidgen of scepticism traceable beneath his thick antipodean accent. 'Lucky.'

'I was,' I replied, sliding my jumper from his grip. 'And yes. Very.'

He looked me up and down, either getting a sense of my build or assessing my dress sense. The elevator doors sucked shut.

'No one else around?'

'It's a quiet beach at this time of the year,' I explained. 'Although a woman did come along as I got her out of the water.'

'Oh yeah? Did she see what happened?'

'I don't know.' He was most definitely a twat and I was completely out of subservience. 'Why? Is there a doubt?'

'No, mate,' he said, shaking his head with a stupid grin. 'No. Mate.' He looked me over again, then seemed to come to an understanding with himself. 'Nah, I'm just fuckin' with yah. Say, who's this Trevor bloke? Was Alice seein' him? Doesn't look like her type.'

Did he think that only he was her type? Would only another chest-beating alpha male have done? Someone he could brawl with to decide who gets to climb the nearest tall building and swat at passing planes?

'I understand they had been, yes,' I said. 'But I didn't really know her, so I couldn't say for sure.'

'Ahh, that's right. You were just runnin' past.'

The elevator door opened again, allowing another nurse out into the hall. I walked through the doors and turned around.

'That's right. Just running past.' I pressed the G button.

'On that quiet beach in the tiny village you both live in.'

I nodded. The doors slid shut and the last thing I saw of Max was his right eye winking at me.

*

The tears that I nearly cried at the elevator were all that came. I sat in my car waiting for more, but though I was able to conjure them to the back of my eyes, they didn't break the seal. I put it down to a numbness and drove off, but as the hours went by and I sat at home looking through the window at the charcoal trees and the rooks lining the limbs, and at the sharp apex of her A-framed roof poking into the sky behind them, I began to realise it was that old familiar blanket settling into place. It had been waiting ever since I ran off down the beach, leaving her to swim out into the lough and the snare of whatever it was that dragged her under.

I lit a fire and watched it climb to life before collapsing in on itself. I added more kindling, let it build up again, then plonked a splintered log on top, after which I sat cross-legged in front of the flames, my chin on my knees, warming my shins until they stung. Outside the twitching corpse of an Atlantic storm blew exhausted winds through the leafless trees, and threw sporadic hailstones sideways at the windows, making sounds like popcorn going off in a microwave.

I had soup for dinner, because it didn't require much of me, and left the unwashed saucepan in the sink. I sat in the armchair in front of the fire and finished *Metamorphosis*, not caring or thinking much about what it all meant. The fire died down and I added the last of the kindling, but had no more logs. I wasn't tired. When the flames again began to subside I looked around the house for things to burn. There was cardboard in the recycling, which singed black first, then contorted, like it was suffering stomach cramps. When that was all gone I tore the pages from *Metamorphosis* and added them, one by one. Then I tossed the gutted spine of the book in and watched the cover blister, fizz and spew out dark smoke like an old diesel engine.

Then it immolated and the flames jetted out sideways, the base of them blue and angry, like a ruptured gas valve.

I woke the next day at two in the afternoon, made coffee and had some toast. Habitually I checked my phone but there was no communication. The next day it was the same. And the day after that.

I'd always said that I run because it kept my head above the parapet, but it occurred to me then, as I sunk into the familiar mud of depression, the error in my terminology. The parapet was a defensive wall. Putting your head above the parapet made you vulnerable. I'd been doing it all wrong.

I stopped running. I stopped shaving. After two weeks I stopped checking my phone. I was nearly out of things to stop doing. After a month I stopped shopping.

At some point in late February, when there were no more tins of soup left in the pantry, I went outside for the first time in a fortnight. By now the days were substantially longer and no matter how late I got up, the sun would still spend a few more hours making its way to the horizon. It even got above the height of the charcoal trees, and on clear days it would descend over a pastel-blue sky that looked cartoonish when viewed through the narrow gap in my curtains.

I shuffled along the cold, wet driveway to the skeletal flower bush that stood all but naked against the chipped white wall. The half-blossomed flower was still there, its pink petals weathered but unbeaten, held tight by the cocoon like grip of the green leathery bud.

I pinched my thumb and forefinger underneath this freak of nature, gripped firmly and pulled upwards. It felt about to pop off when a small van pulled into the driveway. I relaxed my grip on the flower without letting it go. The driver pulled up beside me, lowered his window and observed me curiously for a few moments.

'Is your name Felix?' he finally asked. He wore a light blue collared shirt with an obscured logo on the chest.

I nodded.

'Great,' he said, reaching to the passenger seat. 'I think this is for you.'

He handed me a postcard, then performed a three-point turn and drove away. I watched him exit right out of the driveway, and listened to his tyres, tacky on the wet bitumen road, swiftly fade away.

The picture on the postcard was an old drawing of the Titanic, with black smoke curling out of its smokestacks. I flipped it over and recognised the handwriting immediately.

Dear Uncle Felix

I miss you. I have moved to Jersey with dad and Karen and am going to a new school which is OK. Karen says we can visit you soon. I hope it is really soon. Say hi to the horsey and the doggys.

Love Petra your niece

I took my fingers from around the throat of the pink flower, walked across the garden, down through the dunes and sat on the beach beside the mermaid bath. The tide was out and seagulls were drifting by, cutting tiny wakes through the glassy surface. Above, sporadic rooks crossed the lough, some coming, some going, none making any noises in particular. A fishing boat chugged by, too far away for me to make out the name. I reread the postcard. Tears tumbled down my face unhindered, as salty as the water that claimed my sister, that stole Alice. I let them out, every last one, and sat shivering by the mermaid bath by the time they were done. Then I dipped my hand in it, into the bubbling fresh water that emerged from beneath the sand. I washed my face and felt the sting of the wind on my wet skin.

My stomach grumbled. I needed to buy food. Carbohydrates. Pasta.

—◦ 26 ◦—

Alice

While I was sleeping I had a dream so intense that it felt as if my entire being was wrapped up in it. I was cocooned in its omnipotence and held safe there, carried willingly down whichever unmapped node of my subconscious it felt I needed to visit.

But when I woke the dream ebbed away like the tide. Firstly the outlines of the shapes went, melting into the background until they were indistinguishable. Then the colours left me too, draining away as if through a hole in the bottom of a painter's bucket. I was left with a void of imagery, but with the consolation of an echo of the feeling that accompanied it. I lay there, barely able to move, on a strange bed in an unfamiliar room, clinging to this profound reverence. Every so often I'd make sense of my situation by noticing a tube coming from my arm or a person talking to me, but then those things would swirl down the bucket hole too and I'd return to that dream sensation. For a few days it was the only reality I had and the only one I wanted.

Slowly, however, the real world gained traction. Around me, doctors and specialists asked me questions, told me how I should be reacting, that I wasn't to worry and that I was in good hands. They told me not to rush trying to remember things. I don't know how you can rush remembering. You either do or you don't; there's no effort you can put in. Some memories are cloudy sheaths of secrets, locked in safes with codes so complex there's no hope of cracking them.

They continued to try though and spoke to me like I was worse than I was. No doubt this was largely down to my inability to speak properly, which was incredibly frustrating. But in reality light began to shine on my memories a few days after I woke up. I recognised my parents nearly straight away, as well as Simone and Trevor from school. When I first saw Max my heart jumped with excitement. My mind lit up with happy memories from Brisbane and of the house we shared together, of trips to New Zealand and Thailand. It was like they were all just waiting for a trigger to lurch out of the fog and his face was it. However, then there was something else, cloudier than the earlier memories. Recollections of London and of me sitting home alone, something coming between us. Did we break up? I looked to Max and tried to ask about it, but my speech was slow and the doctors, and Trevor, told me to get some rest.

I had no memory of the incident that put me in hospital, or of almost anything over the last month or so. It wasn't a clear cut though, where I remembered nothing from a particular date forward and most things before then. It was more of a tear. I remembered school, the performance of *Bugsy Malone* we put on and I remembered talking with Trevor about his pending divorce. I remembered a few things about my house – silly stuff like having no WiFi and the colour of the paint in the bedroom, but I didn't remember the house itself nor almost anything about the village.

'You don't remember the beach?' Trevor asked. 'Swimming in the lough?'

'I remember swimming on the Gold Coast with Max,' I replied, though not as quickly and dextrously as that suggests.

Trevor seemed dismayed by this, but what else could I say other than what lit up in my mind? My memories of him were mostly clear, I thought. We got on well at school and I remembered fancying him a little, wondering what I would do if his divorce came through and he made a move.

One of the only other things I could recall from the village was a vague image of birds. It wasn't a specific memory of anything in particular, rather *something* to do with birds. And a pineapple. Black birds, a pineapple and Russell Crowe. I didn't articulate this as I didn't know how to. Fog drifted over large parts of my mind and I had the impression unnatural connections were being made in desperation.

Soon they started bringing in people I apparently had more incidental and recent connections with. The specialist hoped that they might spark my short-term memory. But they may as well have been actors auditioning for roles in my life, as there was nothing I saw in them that I could recall. The first was a man who looked to be in his late forties, with short, dark hair, big arms and a thick chest.

'Hi Alice,' he said. 'Do you remember meeting me when you arrived in Rathmullan? I gave you the key to your cottage.'

I could only smile at him politely, or try to, since my face didn't really work. 'No,' I said. 'Sorry.'

'Try, Alice,' the specialist insisted, as if squinting or gritting my teeth might turn this stranger into an old friend.

The next was another man, perhaps five years younger, a balding scalp above a round face. He looked nervous but Trevor, who was acting quite differently to how I remembered, shepherded him to my bedside and encouraged him to speak to me.

'How you doing there, Alice?' he asked.

'Fantastic,' I answered, though I suspect the tone was lost in my delivery.

'You remember Connor don't you, Alice?' Trevor asked.

I studied his face, attempting to give the impression of *trying* so that the specialist wouldn't ask me to, but it quickly felt awkward. Staring at strangers' faces while they pretended to be your friends was horribly disconcerting.

In between these visits the doctors took blood samples and adjusted my tubes, making it look as though they were helping. But what could they do, really? They said themselves that my recovery would depend on how badly affected my brain was and beyond that on my willpower. Yet still they hovered around and studied me, huddling together every now and then to look at a chart. On one occasion I witnessed a doctor come in and take the specialist who was always on about me trying to remember things, aside. They spoke for a few moments, then both looked at me in a way that you learn quite quickly in hospitals means something unexpected has been found. They whispered for a few more moments and then the specialist shook her head and the doctor nodded. But what it all meant, they didn't share with me. The specialist just returned to my bedside and continued with her questions that I didn't have answers to.

'Do you remember what colour car you drove?'

'No.'

'I bet you had a favourite dress you wore on special occasions.'

'Probably.'

'Did you have a boyfriend in Rathmullan, Alice?'

'I don't remember.'

The next day they brought in yet another man. I wondered if there was anything they weren't telling me about any of them. This one was a bit closer to my age, with a full head of black hair and a furrowed brow, as if he spent most of his time worried about one thing or another. My mum got up and hugged him as soon as he entered and said something to him that I didn't quite catch. Then my dad shook his hand before returning to my side. It was a strange scene but in some ways typical of the way people were acting around me. I just wanted them to be normal. It was difficult watching dad nearly crying and Trevor fussing about. I felt fairly normal inside, I just couldn't remember everything or walk properly. But I was the same person and I was going to get better.

The black-haired man approached my bedside cautiously and then looked me over as if considering a disappointing selection of cold meats. When finally he got round to looking me in the eye he said something inane like *how are you?* Seriously, how did I look like I was? I didn't recognise him at all and was quite tired of being paraded like this. I glared back at him, trying to repel his penetrative stare. Then there was a flash, like lightning behind a cloud behind a mountain. It didn't bring any memories, just the suggestion that there was one somewhere. It confused me briefly and then the feeling of it was gone. I squinted at the man again, trying to recall what had just happened, but the clouds thickened and whatever was there was lost.

I asked my dad for a drink of water and hoped that would be the end of the parade, but the counsellor insisted I try some more. She gave me some prompts, again something to do with the beach and swimming, but being told to recall these activities and this place of which I had absolutely no recollection was extremely frustrating. It made me feel like everyone in the room was in on a joke of which I was the butt. I turned to the man again, pretended to try and then looked to Trevor, who was hovering nearby as always. I told him I was going to go to school tomorrow. Thankfully he took the bait and soon the black-haired man was gone.

There was one last guest. This time it was a beautiful woman of about thirty with long braided hair, along with her handsome boyfriend who wore a denim jacket with a woollen lining. She was sweet and bubbly and talked to me like I was normal and nothing was wrong.

'We got engaged!' she told me, brandishing a silver ring on her left hand.

I smiled back and said congratulations. It was a shame I had no idea who she was.

*

Then one day the specialist and one of the doctors entered my room like a pair of bumbling secret agents. The specialist asked my mum if she could slip in beside the bed and run a few tests. Then, as she waved her finger in front of my face and started talking in a pathetic attempt to distract me, the doctor whisked my mum outside.

'Your friend Trevor seems nice,' the specialist said.

'Mmm,' I replied.

'Lovely eyes.'

'I guess,' I replied.

'He seems very fond of you.'

'Where's Mum?'

Shortly the door opened and my mum entered with a startled look on her face. The specialist abandoned her inquisition and moved aside so mum could retake her place by my side. She rubbed my arm and tried to smile at me.

'What's wrong?' I asked.

'Oh Alice,' she began, tears filling her eyes. 'Alice, you're pregnant.'

As she leaned in to hug me I had a sudden sense of déjà vu. But it came with what felt like real memories. A clinic, an ultrasound, a blue jacket. I struggled to make sense of it all. And then, just as the memories came they went again and I was left grasping at the echoes they left.

'Max,' I said in desperation.

'Max is the father?' Mum asked. 'Are you sure, Alice? He said he hasn't seen you for over six months.'

'Max …'

My mum looked across at the specialist and said, 'He's a good boy, he wouldn't lie to me.'

The doctor, a woman in her thirties, bit her lip.

'What about Trevor, Alice?' the specialist asked. 'We were wondering if maybe you were more than just friends. Do you remember?'

Another sudden burst of memories. A fire, Trevor's eyes, his hairline, a discussion about condoms.

'Trevor?'

Right on cue the door opened and Trevor, Max and my dad walked in with cups of coffee and grins that quickly fell away.

'What is it?' Trevor asked.

'Peter, you better sit down,' my mum said.

Dad rushed to my side and looked me over like he might be able to fix the problem, whatever it was, by thumping it with the base of his fist.

'Is she okay?' Trevor was in his last few moments of innocence.

Mum was suddenly very matriarchal. 'Well, Trevor,' she explained, 'that depends on what you can tell us.' Then she turned to Max. 'And you, Maxwell.'

'What the bloody hell's going on, Sophie?' Dad blurted.

'Peter,' mum breathed out purposefully, 'our daughter is pregnant and she can't remember who the father is.'

My dad looked me over, suddenly unlike the worried father he had been since he arrived and instead like the man I knew growing up, only with a sadness that he betrayed with the smallest tear in his right eye.

'My girl,' he whispered, and I could just about feel his hand touching mine.

Then he turned to Max and fixed him with a glare.

'Peter, I promise,' Max said, his palms exposed in front of him. 'I haven't seen her for donkey's. And I've got Lucy at home. She's three months herself.'

Dad's glare took in Max's story, then slid over to Trevor. It was the first time I'd seen Trevor look terrified. His hazel eyes widened and he ran his hand through his hair. Though the memories I'd just experienced had already faded away, the one about his hairline came flashing back.

'Jesus, Mary and Joseph,' he uttered.

The next few minutes were a blur that I struggled to keep up with. All this new information was careening into my brain and scrambling for footholds to hang on to. A lot fell away, lost for the time being into foggy wastelands, but some managed to find familiar ledges. Max, for example, and his pregnant girlfriend. It fit, somehow, and though I wasn't exactly sure how, I was able to hang on to it as information that made sense.

Then there was Trevor. When I concentrated on his face I

could just about recall seeing it up close, his smell and the way he breathed through his nose. It was awkward having these tiny, faint memories, as otherwise I only recalled him as a colleague and friend at school. It was as if he had had a relationship with me while I was unconscious, and I definitely wasn't comfortable with the knowledge that he could remember sleeping with me yet I couldn't with him. The whole thing made me feel sick.

But there was nothing I could do. Everyone else was talking fast and I could only lie and watch them, ignored as I tried to ask for clarification.

'Why didn't you mention this, Trevor?' my mum asked.

'It didn't seem appropriate.'

'You were dating my daughter. How was that not appropriate?'

'Well it was early days—'

'You going to support my grandchild, son?'

'Of course, Peter. Of course ... When she gets better we, er, we could get married. I mean, with your permission.'

'Please tell me that wasn't your proposal.'

'We hadn't discussed it, obviously, but, it's the right thing to do.'

'Don't you already have kids?'

'Yes, two—'

'How you gonna support a third child on a teacher's salary?'

As this went on, my eyes settled on the doctor. She was politely letting the discussion go back and forth, as if she knew they had to get it out of their systems. But it was obvious she had something to add. She turned to face me, our eyes met for a moment and she smiled sympathetically. I already knew what she was going to say.

'I can't have it,' I uttered through my half-paralysed face.

Nobody heard me.

'Can I?'

My mum placed her hand on my arm instinctively but

continued to focus on Trevor and my dad. The doctor studied me from the foot of the bed, squinted, then cleared her throat.

'If I may intervene,' she said firmly.

The room fell silent.

'Alice's condition,' she explained, 'is fragile. The early stages of pregnancy are the most delicate, and she has been through a significant trauma. Frankly, it's a miracle the foetus has survived this long.'

'My girl is strong,' my mother said proudly.

'She is. But her body's priority is itself,' she paused, 'and she has a lot of healing still to do.'

Max had moved himself to the corner of the room once Trevor claimed ownership of the child inside of me. However, now he stepped forward again.

'So carrying a baby is going to mess with her recovery?'

'To a degree, but it's the foetus that's most at risk.'

'You mean it might be born fucked up?'

'Maxwell!'

'He's right,' my dad said, suddenly a doctor. 'That's what she's getting at.'

'What I'm saying,' the doctor interjected, 'is that there are risks to both Alice and the foetus.'

Max, again, cut to the chase. 'So she should abort.' He said it as if giving directions to the clinic.

'Perhaps Trevor would like a say in this,' my mum added pointedly.

'Jesus, Mary and Joseph.'

'Stop bringing them into it,' Dad replied.

'You can't,' Trevor muttered, 'I can't . . .'

'Speak up! What can't you do?'

'Abort a baby—'

'You don't have to abort anything,' Dad answered sternly. 'My daughter does.'

'No.' Trevor shook his head. 'She can't. Not in Ireland.'

'What are you talking about?'

'It's the law.'

'Her life's in danger!'

As Trevor stood there shaking his head I struggled to comprehend that I had been naked with him. Somehow now, bedridden and paralysed, I saw him more clearly than I evidently did while able of body and mind a month ago. There was no way I was going to marry him and the thought of having his baby was equally repulsive.

'It's my choice,' I said as best I could.

Trevor continued to shake his head, 'No, Alice,' he said quietly. 'It's not.'

I looked to the doctor for confirmation, like she was the judge and jury in the matter.

'The foetus isn't a risk to your *life*, Alice,' she said, with the slightest hint of apology.

*

That afternoon I forgot I was pregnant. Mum reminded me as she fixed the flowers in a vase by my bed, but then I forgot again until after dinner, when Max came to say goodbye.

'How's this sound?' he said. 'If mine is a girl, I'll call it Alice, and if yours is a boy, you call it Max.'

'My what?'

He shook his head and gently tapped my stomach through the sheets. I still didn't fully grasp what he was saying, but nodded anyway.

'You know what?' he went on. 'I actually thought it might be that guy who pulled you from the water.'

I had no idea who he was talking about.

'He looked more your type. You know, worried.'

'You're not worried,' I managed to reply.

'Maybe that's why you left me.'

A rush of memories fell from the fog: Max cheating on me, me getting pregnant, having an abortion. But the fog quickly descended again and I grappled to try and make sense of their content.

'I left you because ...' I wanted to tell him what I thought was true but the memories jostled for position, perhaps in fear of being forgotten again, and the words got caught up in my mouth. In the end all I managed to utter was '... abortion.'

Max looked confused. He began to speak, then squinted and shook his head.

'You can't get an abortion here, Alice,' he said. 'And look, to be honest, you're probably not going to need to. The doc reckons you'll lose it soon anyway.'

That's when I realised he was talking about a baby that was inside me now, not back then. Trying to keep a hold of where and when things were was very difficult. But I recalled the discussion now, if tenuously, about Trevor and me. And I felt the horrible weight of what it all meant descend on me again.

'Ah shit,' Max said. 'Sorry. I'm not good with all this. Lucy says I speak before I think. I'm not sure I really think at all.'

He knew himself better than anyone.

'Tell me about Lucy,' I said, wanting to forget my predicament.

*

That was the pattern for the next few weeks. Someone or something would remind me of the human growing inside me and I'd be thrown into a mild, bedridden panic. Then the familiarity of the memory would occur to me and the panic would subside, replaced by worry. I'd dwell on it for a while, get distracted by something new, and it'd be forgotten again.

By the time they moved me to the specialist care facility though, my feelings began to change. I felt sorry for the unborn child, already up against it by having a half-paralysed mother; the least I could do, if my body wasn't going to help it out, was try to remember that it existed. But the more I grew used to the idea, the less everyone else seemed to want to talk about it. I'd mention it to the doctor and she'd breeze over it and ask whether I had any more feeling in my hands. Trevor stopped coming to see me, and even my mother, before she went back to Australia, told me to just worry about my own recovery and let everything else run its course. Soon it came to feel like this bizarre little secret I was keeping from everyone.

*

The plain white walls of the specialist care facility were enough to send anyone brain-dead, let alone someone with a head start. I hated it. It felt like a retirement home. They talked to me as if to a child unaware of the dangers of sharp edges. I was improving slowly, but I had the impression that unless I suddenly sprung out of bed and sung like Kylie Minogue, all anyone saw was an invalid. If I could have gripped a pen strong enough, long enough, I would have written out exactly how I felt.

When they moved me there I was told it was to help stimulate my recovery. But around me were people with half their faces not working, those who flew off the handle at the slightest aggravation, and others who needed two nurses just to plonk them in front of the television each morning. It was more depressing than stimulating.

Soon they started bringing in stuff they claimed was from my 'old life'. I didn't recognise a thing. Instead I felt resentment for being pushed this way and that, for being talked down to, for being treated like I was the same as the invalids sitting in front of the television all day. I could do all the things they wanted me to do, just not yet.

'Do you recognise your flippers today, Alice?'

My rehabilitation nurse's name was Siobhan. She was a kind woman in her mid-fifties, with short white curly hair and a slim figure. She was still quite beautiful, I thought, but she must have been stunning in her twenties. Some days I despised her while on others she felt like a friend. When she flapped those stupid flippers in front of me it was the former, but when she talked to me like a normal person I relaxed and could feel the memories I had lost crying out behind a grey foggy mist.

Siobhan would strap me in to a ridiculous contraption and

together we would plod past the other patients' rooms, their befuddled faces staring out at me, on past the television room and the snack machine, through the block of pale light that spilled lethargically through the glass doors of the foyer, and on down to the end of the hall. There we undertook an elaborate turning manoeuvre and headed back. When we first started, I couldn't make it to the TV room, but after a month or so I could conquer the full journey. We didn't set any land speed records along the way though, so Siobhan had plenty of time to tell me about herself.

'I was married once,' she said the first time we paused for a break.

'Were you?' I replied, though wanted to add *for how long, where did you meet him, did you have any kids, you say 'once', so what happened to him?* My brain worked faster than my mouth but Siobhan seemed to understand.

'Oh yes,' she answered. 'He was a fisherman out of Rathmullan. That's where you live. That's where I first met you.'

She told me this a number of times, but I usually forgot. Apparently she was there when I was rescued, even called the ambulance. She said a nice young man helped me from the water and breathed air into my lungs to keep me alive. Apparently he came to visit me in the hospital, but I didn't remember the rescue or the man. I didn't remember the water or the swimming or the beach or anyone from the village. Every time someone mentioned them I could feel a drawbridge being pulled up in my brain.

But when she told me of her husband she made it sound almost like a fairy tale, and for some reason I was able to hang on to some of the details. When I saw her the next day I would remember parts of it and then ask her to tell me again so I could fill in the blanks. With each retelling I could feel the roots dig in a little deeper and the images her words created forming bolder outlines.

'We went to the same school in Letterkenny,' she explained.

'He was a couple of years older than me and got the same bus home as I did every day. But he was a shy boy and wouldn't speak to me or anyone else. Some of the students said he was odd, that something was wrong with him, but mostly everyone left him alone and being that he was quite tall and broad-shouldered, none of the boys teased him. He got off a few villages before me and, unlike the rest of us, he never looked up to the windows as he walked off to give a final wave to a friend. I never saw him speak to anyone, at school or on the bus.

'One Saturday I was with my mum and our car broke down trying to drive up an icy hill on the edge of his village. She managed to park it on the side of the road with the back bumper up against a tree, and then went off to get help. It was cold so mum told me to wait in the car – you didn't need to worry about bad people in those days. I wrapped myself up in some blankets my dad kept in case of emergencies just like this, and I sat in the front seat and waited, watching the snow-flakes fall like they'd been shaken out of a sack in the sky. I don't know how long I was asleep for when suddenly the door swung open and I was wrenched out and thrown to the ground. Moments later a lorry came sliding down the hill and smashed into the car, squeezing it against the tree like an accordion. I looked up and there was Felix, standing over me.'

Every time she told me the story she paused at this point and glanced at me. I would smile and nod and tell her I remembered.

'But please tell me the rest,' I'd say. New memories felt warm inside my head and that warmth felt like it might burn the fog away. I wanted to add more logs to the fire.

'Felix gave me his hand,' she continued, 'and I wrapped my fingers around his. He didn't say anything, just helped me up and smiled. But our eyes were locked together and I knew then, in a way I didn't understand as a young girl, and barely understood any better as a woman, that we were in love. My mum was running down the hill by this stage, slipping and falling herself. She gathered me up in a big hug, apologising for leaving me alone. But I was fine. She didn't know Felix had saved me so gave him short shrift, assuming he was a nosy bystander. He drifted away before I could explain and by then there were other things to worry about, what with the car being wrecked and so on.

'Anyway, from then on, Felix always looked out for me. If the bus was full and I didn't have a seat, he would give me his. When I was running late, he would stand in front of it, pretending to do up his shoelace so it wouldn't drive off without me. And he always glanced up at the window as he got off, catching my eye. I would spend the whole day looking forward to that one moment.'

When she first told me this part, about the eye contact, I felt a flash of something, like lightning that never leaves the cloud. It was fleeting and impossible to grasp but it was definitely there. I rested my hand on my stomach and continued to listen to Siobhan.

'Felix finished school and for two years he was no longer on the bus; but twice, three times a week, as it passed through his village, he would find an excuse to be near the stop when it did. Then in my last year all my girlfriends encouraged me to get off at his stop the next time he was there. So I did. The bus drove off and I stood there, not knowing what to do. He just looked at me and I looked back, then I thought this is silly, so walked up to him and told him he had to say something to me or else I was never going to look his way again. He pulled out a notepad and pencil from his pocket and wrote, *Sorry, I can't speak, my voice doesn't work. Never has.* He handed me the notebook and shrugged his shoulders in apology. I took the pencil and wrote, *How will I know when you want to say something?* And he wrote back, *I'll squeeze your hand.*'

Sometimes Siobhan would squeeze my hand when she told this part. It was a little thing but it helped make the story real.

In many ways the distant sensation of her grip was kind of like my memory – there, but only just.

'He showed me to his house where he lived with his mother. His dad had disappeared when he was very young. His mother was a wonderful woman who spoke lovingly of her son, of everything he did around the house, his love for fishing. I spent more and more time with her and learned of the things she had tried to get his voice to work. Initially she had prayed, but when that got her nowhere she experimented. She tried hanging horseshoes from his bedroom door, wearing her stockings inside out, visiting holy wells, collecting bullaun stones, astrology, tarot cards. Nothing worked and by the time I started seeing him she had accepted he would never speak; however, she had become fascinated by superstitions and folk tales. We would sit around talking about them all evening, Felix listening in and chuckling in his muted way. He would squeeze my hand and write, *My mum is a bit crazy, sorry.*

'In time we got married and got ourselves a house in Rathmullan. Felix's mum would come over for dinner and we would talk about whatever silly superstition she had read about that week. It was good fun. She passed away ten years ago now. Felix ran his boat in Lough Swilly and out into the Atlantic if the weather allowed it. We had a good life. Often we both used the notepad to communicate. You'd be surprised how tender you can be when writing a note to someone. Just adding their name can make all the difference. Even with simple things, I'd still write *Felix. Tea?* And he would write back *Siobhan, you're an angel.* He had been doing it all his life so was much better at expressing himself than I was. To compensate I learnt a little calligraphy.'

When she got to this point in the story she would always pause and, depending on how she felt, either go on to tell me what happened when he died, or change the subject. I remembered well enough though. He went out fishing one morning and his boat was found two days later, overturned and sinking near the lighthouse at Fanad Head. Felix couldn't swim.

'I tried every superstitious trick in the book to bring his body back to me,' she explained when feeling up to it. 'Burning a candle all the way down, giving away precious heirlooms, offering money to the sea witch. I even took up swimming in the lough, just like you, in the hope he might have been a selkie and he'd come to me as a seal. It took me the best part of two years, but in the end I had to accept he was gone. I wrote him a final note and threw it into the lough.'

*

I had a calendar in my room but as my short term memory improved I was able to wake up in the morning and remember not just where I was, but what time of year it was. I could look out the window and see the trees were more knobbly than they had been a week ago. I could tell that the sun was longer in the sky and the blue that accompanied it – on rare clear days at least – was a lighter shade than it had been. Insects started to appear. You don't notice these things, not in the detail I did, unless you're seeking evidence of change. With the first butterfly of spring I felt not just the warm glow of nature's re-emergence, but of my own.

There was, of course, one other sign that time was moving steadily along: my secret was making my tummy bigger. For the three months I'd been in the facility, no one had wanted to discuss it, hoping, no doubt, that it would just go away. Even Siobhan, in every other way my ally, had avoided the topic. But as my clothes started to show a bump that couldn't be ignored, things began to change. The doctors started doing more tests and actually mentioned the baby as a thing that existed. Then Trevor visited.

Until that point I hadn't seen him since moving into the facility. He had sent flowers early on, along with a card and a forgettable message that I suspect was written by the florist. But I hadn't replied to thank him and, with a little help from my colander memory, had all but forgotten about him. But now he edged into my room cautiously, like I might have rigged a tripwire. He said hello and, realising I wasn't armed, looked me over as I rested in my bed following a session with Siobhan. Raindrops ran down the window in stops and starts, like the see-through husks of empty cars in traffic.

'You probably don't remember,' he started, 'but before your accident, you nearly had another one.'

'I drowned?'

'No,' he said, adding humbly, 'I got there before you went under.'

'Oh. Well, thanks.'

'And then about a week or two later it nearly happened again.'

'I thought I loved swimming,' I replied. 'Sounds like I was terrible at it.'

'You were a brilliant swimmer,' Trevor acknowledged, 'you just had some bad luck.'

When he spoke like this I felt less inclined to hate him for making me pregnant.

'That was the length of our relationship,' he continued. 'It started with one near drowning and ended with another. Less than two weeks.'

I was shocked. All this time, even as I'd tucked the very existence of Trevor away to the shifting sands part of my memory, I had assumed our relationship had gone on for months.

'That's why you haven't visited,' I said, only then realising it had bugged me. 'But why did . . .'

'We break up?'

I nodded sheepishly. I had a nagging suspicion his kids may have been an issue for me. Or his hairline. Possibly his age. Looking at him now I could see so many reasons.

'I . . . I ended it,' he said.

'You?'

'Why is that so surprising?'

I chuckled. The first time in ages. 'It just is. Why didn't you want me?'

'I did. But it was too soon after my divorce and, honestly Alice, I didn't think you really wanted me. We were friends and you were lonely.'

'You took advantage, you bastard.'

'I was lonely too, just in a different way. I missed the companionship of ...'

'A marriage?'

'I guess.'

A gust of wind blew some raindrops onto the window and slid a plastic chair in the courtyard a few inches.

'Cards on the table, Alice. Do you want to have this child?'

I paused. 'Don't you?'

'The Catholic in me does. But the Catholic in me also expects a child to be a product of marriage, and of marriage to be to the grave. There's a whole bunch of stuff.' He leaned in a little closer. 'A little secret, Alice. I'm not much of a Catholic.'

'What are you saying?'

'I guess that, you know, if you want to take care of it, then I would ... help.'

'An abortion? But I thought the law ...'

'The law applies in Ireland and the north. But in England or Wales—'

'But, how ...'

'I could take you out for a few days. I've already spoken to the doctors; they say you're strong enough to spend a few days out in someone reliable's care. I can make all the arrangements, get us tickets to London. We could be there and back again in a couple of days. You could leave on a Friday and make a long weekend of it.'

I hadn't realised as I could barely feel it, but I noticed now that my hand had slid down to my stomach and was resting on the small bump there. Trevor continued to focus on my face.

'I loved it when we were friends, Alice, without the complications. We had a laugh. I think you preferred that too, even during those two weeks. It'd be nice to have that again, don't you think?'

I nodded slowly.

'I could help you get better. Get you swimming again – it's bound to be good for your recovery. And you'll be able to return to teaching sooner. I can help with staging another play. You were so great at that. Do you remember *Bugsy Malone*?'

Again I nodded. I could remember *Bugsy*, more or less, and the joy I had in watching it come together. I missed that. I missed my old life – moving freely, chatting and flirting, being responsible for kids for only six hours a day. At least I was pretty sure I did. My memory wasn't that great.

Trevor's big hazel eyes were on mine. I felt a tremor of memory come back to me, though couldn't place it exactly. Was it Trevor the brief lover or Trevor the friend? He took my hand from my tummy and held it between us.

'I want what's best for you. I want the old Alice back.'

'Me too,' I replied, and though it made me sick to my stomach, I knew it was the right thing to do.

*

I put myself in Trevor's hands and tried to move the thought of the child inside me to the same crumbly ground that I had put Trevor on previously. It was definitely the right thing to do. He couldn't afford another child. I couldn't. What kind of family would it be brought up in? I'd have to move back to Australia and get my parents' help. Then it'd truly be a child without a father. No, this was the right decision. Definitely.

As Trevor made the arrangements I continued my recovery otherwise. I could walk with the aid of a Zimmer frame now, holding myself up with the strength in my arms and moving with that in my legs. Siobhan and I abandoned the hallway and ventured outdoors, burning laps around the facility while I pulled faces at the less able patients inside.

Soon there came talk of taking me to the village and putting me in the water for a swim. I was as reluctant as the counsellor, who worried it might do more harm than good.

'It's likely now,' she explained to a semicircle of nodding boffins, 'that Alice's remaining memory loss is trauma-based. Putting her in that environment again risks shutting the door to those memories permanently and possibly even causing regression.'

I often wondered how someone became an expert on something they had no first-person experience of. She even said herself that there was more they didn't know about the brain than they did. Yet she was the one everyone deferred to. On this matter, though, I was happy to go along with her. I had no fear of the water, because I had no memory of it, but the horrible green wetsuit and the silly flippers looked ridiculous. I couldn't imagine how a person walked in those things, especially when they struggled to walk without them. Splashing foolishly in that get-up while Siobhan tried to keep my head above water, did not appeal. What if someone I once knew saw me?

'Considering how her short-term memory is improving,' the counsellor continued, as if I wasn't there, 'and that she seems to have most of her memories from before the incident, it's perhaps not that essential, certainly not right away, that she remembers everything from around the time. After all, most of what she's missing she can pick up again just by seeing her home. She remembers her fellow teachers and by all accounts these are the most significant relationships she built up while living there. Everything else is domestic – the whereabouts of household items, how to get to the shop, how much heating oil is in the tank. All things she can relearn without any harm done.' She shrugged her shoulders dismissively. 'I'm inclined to think that we don't need to risk pushing a traumatic memory to the fore when the benefits of doing so are negligible. If she doesn't go swimming again, does it really matter?'

'Perhaps a visit to the village though,' Siobhan suggested, 'just to see her home and maybe the beach.'

I felt absolutely no connection with this place they called my home and wasn't sure I wanted one. Once I was walking by my own volition again, especially with my secret taken care of, I intended to get out of this facility and return to work at the school. If Rathmullan risked triggering a regression I saw no benefit in going there. I would move. Trevor had mentioned something about a spare room in his flat.

The counsellor considered Siobhan's suggestion for a moment and then nodded. 'Okay. Let's start at the house and go from there.'

*

It all came together quickly. The Rathmullan visit was arranged for a Wednesday and assuming there were no issues stemming from it, Trevor arranged to take me away the following Friday. I could begin my life again in just a few days.

*

The day of the visit to Rathmullan turned out to be the first properly warm day of spring. I was helped into the van under gorgeous blue skies and along with Siobhan, the counsellor and a driver, began the journey.

The road curled through glorious Donegal countryside, revealing all the sights I'd missed during my incarceration at the facility. The bolshy, fertile grasses of a farmer's paddocks; the flashes of virgin white wool on his sheep; the rocks of a hillside outcrop, jutting from the green canopy of shrubs like old bones hidden by seaweed.

We passed through Ramelton and continued along the western coast of Lough Swilly. Siobhan provided little anecdotes about places and people along the way.

Soon the muddy shore became littered with rocks and the far side of the lough blurred by a thin veil of mist. By the road signs I gauged the Atlantic coast was still some distance off, but the widening body of water gave the impression of moving towards something large and overwhelming. Every now and then, when Siobhan gave her a chance, the counsellor would chip in.

'Do you recognise that river, Alice? How about that old house there?'

The closer we got to Rathmullan, the more pressure I felt to remember. But it was all new to me. Luckily Siobhan kept talking most of the time, recounting stories of how a particular stretch of coastline related to her and Felix somehow. In this way I was ferried to the place of my lost memories, on the wings of Siobhan's happiest ones.

Finally we entered the village and Siobhan fell quiet. I anticipated the counsellor pointing things out, enquiring about my recollection, but for the first few bends no one spoke. We drove past a large waterfront restaurant that looked as though it had been closed down for the winter. I'd expected a yellow sandy beach but the coastline in front of it was muddy and strewn with rocks and seaweed, like it had been since Ramelton.

A small general store on the left and then a short hill with a paddock and a smattering of bushy trees on the right. None of this was familiar. The road curled to the right, past an antique shop with an old wooden bench out front, turned on its side, a post office and the ruins of an old church. Then the beach appeared again, still no prettier than before. A long pipe of some kind shot out into the lough, its hide laced with clumps of brown seaweed and a sheath of green slime. Was this really the place I went swimming? No wonder my brain wanted to forget it.

We crested another hill upon which sat a pub, its doors pushed open at the moment we passed by a light-haired man with an amused face. A brief glimpse into the world inside – large windows looking across the water, heads sitting at the bar, a jacket hung over a bannister.

'Had a few lovely meals in there with my Felix,' Siobhan muttered, her voice melancholy and reflective.

'Did you ever go, Alice?' the counsellor asked, seemingly buoyed by the reintroduction of conversation.

'I don't remember,' I replied.

Siobhan touched my knee. 'We've all forgotten a few nights in there, my dear.'

Beyond the pub the view opened up again, revealing a car park, jetty, boat ramp and, stretching out in complete contrast to the coastline that preceded it, a gorgeous orange beach, spotted with people. I felt a pulse, something well out of reach, like the evaporating tail of a single drumbeat.

We turned left onto what must have been the high street. Another pub on the corner with three people visible through the window. A cafe on the left with more heads wobbling in close proximity, a fish and chip shop and a restaurant. Again a pulse, maybe stronger, but not revealing anything. Not even teasing. I wondered if it was nothing at all, just my excitement at being away from the rehab facility. We turned right at the end of the road.

'What a lovely looking church,' the counsellor said. No doubt she was expecting me to look in the hope I might recognise it. A new tactic. No more effective.

On the right a cemetery occupied a large block, curling over a slight rise and disappearing into a wood. Again the pulse. Again nothing with it. It was like being five miles from a festival I didn't know was on.

We drove out of the main part of the village, then, as the road bent to the left, took a smaller road to the right. Either side seemed occupied by relatively new buildings; holiday homes, I imagined. Very few cars were in the driveways. We continued half a kilometre down this road then slowed and turned into a collection of cottages with sharp A-shaped roofs. The driver pulled up next to a small red vehicle that wore a liberal sprinkling of twigs and bird droppings.

'That's a sweet little car,' the counsellor said.

Siobhan pushed open the door of the cottage and checked the air inside, then gave the all-clear. I looked around the foyer, taking in the coat rack, the staircase to the balcony, the dining table with two half melted candles. Two pulses but no images, no recognition. I caught the counsellor watching me. She didn't say anything but, for the first time, didn't look like she wanted to either. Perhaps she was thinking what I was thinking. If this was my home and nothing was rushing back, what was it going to take?

Even if I couldn't remember it, it was fascinating to see how I lived – tea towels neatly folded in the third drawer down, saucepans stacked like Russian dolls, a spare bottle of each cleaning liquid. These things were actually familiar, but not from here. This was how I had kept all my kitchens since my twenties. I opened the pantry door expecting, and finding, Vegemite, cinnamon and bay leaves. I never ran out of these ingredients.

Upstairs the bedroom walls were painted eggshell-yellow, the colour I recalled when I came out of the coma. On the floor beside the bed was a blue dress, next to it a bra. I felt another pulse, the strongest yet, but still there was nothing that came with it. I had been sceptical about coming, feeling that my brain had given up all it wanted. But now that I was here I could feel the lost memories clambering in the fog, like drunks trying to get up an icy hill before the train leaves. They may not have been important, but it still felt like a piece of me was nearby, just waiting for the right catalyst to push open the door.

We walked through the cottage but nothing else brought about any reactions. By now the counsellor wore a look of acceptance and had stopped pointing out how nice things were. She made some notes in her Manila folder as Siobhan and I tried, and failed, to start the car, then joined us outside.

'Shall we take a walk down to the beach?'

We made our way along a firm gravel path, until we came to a trail that cut through the dunes. It was tough going here as I was still using a Zimmer frame and the rubber feet dug into the sand. We ploughed on though and, after a few testing moments up some short hills, finally reached the beach.

A pulse. No image.

It really was quite gorgeous and with no signs of mud, slimy pipes or seaweed covered rocks, it made much more sense that I may have swum there. I struggled over the soft sand and then looked both ways down the beach. Back towards the village there was a handful of people staring out across the lough, dogs ploughing into the water after sticks, and a shimmer of sand hovering in the air, holding them in place like a grainy TV screen. In the other direction the beach curled around to the left, disappearing behind the grassy dunes. There were less people in this direction, which surprised me given the lovely conditions. Perhaps they were all in the village, indulging in their first ice creams of the season. A man with dark hair was making his lonely way towards the bend in the beach, while by the waterline, a little to our left, a young blonde girl was carving letters into the sand while her mother stood by and admired her work.

We walked slowly towards the water, me pushing the stupid Zimmer frame out in front then willing my legs to catch up. I could make out prints along the way, little fat U's dug into the firm sand with a divot kicked out behind it. Only a couple of metres further down the beach the same tracks were there again, this time pointed in the other direction.

'Oh, there must have been a horse,' the counsellor observed. Not much escaped her eagle eye.

We reached the shoreline and peered into the shallow water. Siobhan placed a gentle hand on my shoulder. The pulse I'd felt at the dunes had returned now, like the beating of a drum behind a curtain, heard from the foyer of a concert hall. There were no images but there was a pressure. A blister wanting to burst. I saw a patch of seaweed, no bigger than a dinner plate, lurch listlessly in the tiny shore break. A sweat broke out over my skin, chilled by the light breeze. I struggled to breathe.

'Shall we walk a little this way?' The counsellor suggested, either oblivious to my reactions or fiendishly wanting to encourage them. Siobhan's hand caressed my shoulder blade.

We turned left and approached the mother and child who had been writing in the sand. By then the artwork was complete and they were admiring their achievement. The girl's hair danced in the breeze, coming to rest after each movement against her red jacket, which she wore unbuttoned. As we neared, a feature in the sand became apparent – some kind of hole with water flowing out of it, eroding shallow furrows all the way to the waterline.

'How are you feeling?' the counsellor asked.

'Confused,' I answered instinctively.

I felt the counsellor's head turn, far quicker than the way she usually moved.

'Why's that?' she asked, a curiosity in her voice, almost a timbre of surprise.

'That girl's hair,' I explained, though didn't have any other details to offer. There was something about it that was causing the pulses to quicken, the drum to grow louder behind the door.

'It's lovely,' the counsellor observed. 'The same colour as yours.'

Was she suggesting that was my confusion? I was simply seeing myself in this girl? The pulse slowed, the beat quietened. But as we approached it increased again. The little girl looked up at me and stopped what she was doing, clipped short the conversation she was having with her mother.

'... holidays, Dad will let me stay with uncle ...'

She had a blue and purple dress beneath her jacket, the bottom of which seemed designed to look like a fish tail. Her eyes matched it, milky blue lidos of innocence that watched me hobble by slowly.

Beside them, written in the sand, were two names:

Petra
Karen

The pulses increased, the door swelling with the pressure, desperate to burst open. I began to shake. Was this the counsellor's trick? Did they know about my plan to escape to London with Trevor and get an abortion? Was this girl a plant? Did they know the sex of the child inside me? Did I know? Had I always known? I rested on the Zimmer frame and tried to get my thoughts in order. It didn't make sense. There was something else going on. I could feel myself noticing something, just couldn't identify what it was.

I cast an eye over the sand feature, the bubbling water emerging mysteriously from underground, the rivulets cascading gently towards the lough. The writing in the sand, the curl of the letters and the stick dropped next to them. None of it pushed any more firmly at the door. Perhaps the mother? I studied her face as briefly as politeness would allow. She smiled back. She had brown hair growing through blonde dye and eyes the colour of wet sand. She seemed young. Too young, perhaps, to be the girl's mother. Maybe an older sister, or that word – uncle – maybe she was the child's auntie. None of which pushed the door open.

The girl approached me cautiously. She had something in her hand which she had plucked from behind her ear. She offered it to me nervously, her eyes as wide as the lough, her lips ever so slightly apart, quivering with words she was too nervous to say. Bravely, she forced them out.

'What happened to your tail?' she asked.

In her hand was a rose, the petals a deep, robust pink. It must have grown in a greenhouse.

'This is for you,' she said.

I reached forward, the drum thundering behind the door. There was something here that I needed to identify. It wasn't the rose. It wasn't the girl or the young woman, the name's in the sand. It was ... a sound. Above me – the sound of a child's toy, trodden on, falling from a bridge. I wrenched my head back as best I could and saw, circling above me, low, excitedly, two black rooks – Cameron and Russell.

The door exploded open and knocked me to my knees. Pictures flooded through my mind. Everything was there – swimming, Trevor, Janet, the cave, the bottle. I lay on the sand as the women rushed to help me. And through them, through the huddle of bodies, at the bend in the beach, looking back, I saw a black-haired figure turn and put his hand to his forehead to shade his face from the sun. As they helped me to my feet I saw him start walking back. I saw his pace quicken. Saw him break into a jog. I saw Felix running to me.

Acknowledgments

Thanks to Barbara Napthine, Virginia Leatherbarrow and Claire Goddard for reading early versions of the manuscript, and providing vital feedback and the encouragement to see it become a novel.

Extra special thanks to Kate Shelper for being a valuable friend, an early, enthusiastic reader, for providing essential guidance on a few technical points, and for twice rescuing me from my hermitage during the cold Irish winter. On this latter point thanks also goes to Emmanuel Martin for always being available on the end of the phone. It is perfectly apt that your beautiful illustration adorns the cover of this book.

A warm thanks to Alessandra Milani for support, encouragement and ultimately understanding during the difficult period that preceded my going away to write this.

Alison Watkins was generous and extremely helpful in providing my accommodation at Fort Royal, and for this I'm extremely grateful.

And finally my gratitude to the village of Rathmullan in County Donegal, which for six cold, wet months provided the canvas upon which this story was imagined.

Lightning Source UK Ltd.
Milton Keynes UK
UKHW010649140720
366515UK00001B/285

9 781789 630992